DEATH
OF THE
BLACK
WIDOW

James Patterson is one of the best-known and biggest-selling writers of all time. His books have sold in excess of [0] million copies worldwide. He is the author of some of the most popular series of the past two decades – the Alex Cross, Women's Murder Club, Detective Michael Bennett and Private novels – and he has written many other number one bestsellers including non-fiction and stand-alone thrillers.

James is passionate about encouraging children to read. Inspired by his own son who was a reluctant reader, he also writes a range of books for young readers including the Middle School, Dog Diaries, Treasure Hunters and Max Einstein series. James has donated millions in grants to independent bookshops and has been the most borrowed author in UK libraries for the past thirteen years in a row. He lives in Florida with his family.

J.D. Barker is the international bestselling author of numerous books, including *Dracul* and *The Fourth Monkey*. His novels have been translated into two dozen languages and optioned for both film and television. Barker resides in coastal New Hampshire with his wife, Dayna, and their daughter.

A list of more titles by James Patterson appears
at the back of this book

JAMES PATTERSON

& J.D. BARKER

DEATH
OF THE
BLACK
WIDOW

PENGUIN BOOKS

PENGUIN BOOKS

UK | USA | Canada | Ireland | Australia
India | New Zealand | South Africa

Penguin Books is part of the Penguin Random House group of companies
whose addresses can be found at global.penguinrandomhouse.com

Published in Penguin Books 2022
001

Copyright © James Patterson 2022
Excerpt from *James Patterson by James Patterson: The Stories of
My Life* © James Patterson 2022

The moral right of the author has been asserted

Typeset by Jouve (UK), Milton Keynes

Printed and bound in Great Britain by Clays Ltd, Elcograf S.p.A.

The authorised representative in the EEA is Penguin Random House
Ireland, Morrison Chambers, 32 Nassau Street, Dublin D02 YH68

A CIP catalogue record for this book is available from the British Library

ISBN: 978–1–529–15738–3
ISBN: 978–1–529–15739–0 (export edition)

www.greenpenguin.co.uk

There are mysteries which men can only guess at, which age by age they may solve only in part.

—*Bram Stoker*

NOW

1

COULD A BUILDING SWEAT?

If someone were to ask him, Walter O'Brien would say no. But that was exactly what the square brick structure on the corner of Park and Woodward in downtown Detroit appeared to be doing. The faded red brick had a dull sheen on it, the moisture reflecting the streetlights, the neon from the sign above, and the headlights of the cars as they rolled by, oblivious to what was coming.

Walter wanted to throw his damn binoculars. "Why is there traffic? Shut that shit down."

Lincoln Sealey's gruff voice replied in his earbud a moment later. *"We can't."*

"Why not?"

"Because nothing's happened yet."

They'd had this argument more times than Walter could count, and as much as he felt like he could win this time, it wasn't worth the aggravation. Something would happen soon enough.

He looked at his watch.

Nine fifty-two.

The neon sign continued to blink on and off, pink and purple reflecting off the surrounding buildings and glowing in the street.

CLUB STOMP.

Eight minutes.

At fifty-seven, Walter shouldn't be out here. He heard the various pops and creaks of his joints as he stood and looked out over the edge of the rooftop. His damn leg screamed. Gripping his cane, his palm was greasy with sweat.

Five stories up.

Across the street from the club.

Direct line of sight to the front entrance.

What passed for music these days churned from inside, seemed to rattle the air. This unforgiving *thump, thump, thump, thump*, with no break between what could loosely be defined as songs. He missed guitars. Melodies. Harmonies. He remembered when Detroit was all about the music. Music and cars. Now it was someplace you only visited if you were looking for cheap real estate.

A bouncer stood at the entrance, checking IDs with a penlight while another worked his way back through the line of about thirty people waiting behind a faded red rope. His job was apparently to pluck the best-looking girls from the wait and escort them directly in. Both bouncers were ridiculously large. The biceps on the one at the door looked bigger than Walter's head. He had some kind of tattoo that started behind his left ear and crawled up his bald scalp. Walter couldn't tell what it was. The tattoo seemed out of place with the man's three-thousand-dollar suit.

Walter spotted Sealey on the roof of the federal building kitty-corner. Dressed all in black, lying on his stomach, propped up on his side so he could scan the crowd through the scope of his rifle positioned in a break meant for storm drainage. The rifle was a Paratus-16, a folding semi-automatic takedown sniper rifle that traveled in a case not much larger than a lunch box.

Red Larson came through the rooftop door about twenty feet behind Walter, quickly scanned the roof, checked his sight line to the club, and began assembling a rifle identical to Sealey's. He spoke as he worked. "I phoned in 'shots fired at a convenience store' about a block down the road on Woodward. Said it sounded like automatic weapons. Maybe more than one. That should get the locals close and bring in the press. I didn't get a chance to check the radio, but the Thirty-Second Precinct is less than two miles from here."

"We need ambulances, not cops. Cops will get in the way."

"They'll send ambulances, too. Standard procedure."

"You should have said heart attack, not shots fired."

"We'll need more than one ambulance."

He was right. Walter dropped it. "Did you destroy the phone?"

Red gave him an aggravated glance, plucked the cheap burner phone from his jacket pocket, cracked it in half, and threw both pieces over the side of the building. "Yes, Mom. Absolutely."

Walter just shook his head.

Rifle assembled, Red lowered himself to his belly, cringing as his body made more noise than Walter's had. Red had

5

eleven years on him. "This is a young man's game, Walt. None of us got any business being out here."

"We've got unfinished business."

Over their earbuds, Sealey said, *"It's not too late to go back to my motel and catch the end of the Tigers game."*

"I'm saying," Red replied.

Walter felt a tickle in his throat, pulled a handkerchief from his pocket, and caught the cough. Loud, but not as bad as some of the others. He shoved the stained cloth back into his pants before Red could see the blood. As if Red didn't already know what was happening to him. Sealey, too, for that matter.

More unfinished business, he supposed. That one was on track to take care of itself.

He tapped Red's foot with the toe of his shoe. "When did it rain last?"

"I look like the weatherman to you?"

"The building looks wet."

"It's Detroit," he muttered, as if that was some kind of definitive answer needing no further explanation. "How's our time?"

Walter looked at his watch. "Three minutes."

"She's inside?"

"That's what I've been told."

"You sure about this?"

Walter wasn't sure about much of anything, but he wasn't about to tell Red or Sealey that. The last thing any of them needed was an excuse to back down. Instead, he asked, "You took care of the back door, right?"

It was a stupid question. He'd watched Red tack weld the door less than half an hour ago.

"Only way out is through the front," Red replied anyway.

"You're both loaded with regular rounds?"

Red tapped a spare clip on the ground to the left of his rifle. "Got regular in chamber. Oxys right here on deck. I'm not eff-ing senile. Not yet. We've got this."

"You sure you don't need two guns?"

He *tsk*ed. "I can change them out fast enough."

"I hear sirens," Sealey interrupted. *"Two, maybe three black-and-whites. Coming in from the west."*

Locals responding to Red's call.

"Copy," Walter said, although he couldn't hear them yet. He looked back at the club. "Things looked wet in Chicago. Same with that little pissant town outside of Reno back in '94. A couple of the others, now that I think about it."

Red shrugged. "Could be something, or could just be you wanting it to be something. Doesn't really matter, unless we find a way to use it. If we end this tonight, no reason to give it another thought, anyway. I vote we go that route. I don't want to do this shit again."

"It's raining like a bitch out west," Sealey told them. *"Probably passed through here first. Drop it and stay sharp."*

Walter looked at his watch again. "Time."

Retrieving a burner phone from the pocket of his pants, he dialed the number he'd written on his palm in black marker.

A male voice answered, shouting over the music. *"Club Stomp!"*

Walter spoke slowly, doing his best to keep the anxiety from his voice. "I've planted a bomb in your club. You have two minutes to get everyone out, or you're all dead. Do you understand?"

"A bomb?"

"Do you understand?" Walter repeated.

7

"Yes, but—"

Walter disconnected.

Unlike Red, he didn't destroy this phone. They'd need it. He dropped it into his pocket.

A moment later, the loud thumping music stopped.

The world went suddenly quiet.

There was some kind of announcement inside. Too muffled to make out the words.

"Here we go," Sealey said softly in their earbuds.

Walter's finger rolled over the rough, nubby burn scar on his left wrist. He raised the binoculars and focused on the door. "Stay sharp."

"You're sure about this?" Sealey asked.

Walter thought about the text: *Club Stomp 10PM. I miss you.* "I'm sure."

The first bouncer's phone rang.

He raised it to his ear with a beefy arm and listened.

He hung up a moment later, said something to the second bouncer that caused him to dart around the side of the building toward the back door. He then spoke quickly to the crowd, sent them scattering across the block like rats fleeing a sinking ship.

A girl appeared at the entrance. The bouncer pushed her, and she ran out. Dark hair cut just above her shoulders, black dress.

"Brunette, twentysomething, white!" Sealey called out.

"Agreed!" Red replied.

"Skip," Walter ordered, although he wasn't 100 percent sure. No way he could be.

Two men rushed out the door behind her and darted for the parking lot across the street. Walter and his team ignored them.

Screams from inside the club.

Everyone rushing toward the front now.

Screaming was good. It would drown out what would come next.

Another girl appeared in the doorway. Eyes wide. Confused.

"Blonde!" Sealey said. *"Hazel eyes!"*

"Blonde, hazel eyes, concur," Red said.

"Skip," Walter said again.

Two more girls came through the door. Each holding up the other. The one on the left had a deep red patch growing at the thigh of her jeans; the other had a bad cut in the arm from maybe a knife or broken bottle. Blood was rolling off her fingertips as the bouncer shoved them both forward and pointed at the parking lot.

"Skip," Walter ordered before the others said anything.

Sweat trickled down his forehead and got in his eye. He wiped it away with the back of his hand and pressed the binoculars tighter.

Walter had checked out the club yesterday. Said he was there to check a gas line and walked right in. The entrance was a single glass door, narrow, and it led to an even narrower hallway with a cashier on the right and a glass display case housing the club's licenses on the left. It opened up once you got beyond the cashier, but the doorway itself, the only exit with the back door welded shut, was a funnel. He estimated there were at least two hundred people inside, possibly more. Tough to say on a Thursday. When he closed his eyes, he could imagine them all in there, running, pushing toward that door, trampling one another trying to get out.

Three more men ran out. Kids, really. Barely legal.

His team ignored them as two more girls appeared: One Black, the other Hispanic. They were coming faster now, everyone trying to get out.

The Black girl had a cut on her cheek and maybe a broken arm. Hard to tell, but she was cradling it. The girl helping her was in a short red dress and was missing a shoe.

Sealey ignored the injured girl and described the other. *"Hispanic. Brown hair, two inches over shoulders. Green eyes."*

"Green?" Red huffed. "You sure?"

Walter didn't hesitate. "Sealey, take the shot!"

Sealey fired.

The bullet entered the Hispanic girl's arm just below her shoulder and came out the other side. It cracked against the cinder-block wall with a puff of dust and chipped concrete. She dropped the other girl, grabbed her shoulder. Blood leaked out between her fingers.

"Negative," Sealey said, an edge to his voice now. *"She's injured."*

"Shit," Walter said as four more people came out the door. Three male, one female.

"I've got no visual on the female," Red said. "Those guys are blocking my view."

"Same," Sealey said.

Walter could definitely hear the sirens now. They were close. "Wing one of the guys if you have to—get a visual on the girl!"

"You sure?"

"Shoot, goddamnit!"

Red Larson shot.

The boy in the front rolled to his left and fell away, clutching his ankle.

Sealey quickly called out, *"Strawberry blonde. Pink streak on left. Blue eyes."*

"Her left or your left?" Red quickly replied.

"What?"

"The streak!"

"Her left! Her left!"

Red blew out a breath. "Agreed."

"Skip," Walter told them.

The screams were loud now.

The bouncer had realized someone outside was shooting and was now trying to keep people from running out. But even at his size, he was little match for all the bodies pushing against the door.

Sealey's voice crackled in Walter's earbud. *"I can see the locals. They're coming in from Woodward hot, didn't even bother to stop at the convenience store Red mentioned. They're heading straight here. I see six — no, eight — cruisers. No SWAT, not yet."*

Five more people ran out of the club, the pressure of the crowd behind them propelling them through the door and past the bouncer.

One of the guys from the last group was crouched down, pointing up at Sealey's rooftop, shouting at the bouncer.

"This isn't working," Red quickly said. "We've got too many coming out!"

Walter squeezed his cane and quickly turned, started toward the stairs. "Shoot up the entrance! Keep them inside! Sealey, reposition — you've been spotted — I'm going down there!"

He limped into the open stairwell and started down; his chest began burning before he made it halfway. By the time he reached the ground level and pushed through the door out onto the sidewalk, he was coughing again. Blood stained his chin.

As the door swung shut behind him, three Detroit PD squad cars squealed to a halt on Park. Four more came in from Woodward. One ambulance. No, two. More sirens screamed in the distance.

Walter looked up and down the various roads and cursed when he didn't see it. "Where's the truck?"

No response.

"Where's the damn truck!?"

"Couple minutes out," Sealey replied. *"Five. Maybe ten."*

Too slow. Shit.

Walter shook his head. "Nobody makes a move without my order. This isn't a firefight with the locals. I don't want it to turn into that. Remember your instructions."

"You're sure about this?" Red asked. *"This is what you want?"*

Pivoting on his cane, Walter stumbled toward the center of the intersection, lowered his broken body until he was kneeling on the ground, and set his cane at his side. He had both hands above his head when a patrol car skidded to an awkward stop about ten feet to his left.

What Walter wanted didn't much matter anymore. He'd be dead in an hour.

1986

... Walter O'Brien, 22 Years Old

CHAPTER

2

"YOU SURE YOU HEARD SCREAMING?"

The elderly woman from 1A clearly didn't like cops. But she had only needed a moment to size up Officer Herb Nadler from behind the safety chain on her door before deciding he wasn't a threat. She unlatched the chain and stepped out into the hallway to get as close to his face as her five-foot-nothing frame would allow. She barely gave Walter O'Brien a second glance, flat-out dismissed him before bobbing her head back at the stairwell. "I ain't never said it was screaming; I said howls. Up in 2D. You need to do something about it. Can't let it go on another night."

"Howls? What, like a hurt dog?" Nadler asked.

"Yeah, but not a dog. It was a person."

"You're sure?"

"Think I would have called if I wasn't?"

Her faded pink terry-cloth robe fell open again and she made no effort to close it. She was wearing a ratty Harold

Melvin & the Blue Notes T-shirt beneath the robe along with a pair of cutoff gray sweatpants. No bra. And that was unfortunate, as her no-bra days had ended at least fifty years ago. Purple curlers were knotted up in her hair, several held with rubber bands.

Standing a few paces behind his new partner, Walter tried to unsee the image burned in his retinas. He hitched up his gun belt, the weight of it a constant reminder that the size was wrong. The duty officer back at the precinct had insisted he had nothing smaller when he handed the belt to Walter along with two pairs of handcuffs, knife, mace, radio, spare batteries, baton, flashlight, and other assorted odds and ends. At least thirty pounds' worth of items, and that was before Walter added the Smith & Wesson revolver and spare ammunition he'd received the day before.

The woman shifted her considerable bulk from her left foot to her right. "This nonsense has been going on for the better part of two weeks."

"Why didn't you call sooner?"

"I called eight times. You're the first ones to show up. Why didn't *you* come out sooner?"

Walter's partner gave her a blank stare. Walter knew what the man wanted to say because he'd said it in the car on the way over here—*It's snowing balls outside and cops who venture into the Forest Park corner of Detroit after eleven tend to get shot at. Half the calls that come in from this shithole are bogus, just a ploy to get a cop to drive out so the bangers have someone in uniform to shoot at. Most situations out here tend to resolve themselves, and it's always best to question the survivors at the hospital when it's over rather than arrive early and take part in the big show.* Nadler had gone on like that for the twenty minutes it took to get here, breaking it up with complaints about having to haul a rookie like Walter (out on his first night, no less) with him on this death march.

"It's quiet now," Walter pointed out, looking up the stairs.

Her eyes became narrow slits. "And you think that's a good thing?"

A little boy, no more than two and wearing nothing but a loaded diaper, wandered out of the apartment, wrapped his arms around the woman's leg, and stared up at them.

She patted the boy's head. "I'm gonna get back inside and put this one to bed for the third time so his momma's got a chance at seeing him between jobs. You all get up there and take care of whatever the hell is going on, 'cause it ain't right and nobody in the building wants to listen to it no more."

With that, she ushered the boy back in and slammed the door behind her, leaving Nadler and Walter alone in the hallway.

Nadler looked back up the steps. "Ready to protect and serve?"

Walter hitched up the belt again and swore when it dropped right back down.

Nadler rolled his eyes. "Goddamn rookie pranks. Gonna get someone killed if they don't stop that shit." From his own belt, he took out a knife and held it out to Walter. "Punch out another notch before all that crap falls off you. They love to send you guys out on your first night with a belt too big, loaded up like a private marching off into the jungle on his first tour. You don't need half that shit. When we get back out to the car, I'll show you what you really need to carry. The rest can go in your locker. Tell anyone I helped you, and they'll just do something else tomorrow, so it stays between us, understand?"

"I'm fine," Walter said, turning toward the stairs.

"Look, you wanna wind up with that thing around your ankles while someone's shooting at us, be my guest. If not, take the goddamn knife, hitch that thing up right, and save us both the paperwork."

Walter grabbed the knife, punched out a new hole, and refastened the belt. He dropped the knife back in Nadler's hand without a word.

"You're welcome."

Nadler returned the knife and unsnapped the leather clasp on his revolver. He rested his hand on the butt. "Your gun stays put. You don't draw unless I tell you. I don't want you shooting anybody on your first night. Most likely, we're looking at junkies holing up on an extended trip. A lot of 'em score horse around here, then lock themselves in and don't come back out unless they run out of food or need to score again. I know of at least three dens just in this building where nothing else but that goes on. You go in there, you'll find twenty bodies all lying around in their own filth, half dead, stoned out of their gourds. Most are harmless, but don't let anyone spit on you. If they do, don't let it get into your eyes or your mouth. You get it in your eyes or your mouth, you find the nearest sink and wash that shit out. They got whores around here with so many diseases the rats cross the street when they get too close. Take something like that home to your girlfriend, and she's liable to cut off your pecker if it don't fall off on its own."

Walter glanced back at the closed door for 1A.

Nadler guessed exactly what was going through his head. "You'll be arresting that kid before you know it. Ask his momma or his grandma there. They know what's up. Just hope he sees you around enough to know your face and hesitate if he ever draws on you, so you can get a shot off first. Us versus them, rookie. Don't ever forget that. Day you forget that is the day you die. Come on…"

Nadler started up the worn steps then, one chubby hand on the rail, the other on his gun.

Walter's hand had drifted into his pocket. He rolled his fingers over the worn leather of the small dog collar he kept there. He traced the creases, the tiny holes, the edge of the metal tag. "Here we go," he said softly, before following Nadler up the stairs.

CHAPTER

3

THE SECOND FLOOR LOOKED no different than the first. A hundred years' worth of paint covered the walls, peeling wallpaper beneath that. The stale air stunk of piss, and if not for the yellow light of the fluorescents dangling from the ceiling, the shadows would devour the space, making way for the roaches, spiders, rats, and mice Walter could feel watching him.

At the top of the steps, Nadler stepped over a discarded condom and looked left and right before moving cautiously out into the hallway.

Six apartments on this level.

2D was the second door on the right.

He gestured for Walter to move past him and stand on the far side of the door, then gave it a heavy-handed knock before stepping to the side himself.

Never stand directly in front of a door—they drilled that in at the academy. *If bad guys decided to shoot, they tended to aim for the center.* This thought passed through Walter's head as he pressed himself against the cracked drywall beside the door, fairly certain it would do nothing to stop a bullet if said bad guy had shitty aim or fired high and to the right instead.

Nadler drummed his fingers over the butt of his revolver and let several seconds tick by before beating on the door again. "Police! Open up!"

If anyone moved inside, they were quiet about it.

Down the hall, the door to 2E opened a few inches, enough for a lanky Black teenager to get a look at what was going on. The teen's eyes met Walter's and he hesitated as he started to close the door, saying, "He got a girl in there."

"Who?"

"I don't know his name. Some white dude. Been there a couple months."

"Him or the girl?"

The teen didn't answer. Instead, he closed the door, and several locks clicked into place.

Walter looked over at Nadler.

Nadler was chewing the inside of his cheek. "He said he's got a girl in there. He didn't say against her will. Could just be a pro polishing his knob. Can't go in without probable cause."

Walter looked back down the hall at 2E. "Should I get him back out here? Get something specific?"

Nadler turned back to the door of 2D without replying.

"He wouldn't have said that if he didn't think she was in trouble," Walter continued.

"You're reaching, kid."

"Then why isn't anyone opening the door?" *Christ, Nadler's scared,* he realized. *Some role model they saddled me with.*

Walter hammered at the door with the back of his fist. "We know you're in there! Open the door. Now!"

Nadler didn't like that one bit. He glared at Walter and shook his head. "Goddamn rookie," he muttered. "Wanna get killed on day one?"

From behind the door came a thump.

A loud thump. Something falling.

Something large enough to be a body hitting the floor, Walter thought.

That was followed by a short scream—muted and quickly silenced.

Here we go.

At this, Nadler perked up. He eased his revolver from the holster and moved to the opposite side of the hallway, leveling the barrel on the door. "Detroit PD, we're coming in!"

Walter didn't give a shit what Nadler said; he wasn't going in unarmed. He unsnapped the safety strap and took out his revolver.

Nadler jerked his head toward the door and raised his eyebrows as if to say, *Okay, kick it in, hotshot.*

Walter took a step back, gave a three-count, and kicked the door below the knob—*three inches below the hardware, heel first, follow through with body weight.* Academy 101.

The frame splintered and the door jumped, but it didn't open. Something was holding it near the top, probably a dead bolt. He had to kick it two more times before it finally gave and burst in on the room, bounced off the wall, and nearly slammed shut again.

Nadler moved fast. Far quicker than Walter expected. Gun leading the way, he burst through the door, into the apartment, crouched, and spun in a semicircle, taking in the room.

Walter followed.

Small living room with a tiny kitchenette on the right.

A ratty brown couch sat against the far wall facing a nineteen-inch television on milk crates. An open pizza box on the floor, two slices left. The cheese was crusty and covered in white mold. The room smelled of spoiled milk. There were crushed beer cans scattered about and a lamp with a bare bulb burning in the corner, casting sharp shadows over everything. The kitchen counter was buried under old take-out containers and trash.

No guy or girl, though. Not in this room.

With his gun, Nadler pointed at the dark doorway leading into what had to be a bedroom in the back.

They'd practiced this drill a million times in the academy, and Walter let his training take over. Like leapfrog—partner first, then you, then them. *Secure every room as quickly as possible. Move fast. Don't give your bad guy a chance to react.*

Walter crossed the small room, passed by Nadler, and entered the bedroom while crouched low. He moved so fast he nearly tripped over the body just inside the door.

A man.

Wearing only a pair of stained boxers, the man was lying facedown on the hardwood, one arm up over his head, a rusty steak knife wrapped in his thick fingers, the other arm pinned under his sizable belly. His greasy gray hair was matted and damp with blood from a fresh crack in the back of his skull.

Walter knelt and felt for a pulse.

Nothing.

The man's neck was warm, though. He hadn't been dead long.

Walter could make out nothing in the thick darkness but the soft lines of a mattress on the floor with a box or nightstand beside it, maybe another milk crate. He couldn't tell.

Nadler came in behind him with his flashlight out. The beam cut over the body, drifted over an empty closet, and fell on the bed. The mattress wasn't on the floor but on a low metal frame. Ropes were tied at the four corners. One was soaked in blood and frayed at the end as if chewed through. No sheets. The mattress was covered in stains and smelled of waste.

Nadler swept the rest of the room. The flashlight beam landed on another door at the back — this one closed.

Bathroom?

Had to be.

As Nadler crossed the room, something crunched under his shoes, sounded like glass. His foot caught, he nearly tripped, and when he hit it with the light, Walter realized it was another lamp. The bulb was shattered and the frame was bent at an odd angle in the heavy base. Possible murder weapon.

Nadler carefully stepped over and positioned himself at the edge of the bathroom doorframe before gesturing for Walter to open the door.

Avoiding the body and the mess on the floor, Walter went to the door and gripped the knob.

Nadler counted, and when he hit three, Walter gave the knob a fast twist and pulled the door open.

They both saw the girl at the same time, caught in the beam of Nadler's flashlight.

Early twenties at best.

Nude.

She was on the floor, wedged between the sink and toilet, her knees pulled up against her chest and her long, dark hair, twisted with knots, covering half her face. She looked up at them, a frantic heat in her eyes, every inch of her body quivering.

"I didn't mean to," she said in a sheepish voice, looking beyond them at the body of the man. "Please help me?"

CHAPTER

4

WALTER REACHED INTO THE room and fumbled with the switch. A single bulb filled the small windowless space with harsh, cold light. The girl pinched her eyes shut against it. She pushed farther back under the sink.

It was then he saw the pair of handcuffs dangling from under the sink, one side fastened to the water pipe, the other open. A thin piece of rusty wire on the floor, some kind of improvised lockpick.

Droplets of blood covered her cheek, blended with soft freckles on her bare shoulder.

"Whoa, it's okay. We won't hurt you." Walter holstered his weapon, took off his jacket, and knelt, but when he tried to drape it over her, Nadler stopped him and indicated the blood. It was still wet.

"Evidence," he said in a soft voice.

Walter covered the girl anyway. He brushed the hair from her face. "Everything's going to be fine. You're safe now."

She opened her eyes, hesitant against the light, cautious, and looked up at him. They were deep gray, dark pools unlike any Walter had ever seen. He didn't realize he was staring into them until Nadler cleared his throat and pointed at the bathtub.

A ratty green quilt and pillow were bunched up in the corner. Several candy bar wrappers were scattered around the floor. Walter spotted a half eaten loaf of bread, too. Someone had haphazardly scrubbed the tiles but only left swirl patterns in the grime. The towel on the floor next to the tub was crusty with what looked like blood in one of the folds. The rusted mirror frame above the sink was empty, the glass long gone.

Christ, he kept her in here. The fucking monster kept her in this room chained to the wall.

Standing behind Walter, Nadler asked the girl, "What's your name?"

She didn't seem to hear him. Her gaze lingered on Walter. Then she looked down at the jacket. Her hands curled around the edges and pulled it tight, covering herself as best she could. She gripped it so tight, the zipper dug into her palm.

Walter didn't realize he was reaching for her until his fingertip brushed her ankle. She didn't shy away from his touch, but instead pressed her foot against his hand. She felt so cold.

An uncomfortable edge filled Nadler's voice. "Go down to the car and call this in, O'Brien."

Walter shot him an irritated glance.

"Now," Nadler insisted.

Her hand shot out from under the jacket and grabbed Walter's wrist. Her fingers were small, delicate, but she squeezed him like a vise. "Please don't leave me."

Nadler groaned. "Christ, okay. You stay, but don't touch anything. I'll be right back."

Before Walter could reply, Nadler turned and crossed back out of the room, carefully stepping around the body, lamp, and broken glass on the floor. Walter heard voices out in the hall, which grew muffled as Nadler pulled the damaged door shut behind him.

He and the girl were alone then, and the apartment went oddly still.

Why is it so cold in here?

For the first time, Walter heard an air conditioner running. When he turned, he spotted an ancient window unit spurting out air cold enough to see even in the dim light.

It's maybe twenty degrees outside. Why is this guy running the air-conditioning?

"Amy," she said so softly that at first Walter wasn't sure she'd spoken at all. "My name is Amy Archer."

He cleared his throat. "I'm Walter. Walter O'Brien."

"I killed him, didn't I?"

Walter saw no point in lying to her. He nodded.

She tried to shrink deeper into the alcove, but there was no place to go. Her bare feet only slipped on the filthy floor, leaving streaks.

"He would have killed me if I didn't…"

"It'll be okay, Amy. Nobody will fault you for self-defense, I promise," Walter assured her again. His gaze fell on the half eaten loaf of bread. Mold was growing on one side, built-up moisture creating a haze on the plastic. "How long have you been here?"

She shook her head. "I'm…not sure. Two weeks, maybe three?"

"Can you tell me what happened?"

A tear slipped from her eye and rolled down her cheek. "He's a taxi driver. Or at least he said he was. He picked me up downtown, near Eastern Market. I gave him my address, but instead of taking me home, he headed north. When I told him he was going the wrong way, he pulled over and sprayed something in my face. I don't know what it was, but I blacked out, and when I woke up..." Her voice dropped off, and she looked at the handcuffs dangling from the water pipe. "He kept me in here when I wasn't on the bed."

"Did he...?"

She understood what he meant, hesitated, and nodded softly.

She was holding his hand. Walter wasn't sure when that had happened. He didn't remember reaching for her again, didn't recall her slipping her hand into his. She felt warmer now. That was good. "How about you come out of there?"

She looked at the side of the toilet and the sink, her gaze lingering on the handcuffs for another moment, before finally nodding.

Walter helped her out of the small space to sit on the edge of the bathtub.

She glanced down at her naked body, crossed her legs, and pulled the jacket tighter. A blush filled her cheeks, and she turned away from him, looking embarrassed.

"Where are your clothes?"

"I don't know what he did with them."

Wondering how long Nadler would be, Walter looked back over his shoulder. "If I look for them, will you stay here?"

"Can't I go with you?"

"I'll be right outside the door where you can see me. It's better you stay in here."

Her hair had fallen back in her face, and he brushed it away, tucked it behind her ear. She pressed her cheek into his palm, and for one brief instant, her mouth formed a smile. The color had returned to her lips. They were a deep red. She had an exotic look about her, European or maybe Mediterranean. Walter couldn't put his finger on it.

He didn't find her clothes, but he turned up a pair of red sweatpants and a faded Detroit Lions T-shirt, both extra large.

He crossed back into the bathroom and handed them to her.

She shrugged off the jacket and quickly got dressed.

When finished, she stood there and glanced up at him, a grateful look in her eyes.

Walter wiped a speck of blood from the side of her face. He couldn't help himself.

"HIS NAME IS ALVIN SCHALK. Thirty-one years old. Unmarried. Loner. No priors. Cab driver for Detroit Metro Taxi. His residence is listed as 83 Cambridge, not this place. According to the landlord, nobody lives here. My guess is he just used this apartment as a sex den."

Walter and Nadler were standing over the body in the bedroom with Detective Freddie Weeden of Detroit Homicide.

Walter couldn't help but look over at Amy.

The detective had asked her to stay in the bathroom until paramedics arrived. They'd take her to the hospital soon, where they'd perform a rape kit exam and see to her injuries.

Amy must have felt Walter's eyes on her—she glanced up and caught him watching.

"We also found an unplugged freezer in the basement with two bodies inside, wrapped in quilts. Decomp so bad I couldn't tell you if they were men or women. They'd been there awhile. Won't know cause of death until the medical examiner gets a look." He nodded toward the bathroom. "She's not his first, that's for damn sure. This guy had a system in place. That comes from practice. I wouldn't be surprised if we find more back at his house. I'm waiting on a warrant. His cab is MIA, but I'm sure we'll find something there, too, when it turns up."

Evidence markers littered the apartment, and they'd brought in some lights. A photographer was systematically documenting the scene, the bright flash of his camera going off every few seconds. He was leaning over the bed now, capturing images of the ropes, particularly the frayed one, the one that looked chewed. Evidence marker 43. Weeden had asked Amy about that rope, but she hadn't answered. Instead, her face had filled with horror, her eyes with tears. He'd let her be after that.

"How do you know the freezer is Schalk's?" Walter asked.

Weeden rolled his eyes and looked at Nadler. "First day?"

Nadler nodded. "Yep."

"Fuck you both," Walter muttered.

Weeden said, "Educated guess. We'll tie it to him with prints. This isn't the best neighborhood, but it's still pretty rare for residents to stash stiffs in their basements, kid. Frankly, most have no problem shooting each other in the street right out in the open and leaving 'em there. Hiding a body takes time, means this guy planned." He nodded toward the bathroom. "I tried to interview her but she clammed up. She say anything else to you?"

Walter shook his head. "Only what I told you."

"She's still in shock," Weeden surmised. "Lucky for her, you two yahoos showed up and distracted him by beating on the door. She would have ended up in that freezer if you hadn't. No doubt about that." With the toe of his shoe, Weeden nudged the broken lamp on the floor, inches from the man's cracked skull. "She saved the taxpayers some dough."

Walter thumbed the dog collar in his pocket. "Where the hell are those paramedics?"

If the girl was listening, she made no indication. She was looking off to the side, either lost in memories or attempting to forget them.

The broken apartment door swung open again. Half the building seemed to be standing in the hallway, trying to get a look inside. Nadler kicked it shut and braced it with an evidence case.

"She shouldn't have to sit in this place. We'll take her," Walter told Weeden.

"Huh?"

"To the hospital. We can take her. Do we really need to wait on an ambulance?"

"Rookie might be right," Nadler agreed. "Why waste a bus? They got better things to do."

Weeden thought it over, then said, "I need one of you on that door. Can't spare you both."

"Looks like you're on door duty, O'Brien," Nadler said flatly. "I'll go."

"She likes the rookie," Weeden pointed out in a low voice. "They keep making googly eyes at each other. I vote he goes. Might open up to him, tell him something we don't know yet. Three weeks locked up with this creep, who knows what he said to her. Might lead us to his cab, more bodies, who knows."

Nadler was shaking his head. "He's only been on the job

three hours. I don't need the ass chewing that'll come with him fucking up on my watch."

"She's not going to talk to you," Weeden replied. "You've got the same hair and beer gut as our dead guy. You might as well be his long-lost brother. Hell, *I* don't even want to talk to you."

"Fuck you."

"I'll take her," Walter interjected. "It's two miles. Not even."

"I'm not—"

Weeden clucked his tongue impatiently. "A hundred years ago, you were a rookie, too, Herb. Give the kid a break. My crime scene, my call. If he can get her to talk, I want to give it a shot." Before Nadler could respond, the detective pulled a microcassette recorder from his pocket and held it out to Walter. "She says anything, get it on here. Take her directly to Emergency and ask for Dr. Lomax. I'll call ahead and tell him you're bringing her in."

Nadler stared at Weeden for a moment, then angrily fished the keys from his pocket and tossed them to Walter. "Drop her and come right back. No bullshit."

Walter gave him a quick salute, led by his middle finger. "Sir, yes, sir."

CHAPTER

6

ALTHOUGH AMY RODE IN the back, her eyes found Walter's in the rearview mirror, and the strange grayness of them only seemed to intensify in the dark. Each time they passed under a streetlamp, the light washed over her like a brush, repainting her on a canvas of shadows.

Walter fumbled with the microcassette recorder, managed to hit the red Record button, and set it on the seat beside him.

"Are you okay back there?"

She looked back at him but said nothing. She was still wearing his uniform jacket, now over the T-shirt and sweatpants. One of the investigative techs had found her an old pair of tennis shoes. Not a perfect fit, but close enough. Better than no shoes at all on a night like tonight. It was cold and growing colder by the minute as angry gusts came off the Detroit River. The snow was coming down sideways and only getting worse.

Something about her seemed oddly familiar.

Walter cleared his throat. "This is going to sound a little crazy, but have we met before?"

As soon as he said it, he wished he could take it back. It sounded like a bad line at a bar.

In the rearview mirror, she gave him the same look he'd probably get if he asked that question in a bar, then a gentle shake of her head.

They passed through three more intersections in silence. "What's going to happen to him?"

Walter slowed and changed lanes in order to get around a Volkswagen Bug going half the speed limit. "Who?"

"The dead guy."

"Once they're done processing the scene, they'll transport him to the city morgue."

"Will he be autopsied?"

He met her eyes in the mirror. "Probably. Why?"

"Just curious."

Walter weighed his words. He didn't want to spook her. "They tend to do one anytime a death isn't ruled accidental. In a case like this, it's just procedure."

"I didn't mean to kill him. I was only trying to get away."

"I know." He made a left on Wilmont and eased into the middle lane. "Were there others?"

"Other girls, you mean?"

"Yeah."

She shrunk a little lower in the seat and looked out the window. "That first night, I smelled perfume on the bed. Not much, but when I said something to him about it, he bagged up the sheets, the only pillow, and took it all out of there. Said he dropped everything in the incinerator. Someone carved J.K. into the bottom of the sink, too."

"J.K.?"

"It looked like it had been there awhile. I saw a bra next to the bathtub the first night he locked me in there, but it was gone the second night." Hesitating for a second, she added, "Do you think that's who they found in the basement freezer? Was it J.K.?"

"You heard that, huh?"

"That detective was very loud."

"We'll know more after we identify the bodies."

"More autopsies…"

"Fingerprints, most likely."

Her eyes met his again in the mirror. "Is that possible? That detective said they were…bad."

In training, Walter had learned how a medical examiner could sometimes remove the skin from the hand of a deeply decomposed body and wear it like a glove in order to obtain prints, which he'd found fascinating at the time—but it wasn't the kind of thing you told a girl who might have been days from ending up in that freezer herself.

That realization must have come to her anyway. When Walter glanced back, Amy's face had grown pale and she'd covered her mouth with her hand.

"Oh, no, are you—"

She nodded quickly. "Pull over—I think I'm gonna be sick."

"Shit—hold on…"

With the snow growing heavy, traffic was moving particularly slow. Fumbling the switches on the dash, Walter gave the siren a quick chirp and flicked on the red and blue flashers. In the back seat, Amy shrugged off his jacket and grasped the door handle. She quickly discovered you can't let yourself out of the back of a cruiser.

Walter jerked the wheel to the right, crossed the lane at a sharp angle, and slid to a stop against the curb. He jumped out and stumbled through the snowdrifts left by the plows the night before to tug open Amy's door.

She was hunched over, one hand still over her mouth. He tried to help her as she scrambled out, but she shrugged him off. He stepped aside, clearing her path to the bushes—as Amy brought her left shoulder up into Walter's gut, knocking the wind out of him and sending him tumbling into the snowbank. The toe of her borrowed shoe connected with his lower back, and Walter felt a sharp pain in his kidney. He rolled to the side, both hands up, ready to block another blow. But Amy was no longer standing there. She was darting across Wilmont, dodging the slow-moving cars.

Scrambling to his feet, Walter tried to shout but coughed instead. He ran after her, narrowly missing a green station wagon and black sedan in the street. On the other side of Wilmont, he spotted her again, nearly a hundred feet down the sidewalk already. How was she so fast? Amy pushed by several pedestrians and ducked down an alley, running between a laundromat and a Chinese restaurant.

The alley was about fifty feet deep and ended at a brick wall. He reached the opening in time to see her scurry over some crates onto a dumpster.

"Amy, stop!"

She didn't even turn. Pushing off with both hands, she swung over the top and disappeared behind the wall.

Walter followed after her, but by the time he scrambled over the crates and reached the dumpster to peer over the wall, there was no sign of her. The falling snow made quick work of any tracks she'd left behind.

NOW

7

THE PASSENGER-SIDE DOOR of the patrol car flew open, and a female officer leaned out low. "Get in the back, now!"

Walter didn't look at her. His gaze remained on the pavement. "I'm not going to do that. You don't understand what this is."

"No? Get in the car and explain it to me, before you get yourself killed!"

Two shots rang out.

Hard cracks.

Both wheels on the driver's side of the car went flat.

A third shot pierced the hood, and the engine seized and went silent.

Someone tried to squeeze out the front door of the club, and another shot hit the brick inches from their head, sending dust into the air. They quickly shuffled back inside.

The bouncer was huddled behind the brick valet stand

to the left of the club's door, his eyes searching the rooftops across the street, the direction of the shots.

The driver of the patrol car yanked the microphone from the dash. "Twelve eighty-four. Vehicle disabled. Multiple shots fired. Establish——"

Another shot. Red's expert marksmanship. The bullet tore through the windshield, the dash, and the center of the radio. Sparks rained out, and the officer dropped the microphone with a squeal of profanity.

Through all this, Walter kept his eyes on the pavement.

When he spoke, his voice remained calm. "Both of you need to exit that vehicle, walk over to your friends, and send back whoever is in charge."

The female officer's name badge read RODRIGUEZ. Sinking low in her seat, she glared at Walter.

When she didn't move, Walter turned to her. "If you don't do as I'm saying, the next bullet from my snipers will split your partner's skull in two."

"*Your* snipers?"

Walter looked back down at the pavement and fought the tickle in his throat. "Five…four…three…two…"

"Okay!" her partner blurted out. "Okay!" He unfastened his seat belt, clicked open the driver's-side door, and slid out to the blacktop as if melting from the seat, as low as he could get without crawling, his head turned up toward the surrounding buildings. "They won't shoot!?"

"Not if you hurry."

He took a deep breath and looked back at his partner through the interior of the car. She was still in her seat. She gave him a soft nod but didn't move.

He was gone then, scrambling across the intersection in a low crouch. Barricades had gone up on Woodward. When the officer reached them, he dove through and vanished into the growing crowd of first responders.

Rodriguez remained in her seat.

"Don't make me kill you. Go."

"I could hit her in the arm or knee," Red said in the earbud. *"It doesn't have to be a kill shot."*

"If she doesn't exit the vehicle, she dies," Walter said calmly.

Her head swiveled and she quickly took him in, spotted the earbud, then looked from him to the buildings. "What are you doing?"

Walter just shook his head. "Go. Send over your supervisor."

This time she did. Unlike her partner, though, she unfastened her seat belt without any sign of panic. She climbed out of the disabled car and went to where the other officers waited, not at a run, but at a slow walk, stopping at the midway point to look back at Walter, then at all the surrounding roofs and windows.

"That one's got balls," Red said.

"Keep moving around, multiple floors like we discussed," Walter replied. "We don't want anyone to get a bead on you."

At the back of the growing police presence, SWAT arrived.

A large armored black van.

The back doors opened, and six officers dressed in full tactical gear jumped out, lining up in a ready stance along the side. A seventh climbed out after them and glanced at the entrance to the club, where the bouncer huddled near the door and various clubgoers were taking cover around the intersection.

Walter watched Rodriguez cross the barricade and push through the officers. She went straight for the SWAT van. For the seventh officer. Rodriguez gestured back toward Walter several times, but they were too far away for him to make out what she was saying. One by one, the heads started to turn in Walter's direction as she spoke.

All these people were from Detroit PD, but Walter didn't recognize anyone. He'd been out of the game too long. The last one was clearly in charge, though. The boss kept watch on Walter as Rodriguez debriefed, then rounded the vehicles with a swagger—something between urgency, confidence, and caution—and approached with one hand resting on the gun in the hip holster. No indication of worry about getting shot.

Up close, Walter saw she was maybe fifty, with short-cropped dark hair flaked with bits of gray and a scar above her left temple. She stopped short of Walter and looked back toward Rodriguez. "Did you frisk him? Anyone?"

When nobody answered, she shoved a foot between Walter's legs and kicked them apart. "You carrying any weapons?"

With the sudden shift in weight, Walter nearly fell over. His right thigh cramped under the added strain. Pain sliced up his back again and gripped his spine. He looked over at his cane lying on the ground at his side but didn't reach for it. From between clenched teeth, he said, "Careful, I've got a bum leg."

"I asked you a question."

"No weapon, no."

The commander moved on to Walter's right ankle, then his left. She tugged open Walter's coat and frowned. "What the hell is this?"

"A bulletproof vest."

The woman slid a finger under one of the metal clasps, pinched the thick material on Walter's shoulder, and frowned. "From what decade? That thing must weigh fifty pounds."

Walter shrugged. "If it ain't broke…"

The commander moved on to Walter's pockets. She took Walter's burner phone. When she found nothing else, she stepped back. The scar above her temple was marred with several frustrated creases. "Do you want to tell me what's going on?"

When Walter opened his mouth to answer, another cough came—deep and wet, from his lungs. It felt like shards of glass as he choked it up. He'd managed to turn his head and cough into the crook of his elbow, but when it relented and he pulled away, red spittle dotted his coat sleeve.

"Je-sus," the commander muttered. "What's your name?"

"O'Brien," Walter told her. "Walter O'Brien."

In the commander's hand, Walter's phone began to ring.

Sealey.

"Go ahead," Walter said. "Answer it."

The woman eyed him for several seconds, then looked at the phone, studied the screen, and tapped Answer. "This is Commander Rigby with Detroit PD. Who am I speaking to?"

Walter heard Sealey through his earbud.

I'm only going to explain this once, so I need you to pay careful attention, Commander Rigby. I have snipers positioned throughout that intersection, all the surrounding buildings. Some of the best shooters in the world. Think of them as enforcers. As long as you do as you're told, I won't ask them to fire a single shot. You don't, and you'll witness some of the best marksmanship of your career. Every bullet they place, every life they take, will be on you. You are in control of that. You are in control of only that."

Still on the ground, Walter said, "I'm getting up. My knees can't take this."

Rigby shot him an irritated glance. "Stay the hell down! You're not in charge here."

With two fingers, she pointed angrily at a couple of SWAT officers behind the barricade, then at Walter. Both officers raised their weapons, AR-15s by the look of them. They pointed the barrels toward Walter.

Walter shifted his weight. The cold blacktop bit into his knees. A sharp pain shot up his bad leg and ended somewhere in the middle of his spine. He chewed his lip and did his best to ignore it.

"You don't want to test us," Sealey said.

Red fired.

The bullet struck the pavement a few inches from Rigby's left shoe. She barely flinched.

Red fired a second time. This shot hit the barrel of one of the AR-15s. The rifle twisted from the man's grip with a sharp *clang!* and jerked to the side.

Walter hadn't seen Red shoot in a while. It was a thing of beauty.

"You've got a job to do, Commander Rigby, and that job isn't to harass the man in front of you. Your job is to contain this. Nobody moves, nobody leaves without my permission. Nobody exits that club. My enforcers are in place to ensure you do that job properly. If everyone does as they're told, everyone walks away from this. You don't bring in air support. You don't make any move against my people. You do, and bad things will happen."

"What do you want?"

"That's simple. There's a woman inside that club. She's responsible

*for the deaths of hundreds of people. We want her. She surrenders,
and nobody else has to get hurt."*

"I'm not allowing *anyone* to get hurt," Rigby replied. "And
I'm certainly not going to turn someone over to whoever
you are."

*"This isn't a negotiation, Commander. Earlier tonight, we placed
a bomb inside that club. How many people do you think are still in
there? In one hour, if she isn't in our custody, it will detonate. One or
many is the only choice I'm going to give you tonight. We get her, or
they all die. Fifty-nine minutes. Hold on to that phone. You'll receive
additional instructions shortly."*

Sealey hung up.

Over Walter's comm, Red said, *"You forgot to ask for a
hundred million dollars in unmarked bills and a jet to Tahiti."*

Rigby stared at the phone in her hand, then at Walter.
Without a word, she dropped it in her pocket, took out her
own, and quickly dialed a number as she crossed back over
toward the SWAT van, ignoring Walter and the multiple
weapons pointed at both of them.

Walter ignored all the guns, too. He reached for his cane
and used it to get back to his feet. The officers holding the
AR-15s tensed but did nothing as he stepped over to the
abandoned patrol car and settled into Rodriguez's spot in
the passenger seat. "Much better." He was facing the police
barricade on Woodward and the entrance to the club was
on his right.

At the SWAT van, Rigby spoke to her team. Three of
the patrol officers had joined them. They were too far off
for Walter to read the insignias on their uniforms, but they
were most likely the ranking officers. He'd lost track of
Rodriguez.

"You ever see a female SWAT leader?" Red asked.

"Times they are a-changin', boys," Sealey replied.

Walter knew both Red and Sealey had all these people in their rifle sights and would take them out if things went sideways. They wouldn't risk the woman getting away because of bureaucratic bullshit. Between the SWAT team and the patrol officers, Walter counted twenty-six law enforcement, four EMTs, and at least thirty civilians scattered about, probably more. The first news truck was working its way closer, two wheels on the sidewalk to round the standstill traffic. The last thing they wanted to do was take out innocents, but they would if they had to.

Rigby stomped back over a moment later, her haggard face wrapped in a scowl. "Who is this woman you're after?"

Before Walter could answer, a deep-throated engine growled from the opposite end of the intersection. A large dump truck lumbered through the wooden police barricades, cracking them like toothpicks, and rounded the front of the club. There was a snowplow attached to the front and DETROIT PUBLIC WORKS stamped across the doors in faded green letters. Salt sprayed out the back of the truck, coating the blacktop, sidewalks, and whatever else was in its path. Everyone watched in confusion as the plow caught the corner of a patrol car and effortlessly pushed it aside, kept going. The heavy vehicle then rumbled around the front of the club, turned, and vanished down the opposite side of the building across Park, leaving thick clouds of black smoke in the air and salt on everything else.

Rigby took several steps forward, her mouth hanging open. "What the hell?"

About damn time, Walter thought.

In his earbud, Red said, *"Now we've got a party."*

1992

Amy Archer

Alvin Schalk
Two bodies/basement freezer

... **Walter O'Brien, 28 Years Old**

8

"YOU'RE DOING ANOTHER SHOT, or I'm playing the song again. That's the rule."

Walter turned on his barstool to face Herb Nadler and felt the room tilt slightly to the left. When his vision caught up with the movement, he found three Nadlers standing next to him, holding shot glasses. He focused on the one in the middle. "I can't do another shot. I gotta work tomorrow."

The words came out as *I candzo nudder zot,* but Nadler understood. These were the words of his people. He rolled his eyes, held up the shot glass, and yelled at the crowd, "O'Brien won't do another! Billy, drop the quarter—this one is all on him!"

From the jukebox in the corner of Mig's Tavern, Billy Preston shouted something back, then turned to the jukebox, half the beer in his mug sloshing down over his hand and onto the floor. A moment later, the opening beat of

"Eye of the Tiger" by Survivor clapped through the bar's speakers for the eighth time amid a flurry of boos and shouts.

Walter rested his elbows on the bar and buried his face in his hands.

Mig's had been a cop bar for forty-three years. On any given night, it was filled with Detroit's finest from the four surrounding precincts. This Wednesday night was no different. The beer was cheap, the watered-down liquor cheaper, and the company a mix of uniforms and officers in street clothes. Nadler had taken Walter here the first night they'd met, and it was only fitting they spend their last night as partners here, too.

Nadler smacked him on the back. "You, my friend, may have to work tomorrow, but not in uniform. And as your soon-to-be former partner, it's on me to send you off to your first day on the job as a detective for Detroit PD properly."

Nadler then drank both shots and slammed the glasses down on the bar top.

Walter raised his index finger and signaled the bartender. "Water, kind sir. Just water."

The man smirked, filled a glass from the tap, and slid it in front of Walter, who drank it down in a single gulp.

Nadler frowned. "Seriously?"

"I gotta go."

"Six years together, and you're going to let it end like this? Just walk off into the sunset? Let me see the shield again."

Walter sighed and pulled the gold badge from his back pocket. "The sun set like four hours ago."

Nadler whistled and scooped it up. "It's so shiny."

Before Walter could get his badge back, Nadler took

several steps away from the bar and held it over his head. "Billy, shut that thing up!"

The jukebox screeched and went quiet.

"I need everyone's attention!" Nadler shouted. "Eyes front. This is some important shit I am about to bestow on all of you!"

"Herb's using big words, cut him off!" someone shouted from the back.

Nadler cleared his throat. "For six torturous years, I have been tasked with babysitting Officer Walter O'Brien. During that time, he has written more than twelve hundred tickets, arrested six hundred twenty-three upstanding fellow members of our fine community, received three citations, two accelerated promotions, and been shot at twice. He's drawn his weapon fourteen times and saved my skin at least once. I taught him everything I know, and luckily, he had the common sense to ignore all that and learn from others so he could get out of uniform and move up the ranks. I've got twenty-two years in blue, and I'm pretty sure the powers that be have no intention of changing that."

"Didn't he lose one, too, Herb?" Billy Preston shouted from the back.

"Ah, yes." Nadler nodded. "The girl who got away. The tiny little thing who beat the hell out of our boy on his first night out of the gate and ran off on him. At least she taught him how to take a punch. The point is, our boy got back up, dusted off, and kept on going. Not easy to do in this line of work, and he did it like a pro. For six years, he's been nothing but a pro." Nadler raised the gold shield high above his head. "I could have not asked for a better partner, I'm gonna miss him, but I wish him nothing but the best as he moves on to the next chapter of his life. If you got 'em, raise 'em up, folks. Join me in toasting the latest addition to the Homicide Division of Detroit's finest!"

"You don't have a beer, Herb!" someone pointed out.

"I don't have a beer," Nadler repeated, glancing at his empty hand. He quickly grabbed a random glass from the table next to him and held it up.

The bartender had slipped a Coors draft in front of Walter, and he raised it along with everyone else, mouthed the words *thank you* to Nadler, and drank it down.

Twenty minutes later, he was on the sidewalk walking back to his apartment on Benton. Nadler and some of the others had tried to put him in a cab, but it wasn't far and he wanted to walk, give his head a chance to clear and savor the moment. The August air was warm and still slightly humid from the earlier drizzle. It had rained just enough to wash some of the city's stink away. He glanced up at the clock on the side of Hartington Savings and Loan and realized it was eight minutes until midnight.

Six years from rookie to homicide detective was no easy feat. He'd worked his butt off to make it happen, and he'd be one of the youngest in the department. He knew that meant an uphill battle in his future, but it wouldn't be his first, and at that particular moment there was very little he felt he couldn't take on.

Except the damn sidewalk, which kept shifting under his feet, while the buildings swayed gently with the wind. And why was everyone else suddenly walking so fast?

Or was he just walking slow?

Maybe he'd drunk a little more than he should have.

That might be it.

A bus stop shelter came up on the right side of the

sidewalk, and Walter half fell, half settled down onto the bench.

An elderly woman was sitting on the far end. She gave him an odd glance, then turned back to the paperback in her hand. *Different Seasons* by Stephen King.

"I'm a homicide detective," Walter told her, not exactly sure why, but the words felt good rolling off his tongue.

She marked her place in the book with her thumb and looked back over at him. "I'll be sure to keep that in mind if I decide to kill someone."

"I'm a homicide detective at twenty-eight years old."

"Good for you."

"What do you do?"

She stared at him for another second, looked him up and down, then returned to the book as she spoke. "I sit in this shelter every couple of nights and wait for Giovanni's to close, and sometimes they give me a bite to eat. Whatever they got left over. That's what *I* do. How about you leave me alone so I can get back to that?"

Walter noticed her clothing for the first time. The holes in her sweater. The worn shoes that looked two sizes too big. On the sidewalk across from them stood a shopping cart loaded with various odds and ends, bottles and cans, all loosely covered with a tattered blue blanket.

"You're a detective now, at twenty-eight," she muttered under her breath. "I'm fifty-six. What do you think you'll be at fifty-six? Ain't none of us really know till we get there."

"I'm sorry," Walter heard himself say, knowing it was the wrong thing to say but too late to take it back.

She huffed but didn't reply. She returned to her book, shaking her head.

The bus stop shelter faced Giovanni's from across the sidewalk.

Nearly every table was full, even though the Italian restaurant would be closing soon. A completely different world not more than ten feet away, with dozens of laughing and smiling faces inside—mostly couples, a mix of young and old, tiny islands of red-and-white-checkered tables filled with wine, pasta, and pizza.

When Walter's eyes landed on her through the glass in that crowded dining room, a voice in the back of his mind immediately whispered that it couldn't possibly be her. Not now. Not after six years. But even as this thought attempted to take hold, another voice told him it was.

It was her.

Amy Archer.

The girl who got away.

CHAPTER

9

AMY ARCHER.

She was sitting with a man at a small table on the far left side of the dining room, tucked up in the corner. The man's back was to the picture window, and she faced him, a glass of wine in her hand and a smile on her face. She wore a red dress, and her chestnut hair was feathered back to one side, clipped in place above diamond earrings. Only a hint of makeup.

Walter vividly recalled his fingers in her hair, tucking loose strands behind her ear.

The touch of her skin against his palm.

And those eyes.

There was no mistaking her eyes.

Even from this distance, from the shelter across the sidewalk outside, he knew those eyes. The deep grayness of them. They pulled at him, and he was nearly to his feet before he even realized that he had started to stand.

It couldn't be her, though, could it? All these years later? *It's her. You know it is.*

He forced himself to settle back down on the bench. The man across from her must have said something funny—the girl leaned forward over the table and laughed, then rocked back in her seat, somehow managing not to spill the wine.

Back in that apartment, beneath the grime and filth of captivity, he'd known she was an attractive girl. He'd seen glimpses of it. But now it was undeniable.

She *radiated* beauty.

As Walter watched her, he realized he wasn't alone—half the men and several of the women in the restaurant were watching her, too. Stealing glances whenever they could, unable to help themselves.

If she was aware, she didn't acknowledge it. She looked at the man across from her as if he were the only other person in the room. Walter could see her foot resting against his under the table.

The man raised his hand, signaled their waiter. He twitched his fingers, signing the air with an invisible pen.

The waiter nodded, disappeared for a moment, and returned with their check in a black leather case.

The man paid with a credit card. Then the two of them stood and started for the door.

The back of her red dress was cut low, revealing the small of her back. Those who had been stealing looks gave up the pretense and simply stared as she walked by, moving with the grace and fluidity of water in tall, elegant red heels.

Her companion held the door for her as the two of them stepped out onto the sidewalk. He then slipped his hand down her bare back and pulled her closer for a kiss, right there in front of that large picture window as if to show all those watching that she belonged to him.

Walter had never been a jealous man, but in that moment he hated that guy. Every ounce of his being wanted to be him. He wanted to know the feel of her lips, the taste of her breath. He wanted to feel her body pressed against him in that slinky dress.

Watching her return the man's kiss instead of rebuffing him might have been worse. She stood on the tips of her toes to meet his lips, eyes closed, leaning into him. Her hand drifted down his chest, to the growing bulge in his jeans. She turned and led him by the hand, west, toward Oakton.

Walter realized he was gripping the edge of the bench seat tight enough to turn his fingers white. The woman beside him noticed. She was watching him. Watching him watch *them*.

"Maybe it's best you go home and sleep it off, Detective."

But when he stood on drunken legs and started down the sidewalk, Walter had no intention of going home. Though he cursed himself for leaving his gun there.

10

WALTER FOUND THEM IN an alley about three blocks from the restaurant. He'd lost sight of the pair on the sidewalk and would've almost missed them in the alley if not for hearing the man's voice from behind a dumpster about ten feet back. He spoke too low for Walter to make out exactly what he said, but when he grunted, the sound echoed off the surrounding brick. This was followed by a soft exhalation and a gasp.

Walter paused at the mouth of the alley and listened.

He pictured Amy pressed up against the wall, her dress hitched up, underwear pushed aside. Standing on one leg with the other curled around this other man who wasn't him. Walter imagined the scene so vividly he didn't realize he'd closed his eyes until he opened them and found that he'd closed the distance to that dumpster by more than half. Rushed breathing inched through the silence, and when Walter closed his eyes again he heard her whispers at his ear, felt her breath slipping over his face and neck.

"What the fuck?"

Walter's eyes snapped open. The man was standing there. His belt was undone, but he'd hitched his pants up. He'd come out from behind the dumpster and was glaring at Walter. "What the fuck?"

Behind the man, the red dress was pooled on the ground, a single red pump lying on top.

Walter caught a glimpse of a bare leg as the girl silently edged deeper into the shadows. In his mind, he saw her tucked between the sink and toilet in that bathroom all those years ago. He remembered—

The man slammed Walter in the center of his stomach with the heel of his palm.

Walter felt the air rush from his lungs and he stumbled backward, tried to keep his footing, but tripped and landed hard on the asphalt.

"You drunk piece of shit. This is how you get your rocks off? Perving around in alleys?"

He took three hurried steps and kicked Walter in the side, caught him just below the ribs. Walter pulled his knees up and twisted to the right, tried to get his badge out of his back pocket, but another blow came. A third after that.

Amy, tell him to stop, he thought.

She didn't. She had to be watching, but she didn't say a word, didn't make a sound.

The man was shouting now. He kicked him again and again. Ribs, kidneys, thigh, shoulder. The blows came so fast and hard Walter only managed to block a handful. It was the kick to his chin that hurt most, that one sent his world to black.

11

"**JESUS, WHAT THE HELL** happened to you?" Lynn Crowley set down her mug of coffee and stood from her desk. She crossed the small, crowded room that served as her office outside Evidence and got a better look at Walter through the barred window.

He wanted to tell the evidence clerk to lower her voice, not because he was worried others might hear—Detroit PD stored evidence in the basement of headquarters on Beaubien Street—but because despite the handful of aspirin he'd swallowed when he finally made it back to his apartment, damn near every sound he'd heard since waking this morning seemed to amplify and rattle around in his head.

When he'd come to in the alley, he'd been alone. It took a moment before he realized where he was and exactly why he was drooling on the pavement. Then the pain came. Nearly every inch of his body ached, numbed only by the copious amounts of alcohol still working through his system. Albeit only in fuzzy pieces, he remembered what had happened—leaving the bar, sitting outside the restaurant, following—

Could it have really been her?

He wanted it to be Amy, and he supposed that made it less likely. He'd been looking for her for a very long time, and he'd seen her before—in line at the grocery store, next to him in traffic, sitting at the DMV, walking along the sidewalk—but the moment he'd get close, he'd realize it wasn't her; it never was. Always just some cheap facsimile.

But last night? That was *her.*

Walter figured he'd been unconscious for about ten minutes. Maybe fifteen. He'd seen it was a little after midnight when he'd stumbled out of the alley back onto the sidewalk. He'd taken a beating, no doubt about that, but nothing seemed to be broken, and moving seemed to help with the pain, like working a strained muscle. He'd shuffled back to his building, managed to get his key into the lock, and dropped onto his couch after the aspirin.

The clanging of his alarm clock woke him at five thirty, and after a tenuous shower, several bandages, and more aspirin, he'd made his way into Detroit PD with a black eye, a cut under his chin, and a bruise the size of Delaware wrapped around his torso.

From behind her barred window, Crowley snapped her fingers in Walter's face. "Walter, you with me?"

"Yeah, sorry. Got jumped on my way home from Mig's last night."

"Bastards did a number on you." Crowley reached through the bars and gently turned Walter's chin from side to side to get a better look. "Nothing a little time won't cure, but still, ouch."

Walter fished a scrap of paper from his pocket and slid it through the window to her.

She read aloud the case number, tapped the paper with the tip of her finger, and narrowed her eyes for a moment. "Hmm. Detective Weeden, tenement building in Forest Park, rape vic, right?"

"I don't know how you do that."

She shrugged. "Date and badge are in the case number. The rest isn't so hard. Give me a second."

She turned and disappeared into the large evidence room behind her office and came back a few minutes later with a battered file box, a clipboard resting on top. She buzzed her outer door open and handed the box to Walter, nodding at a small table behind him. "Can't leave my sight, but you can go through it right there. Just remember—"

"Everything that comes out of the box goes back into the box. Yeah, yeah, I know the drill," he finished for her.

He scribbled his name, badge number, and date on the clipboard, handed it back to her, then took the box over to the table.

At one point, the lid had been secured with tape, but after years of opening and resealing, the tape was peeled back and gummed up with so much dust it did nothing but dangle from the sides like ratty pigtails.

There wasn't much in the box.

The lamp, wrapped in plastic, took up most of the space. He carefully removed it and set it aside. Underneath were bags containing the handcuffs, the ropes from the bed, an envelope of photographs, and several swatches of material cut from the mattress. The dried blood had taken on a dark rust color over the years, the rest of the cloth stained yellow. There were also small tubes containing Q-tips with blood samples and a fingerprint card for Alvin Schalk.

At the bottom of the box was a copy of Detective Weeden's typed report. Walter fished it out and scanned the text. He lowered his sore body into a worn wooden chair and read it a second time, much slower. None of it made sense.

CHAPTER

12

THE PAPER WAS STIFF and crinkled in Walter's hand. The initial report was dated Tuesday, February 18, 1986—a little over six and a half years ago.

The body of Alvin Schalk (31, unmarried) was found dead of apparent blunt force trauma to the head by officers Herbert Nadler and Walter O'Brien in response to a neighbor's noise complaint. Schalk's body was on the floor of apartment 2D in a tenement building at 186 Rivard in Forest Park. The apartment was not leased in Schalk's name. It should have been vacant. A lamp found next to the body is the suspected weapon.

An asterisk next to that entry led to a handwritten note in the margin stating that Schalk's blood, hair, and skin from his scalp had been found on the base of the lamp.

A young white female (Amy Archer), discovered nude in the bathroom, admitted to delivering the fatal blow. Evidence (handcuffs) pointed to her having been restrained earlier. She claimed Schalk, an employee of Detroit Metro Taxi, abducted her with the use of his taxi and held her captive for at least two weeks. She appeared to be in shock and was unable to provide exact dates, only that he had picked her up near Eastern Market and drugged her. Signs of apparent sexual assault were visible both on her person and on the bed where additional restraints (rope) were found.

All that was fairly clear, nothing Walter didn't already know. It was the additional notes that confused him.

ADDENDUM—2/18/86: While in transit to Detroit General Hospital, murder suspect Amy Archer escaped police custody and fled. BOLO issued—white female, short blond hair, green eyes, approximate age 15–18, 5'6" in height. Last seen wearing red sweatpants, Detroit Lions T-shirt, white tennis shoes, near the intersection of Wilmont and 18th.

Weeden's physical description was all wrong. There was a photograph attached, but Amy's face was blurry. Probably one they had taken back at the apartment where she was found. It was impossible to make out the details in the photo, but Walter remembered her vividly—she'd had shoulder-length brown hair, not short blond. Gray eyes, not green. And her age—Walter was certain she was twenty-something, no chance she was in her teens.

How did Weeden get something as basic as her vitals wrong? Had he even actually issued any BOLO? Walter didn't remember seeing it; that's why he…

Walter turned the page.

ADDENDUM—2/18/86: Transporting officer, Walter O'Brien, was given a microcassette recorder in the event Archer said anything useful during transport. Upon playback of the tape, only O'Brien can be heard speaking, most likely due to poor placement of the recorder or because Archer was in the back of the patrol car. See attached report from O'Brien for details of their conversation.

ADDENDUM—2/18/86: Schalk's cab located behind Carmine's Drugstore on 49th, substantially vandalized. All windows shattered. Plexiglas between the driver and passenger compartments cracked and left on the floor of the front passenger seat. Due to extended exposure to the elements, no retrievable prints found inside. Per store employees, the car had been there for nearly three weeks. Nobody phoned it in. Bad neighborhood. Cars routinely abandoned in this lot, and the tow company comes on the first Tuesday of the month.

ADDENDUM—2/18/86: Interview with Schalk's dispatcher (Ralph Kanton) at Detroit Metro Taxi. Schalk last reported to work on 1/31/86, called in a fare pickup at 653 Orleans Street (Eastern Market area—possibly AA) at 9:46 p.m. Absence noted two hours later, dispatch unable to reach him on radio. Kanton claims he phoned Schalk's disappearance in to Detroit PD, but I was unable to find a record at the watch desk. The cab was reported stolen on 2/1/86.

Per the dispatcher, Schalk had a history of substance abuse and sometimes disappeared for days at a time. He'd been reprimanded twice (copies attached), and a third would mean termination. They'd phoned his home several times without response. Two coworkers stopped at his residence (83 Cambridge Drive, Detroit MI 48214), but both reported nobody home / no answer at door (copies of dispatcher notes attached).

ADDENDUM—2/18/86: Search warrant for Alvin Schalk residence issued by Judge Harold Shummer and served by Detective Weeden (badge 8674), four uniforms, and five members of SWAT. No answer at door, breached by SWAT. Two-bedroom single-family dwelling. Nobody found in or around home. Spoiled food in kitchen. No evidence of additional abductions in or around premises. Presumed criminal activity appears contained to the Forest Park apartment. Nothing useful learned from neighbors—usual fodder—quiet guy, kept to himself. Last seen sometime in January, exact date unknown.

ADDENDUM—2/19/86: Per Officer Herbert Nadler, resident in apartment 2E of 186 Rivard Street stated, "he [Schalk] had a girl in there." Despite attempts to speak to resident of 2E, they are not answering the door. Neighbors in 2A and 2C had no recollection of anyone entering or leaving 2D in more than a month, both thought the apartment had been empty but admitted to hearing sounds in there ("an animal in pain"). Resident of 2B states seeing an unknown female (Black, mid-twenties) leave 2D on at least one occasion the previous week, approximately 2/10, but could not provide specifics.

ADDENDUM—2/21/86: All fingerprints located in 2D match Schalk. Prints on lamp too smudged to be useful. No other prints discovered. Apartment possibly wiped down recently?

ADDENDUM—2/22/86: Five "Amy Archers" found in the Detroit area; all five accounted for, none matching description of our missing "Amy Archer." BOLO amended and extended to all Wayne County.

ADDENDUM—2/23/86: Autopsy completed on Alvin Schalk (attached). COD = blunt force trauma to occipital bone/cranium. Additional unrelated/abnormal findings (see report).

ADDENDUM—2/27/86: Analysis on blood found on mattress: Type B, male, not female. Schalk also Type B. Either Schalk's blood or possible unknown male victim?

ADDENDUM—3/2/86: Amy Archer BOLO extended statewide.

That was the last of Weeden's notes. If Amy Archer had ever been found, there was no record of it here.

Walter scanned the attached copies of the reports from Schalk's dispatcher—the missing cab, the abandoned job, the reprimands. Nothing useful there, not really. They painted a familiar picture of a man Walter had seen a thousand times in his six years on the force. Someone going through the motions to survive.

The autopsy report was five pages long and included a sketch of Schalk's body with details of the fatal wound noted near the skull. A paragraph on the third page was circled with a large question mark next to it. Autopsy revealed that Schalk's left arm was riddled with cancer and blood clots, which the medical examiner noted as extraordinarily unusual to only present in a single arm, but there it was. Nothing further.

Neither the microcassette recorder nor the tape were in the box.

Walter flipped back to Weeden's description of Archer: *White female, short blond hair, green eyes, approximate age 15–18, 5'6" in height. Last seen wearing red sweatpants, Detroit Lions T-shirt, white tennis shoes, near the intersection of Wilmont and 18th.*

Aside from that first call, he'd never worked with Weeden again. Was he a sloppy cop? Did he mix Amy Archer up with another victim? That seemed ridiculous, but the alternative was that he'd intentionally included the wrong description, which made no sense, either.

Something else was missing.

Walter went through the box a second time to be sure, then looked up at Crowley's window. "Hey, Lynn?"

She was reading a paperback. "Yeah?"

"Weeden found two bodies in a freezer on this case. Down in the basement. I don't see anything on that here. Any idea where that file might be?"

She picked up the scrap of paper with the case number and flicked the edge. "I didn't see anything else back there but I can look again. Do you want to wait?"

"Sure."

She twisted off her stool and started toward the evidence room when her phone rang. She reached back and scooped up the receiver. "Evidence."

Her head bobbed. She looked over at Walter and nodded. "I'll let him know."

When she hung up, she said, "Captain's looking for you."

13

WALTER TOOK THE ELEVATOR up to the third floor. When the doors opened on the Homicide Division bullpen, unfamiliar eyes landed on him from the dozen metal desks stuffed into the space, placed anywhere they could find room. There were several grunts, a couple of quick one-liners about the eye, muffled laughs. A wadded sheet of paper bounced off the wall a few inches from his head. His new coworkers, same as the old. Newbie rookie all over again.

Made primarily of glass and crooked window blinds, the captain's office stood like an afterthought on the back wall of the large room. It was crammed between a series of file cabinets on one side and a counter with a coffee maker that looked like it hadn't been cleaned since Nixon on the other. Walter filled a disposable cup, sniffed, and left it sitting on the counter. Coffee wasn't supposed to smell like warm cheese. This brought several more comments from the desks behind him.

Without looking back, he straightened his tie and knocked on the frame of the half-closed office door.

Captain Jerome Hazlett was standing behind his desk, the phone pinched under his chin, scribbling on a notepad. He glanced up at Walter through the glass and bent blinds and motioned for him to come in.

Hazlett was somewhere in his mid-fifties, with thin gray hair shaved short, and skin as dark and smooth as an eggplant. With about thirty extra pounds on his six-foot-five frame, he barely fit in the room. His voice was so deep the furniture seemed to rattle with it.

There were two wooden chairs in front of the desk, both buried under stacks of manila folders. More files and boxes cluttered the floor. Walter squeezed inside and nudged the door closed. A file with his name on it was sitting on the captain's desk.

When Hazlett finished his phone call and hung up, he looked Walter over but said nothing about the black eye. "I'm pairing you up with Wes Brayman. He's got two decades here in Homicide, patrol before that. He's not a fuck-up like some of the others out there." He waved a large hand toward the desks outside his office. "Keep your head down and listen to him, do what he says. Learn from him. I don't want to hear about any problems with you. I've got enough of those already. You become a problem, and I'll have you back in uniform before the week's out, understand?"

"Yes, sir."

"Herb Nadler and your watch commander both said good things about you; that goes a long way. Tells me a lot more than the selective crap in here." He tapped on Walter's file with a long finger. "Keep your head down and keep doing what you're doing, and you'll be all right. You run into a problem, you take it to Brayman first. You run into a problem with Brayman, try to work your shit out. I don't want to hear about it. I hear about a problem with you from someone else, then you and I will have a problem, understand?"

The number of times that Hazlett said the word *problem* wasn't lost on Walter.

"I don't cause problems."

"Exactly. You don't. Not under my command."

Hazlett tore the top sheet from his pad and handed it to Walter. "Got a body found at the Edison downtown. Brayman's already out there. ME's on the way. Get a patrol to give you a lift and meet up with him. Follow his lead."

Walter knew the Edison Hotel by reputation. It was one of many hotels downtown that primarily rented by the hour for cash. Regular bang and dash.

Hazlett picked up his phone and started dialing a number. When Walter didn't move, the man frowned. "You need something else?"

"I didn't see Detective Weeden when I came in. I was hoping to talk to him."

Hazlett's frown grew deeper. "Weeden? Weeden's been dead going on five years now. Ticker gave out while he was sleeping. We should all be so lucky. What did you need with him?"

Walter considered explaining, then thought better of it. "He's just somebody I knew from a while back."

"Sorry." Hazlett finished dialing his number and pressed the receiver to his ear. "Tell Brayman I want a report by four. And close the door behind you."

14

THE EDISON HOTEL STOOD on the 1200 block of Arlington between a former Pizza Sal's and a laundromat, both abandoned and boarded up years ago. Half a dozen people stood outside a homeless shelter across the street—several smoking, two wrapped in blankets, all taking in the early-morning show.

The Edison's heavy glass door squeaked as Walter tugged it open and stepped inside.

He'd taken two more aspirin on the drive over and they'd taken his hangover from a sledgehammer pounding on the inside of his skull to something more akin to a rubber mallet. He made a mental note to thank Nadler for being an insufferable ass the next time he saw him.

The cage surrounding the manager's desk in the lobby was as old as the crumbling plaster on the walls and ceiling, an original fixture of the building.

The man inside that cage looked old enough to have been an original fixture, too. With wiry gray hair and cloudy eyes behind thick, round glasses, he sat perched on a stool, watching a small black-and-white television with a half-eaten breakfast sandwich in his hand.

Before Walter could say anything, the old man pointed a bony finger at the stairs to his right and said, "Third floor."

Walter nodded, gave the dog collar in his pocket a gentle squeeze, and started up the steps.

The door to room 305 stood open, yellow crime scene tape hanging limply from the frame and a uniformed officer positioned outside.

Walter took out his badge, showed it to him, and stepped inside.

He'd expected to find the room full of people, but there were only two in the room, only one of those two alive.

The live one wore a rumpled brown suit and matching loafers. A Black man with close-cropped salt-and-pepper hair and a neatly trimmed goatee, he was older than Walter had expected. Probably somewhere in his mid- to late fifties. He stood between Walter and the dead man on the bed, partially blocking his view.

Walter cleared his throat. "Detective Brayman? I'm—"

Without looking back at him, Brayman extended his arm and held up his hand, his index and middle fingers extended. "Shh."

Walter stepped deeper into the room and cocked his head. "Why? I don't hear anything."

"I said *shh*, damn it. Just stay right there. Don't move."

"What are you—"

"Another word, and you can wait outside," Brayman said, slowly circling the man on the bed. "I need to think."

Walter opened his mouth, ready to argue, then thought better of it when he got a view of the body.

The dead man was naked, spread-eagle on the bed, his head twisted oddly to the side and his mouth open as if caught in some perpetual silent scream. Both his eyes were open, milky, covered in haze, most likely cataracts—untreated and advanced. His right arm was outstretched, as if reaching for something on the nightstand. The left was at his side. The peeling wallpaper behind his head looked like it was reaching down for him.

Walter's stomach lurched. "Where are his fingers?"

Brayman shook his head. "Christ, are you going to be one of those?"

"One of those?"

"One of those who can't follow simple instructions."

"What, like you say sit, and I'm supposed to sit?"

"Exactly like that."

"Then, yeah. I'm gonna be one of those."

No problems, Captain Hazlett had warned him.

Walter drew in a deep breath, held it for a moment, then let it back out. "Let's start over. I'm Walter O'Brien. Your new partner."

He extended his hand, but the detective didn't take it. Instead, Brayman turned back to the body on the bed.

"How old would you say this guy is?"

Walter went to the edge of the bed and got a better look. "Seventies?"

"The astute young man at the desk downstairs said the guy who rented this room was in his thirties."

"The Crypt Keeper down there is older than this guy. Maybe even older than you. Place like this, he doesn't see any more than he has to and remembers less. Doubt we can take his word for much. Did you walk him up here?"

Brayman nodded. "Manager says this isn't the guy who rented the room."

"Okay. So the guy who rented the room killed this guy and left him here. Mystery solved."

Brayman nodded toward a pile of clothes near the window. "Except the manager told me the guy who rented this room was wearing tan slacks and a red sweater, just like those. He also said that guy came up here with a girl."

"Grandpa here came up with a girl? Good for him."

"The *thirtysomething* man who rented this room, wearing those clothes, came up here with a girl."

Walter said, "Okay…so our guy left here with the girl, swapped clothes with the old guy, and left his?"

"Why?"

"I have no idea."

"Exactly. So be quiet. I need to think."

Walter took a latex glove from his pocket, slipped it on, and went to the pile of clothing. He pinched the tan pants between two fingers and lifted them into the light from the window, then went through the pockets. After a few moments, he said, "No wallet. No nothing. Do we have a name?"

"Paid cash. According to the guest register, his name is Paul Newman. So no, we don't have a name."

Walter dropped the pants and went to the dresser opposite the bed. The dark wood top was scuffed and scraped from years of abuse. There was an indent where a television had once sat, but nothing was there now. The dust had a fresh swirl pattern to it. "Someone wiped this down."

"Someone wiped down everything in this room. Every

surface. There's a towel on the floor in the bathroom. I think that's what they used." Brayman turned to look Walter in the face for the first time and got a look at his black eye. "So I need to teach you to solve homicides *and* how to fight? Remind me to thank the captain."

Walter ignored the dig. "You said *they*. So you agree there were two others?"

Brayman crossed back over to the window and studied the latch. "I'm not agreeing with anything. In this line of work, if you make assumptions, those assumptions start to color your theories. Say I agree with you that we're looking for a man in his thirties and a woman. We put that in a report, and it's carved in stone from that moment forward. That's all anyone looks for. What if three other people were in this room? *Five* people? What if they came and went through the fire escape here? Our man downstairs didn't see anyone leave, so how did they get out?" He gestured at the man on the bed. "For that matter, if he didn't walk through the lobby, how did this guy get in?"

"Nobody came through that window. It's locked from the inside. I already looked." Walter stepped into the small bathroom and was looking at the wall behind the chipped porcelain sink. "Someone smashed the mirror."

"We don't know that's related. Could have happened a month ago."

"It's fresh. There's glass in the sink, all over the floor."

"Maid service here might not be up to your usual standards. Other than our perp wiping away prints, I don't think this room's been cleaned in a year."

"It is a grungy fucking room." Crossing back over to the bed, Walter took in the sheets. They were yellow and looked stiff, covered in stains. "Oh, man, who the hell even lays down on that? I feel like I need a shot just standing here. Any idea on COD?"

Brayman shook his head. "At first I thought broken neck. That's a rough angle. But it's not. I don't see any visible wounds other than the fingers, and there's not much blood so I think that happened postmortem."

Crouching down, Walter got a better look at the man's hands. His stomach lurched, and he felt his headache attempting to beat its way back. "Gotta be trying to hide his identity, right? Why else would they cut his fingers off?" He gestured toward the nub above the knuckle where the man's right pointer finger used to be. "What did they use? Too sloppy to be a knife. Look how ragged these cuts are."

Brayman went silent for several beats, then stepped closer. "I think someone bit them off."

"No way."

"Look at the way the skin is torn at the edges, the ridges. How it tapers out from what's left of the joint bone, like a point. That's consistent with someone biting down hard at the knuckle, then pulling back as they apply pressure." To demonstrate, he put his own finger in his mouth, clamped down on it with his teeth and mimicked jerking his head back. "It would take a lot of force, but it could be done. Especially if the person who did it was tweaking."

The man's skin was covered in age spots and tinged a strange shade of greenish white. His legs looked like toothpicks draped in diseased flesh. "Can we cover his—"

"Nope."

"We've got a tattoo here near the sternum," Walter pointed out. "A four-leaf clover. That might help with an ID."

There was a knock at the door, someone from CSU holding a camera. "Can we get in here now? We've got a shooting downtown and a home invasion after that. I need to get my people moving. The ME just pulled up, too."

Brayman nodded softly, then turned to Walter. "I'll stay in here. I want you to go room by room, question whoever else is still in the hotel, then get a statement from the manager. Let's see if he contradicts anything he told me."

"Not a chance. Get a uniform. I want to hear what the medical examiner has to say."

"I want *you* to do it. Uniforms always miss something."

Walter nearly told him he was a uniform just yesterday. Some of the best cops he knew were uniforms. Wasn't worth the trouble. He stood and started for the door. "I'm not gonna like you, am I?"

"Probably not."

15

THAT NIGHT, WALTER HADN'T been able to sleep. He tried, but he was too wired from the day. When the plastic numbers of his alarm clock rolled from eleven twenty-three to eleven twenty-four with a soft buzz, he'd given up, got dressed, and gone for a walk.

Wes Brayman was an ass, but he knew what he was doing, and every time his new partner got under his skin (which was a lot, possibly a record for a single day), Walter reminded himself of that. This was someone who could teach him, he was sure of that, but he also knew he couldn't let the man walk all over him. Walter knew what he was doing, too. Brayman would see that.

He'd make him see it.

When he left his apartment, he had not intended to return to Giovanni's. His mind had been busy working the details from the Edison—the dead man on the bed, the missing fingers, the possibility of multiple perps. Aside from the manager, nobody had seen anyone come or go. He'd beat on every door like a good little officer before heading back to the room, where he'd caught the tail end of the medical examiner's initial thoughts: their vic had been dead for about six hours, and most of those "age spots" were actually melanoma—their vic had a serious case of skin cancer. And the ME agreed with Brayman that the fingers had been bitten off.

Walter had been so lost in his own head, he'd been wandering the streets aimlessly, paying just enough attention to keep from stepping out into traffic.

Amy Archer kept popping into his mind.

Between thoughts of the Edison murder, he'd see her—laughing in the restaurant, kissing that guy, against the wall in the alley—her; each time, he'd forced the thoughts out, returned to the Edison, then she'd creep back in like some whisper.

He didn't remember walking back to Giovanni's, not exactly. But when he finally did look up to get his bearings, the restaurant was to his left and the bus shelter was on his right. He dropped onto the empty bench, no sign of the homeless woman from the night before.

The night had grown chilly, the sidewalk was nearly deserted, and there were far fewer people inside the restaurant than there'd been last night. Only three tables were occupied. He stared at her table, empty now.

Did he expect her to come back?

Show up with her date from the night before, plop down at the exact same table, and pick up where they left off?

He knew that was ridiculous, but here he was.

Waiting.

And for what, exactly?

It couldn't possibly have been her.

You're an idiot. It wasn't her.

Go home.

But what if it was?

It wasn't.

What if it was?

He had been drunk. *Very* drunk. His mind might have wanted that to be her, but there was no possibility it was. Maybe that's why he was here. He needed to see that it *wasn't* her. Prove it to himself so he could close that door in his head and get back to what he was supposed to be doing—working his first homicide as a detective.

Walter recognized the waiter who'd brought their check last night. Tonight's smaller crowd no doubt meant fewer tips, and he didn't look too pleased about it. He said something to the hostess, then disappeared through a swinging double door at the back.

Where the hell did the waiter go?

Giovanni's closed soon. He could stay and catch the waiter on his way out, maybe ask him—

What?

What exactly would he say?

Hey, last night when I was practically passed-out drunk on this bench, I thought I saw someone I knew inside. I tried to follow her and got my ass handed to me by her boyfriend. Don't suppose you could put me in touch?

It couldn't be her.

It was her.

Walter drummed his fingers on the bench seat. Brayman wanted to get an early start and had told him to be at the precinct by seven. Walter planned to beat him, get there by six. Search through older cases and see if he could find others with missing fingers. He figured that would be their best bet at a starting point.

The waiter still hadn't come back. What if he'd left out the back?

One of the couples rose to leave. The hostess had given them their check, not the waiter.

Go home.

"Fuck it," Walter muttered.

He didn't go home. He crossed the sidewalk and entered Giovanni's.

16

THE HOSTESS GLANCED at a clock on the wall before smiling at him. "I'm sorry, sir, we're closing in a few minutes. I'm afraid we're not seating anyone else tonight."

"I need to see your credit card receipts from last night." Walter took out his badge and pointed at the table in the corner. "Everyone who sat at that table. I'll need to speak to the waiter, too."

She stiffened at the sight of the badge, glanced at the table, then toward the kitchen. Behind her eyes, Walter could see her mind churning through every possible infraction she'd ever committed in her life. The truly guilty ones attempted to conceal their feelings, put up a wall. The innocent ones always looked guilty as hell.

Walter smiled and put his badge back in his pocket. "Don't worry, neither of you did anything wrong. I'm just following a lead."

Relieved, she nodded and quickly regained her composure. "I can get the receipts, but I think Jake left."

"If he did, I'll need you to bring him back in."

With another nod, she disappeared through the kitchen door.

The handful of remaining customers were watching him, surely listening. Walter was completely overstepping and he knew it. This was the kind of thing that could cost him his gold shield and dump him back in uniform, or worse. He turned his back on them and faced the kitchen. The less they saw of him, the better.

The hostess returned holding a stack of receipts, the waiter following behind her. She must have caught him halfway out the door. His tie was hanging loose around his neck and a pack of cigarettes bulged from his shirt pocket. He awkwardly tucked in his shirt as he shuffled back into the dining room to Walter. "Can I help you?"

"What's your name?"

"Jake. Jake Marson."

"How long have you worked here, Jake?"

"Like a year, little less."

The hostess sorted the receipts on an empty table, separated them into two piles. She slid the smaller of the two stacks toward Walter. "That's everything for table 4."

Walter spread them out and quickly handed back the receipts that listed three or more guests. He lined up the remaining four receipts in front of Jake. "Which one was a woman—Caucasian, early twenties? About five four, shoulder-length brown hair, gray eyes. She was with an older man, probably mid-thirties."

The waiter's eyes narrowed, and he studied the receipts.

He pulled them closer one at a time. "Last night, you're sure?"

Walter nodded. "She was wearing a slinky red dress, cut real low in the back."

The waiter's finger drifted over the text. "I don't suppose you know what they ordered?"

"I know she had red wine."

"All four of these ordered wine."

"They would have seemed…out of place to you. She was out of his league, know what I mean? But they were clearly together."

"Brown hair, gray eyes…"

"Red dress. Yeah."

"I just don't remember…"

How can he not remember? Is he covering for her for some reason?

"If you're lying to me, holding back for some reason, you could get in serious trouble," Walter insisted.

"Dude, why would I lie?" Jake tapped on the second receipt. "This receipt was the Parsons. They come in a couple times each week, and he always orders the Cena di Domenica. I know it wasn't them." He slid that receipt off to the side. "I guess it could be any one of these three, but I don't remember anyone like that, not last night. You sure I waited on them? Last night was busy. We all wear the same getup. Are you sure it was that table?"

"I'm sure."

You were drunk. How sure are you really?

No, he was certain. That table. This waiter. Walter slid the remaining three receipts toward the hostess. "I'm gonna need copies of these."

17

AT TWENTY AFTER SIX the next morning, Walter was one of only five detectives in the homicide bullpen. He'd remembered to bring his own coffee, and he sure as hell needed it—he'd only managed to get maybe four hours of sleep.

By the time Brayman came through the door twenty minutes later, holding an armload of files, Walter was busy tacking eight-by-ten photographs from the Edison up on a board. He'd found the photos sitting in Brayman's inbox, someone having developed and dropped them off during the night.

"I wanted to get a head start," Walter told him.

Brayman studied the photographs for a moment, grunted, then set the file folders on his chair. "I've been in records since five. These are all the cases I could find in the past ten years where fingers were removed."

Damn it.

Walter eyed the large stack. "How many?"

"Twenty-nine."

"Jesus."

"Detroit's a mob town," Brayman reminded him. "It's not uncommon to find missing fingers or teeth. Sometimes both."

"You think this was a mob thing?"

"Nope. So I want to go through these and try and isolate any that don't seem mob related. We'll focus on those."

"You said twenty-nine. There's more like fifty or sixty files here."

"Mob guys tend to bring tools. They don't bite off the fingers. I pulled all the cases with severe biting, in case this is some kind of escalation from someone in the system."

"What, like a fetish thing?"

"A fetish implies some form of sexual gratification from the act. I don't think that's what we have here."

Walter agreed. "Okay, so you're thinking someone trying to conceal our vic's identity, not smart enough to bring his toolbox, but willing to improvise in a pinch because chewing someone's fingers off is better than risking an ID."

"Precisely."

Brayman divided the files into two piles and slid one stack to Walter.

Walter frowned. "Why do I get organized crime?"

"You'd rather go through the biters?"

Walter shook his head and pulled the files closer. "No, it's fine. I'll go through these. Says a lot about you, though, wanting to search the sex crime files over mob. Probably some kinky shit in there."

"Hardly. You wanna switch, we'll switch."

Walter settled down into his chair, took a sip of his coffee, and started flipping through the first file. "Nope. I don't want to get between you and your kicks. At your age, I'm sure they're hard to come by."

Brayman sat on the corner of the desk and glared at him. "How old do you think I am, exactly?"

Without looking up from the file, Walter said, "I think when Lincoln was shot you might have been the first to roll into Ford's Theatre with your musket out."

"I'm fifty-four."

"Okay."

"So stow the age jokes. Especially the bad ones."

Walter closed the first folder, set it aside, and opened the next one. "Well, if you don't want me to treat you like the second coming of Grandpa Munster, then how about you don't treat me like a rookie and send me on door-to-doors? I'm damn good at my job. That's why I'm sitting here."

"I didn't intend to imply—"

"You've got experience, I respect that, but I've got a solid arrest record behind me, couple citations from the brass. When I came up for promotion, three different departments wanted me. I *chose* Homicide. Don't dismiss me because you think I'm some wet-behind-the-ears newbie who can't tell his ass from his head."

"Fair enough. You're right."

Walter opened his mouth, ready to argue, before realizing the man had agreed with him.

Brayman rounded his desk and settled into his chair. "I shouldn't have been so dismissive yesterday. I apologize."

"Seriously?"

Brayman smirked. "No, of course not. You've had your gold shield for what? Thirty-six hours? I've had mine for twenty-one years. Mine says lieutenant on it, yours does not. Yours still has that new-badge smell. How many homicides have you worked? Personally, I lost track of my record more than a decade ago, when you were probably still in the back seat of your daddy's car trying to get your hand up some girl's business."

A memory, plucked from his childhood, suddenly intruded on Walter's thoughts:

Night—his father, standing outside the kitchen window, his back against a tree. A woman in his arms. A woman who wasn't Walter's mother. His father's hand twisted in her hair, holding her close as their lips met. Her palm in his shirt, on his chest. His father glancing at the window, seeing Walter, seeing Walter watching him yet unable to stop.

Walter shook off the memory. Brayman was still talking.

"You were assigned to me because someone higher than you in the food chain decided you might learn something from me, not the other way around. If I need someone to remind me how to write a ticket for jaywalking, I'll ask you. Otherwise, I expect you to keep your mouth shut and do as you're told."

Walter felt the blood rush to his face, but before he could say anything, Brayman added, "Before you get too deep into those files, call down to Vice and get a list of all the known working girls in that area. Anyone they've seen or picked up near the Edison."

Walter shuffled through the paperwork on his desk, found what he was looking for, and tossed the stack onto Brayman's desk. It landed with a thud. "I did that yesterday, jerk-off."

Brayman looked down at the rap sheets. He thumbed the edge of a Post-it Note sticking out from the top.

Walter added, "I also flagged the ones that match the description I got out of the Edison's manager while you were upstairs playing with the lock on the window in *our* crime scene."

"Smartass. You don't want this assignment, talk to the captain. I sure as shit didn't ask to be partnered with you."

From the other side of the room, Captain Hazlett's door opened. With the phone pressed to his ear, he looked around the room, found them, and said loudly, "Your vic from yesterday, old guy missing fingers, right?"

When had the captain come in?

Brayman cleared his throat. "Yes, sir."

"Hang on," Hazlett told whoever was on the line. He set the phone down on his desk and walked over, placed a scrap of paper in front of Brayman. "We got another one. Old woman this time, also missing fingers, found in the ladies' at the Corktown bus terminal. I want you two on it first. I've got uniforms taping things off and keeping everyone out. If it doesn't seem related, come back and I'll give it to someone else."

"Yes, sir."

Halfway back to his office, he added, "And quit piss ing on each other. Work your shit out. Nobody's getting reassigned."

18

BRAYMAN DROVE, WHICH WAS fine with Walter. He was busy flipping through the information from Vice. He'd brought several of the photos from the Edison, too. Primarily close-ups of the severed fingers.

On their way out, Brayman had called the medical examiner's office to get an update on the autopsy. When he couldn't get the ME on the phone, he'd left a message with an assistant.

They were a few minutes out from the bus depot when Brayman cleared his throat and spoke, his gaze never leaving the road. "I think we need to set some guidelines."

"Guidelines?"

"If we're going to work together, we need rules."

Walter rolled his eyes. "Oh, I can't wait to hear this."

"Like a truce."

"Hey, you fired the first shot."

"A cease-fire, then."

"How does that work?"

"We compromise. We both recognize the strengths each of us brings to the table, and we agree to focus on those strengths and try not to get wrapped up in the petty stuff."

When Walter said nothing, Brayman continued.

"I accept that you have a solid record behind you in a uniform. I know Herb Nadler. He told me you're a good cop. Not afraid of hard work. Intuitive. He couldn't think of a single instance where you didn't go above and beyond in all the years you worked together."

Walter felt his anger diminishing, even as he also felt a *but* coming.

"But—he also said you were stubborn, reactionary, cocky, emotional, and sometimes too focused."

"Too focused?"

"As a detective, you need to keep an open mind. You need to see *all* the evidence and weigh it with every decision, not necessarily chase it or let it lead you."

Walter smirked. "So good detectives don't follow the evidence?"

"Good detectives don't let the evidence *lead* them. Like I said yesterday, if you form an opinion and follow it *exclusively*, you do so at the detriment of every other possibility. Give too much weight to a single lead, and there's a good chance you'll go down the wrong rabbit hole because you're neglecting everything else. A good detective creates multiple theories and follows *all* of them, without favoring any one in particular. Laser focus is great when you're solving simple crimes—minor thefts, traffic, domestics, D and Ds—but homicides are rarely simple. You need to unlearn that method. I'll help you with that."

"Uh-huh. And what exactly are you going to get from me in this *compromise*?"

Brayman signaled and made a right onto Howard Street. "People like you. That was the other thing Nadler told me. He said good guys, bad guys, coworkers, they all seem to like you. I've...I've never been much of a people person."

This time, Walter laughed. "No shit."

"The manager at the Edison, he gave you a far more detailed description of the girl and the man who went upstairs with her than the one he gave me. He *talked* to you. He only told me enough to get me out of his hair. There's a difference. Nadler told me that was one of your superpowers and I wanted to see it for myself."

"I didn't get much."

"You learned we were looking for a white girl, late teens to early twenties, narrowed down that pile of rap sheets to what, half a dozen?"

"Nine out of forty-eight."

"Without you, I'd still be looking at all forty-eight," Brayman said, turning into the bus depot parking lot.

Several patrol cars were parked under the large portico, lights flashing. Brayman parked behind them, and they were directed to the restrooms on the east end of the building, inside the main terminal. Four patrol officers were stationed there and the entire area was roped off with yellow crime scene tape. They ducked under and followed the echo of voices into the women's restroom.

Four more uniformed officers were standing inside, but nobody Walter recognized. One of them pointed toward the last stall on the right. "She's in there, the handicap stall."

Another officer was holding a box of latex gloves. She handed a pair to each of them.

"Who found her?" Brayman asked, walking toward the back, tugging on his gloves.

"A mother and her little girl. They're both pretty upset. We've got them stashed away in an office down the hall."

Brayman reached the stall first and stood there quietly for a moment, then told the patrol officers, "Everyone out, please. Wait in the hall."

As they shuffled out, Walter stepped up beside him and got a look. "Oh, man."

The smell that wafted out was a mix of rot, decay, waste, and something sickeningly sweet.

Walter covered his nose with the sleeve of his shirt. "How long do you think she's been here?"

"Hazlett said they found her just before six a.m."

"That's when they found her," Walter said. "How long has she *been here?*"

"I don't..." Brayman's voice trailed off as he stepped into the stall, careful not to touch her.

The woman's body was on the toilet, leaning back against the wall. A few thin wisps of gray hair remained on her skull, but most of it was on the floor around her feet, as if it had somehow fallen out in clumps. As they stood there, Walter watched several more loose strands fall to the ground. The harsh fluorescent light showed her bare skin was dry and puckered, with an ashy tone as if baked in the sun, stretched over frail bones. Her eyes were open, but like the victim from the Edison, the color was unrecognizable through the milky haze of thick cataracts.

Walter's eyes began to water from the stench. "On patrol, we got called out on a lot of wellness checks—old people living alone—neighbor hadn't seen them for a little while, got worried, would call us. Nadler always checked the mailbox first. If there was a stack of mail, we knew what to expect inside. More times than I can count, we'd roll up and find the mailbox overflowing and a body in the house. Heart attack, stroke, slip-and-fall…sometimes there for a day or two, other times could be weeks or even months before someone noticed and called it in. This one's been dead a long time."

"Well, I don't see a stack of mail." Brayman tentatively reached into the stall and placed two fingers on the woman's neck. "And she's still warm."

"No way."

"Body temp usually drops about two degrees per hour after death — it can't be more than seventy in here, and I'd be willing to bet this woman's temp is still above ninety."

The dead woman's right arm dangled at her side, her left folded on her lap. Brayman gently picked up her left wrist, raised it several inches, and watched it drop back down when released. "No rigor."

"Rigor peaks at what, twelve hours? It's gone in a couple days. I bet she's been dead at least a month. Rigor's long gone."

"So you think that after she died, someone kept her warm, then brought her in here, carried her through the main terminal past who knows how many people? And look at her dress—"

She wore a black cocktail dress with thin shoulder straps. Short. Her withered legs exposed like twin twigs.

Walter nodded. "Yeah, it's all wrong. She's got to be what, in her seventies, eighties, maybe? That dress is something a girl in her twenties wears on a night out. Same with the shoes. Older women don't wear heels like that. Even the earrings look wrong." He paused, then said, "The clothes with our Edison vic didn't make sense, either. Maybe our perp has a strange clothing fetish? Redressed her post-mortem for some reason?"

"She died in that dress. I can see stains around the edges," Brayman replied. "Muscles relax at death, bowels release. She defecated recently, right here."

"I think I'll take your word on that."

Using the toe of his shoe, Walter snagged the strap of the woman's small black purse from the floor, tugged it closer, and picked it up. It was open. He riffled around inside. "No wallet or ID. We've got lipstick, eye shadow…" He took out a small canister and held it up. "Pepper spray and, holy shit—" Reaching back inside, he took out a wad of cash. The bills were rolled up and held together with a rubber band. "This wasn't a robbery. There might be a grand here. Three condoms, too. Could she be a working girl? Woman, I mean? Working woman? A working grandma? Christ, is that a thing?"

Brayman was studying what was left of her fingers. "Let me see one of those photos from the Edison. Our other vic's hand."

Walter handed the best close-up to Brayman, who held it up next to the woman's hand.

"They're bitten off for sure, right at the first knuckle. Same as our first vic. We'll need a mold to match teeth marks." When he lifted her hand, he paused, set it back down, and did it again. He did this several more times before turning back to Walter. "I think rigor is starting to set in. She definitely died within the past few hours. I'd bet my life on it."

Walter took in her appearance again. It wasn't possible. She looked like a damn mummy, easily dead for months. If someone told him she'd been dead for a year, he wouldn't be surprised. But only a few hours? "What the fuck is this?"

Brayman didn't answer. He didn't say anything, only shook his head.

19

WHEN WALTER O'BRIEN STEPPED into his apartment at a little after seven at night and dropped the mob files on the kitchen counter, he could still smell the woman's body from the bus depot, like the scent had followed him home. Not the dry, rotten scent, but the sugary odor he had detected beneath, and which had seemed to intensify the longer they were at the bus depot.

While Brayman had supervised the techs from the crime unit and waited for the ME, Walter had spoken to the woman and daughter who'd found the body. Thinking they were alone in the bathroom, the mother had led her four-year-old to the open door of the handicap stall for the extra space—she'd managed to pull her daughter away when she spotted the dead woman, but not before the little girl got an eyeful.

He'd talked to the bus depot custodian next, a Guatemalan man in his fifties, who swore the woman hadn't been there when he'd cleaned the bathroom just before five a.m. He'd shown Walter a clipboard and pointed at the line that said 4:57 with today's date next to WOMEN/RESTROOM 3. There were no cameras to back him up—the three installed in the terminal hadn't worked for months—but the station manager said the man was reliable and he had no reason to doubt him. That meant the body had been there for less than an hour when the woman and girl had found her.

Neither the two people working the ticket counter nor the security guard had seen the woman come in, and all three insisted that an older woman dressed like that would have stood out, particularly at that early hour. Hell, *anyone* dressed like that at any time at the bus depot would have stood out. As for whether someone had carried her body in (maybe in a large bag or suitcase), nobody had noticed that, either, and the security guard was quick to point out he would also have noticed someone passing through with luggage large enough. However, the manager admitted that unlike the custodian, the security guard *did* have a habit of napping between four and six in the morning. Walter was more inclined to believe someone had rolled the body right by the security guard in a beat-up suitcase than he was to believe the woman had walked in on her own.

Dead end.

Dead end.

Dead end.

Back at home, Walter pressed his shirtsleeve to his nose and sniffed.

That damn smell.

He took a quick shower, but the odor was still there. He picked his clothes up off the floor, emptied the pockets, and shoved everything deep into his overflowing laundry bag, buried them at the bottom before putting on a pair of jeans and a fresh oxford.

The wadded-up receipts from Giovanni's were in his hand along with the dog collar as he made his way back to the kitchen, took a beer from the refrigerator, and looked at the stack of mob-related files. He'd told Brayman he'd go through them tonight. He planned to run through his homework, the files on various bite victims, while waiting for the preliminary autopsy findings on their Jane Doe. They'd compare notes first thing in the morning.

A partial address in his scribbled handwriting seemed to glare from the topmost receipt, an apartment no more than ten minutes away on foot. He could easily check that one and be back home in under an hour. Plenty of time to review the files.

Plus there was the smell. Still there. Faint, but hanging on. A quick walk, some fresh night air—that would be enough to get rid of it, get it out of his head.

One hour.

No more.

Then the files.

Walter finished the rest of the beer, fastened his secondary weapon to his ankle—a small .380—and was out the door. He moved fast, before his common sense had a chance to weigh in.

He managed to get to the apartment in eight minutes, not ten, but when an older man answered the door, he knew he had the wrong place. After seeing Walter's badge, the man nervously confirmed that he and his wife had eaten at Giovanni's for their twenty-second anniversary. Walter congratulated him, thanked him for his time, and without further explanation was back out on the street, looking at the second receipt. If he hurried, he had time.

Damn it, Walter, this is stupid.

He went anyway.

He took a cab to the Newport Village Apartments on St. Antoine, an eighteen-minute ride, and told the car to wait for him. This, too, was a bust. Although nobody answered the door, the next-door neighbor told him a Hispanic couple and their four kids lived there.

By the time Walter got back in the cab, he knew he wouldn't be going home until he checked out the final address. If he didn't, he wouldn't be able to focus. It was best he just got this out of his system. Prove to himself that it wasn't her, couldn't have been her. Then, and only then, could he give 100 percent to his current case. That's what he told himself, and that, too, was stupid, but it was enough.

The drive to the final address took a little longer, nearly half an hour. Not an apartment, but a house in Dearborn Heights—the suburbs just outside the city. A two-story colonial with a perfectly manicured lawn and a black Volvo in the driveway.

Walter had his badge out when the man opened the door.

That might have been why the man turned so white.

He looked first at the badge, then at Walter's bruised face, and seemed to shrink in the open doorway. "I had no idea you were a cop."

CHAPTER

20

AMY ARCHER'S DATE.

Walter nearly gave his name and told him he was with Detroit Homicide, then thought better of it. He put the badge back in his pocket before the man could get a good look at his number. The last thing he needed was this guy picking up the phone and calling his new captain. Instead, he said, "Are you Michael Driscoll?"

He nodded.

"You and I need to talk."

From somewhere behind the man, a female voice called out, "Who is it, Mike?"

Amy?

Driscoll turned a shade paler and called back over his shoulder. "It's a police detective. He's here about the mugging the other night. I'll talk to him outside. Get the kids ready for bed. I'll help you tuck them in when we're done. Shouldn't be long." Before she could respond, he stepped out on the porch and pulled the door closed behind him. His voice dropped lower. "Look, cop or not, you were drunk off your ass and you had no business creeping up on us like that."

"You assaulted a police officer."

"You didn't identify yourself. You could barely walk." He looked nervously at Walter's black eye, the bruise under his chin. "Christ, you would have done the same thing if somebody snuck up on you like that while you were…"

The curtain on a window off to Walter's left moved aside and a woman's face appeared in the glass. She frowned, then the curtain dropped back into place. Mid-thirties, not overweight but carrying a couple of extra pounds. Her hair was pulled back, and she was wearing a baggy T-shirt.

Not Amy.

Walter got it then. "The girl wasn't your wife."

Before Driscoll could answer, he turned and coughed into his elbow. A ragged, wet cough that seemed to go on forever. When he finally looked back at Walter, his eyes were moist, red, and puffy. He looked sheepishly down at the cuts on his bruised knuckles. "I told my wife I got jumped on my way home from work. Said I managed to fight them off, but not before they got my wallet and credit cards." He shook his head. "Fucking stupid, but I used it to explain where the money went."

"Who was she?"

He hesitated, one eye on the house. "She told me her name was Amelia. Amelia Dyer."

"How do you know her?"

Again, Driscoll fell silent, and his gaze dropped down to his feet.

Walter started to edge past him toward the door. "Maybe

I should just talk to your wife. You know, for the report on the mugging. Always good to be thorough."

Driscoll held his arm out to block Walter's path, but this only brought on another coughing fit. The man nearly doubled over. He braced himself on the doorframe until it was over. "Sorry, I think I'm coming down with something. I haven't been sleeping well."

Walter took a step back. Whatever this was, he didn't want it. "Who was she to you?" he repeated, growing impatient.

"I tell you, how do I know you won't arrest me?"

"Forget the assault, that's not why I'm here." Walter lowered his voice. "Look, I was off duty leaving a bar and I recognized her. I needed to ask her some questions about a case. That's why I followed you. Help me track her down, we forget the rest," Walter assured him.

"No talking to my wife?"

"Not if you cooperate."

Driscoll considered this. Finally, he looked back at the window and sighed. He ushered Walter out into the driveway next to the Volvo. "She's nobody, just some escort," he said in a low voice. "My wife and I have been going through a rough patch, and I just needed a break. A buddy at work gave me her card, told me she was discreet. She offered something she called the girlfriend experience."

"The girlfriend experience?"

"Five hundred bucks, and she meets you somewhere, acts as if she's your girlfriend—dinner, drinks, hotel—she pretends you've been out a few times but the relationship is still new, in that honeymoon phase, where you still do things like—"

"Sex in an alley," Walter interrupted.

"Yeah. I got to Giovanni's with no idea what she even looked like. She knew me, though. I have no idea how; I didn't give anyone a description. I stood there next to the hostess station like an idiot, almost turned around and left, then she waved at me from the table. No turning back then. Not that I wanted to. I mean, you saw her, right? I did a couple shots with dinner to loosen up. She made it easy. We talked about damn near everything. Started with small talk, then went into work, even talked about my problems at home. She didn't judge, just listened. I felt like I'd known her my entire life. Dinner was incredible. Like the perfect date. I hadn't felt that way for years." He looked over Walter's shoulder at the taxi waiting in the street. "You took a cab here?"

Walter ignored him. "Where did you go after the alley?"

"The Huntley. I booked a suite there." Driscoll's skin was pasty, and although he was shivering, thin beads of sweat were trickling down his scalp.

Walter knew the Huntley; it was way out of his league on a cop's salary. "Anybody see you there?"

Driscoll grinned. "*Everybody* saw us there. Girl as beautiful as her, people can't help but look. I got her upstairs fast, couldn't risk someone I know spotting us. I had a bottle of Macallan's waiting up in the room, and I drank way too much; the rest of the night is a blur. I fell asleep, passed out, something, but when I woke up it was nearly five in the morning, and she was gone." He looked back at the house. "Look, I need to get back inside. I'm sorry I hit you. I'm sorry for a lot of things I did that night. Who knows, maybe she gave me this damn bug." He coughed again, then wiped his mouth on the back of his hand. "You said you're a detective. What'd she do?"

"Where's her card? Do you still have it?"

Driscoll fished a tattered business card out of his pocket, glanced at it, then handed it to Walter. The card was black with red lettering. "I don't want it. I slipped, but I'm not a cheater. I've never done anything like that before; I'm not that guy. I love my wife. My family. We're just going through—"

"A rough patch," Walter finished for him. "Whatever."

This guy would keep it in check until the remorse wore off, then he'd do it again. A year or two down the road, and Driscoll would be living out of boxes in some cheap apartment trying to piece together how his life came apart.

Walter walked away without another word. Back in the cab, he told the driver, "The Huntley, downtown."

The box of files on his kitchen counter, completely forgotten.

21

BUILT IN THE THIRTIES by the Carmichael family, the Huntley stood on the corner of Barington and Third in downtown Detroit. Six presidents had stayed there, numerous film and television stars, sports celebrities. Jack Tocco, a famed Detroit mobster, had called the Huntley home for nearly two years before relocating to Florida and running the family business from a distance. It was also one of the few hotels in the country with a thirteenth floor, an oddity that brought in its share of tourists.

Opposite the large lobby, the Huntley's restaurant occupied the east end of the first floor. Beyond that was a bar called Retribution, decorated with Prohibition-era memorabilia.

Walter eased onto a barstool and wondered just how long the thirty-odd dollars he had in his wallet would buy him. He declined to see a menu, ordered a beer on tap and water, and asked to use the phone. All three arrived a moment later, and he took out the business card. It was blank other than a phone number with a 313 area code printed in a red font on black paper.

He punched in the number and a male voice answered on the second ring. *"Yes?"*

Careful not to speak too loud, Walter cleared his throat. "My friend Michael gave me your card. I'd like the same girl he had the other night, Amelia."

The voice on the other end went silent.

Although only a few seconds ticked by, it felt like a minute.

When the voice still didn't reply, Walter added, "I'm looking for the girlfriend experience."

Still nothing.

"Hello?"

"Name?"

"Walter."

"Are you aware of the cost, Walter?"

"Yes. I have cash," he lied. "I'm at the—"

"I know where you are. Move to the far end of the bar. Sit on the third stool from the left."

There was an audible click as the man disconnected.

Walter looked at the receiver, then hung up and slid the phone back toward the bartender. He put the card back in his pocket.

Only three other people were sitting at the bar—a couple to his right nursing martinis and a man watching a baseball game on one of the televisions a few stools down from them.

Walter moved to the opposite end and sat where he had been instructed.

Forty minutes later, he was on his second beer when a slim hand slipped around his shoulder from behind and gave him a gentle squeeze. He felt warm breath on the back of his neck, and when he turned, soft lips found his. She lingered for a moment after the kiss and brushed his hair back, a smile on her face. "Hi, handsome. Sorry to keep you waiting. I got caught in traffic."

She set her purse on the bar and sat on the stool beside him, crossing her slim legs and smoothing the silky material of her short black dress down over tanned thighs. Her blond hair fell across her shoulders in loose curls. Her green eyes sparkled.

She was beautiful, but she wasn't *her*.

The bartender placed a napkin in front of her. "Would you care for a drink?"

"I think I would. Vodka and cranberry, please?"

The bartender turned to the bottles at his back, quickly put the drink together, and handed it to her.

She plucked the lime out and set it on the napkin before holding the glass up to Walter. "To the end of a long day and the start of a wonderful evening."

Walter tapped her glass with his beer and took a sip.

She brought her glass to her lips and drank, then rested her free hand on Walter's leg and leaned close to his ear. "Payment will be due in full when we get upstairs. For now, let's just enjoy ourselves. My name is Willow." She lingered for a moment longer, her lips brushing his neck when she eased back.

Walter nudged his stool closer to hers so nobody else could hear him. "I asked for Amelia."

The smile left her face, but only for a second. "If you don't like me, I'm sure they'll send someone else."

"Do you know where she is?"

"I don't know anyone named Amelia."

Walter watched the girl's eyes closely as he described Amy, but there was no sign of recognition. "She was here the other night." He took out the business card and showed it to her as if that would somehow validate what he was telling her, but instead it only made her look uncomfortable.

Willow took another sip of her drink, then placed a hand on her purse. "I think I should go. This doesn't feel right."

Walter grabbed her wrist. "Wait."

This was enough to push her over the edge. Her entire body grew rigid. "Let go. I don't want to make a scene, but I will."

He quickly released her, but the damage was done. "I'm sorry. I didn't mean to do that. It's just…it's important I talk to her."

A soft vibration came from Willow's purse. She glanced inside at the display of a pager, then stood. "If you call back, they'll send someone else. I don't know what else to tell you. I need to go." The smile returned again. "It was an absolute pleasure meeting you, Walter."

Then she was gone. Walter watched her walk out of the bar and into the lobby toward the Huntley's main entrance.

Walter snapped his fingers at the bartender and got to his feet. "Plastic bag, now."

The man's brow furrowed. "What?"

Walter took out his badge and showed it to him. "I need a plastic bag. Hurry, damn it!"

The bartender searched under the counter and came up with a baggie. Walter snatched it from his hand, dumped the rest of Willow's drink, and placed the empty glass inside. He tossed several bills on the bar before running after her.

He spotted her outside on a pay phone about a hundred feet down the sidewalk.

He ducked into the alcove of an electronics store before she saw him, waited for her to hang up, then followed as she continued down the block at a brisk pace.

She turned the corner on Ambrose, and Walter watched her go into the Grainger Hotel—a little less pricey than the Huntley, but still one of the city's best.

Walter went into a sandwich shop across the street and sat at a table near the window.

She didn't come back out until nearly midnight.

When she did, Walter followed again. She walked four blocks to a club called Dreamers, where the bouncer quickly ushered her inside despite the line.

Walter stashed the bagged glass in some bushes at the corner of the parking lot, then flashed his badge at the door to bypass the line and duck into the smoky club behind her. He waited for his eyes to adjust to the lights, a mix of colored spots and lasers, all pulsing in time with the steady beat of some dance track. At first, he thought he'd lost Willow in the thick crowd. Maybe she'd somehow doubled back or slipped out another door. Then he saw her.

Willow was on the dance floor with the girl Michael Driscoll knew as Amelia Dyer.

The girl he knew as Amy Archer.

Her.

NOW

22

THE SALT TRUCK PUSHED aside two other patrol cruisers, missed the valet stand by less than a foot, then rounded the other side of the club down an access road with another gun of the engine. The front of the plow caught several trash cans and pushed them along as if they were nothing. Salt continued to spray everything from the back, leaving a thick swath of white.

Rigby took several steps toward it, then shouted, "Somebody stop that asshole!"

A uniformed officer near the alley started to round the side of his patrol car, and two quick shots echoed—one struck the car's side mirror; the other hit the pavement directly in his path. He jumped back behind the car.

Rigby's head swiveled toward the building behind her and looked up. She glared at the roof like a hawk.

Goddamnit, Red, Walter thought. *I hope you're shuffling around up there. Just because we tell them they can't move on you doesn't mean they won't.*

They were working on it. A spotter had set up shop behind the SWAT van, and he was systematically scanning the rooflines and windows of all buildings with line of sight through a pair of high-powered binoculars. No doubt triangulating shots and isolating positions. Walter was under no illusion they had some kind of upper hand here. At best, they'd bought a little time. In a room not too far away, people much smarter than him were no doubt busy spitballing ways to end this before it got much further along. Walter had spent a good chunk of his life in rooms like that.

The salt truck vanished from sight, and Rigby looked back in the direction it had gone. They could still hear it. She seemed to be trying to piece together the *why* of it all. Walter knew she wouldn't. When it rounded the front of the club on its second pass, another officer started to run toward the cab. Another shot stopped him and sent him back to cover.

"The truck is off-limits," Walter told Rigby. "You need to focus."

"How do I know the bomb is real?"

"You'll get that answer soon enough."

"What kind of bomb is it?"

Walter said nothing.

"You need to give me something."

"No. I don't."

"Who is she to you? This woman?"

Again, Walter fell silent.

"Do you have an ID?"

"No ID."

"What does she look like?"

"I can't tell you that."

"How old is she?"

"I can't tell you that, either."

With each question, Rigby became more puzzled. "Because you don't want to, or because you don't know?"

"Yes."

"That's not an answer."

She's the most beautiful woman you've ever seen, Walter thought. *She's also a fucking monster.*

He shrugged and eyed the front of the club. "That bouncer can leave. At this point, he's just in the way."

Rigby didn't move, only stared at Walter. "Just like that?"

"Get him out of there before I change my mind."

Red's voice crackled in his earbud. *"What if she touched him, Walter? We don't know she didn't. Just 'cause he's outside?"*

Walter didn't reply to that.

Rigby was wearing a bone conduction microphone at the base of her throat. She pressed a finger to the Transmit button and spoke softly.

A moment later, two officers darted out and ducked behind the valet station, got on either side of the bouncer, and rushed the large man back behind the barricade. It was over in less than thirty seconds.

"Thank you for that," Rigby said, and she actually sounded sincere. "Can we talk about everyone else?"

"Nothing to talk about."

"You're looking for a woman," Rigby replied. "Let me get the men out. They're just in the way, too, right?"

"No."

"You think she'd try to slip out with them?"

Walter nearly laughed. "Nobody's mistaking her for a man."

"Then why not? Show some goodwill. It will buy you more time. If you don't know who she is or what she looks like, how do you expect anyone to identify her?"

"She'll contact me."

"Why would she do that?"

"Because she can't help herself." Walter looked at his watch. "You have forty-seven minutes left. Nobody's looking to buy time. If I thought—"

He coughed again. This time, it lasted for nearly three minutes. When it finally ended, he wiped the blood from his mouth, making no effort to hide it.

"Go ahead and work into whatever profile you're building that a dying man has nothing to lose," he told her. "Remember that."

Reaching between the folds of his heavy vest, Walter took out a small USB drive and tossed it to the commander.

Rigby caught it with one hand. "What's on here?"

"Regrets."

1992

<u>ALIASES?</u>

Amy Archer

Amelia Dyer

Alvin Schalk

Two bodies/basement freezer

John Doe/Edison

Jane Doe/Corktown Bus Depot

… Walter O'Brien, 28 Years Old

23

AMY ARCHER DANCED WITH her back pressed against Willow's chest, their arms and fingers twisted together at their sides, moving together more as one than two individuals. Both girls laughed and stomped their feet playfully in time with the music, some song by the Clash.

Any doubts Walter harbored about whom he'd seen the other night vanished. His mind was clear now, and he was certain it was her. This was the girl who'd escaped his custody six years ago. Her face was etched in his mind, and she hadn't aged a day. She was a couple of inches shorter than Willow, and at times the taller girl seemed to envelop her, fold around her. Walter wondered if the two of them were lovers. There was an intimacy in the way they touched each other, something beyond just two friends dancing together. A knowledge. A familiarity. As several men approached, no doubt trying to cut in, they simply laughed them off and moved away. Whatever the men said, they'd clearly heard it all before.

The Clash transitioned to Laura Branigan, and Walter pushed through the crowd toward the bar, careful not to lose sight of the women.

He needed a plan, and he didn't have one.

If Amy saw him, recognized him, she'd run. Finding her twice in three nights had been a combination of police work and dumb luck, and he was under no illusion that he could track her down a third time if she didn't want to be found.

"What can I get you?" the bartender half shouted over the music.

"Water," Walter told him. "And I need to use your phone."

The bartender sloshed a glass of water in front of him and nodded toward the entrance. "Bar phone is for employees. Barstools are for booze. Pay phones are out front. Take your water with you."

Walter tugged out his badge and showed it to him quickly. "Phone. Now."

With a roll of his eyes, the bartender retrieved the phone from a shelf near the register, trailed the cord out behind him, and set it on the bar. "Make it fast. I don't want people to get the wrong idea."

Walter ignored him and dialed.

He pressed the receiver against one ear and covered the other with his free hand.

The line rang six times before Nadler picked up, his voice groggy. *"What?"*

"I found her," Walter told him, squeezing his hand tighter against his ear, trying to block out the pounding music.

"I can't hear you. Who is this?"

"It's O'Brien," he said, louder. "I found her."

"O'Brien? Do you know what time it is? Found who?"

"Archer. Amy Archer."

His old partner went quiet.

"She's at a club downtown."

Nadler still didn't reply. Not at first. When he finally did, he let out a long sigh. *"Are you sure? Remember last time?"*

Walter *did* remember last time. That had been a mistake, but he was sure this time. "I've got her under surveillance right now. She's dancing with some other girl. I need backup. I don't think I should try to bring her in alone. It would be too easy for her to get away in a crowd like this. We need to block the doors, box her in, then drive her out where we can take her into custody safely. If she gets wind that we're onto her, she'll run again. You know she will."

"You're at a club?"

"Yeah, place called Dreamers, downtown. Off Murdock. Can you get down here?"

Again, Nadler said nothing.

"Herb? You still there?"

"Have you been drinking?"

Walter swore under his breath. "I had two beers."

He shouldn't have said that. How many times had he and Nadler gone out on calls for domestics and found some drunk who insisted they'd only had two drinks? Everyone said two. They knew nobody would believe them if they said one, and three meant you were drunk, so two. Always two. "I'm not—"

"Go home, Walter," Nadler interrupted. *"Let it go."*

"Look, I saw the report—Weeden screwed up the description. That's probably why nobody's found her all these years. It's Amy Archer. I'm sure of it."

"Go home."

Walter started to argue and heard a dial tone. Nadler had hung up.

He slammed the receiver down and felt a hand on his arm. He turned to find Willow standing there with a scowl on her pretty face, all pretense of civility gone now that she was off the clock. "What the hell are you doing here? Are you following me?"

The bartender reached for the phone. "Done?"

Walter reluctantly nodded and slid it back to him.

Willow tugged on Walter's shirt and turned him around. She was a lot stronger than she looked. "Why the hell are you following me?"

"Whoa, calm down. It's not what you think."

"No? I bet it's exactly what I think," she fired back. "I think you're some low-life piece-of-shit scumbag who didn't get what he wanted a few hours ago and figured he'd wait to catch me alone and take it for free. I should charge you just for wasting my time earlier. What was your name again? Walter? Maybe I should call my boss, Walter. Tell him where we are and let him explain the rules to you. Him and a few of his friends."

She looked like she was a second away from throwing a punch.

"How about both of you calm down?" the bartender said. He took out two shot glasses, placed them on the bar, and filled them with vodka, lime juice, and something orange. "Two kamikazes on the house. One for the lady, one for our *cop* friend."

This took a second to sink in. Willow's body stiffened. "You're a cop?"

Walter nodded, picked up both drinks, and handed one to her. "Truce?"

She didn't move.

"Look, I'm not on the job right now."

One shot would not kill him, especially if he could use it to take control of this situation without creating a scene. "If I lied to you, it would be entrapment and I'm sure as shit not allowed to drink on the job." He raised the glass to his mouth and swallowed the shot in a single gulp. It burned on the way down, warming his throat and stomach. The drink felt better than he cared to admit.

Walter set the empty down on the bar and nodded toward Amy, who was still out on the floor dancing, her eyes closed and her head tilted back. "I just want to talk to her. That's all."

Willow drank the second shot, shivered, and placed her glass on the bar next to his, bottom side up. "Why?"

"I know her, from way back. It's been a while. She may not recognize me. I assume the two of you have the same…employer."

Her eyes narrowed. "That's who you were looking for earlier? What did you call her?"

"Amelia. Amelia Dyer."

"Uh-huh."

"I know that's not her real name," Walter explained, eyeing the front entrance. If Amy ran, he was confident he could get there first. "I'm not interested in any of that. I don't care what either of you do for a living. A couple questions, and I'll leave you alone, I promise. I just want to know she's all right."

If Willow drew her over, at least got her closer, she was less likely to vanish in the crowd. He should have brought his handcuffs, some way to subdue her.

The bartender refilled both shot glasses and added a third.

Without looking at him, Willow said, "She doesn't drink."

The bartender shrugged. "I don't care who drinks it; I just want all of you to take this away from my bar."

Amy was still dancing, her back to them now. Several guys had crowded around her, and although she ignored them, they obscured Walter's view.

Willow picked up one of the shots and drank it down. "Give me a second."

Before he could reply, she started working her way back through the crowd.

From the booming speakers, a rumbling bass line vibrated Walter's teeth.

The bartender pushed the two remaining shots toward him. "Drink them, or I'm dumping them out."

Walter drank both. Why not. When he looked back, Willow was shouting into Amy's ear and pointing directly at him.

24

AMY ARCHER FACED WALTER and squinted as a strobe light kicked in from above, harsh and bright, flickering several times per second and causing everyone to appear as if they were moving in slow motion. Her eyes locked with his, and Walter was certain she would run. Instead, she cupped her hand over Willow's ear, told her something, then walked toward him.

Whether it was the alcohol, the strobe, or both, Amy seemed to float as she approached, moving with the grace of a ghost in a dress made of a material so thin it was nearly translucent, the lines of her body clearly visible with the bright lights at her back.

Willow remained out on the dance floor, but her eyes didn't leave either of them. Hawklike, she glared at Walter with a nervous contempt, then at Amy with something that resembled worry.

Walter took several steps in her direction and felt his

body sway slightly from the shots. He should have stopped at one.

Three meant you were drunk, so two. Always two.

When Amy reached him, she leaned forward on her toes. Although her black heels added some height, she barely reached his chin. "Willow says I know you?"

The scent that drifted up from her was sweet, floral. Not a perfume Walter recognized, but intoxicating. Lavender maybe? Although she had been out on the crowded dance floor since he arrived—and who knew how much longer before that—she wasn't perspiring. Walter was. He could feel it at his temples, the back of his shirt.

"It's been a long time, Amy."

She seemed puzzled. The smile didn't leave her face, but she looked confused.

"You probably don't recognize me without my uniform. It's been a long time," he repeated. "I'm a detective now."

"Uniform?" Still smiling, she shook her head. "I'm sorry, I don't—"

"You don't have to pretend with me. It's okay. I won't turn you in. I'm just glad to see that you're all right." This wasn't exactly true, but he wanted to disarm her. "I didn't know where you went. I was worried. I'm glad to see you."

"Willow said you called the service looking for me?"

"I'm sorry. I wasn't sure what else to do. I got the number from Michael Driscoll, from…the other night. He said you told him your name was Amelia Dyer." Walter waved a hand dismissively. "I get it, no real names. What should I call you?"

Her head tilted slyly to the left. "What would you like to call me?"

"Amy."

She gave him a soft nod. "Okay, Amy it is. And you are…?"

Walter didn't understand. What game was she playing? She must have recognized him, right? An experience as traumatic as that. She certainly wouldn't forget the first face she saw. The person who took her out of there.

She ran the tip of her finger down his arm and took his hand. With a playful smirk, she tugged him back toward the floor. "Dance with me?"

Where the hell was Nadler with the backup? Was he even coming?

Nadler may have hung up but he wouldn't let me down. This isn't like the last time. Walter had been clear about that.

As loud as the music had been near the bar, it was somehow louder on the dance floor. An incessant pounding beat. Walter didn't recognize the song. It didn't really matter. Each throb got under his skin and shook his bones. The colored lights and the strobes only made it worse—reds, blues, greens, and yellows.

He didn't feel right.

Had there been something in that shot?

Willow appeared, two more drinks in her hands.

Walter shook his head, but when he looked back down at the glasses, both were empty.

Had he drunk another?

The burn was there at the back of his throat, the pit of his stomach, more warm now than hot.

Amy's hands slipped up his chest, and she draped her arms around his neck as she began to sway with the music. She turned around slowly, her back to him, and closed the little space between them, pressed her hips into him until he was moving with her.

He tilted his head down. He could smell her hair, that

same sweet perfume. "You didn't have to run," he told her. "I would have kept you safe."

Although he said the words, he doubted she heard him.

Another body pressed against him from behind, and Walter glimpsed Willow. Her arms went around him and found Amy's waist, pulled the girl closer with Walter in between. Amy was grinding against him, and Walter felt himself grow stiff in his jeans. Her dress was so thin it was like it wasn't there at all. She pressed harder into him, and he felt a hand drift over his thigh, find him, and squeeze. He didn't know whose hand it was, and in that particular moment, he didn't care. His hands roamed up Amy's sides, over the swell of her hips, and his fingers brushed the sides of her breasts. He bent slightly until his lips found the back of her neck.

They were outside now.

An alley, not unlike the one from the other night.

Walter had no memory of leaving the dance floor, the club. Didn't know how much time had gone by.

Just the two of them, Willow gone now.

The music thundered from behind a wall to his left. The air was sticky and hot and Amy was leading him deeper into the dark.

Walter's limbs weren't his own. He willed them to stop; he told himself how wrong this all was. He told himself that when Nadler and the backup arrived, they couldn't find him here, not like this. Yet his body trailed after her with an urgency overwhelming everything else.

At the back of the alley, a dead-end cinder-block wall, she turned to face him, an impish grin on her face. She leaned against the wall and motioned for Walter to come closer. He did. Consequences be damned, he went to her, kissed her shoulder, her neck, behind her ear. He felt one of her legs wrap around his back.

"You don't want to know me, Walter. I'm bad for you."

Her words came so soft he might have imagined them.

He reached up and ran his hand through her hair. He wanted to tell her it was okay. He wanted to tell her so many things, but the words weren't there. A fog muffled his thoughts. His index finger drifted over her cheek and ran across her mouth. She parted her full red lips and kissed his fingertip, her teeth grazing the knuckle under the first joint as she took in more.

"I'll hurt you," she told him between hungry breaths. "I just can't help myself."

She pulled his shirt from his jeans and slipped her hand beneath, caressed the hair on his chest.

He leaned forward, enveloped the warmth of her, and—

CHAPTER

25

WALTER WOKE TO THE shrill sound of a phone ringing. The metal hammer beat on the bells with a violent ferocity.

He was in his apartment, his own bed, naked, his clothing from the previous night left in various piles on the floor, beginning at his front door and ending at the foot of the bed.

He sat up a little too fast, and the room went for a quarter turn followed by a tilt before leveling off. The pain in his head came a moment later, crashing against his temples.

The phone rang three more times before going silent, following a defeated half ring.

He didn't remember coming home.

Didn't remember leaving the club.

Wasn't sure what happened to—

"Amy? Are you here?"

His voice sounded foreign to him, detached.

No answer came.

He rolled to the side of the bed and managed to get his feet on the floor. Managed to sit. "Amy? Willow?"

His apartment wasn't very large. Nobody was there. The files he was supposed to go through last night were right where he'd left them, glaring at him from the countertop.

Walter got to his feet and nearly fell back into his bed.

He hadn't drunk *that* much, had he?

He told himself he hadn't, but the truth was he didn't remember. He needed to dial it back. New job. New partner. He needed to dial it back.

Christ, Nadler would give him an earful for sure.

Nadler hadn't shown up last night. No backup. No nothing. He'd left him out to dry.

Remember last time?

Fuck you, Nadler, it was her. This was nothing like last time.

Nearly tripping over his shoes on the floor, Walter crossed to the bathroom, looked down at the toilet, and promptly threw up.

His stomach lurched and expelled this liquid, yellow, smelly mess, and just the sight and scent of it caused more to follow. Nearly thirty seconds of heaving until there was nothing more, then another thirty seconds as the vomiting continued anyway. Dry heaves as the muscles twisted and contracted.

When it was finally over, Walter took three ibuprofen, brushed his teeth, and got in the shower. He stood there for nearly thirty minutes as lukewarm water rolled over him, slowly coaxing his body back to life.

He might have stayed in there another thirty minutes if the phone hadn't started ringing again.

Walter scrambled out, grabbed a towel, and managed to reach the receiver before the caller hung up again.

"Yeah?"

"Where are you? It's nearly nine."

Brayman.

Walter combed his damp hair back with his fingers. "I'm still at home, going through those files. I don't think they're connected. This doesn't feel like a mob thing to me."

Shit. He shouldn't have said that. What if it was? He'd barely cracked those files.

Brayman didn't reply.

Walter cleared his throat. "Did you find anything in yours? The sex crime stuff? Where are you?"

That was better. Turn the tables.

"I'm at the medical examiner's office. Get your ass down here."

He hung up before Walter could say anything else.

"Well, fuck you, too," Walter muttered, hanging up the phone.

He quickly got dressed and retrieved the small dog collar from the jeans he'd worn last night, gave it a quick squeeze, and shoved it deep into his pants pocket. The business card from Michael Driscoll was gone.

Did I drop it, or did Amy or Willow take it?

Then he remembered the glass with Willow's fingerprints on it from the Huntley. He found it sitting on his kitchen counter, still in the baggie, and grabbed it. How the hell did he get home without losing that? He didn't remember retrieving it from the bushes outside the club.

Walter paused at the small mirror near his door only long enough to get a quick look at himself. The black eye wasn't as bad today, but his skin looked puffy and pale, as if he were coming down with something. His bones ached, too. Maybe he was.

He hailed a cab outside his building and was halfway to the ME's office before he realized he'd left the files behind.

THE WAYNE COUNTY MEDICAL Examiner's Office was a squat brick building on Warren Avenue, not far from Walter's apartment but far enough that it didn't make sense to go back for the files. He'd get them later. The taxi dropped him in the circular drive at the front of the building, and when Walter gave his name at the desk, he was directed to a room near the end of a long corridor on the east side. He pushed through double stainless steel doors and found Brayman sitting on a couch with a copy of today's paper in his hand and a peeved look on his face.

"If you're in the habit of being late, you and I are going to have a problem."

"Sorry. Won't happen again."

Brayman was wearing the same brown suit and tie from the previous day. He hadn't shaved, his face was covered with stubble, and the lines of his goatee were less defined.

"Have you been here all night?"

Brayman ignored the question and held up the front page of the newspaper. The main headline read: DEAD WOMAN FOUND AT CORKTOWN BUS DEPOT, FINGERS MISSING.

"Oh, hell," Walter muttered, skimming the text of the story. "Somebody talked. Maybe the janitor. Shit, they mention both of us by name."

"So it wasn't you?"

"Me? Why would I say anything to the press?"

Brayman shrugged and dropped the paper on the bench. "I don't know. First big case, possible serial. Wouldn't be the first time a detective tried to get his name out there."

Walter was too tired, too hungover, for this. "You really want to start the day picking a fight? I thought we called a truce."

"So it wasn't you?" Brayman said again.

"No, it wasn't me. Was it *you?*"

"Don't be ridiculous."

"Exactly." Walter nodded at the newspaper. "Unless I missed it, there's no mention of our male vic. If I wanted to stoke the press, I would have told them about both. Whoever talked was someone who worked at the bus depot. Probably made a quick fifty. Some nobody asshole."

The stainless steel doors across from them opened, and the assistant medical examiner, Samuel Harris, poked his head out. "She's ready for you."

They followed Harris down the hallway and through another set of doors into an anteroom where he pointed at a stack of disposable Tyvek coveralls, gloves, and masks. "She said you need to gear up. Put your clothes in the lockers there. You can leave your guns, too. Nobody will come in here while the light's on."

Brayman began shrugging out of his clothes.

Walter was looking up at the light Harris mentioned, above the door—a red HAZARD sign burning bright. He considered what that meant for a moment, then took off his shoulder holster and hung it on a hook in the nearest locker. He was hanging up his shirt when Brayman said, "What happened to your chest?"

Walter looked down, assuming he was referring to the bruises from when Michael Driscoll kicked him in the alley, but those were mainly on his back, around his kidneys. Brayman was looking at the center of his chest. A bright, angry red mark about the size of a hand. Walter hadn't noticed it earlier. He brushed it with his finger. The skin felt irritated. "I don't know. Maybe an allergic reaction to something. I'm sure it's nothing."

Walter remembered Amy's hand there, under the folds of his shirt, her palm pressing into him.

"You have allergies?" Brayman interrupted Walter's thought. He unpacked one of the Tyvek suits and stepped in. "What did you eat for breakfast?"

Walter tried to hold on to the memory, but it was gone. Like trying to grab water spurting from a tap. Without answering, he shrugged into one of the Tyvek suits and pulled up the zipper, covering the mark.

Harris helped them both into latex gloves and headgear, then used wide tape to seal up the gaps at their wrists, ankles, and where the masks met the rest of the suit. By the time he finished, Walter was sweating.

They went through another set of doors into the main autopsy theater, where the medical examiner, Jane Ackerman, stood in front of several aluminum tables near the center of the room in a similar suit. "Samuel? Hook them up to the oxygen before you go."

Harris motioned for them to approach the tables and pulled two rubber hoses down from a series of retractable reels mounted to the ceiling. Walter felt cool air fill his suit when Harris attached one of the hoses to a valve on Walter's back.

Ackerman gave Walter a quick glance, then turned to Brayman. "I don't know what you stumbled into here, Wes, but I got half a mind to call in the CDC."

CHAPTER

27

"WHY WOULD YOU CALL the CDC?" Brayman asked, leaning over the nearest table, his voice muffled by the headgear.

The woman from the bus depot was lying on top of the exam table, uncovered. As Walter neared and got a good look at her, he was thankful for the Tyvek suit blocking any chance of smelling the body. Whatever was happening to her most certainly smelled. They hadn't been wearing protective suits when they first encountered her at the bus depot, and he wished now they had.

"Is it contagious?" Brayman asked.

Unlike Walter, who was just fine standing right where he was, Brayman took several steps to get a closer look. The woman's chest had been splayed open with a Y incision beginning near her armpits and ending just above her pubis bone. Her chest plate had been removed along with her internal organs, each of which was on a sample tray on a large rolling table behind her head.

Ackerman shook her head. "Is *cancer* contagious? No."

"Cancer?" A scowl washed over Brayman's face. "This can't be cancer. What kind of cancer does this?" He lifted the woman's arm and ran a gloved finger over the rough skin. It had a mottled look, dry and puckered. A mix of intersecting gray and purple patches.

Ackerman's gloved finger pointed at the inflamed marks on the woman's arm. "This loosely resembles something called Henderson's melanoma, a very rare form of the disease that spreads rapidly throughout the skin. Best I can tell, it started down near her right ankle and worked its way up."

"Melanoma looks nothing like this. Melanoma usually starts with moles and becomes these red blotchy spots. This looks more like…I don't know…an inflamed burn scar, but it's obviously not a burn." He set her arm back down and rounded the table, examining her torso and legs. "It's not isolated, either. Whatever this is covers, what, eighty percent of her body? It's even between her toes."

"Eighty percent when she came in. I'd say closer to ninety now."

Walter took a step back from the table. "This is spreading? Postmortem? How is that possible?"

"I don't know," Ackerman replied. "That's why we're wearing the suits."

Brayman stopped moving and looked back to Ackerman. "Radiation?"

She shook her head. "From an exposure standpoint, there are similarities, but no, that was the first thing I checked. There's no radiation present. She didn't even register a blip on the meter." She glanced at Walter. "To answer your question, it's not spreading anymore; it's already there, it's

142

just becoming more visible as her flesh degrades. Probably due to fluid displacement."

Brayman had rounded the body and was standing at the rolling table with the woman's organs. He was peering down into a microscope, adjusting the focus. "This isn't skin. Where did you pull this sample?"

"That's from her spleen," Ackerman told him.

"Her spleen? Can melanoma spread to the spleen?"

She nodded. "It can, but in this case, it didn't. The cancer cells you're looking at there didn't metastasize; they *originated* in her spleen. They formed independently."

"A woman this age," Brayman said, "it's not rare to have multiple forms of cancer, right?"

Ackerman huffed. "Oh, we'll get to her age in a minute. See those other slides there? I've been taking samples from all her major organs—lungs, heart, liver, bladder, stomach, intestines, thyroid, pancreas—I'm finding cancer everywhere. None of it from metastasization, mind you; all of it seems to have formed organically in the organ where I'm finding it. Rapid onset. I've never seen cancer this aggressive. Her bloodwork came back and also identified leukemia and lymphoma. I have yet to find a single *healthy* cell in this woman's body."

Brayman frowned. "Are you saying our cause of death is cancer?"

Ackerman didn't reply to that; she only raised her eyebrows.

The room went quiet, none of them speaking as this sunk in.

Walter eyed Ackerman, Brayman, the body on the table. This sounded like bullshit to him. "Her fingers were bitten off. Somebody *bit* off her fingers. That *somebody* killed her. You're not gonna convince me she died of natural causes. Cancer. That's ridiculous. She was obviously sick, but that didn't kill her. You just haven't found the real COD yet."

Ackerman gave Brayman a quick glance, then turned to Walter. "Her fingers were bitten off postmortem, within a minute of her passing. I can tell by the clotting patterns, or lack thereof. I can also tell you the melanoma was present in her hands, and her finger joints are cancerous as well. I found several microtumors in her palms and near her wrists. I found multiple forms of terminal cancer throughout her body. Everywhere I look. If the disease didn't kill her, it most certainly would have. Soon. Aside from the fingers, I haven't found trauma of any kind. No drugs in her system." She sighed. "I've got nothing conclusive at this point."

Returning to the far side of the table, Ackerman cocked her head. "Both of you have brought up her age. How old do you think this woman is?"

"Seventies, easy. Eighties, maybe."

Brayman didn't answer. He was busy studying some X-rays on a light box—images of the woman's ribs and skull.

Ackerman gave him a moment to take them in, then stepped closer, "You see it, don't you?"

"I'm not a pathologist," Brayman answered. "I'm not qualified…" His voice trailed away as he examined the images intently, confusion spreading across his face.

"No, but you see it."

Walter's head was starting to hurt again. "See what? What are you two talking about?"

Brayman pointed to the fourth rib in the second X-ray. "See this discoloration here? Near the sternum? That part is cartilage and that side is bone. The color gives us a clear delineation. As a person ages, the cartilage becomes bone. But this can't be…" His face filled with puzzlement.

Ackerman said, "I confirmed it with her skull. I had to be sure. And I'm sure."

"Sure of what?" Walter asked.

Again, they both went quiet.

Brayman finally replied, "This woman can't be more than twenty, maybe twenty-five years old. No more than that."

Walter frowned at both of them, then looked back over at the woman's body and laughed. "Oh, I get it now. This is some kind of hazing thing, right? The two of you trying to screw with the new guy. I don't think we really have time for that sort of thing, do we?"

"Not a joke," Jane Ackerman told him. "She had breast implants, too. Saline, not silicone. Recent." She nodded at another table, this one two over from the woman. Another body covered with a sheet. "Take a look at that one."

Trailing the air hose behind him, Walter went over and tugged off the sheet.

This body was a man, fingers also missing. His skin had taken on the same purple-and-gray hue as the woman's, rippled and mottled. His hair was gone. His face completely unrecognizable. If Walter didn't know better, he'd say the man looked like he was melting. Like the body was dissolving from the inside out and collapsing. He had the same Y incision, and his skull had been opened, but it was the tattoo that Walter fixated on—a small four-leaf clover on the man's sternum.

His voice dropped low. "Is this…"

"It's your vic from the Edison," Ackerman said. "I found the same level of cancer in him—nearly a dozen different types, rapid onset. The only difference is it seems to have started in his arm. He's been dead about twenty-four hours longer, and he's degrading far faster than normal. I'm confident this woman will look like him by this time tomorrow."

"And you're sure this isn't contagious?" Brayman asked her again. The edge had left his voice, and fear had slipped in.

"I don't see how it could be," Ackerman replied. "We're taking precautions anyway, hence the suits, and I'll send samples off to all the appropriate agencies and get their take, but all preliminary indications suggest whatever happened to these people is isolated. He's not much older than her. I'd place him in his thirties at most." Walter and Brayman exchanged glances. She gave this a second to sink in, then said, "There is one other thing. Can you shut off the lights for a second?"

While Brayman went to the switch, she picked up a foot-long plastic wand from the counter to her left attached to a long extension cord.

"Black light?" Walter asked her.

She nodded as the lights went out.

As Ackerman turned on the black light, the room filled with a purple glow. When she held it over the dead man's right arm, a bright ring lit up around his wrist.

Brayman frowned. "What is that?"

"I'm not sure. Like I said, there's no radiation, but from what I can tell, the most advanced cancer started here with him." Ackerman paused a beat, then went back over to the woman's body and showed them a similar mark on the woman's ankle. "And it started here on your bus vic." Rolling the light in a slow circle around the mark, she added, "I can't be sure, but to me this looks like a handprint. Like someone grabbed her ankle. If you look closely, you can see what appear to be finger marks." Ackerman demonstrated by wrapping her own gloved hand around the mark, nearly a perfect match. She nodded back at the man from the Edison. "The mark on him isn't quite as well defined."

Walter and Brayman exchanged a look, but neither said anything.

A phone rang, and Ackerman crossed the room to answer, turning on the lights as she went.

The mark on Walter's chest itched.

When Ackerman hung up, she said, "A suspicious death at the Four Seasons came in about an hour ago. Elderly male. Harris just got there." She hesitated for a second, then added, "I had him check something... I think we all may want to head over."

"Why?"

"It's probably best you see for yourself."

28

OUTSIDE THE MEDICAL EXAMINER'S office, Brayman tossed the Crown Vic keys to Walter and rounded the car to the passenger side. "You drive. I need to think about all this."

Walter caught the keys but made no move for the driver's-side door. Instead, he stood flat-footed on the sidewalk.

"Now what? Don't tell me you don't know how to drive."

Walter knew this would come up and had hoped to say something before it did, but things had already been so awkward between them he'd kept his mouth shut. He looked down at the sidewalk for a moment, then back at Brayman. "I know how to drive. I'm just not allowed right now."

"Not allowed? And why exactly is that?"

Walter blew out a long breath. "About two weeks ago, I got pulled over on my way home. It was around three in the morning. I was tired, dead tired, and I guess I was swerving a little bit. I told the officer I was PD, but he was with the sheriff's office, and you know how they are—he made me walk the line, and when I stumbled he and his partner gave me a Breathalyzer. I should have said no, but I wasn't thinking. I blew .09, barely above the limit. They didn't write it up, so no DUI, but they called my captain and he took my license and stuck it in his desk drawer. Said I'd get it back in thirty days. Told me next time he'd write up the DUI himself."

"Captain Hazlett?"

Walter shook his head. "Captain Morrow from patrol. Hazlett doesn't know. I'm hoping to keep it that way."

"How'd you get here?"

"Cab."

Brayman looked out across the parking lot as if he expected to find the taxi waiting out there somewhere before fixing his eyes on Walter again. "Do you have an alcohol problem?"

"Of course not."

"But you were out drinking last night, right? You're clearly hungover, so don't try to spin some bullshit with me. And you were hungover at the Edison, too. When you first walked in I could smell it on you, like carpet in a frat house."

Walter said, "Nadler and some of the guys took me out to celebrate my promotion, that's all that was."

"I know all about that, and I get it. That's why I didn't say anything. That doesn't explain last night, though. Where were you?"

"I was home. Going through the files you gave me."

"I said no bullshit."

"It's the truth."

Walter couldn't tell him the truth. Brayman wouldn't believe him any more than Nadler had. Not without proof.

"I had a beer or two while I worked, what's the harm in that? Don't tell me you've never had a drink to unwind."

Brayman stared at him for a long moment and finally just shook his head. "Get in the car."

"Are you gonna tell Hazlett?"

"Today, no. But you show up like this tomorrow, and I most certainly will. I'm not no damn babysitter. Try to do this job without your wits about you, and worst case you're liable to get one of us killed. Best case, you just get in the way and slow me down. Either way, I don't need it." He held his hand out. "Give me the keys."

Walter handed them back, and they both got in the car.

Brayman sat behind the wheel for nearly a minute before starting the car and pulling back out onto Warren heading toward downtown. He was thinking either about the case, about Walter, or about both.

They were halfway to the Four Seasons when Walter couldn't take the silence anymore. "If the ME's right, the man on her table is the same guy who rented the room at the Edison. We're not looking for a second younger man anymore."

Brayman didn't reply.

29

AMID SILENT STARES FROM the hotel staff and patrons, a uniformed patrol officer stationed in the lobby told them to take the elevator up to twenty-three. When the doors opened, they followed the voices and crime scene tape to room 2312 down the hall to the right.

Walter paused at the evidence tag on the hotel room door—fresh scratch marks marred the keyhole and lock mechanism.

Picked.

Inside, a Hispanic man walked over, taking a wide step around another man inspecting the carpet. He gave Walter a cursory glance, lingering a second on Walter's bruised face, then turned to Brayman. "Captain gave this one to me, then here comes Brayman and company to yank it out from under me."

"Detective Melendez, this is my new partner, Walter

O'Brien. O'Brien, this is Hector Melendez. Been with Homicide, what? Nine years now?"

"Ten." He reached out with meaty fingers and shook Walter's hand.

"We're not looking to step on your toes," Brayman told him. "We were with Ackerman at the ME's office when the call came in, and she said—"

"I've got enough on my plate," Melendez interrupted, shaking his head. "You want it, you can have it. I don't even know where to start with this one. Give me a pissed-off husband or wife any day." He tapped the edge of the door near the strike plate. "This is a Delco 349, unpickable according to the hotel. Nevertheless, looks like our guy made quick work of it and got in. The last registered guest in this room was eight days ago. Nobody's supposed to be in here." He ushered Walter and Brayman through the door with a wave of his arm. "You caught the woman on the shitter at Corktown, too, right?"

Brayman nodded. "We did."

"Must be your week for weird shit."

The room was larger than Walter had expected, certainly bigger than any hotel room he'd ever stayed in. Grandly appointed with wainscoting on all the walls and a tall coffered ceiling. Artwork and furnishings that made Walter want to shove his hands in his pockets and not touch anything. A four-poster bed sat against the back wall. Aside from a turned-down corner, the crisp white sheets and comforter were pulled tight, not a single wrinkle. A bottle of wine rested in a bucket on the dresser, still corked, the ice long gone, sweat dripping down the sides. Two glasses beside it.

"Room service delivers to unregistered guests?" Walter asked.

Melendez shook his head. "Call was placed from the house phone out in the hallway near the stairs. Ordered it last night for room 2315 across the hall. Male voice, said he was about to get in the shower. Told them to leave it outside if nobody answered. Real occupant of 2315 is an accountant from Tulsa. He was out meeting with a client at the time. Here's the thing. That's not the bottle they delivered." Melendez pointed toward an open drawer in the dresser. "They delivered that one."

In the drawer was an unopened bottle of something called Opus One, an evidence tag placed next to it.

"How do you know?"

Melendez said, "The green sticker on the label. That's an inventory tag from the bar downstairs." He nodded at the bottle in the ice bucket. "No tag on that one."

Brayman knelt and studied the second bottle, also Opus One. "There are tiny holes in the capsule on this one."

"Capsule?" Walter asked.

"The metal seal at the top. Here, here, and here." Brayman pointed.

Melendez said, "We think something's been injected into the bottle. My first guess would be some date-rape drug. Probably did it at home, called room service to get an ice bucket and glasses, then swapped out the bottle. He asked for two glasses, so he wasn't alone."

Brayman studied the wine bottle and glasses for another moment, then looked around the room. "Where's the body?"

Melendez nodded toward the bathroom. "Shower. Ackerman's already in there. Watch your step. We've got broken glass from a busted mirror and we're isolating trace on the floor here."

The tech examining the carpet had placed two strips of tape down, creating a path from the center of the room to the bathroom door, cordoning off a small parcel. The three of them stepped around him and made their way onto the bathroom tile without disturbing whatever he was working on.

They found Jane Ackerman crouching next to her black leather satchel in front of the glass door of a spacious walk-in shower with an oversize whirlpool bathtub at her back. Her assistant, Samuel Harris, was there, too, and both of them looked up as Brayman and Walter came into the room. Ackerman frowned. "Watch your step. Got a lot of water on the floor in here."

"Some kind of struggle?" Brayman replied, taking in the empty mirror frame on the wall and the large shards of glass on the vanity and floor. Like at the Edison.

Walter looked over Ackerman's shoulder into the shower, where the body of a fully dressed man was lying on the tile floor, one thick leg bent awkwardly under him, the other splayed out just inside the open glass door, his clothing soaked. His head rested on a towel; it was bunched up under his shoulders. Water beaded over his pale forehead and dripped from his gray hair. Walter tried to get a look at his hands, but they were under his chest.

"He has all his fingers," Ackerman confirmed, following his gaze. "And I don't see any visible signs of cancer. He appears to be older, like your two vics, but I think he actually *is* older, *un*like your other two."

"How did he die?"

Ackerman placed a gloved index finger on the man's left eyelid and raised it. The pupil was dilated and pointing up and to the right, while his other eye was looking forward.

"I won't know for sure until I get a look inside, but this is indicative of a fatal brain aneurysm."

Walter glanced over at Brayman, then crouched down. He ran his finger through a puddle of water on the floor. "Why does the water look cloudy?"

"It's salt," Ackerman told him. "He's covered in it, or at least he was. The water washed a lot of it away, but we found more when we rolled him. It's all over his skin. Looks like it was in his hair, too. His clothing was soaked in it, saturated and dried. Probably before he got here."

Detective Melendez was standing in the doorway. He craned his head back toward the main room. "We think he died out there, about halfway between the dresser and the bed. Then someone put a towel under him and used it to drag him into the shower. The carpet is filled with salt residue. The cleaning woman found him this morning. Someone wanted to wash the salt away, or at least tried, but it was a half-assed attempt. They didn't bother to rotate the body under the water, so a lot of it got trapped and pooled."

Harris traced the man's face with a gloved finger. "I found minute scratches on his hands, consistent with being dragged across the carpet from there to here."

"I don't get the towel," Melendez said. "You use one to move a body, you put it under the entire body, not just the head and shoulders. This is more like —"

"Like whoever it was didn't want to touch him," Walter said softly.

Melendez shrugged. "Yeah, maybe minimizing trace. There's no wallet, so we don't have an ID," he explained. "Every surface in this room has been wiped down, so we've got no prints." He pointed at a rumpled hand towel next to the sink. "Looks like they used that."

"What's the point of all that?" Brayman said. "This man had an aneurysm out there. Why not just leave him out there?"

Nobody had an answer.

Walter placed a hand on the wall and leaned into the shower to get a better look. "I get that this is weird, but why are we here?"

Harris held a small black light near the dead man's temple. "Because of this."

Under the light, a bright spot appeared about an inch from his left eyebrow, a small oval. It vanished as he moved the light away, then returned when he drew closer again.

Ackerman brought her hand to the man's head. "If those other marks I showed you were handprints, this could very well be a fingerprint."

She extended her index finger, and it was nearly a perfect fit.

What does it mean?

Brayman must have been thinking the same thing, because when Walter looked over at him, his partner was studying his own hand—too large. He made a quick fist, flexed the muscles, and turned back to the ME. "What exactly reacts to a black light?"

"Saliva, semen, urine," Ackerman rattled off. "Nearly all biological fluids contain some level of fluorescent molecules. Most chemicals, oils, plants, organics…"

"You said he was under the water for a few hours. Wouldn't those kinds of things have washed away?"

Ackerman nodded. "They should, yeah. Whatever is causing this is embedded deeper in the dermis. I'll excise a sample when we get him back to the lab and compare it to the others."

In the other room, a female tech was busy packing up her fingerprint kit. Walter recognized her but couldn't remember her name. Joan, maybe? Jane? Something like that. He knew it started with a *J*.

"Give me a second," he told Brayman and the others, and stepped out of the bathroom.

The tech glanced up from her kit and gave him a double take. "Walter? Look at you, out of uniform!"

Walter smiled and got a quick look at her name tag. "How have you been, Jade?"

She looked down at her gloved hands covered in fingerprint dust. "Oh, you know, living the dream."

In the bathroom, Harris had worked his way into the shower and was running the black light over the rest of the body with Brayman and Ackerman hovering. Melendez's large frame blocked most of the doorway.

Walter reached into his jacket pocket and removed the plastic bag, Willow's glass still inside. He lowered his voice. "Can you run this for me?"

"Sure." She started to unpack her kit. "Give me a second to—"

Walter placed a hand on her forearm. "I'd rather you do it somewhere else." Her face grew concerned, and he quickly added, "It's for another case and might not mean anything."

"Oh."

"I'm just following a hunch, and it's a long shot. You do it here, my new partner sees, he might start asking questions. I'd rather not involve him unless it turns out to be relevant." Walter did his best to appear embarrassed. "I just got my gold shield and I want to make a good impression. He thinks I'm chasing my tail, and I'll lose ground with him. You know how that goes, right?"

Jade smiled, took the glass, and set it inside her kit. "You're lucky you're cute, Detective O'Brien. I'll get back to you in a bit. You owe me." She finished packing up and left the room.

A camera flash went off a couple of times in the bathroom, and Brayman came out holding several Polaroids. "Let's go talk to the staff."

BRAYMAN SLID HIS CHAIR closer to the desk. "Can you rewind that?"

Walter stood behind him along with the hotel's manager, all of them huddled in the cramped security office adjacent to the lobby behind the front desk. The hotel's chief of security pressed several buttons on the bulky video recorder. The time stamp read 6:22 the previous night.

A man in a dark suit crossing the lobby holding a paper sack. A moment after he disappeared from the frame, a young woman stepped through the image and vanished after him.

Brayman leaned closer and squinted. "That was him, right?"

The manager looked down at the Polaroid in his hand, then back to the screen and sighed. "I'm sorry, gentlemen, the image quality just isn't that good. These cameras make our customers feel warm and fuzzy, but that's about all they're good for."

"That's him, for sure," Walter said, tapping one of the other pictures against his thigh. "Can you zoom in or something? Why are they so washed out?"

"That time of day, the light coming in from the windows plays havoc with nearly all the lobby cameras," the security chief explained.

"What about another camera?"

"I checked the footage from every camera in the lobby, and this is the best shot we have." The manager rewound the tape again, this time playing it in slow motion.

"Nothing from outside?" Brayman asked.

The manager shook his head. "Our insurance company said filming public spaces created a liability risk. No sidewalks. No streets. Not even the valet area."

"Anything on the twenty-third floor?"

"That camera's been out for about a month. Like I said, this is all we've got." While they could make out some detail on the man, the woman was another story. A glare filled most of the screen as she walked by, making it near impossible to see much of anything.

The security chief froze the image, capturing the woman in mid-stride, several feet from the front desk. She was looking forward, toward the elevators, the direction the man had gone. She wore black stiletto pumps, a dark skirt, and a red button-down blouse. She held a small purse in her right hand.

Walter couldn't make out a single detail of her face. Her hair looked dark, but it could easily be a wig.

Brayman said, "Rewind back to the man again, and freeze the shot."

Brayman leaned in a little closer and pointed down at the man's left shoulder, a bulge under his jacket. "What do you make of that? Almost looks like he's got a gun under the coat. Shoulder rig, like ours."

Walter studied the image for a second, then said dismissively, "I don't see it. I think you're reaching."

"I think this is a man who knows how to pick a lock," Brayman replied. "A thief, or someone on the job. The kind of guy who carries a gun."

"Now you're *really* reaching."

"Okay, hotshot. So what do you think this is?"

Walter turned back to the monitor. "Go back to the girl," he told the security chief.

Her washed-out image returned to the screen.

Tapping the Polaroid on his leg again, he began thinking out loud. "That's the only other person you've got going up to twenty-three?"

The security chief said, "Other than room service, yeah. We alternate floors when booking rooms. The accountant across the hall was here on a multiday stay, but otherwise, that floor was empty. We got your guy going up, room service, and this woman."

Brayman asked, "Is she a pro? Do you recognize her?"

This made both the manager and security chief uncomfortable.

Brayman quickly added, "It's fine, gentlemen. We're Homicide, not Vice."

The security chief shifted in his seat. "I know all the professionals who frequent the hotel. I have to. I can't make out anyone familiar from this footage."

Walter shook his head. "I don't think this was a sex thing. Maybe he's blackmailing her. Maybe she's blackmailing him. There's a million reasons for the two of them to be up in that room together. Remember the wine—if he paid for it, there'd be no reason to drug her."

The manager went on alert. Drugged guests made the papers. "What did you find in the wine?"

Brayman shot Walter an irritated glance. "We don't know. Not yet. We need to wait on the lab. Could be nothing." He turned back to the security chief. "Do you have any shots of her leaving?"

"Yeah. Give me a second."

The lobby image scrolled forward. He twisted a knob on the surveillance system's controller, and it sped up, people flying through the shot. One hour. Two. Two and a half. He slowed down. "It's right around here."

When the image slowed back to a normal speed, the time stamp read 9:08 at night. She walked through the lobby at a brisk pace, but only her clothing was identifiable. Her face was washed out again.

"Sun's long gone," Walter said flatly. "What caused that blip this time?"

The security chief didn't have an answer.

NOW

CHAPTER

31

"WHO THE HELL IS Walter O'Brien?"

Commander Lisa Rigby stood in front of the bank of computer monitors built into the wall of the SWAT van, hovering over the wide-eyed kid who always appeared to her as more of an extension of the equipment than a cop. Russell Hurwitz was only nineteen. By all standards, too young to be out in the field. She'd never seen him with a gun (although members of SWAT were required to be armed at all times while on duty). He wore the uniform, but she was sure if he walked down the sidewalk, people would assume he was playing some sort of dress-up. Like he borrowed the getup from his daddy's closet. A wire hanger filled it more than his lanky frame ever could. Yet, he might be the most valuable person on her team. He'd graduated high school at fourteen. Obtained his first degree by sixteen. And to his parents' dismay (they'd wanted him to go into engineering), he'd had a thing for cop shows and wanted nothing more than to be a part of the action. In the year and a half he'd worked for her, he'd replaced three other officers—essentially her entire tech detail—after proving he worked faster (and was far more capable) working solo.

His fingers danced across the keyboard with a rhythmic *clickity-clack*. "Walter O'Brien is a former cop."

Rigby leaned in closer. "A cop?"

Hurwitz nodded. "Right here in Detroit. From 1986 through 1997. Beat cop, then homicide detective."

"Then what? Where's he been the last few decades?"

"Dunno. His employment record is locked."

"Why would it be locked?"

Hurwitz moved his cursor back to Walter O'Brien's name and clicked on it. The name flashed from yellow to red, and the words *ACCESS DENIED* appeared beneath with a series of letters and numbers. "That lock code is IA," he pointed out. "Internal Affairs."

"We'll need to get his jacket."

"Hard way or easy way?" Hurwitz replied with a mischievous smile.

"Start with the *right* way. Pick up the phone and call IA. Tell them what's going on. If they drag their feet or won't release it, then—"

"Then easy way." His smile widened.

"Yeah," she agreed. "What else you got for me?"

He pointed at the monitor on the top left. "I'm running thermal cameras on all the surrounding buildings. I caught some movement on two of the rooftops when we first got here. One of the shooters was definitely on top of the Moreland Bank building, and I've got another over here in this one—1812 Park—it's a federal building but looks like they took on tenants to fill the space. Thirty or forty different businesses inside—doctors, lawyers, a real estate office—mix of things. This time of night, both buildings should be empty other than maybe cleaning staff, but I've got movement. First on the roof, now inside. Hard to say how many. At least four, probably more. Things are getting hazy."

"Hazy how?"

"I think whoever is moving around inside turned up the heat, office by office. Cranked all the thermostats to full. Between blinds and window tint, there's not much in the way of a visual."

"They knew we'd use thermal, so they're warming the place up to hide their position."

Hurwitz nodded. "Those last couple shots, when the salt truck came around, they came from the third floor of the bank. They busted out the window. Your spotters are in place, but if the shooters keep moving like that, the only way our snipers will tag them will be with dumb luck."

"I'm not above hoping for dumb luck," Rigby replied. "But I'd like to know if the bomb is real or bullshit before I start taking their people out." She was still studying the monitor. "Two to four shooters?"

"So far. There could be more. I'll keep you posted on that."

"What can you tell me about the club?"

Hurwitz brought up a schematic of the club. "It's not very big. Only about eighteen hundred square feet. Most of that is taken up by the bar and various seating areas. The dance floor is only about four hundred square feet, and there are some offices and storage spaces in the back. Official capacity is five hundred. We're running thermals there, too, and I'm picking up about half that. Hard to say—they're all huddled together in groups. Nobody's moving."

"Anyone pick up the phone?"

He shook his head. "I've got the club's hard line on a constant redial. Been at it since we got here, and nobody's touched it. We're blocking all cell signals and transmissions in and out, so if there is a bomb in there somewhere, they'll need someone on the trigger. They won't be able to activate it remotely. Unfortunately, that also limits our communications options."

"If nobody's answering the phone, nobody's moving, there's a good chance they've got people inside. Not just the shooters."

"That would be my guess. Explains what happened with 911, too."

Nine-one-one had received nine calls when the panic started, then nothing. The calls had dropped, and nobody picked up on redial. The club went dark seven minutes *before* the SWAT team's transmission blockers went live. From a red backpack next to his chair, Hurwitz took out a pack of gum. He offered a piece to Rigby, then peeled a stick and popped it in his mouth.

"Did you kill the power yet?"

"Not yet. I've been waiting on your go."

"Do it. Shut down power and heat on the surrounding buildings, too. We can't let them get in front of our thermals."

Hurwitz swiveled his chair slightly to the left, pulled a secondary keyboard out from a cubby in the desk, and hit several keystrokes. "Done."

"What are our ingress and egress points on the club?"

He returned to the schematic of Club Stomp. "Only two doors—the one in front and this one in back. Back door is a metal slab, and it's been welded shut." He loaded up a map of the intersection. "Between utility tunnels and the sewer system, we might be able to get in from underground. I'm still working on that."

"If we need to go in fast, we'll want at least three options."

"You'll have 'em." On one of the other screens, he had set a timer. It currently read forty-four minutes, fifty-one seconds.

"Deputy chief called twice. Wants an update."

Rigby rolled her eyes. "I'm sure he does. Fill him in on whatever we have. They haven't asked for money, but that's probably coming next. Maybe he can speed up things with IA and get us some intel on this guy. What's he doing out there?" she asked. "Let me see him."

Hurwitz cycled through the many images feeding in from the camera array on the roof of the SWAT van. He stopped at the one trained on Walter O'Brien, still sitting in the abandoned patrol car in the center of the intersection. He was facing the club, his lips moving subtly.

"He's in contact with these people," Rigby pointed out. "I saw a small earbud. Think you can isolate the signal?"

Hurwitz huffed. "Does Mona Lisa have teeth?"

"I'm not sure what that means."

"It means yes. Toothless models have never been *en vogue*."

Rigby knew better than to dig deeper. She pointed at the USB drive plugged into Hurwitz's computer. "What did you find on that?"

"Looks like some kind of data dump. Fast and dirty. Unorganized. The dates cover almost forty years—old case files. Photos. Reports. Audio recordings. Video. It's going to take some time to sort it all out."

"Bring in whatever resources you need—we have less than an hour."

"Yes, ma'am."

1992

ALIASES?

Amy Archer

Amelia Dyer

Alvin Schalk

Two bodies/basement freezer

John Doe/Edison

Jane Doe/Corktown Bus Depot

John Doe/Four Seasons

... Walter O'Brien, 28 Years Old

32

BRAYMAN STOOD AT THE board near the back of the homicide bullpen. Walter sat at his desk, his chair flipped around backward, arms folded over the back.

After more than an hour, they'd only been able to come to three conclusions they could both agree on: First, the only real connection they'd found between these three people was the weird marks. Second, all three appeared to have died from some type of natural cause. Third, postmortem evidence indicated none of these deaths were entirely natural, regardless of how they appeared.

"How about assisted suicide?" Walter threw out. "If they knew they were dying and wanted to go out on their own terms, maybe our missing person gave them a helping hand." Walter wrapped his hand around his wrist, his ankle, then tapped the side of his temple with his index finger.

Brayman scratched the side of his head. "We'd find something in toxicology. A sleep-inducing barbiturate to put them at rest, like sodium thiopental. Then something to stop their heart—pancuronium bromide would be my guess. You'd need a paralytic, too, something to prevent spasms and keep the person comfortable."

"How the hell do you know all that? You're like a Black Yoda."

Brayman shrugged. "Crack a book sometime, O'Brien. Preferably one that doesn't require crayons."

Walter ignored the jab and focused on the board. "Could any of those drugs cause the marks? Like a rash at the injection sight?"

"Ackerman didn't find anything like that." Brayman gave him a look. "How's that rash on your chest?"

"Gone, wanna see?" Walter reached for the collar of his shirt and started working the first few buttons. It wasn't gone, though, was it? Fading, but not gone completely.

"No. I don't want to see."

Walter nodded back at the photos of the marks. "If we're spitballing here, let's spitball. Answer my question."

Brayman pursed his lips, considered this for a moment. "In order for a rash to develop, the person would need to be alive; the blood needs to be pumping."

"Not very long, though, right?"

"No, not very long. I suppose that's possible."

"So maybe this is something new. Something the tox screen wouldn't catch."

"Doesn't necessarily look like a rash, though. And there's no injection mark."

"Something new," Walter repeated. "Unknown med,

unknown delivery method, produces unknown result. Does it look like a handprint to you?"

Brayman leaned closer to the photo of the mark on the ankle of the woman found at the bus depot and traced it with the tip of his finger. "That could just be pareidolia."

Walter stared at him.

"Books, O'Brien," Brayman said. "Pareidolia is when you see a face in something where it shouldn't be, like woodgrain or a cloud."

"Like Jesus staring back at you from the grill marks on your toast?"

"Exactly. The brain tries to find the familiar in the unfamiliar. Maybe those marks only look like handprints because our brain doesn't know how else to define them."

Walter got up from his chair and went to the board. "Okay, now we're getting somewhere. What else do you see when you look at these three people? When you look at them in the order they died?"

Brayman took his time, studying all the images in turn. He opened his mouth to say something, then thought better of it and went quiet. He clucked his tongue several times.

"Ah, you do see something," Walter said. "Spit it out."

"I think it's more about what I'm *not* seeing."

"I don't follow."

Brayman pointed at the first two. "Both of these are missing their fingers. Obvious similarity. The third one is not. The first two are riddled with disease, knocking on heaven's door. Our third is older, died of something that looks natural, too, but not like the first two. Cancer, cancer, aneurysm. Even if the first two were assisted suicide, the third doesn't fit. Someone tells you you have cancer, you can plan something. Aneurysm just hits." He snapped his fingers. "The first and third both died in motel rooms, that fits with assisted suicide, but the woman doesn't fit that at all. Nobody wants to die on a toilet."

"So not assisted suicide."

"Nope."

Walter pinched his eyes shut and rolled his head, tried to will his brain to find something they'd missed. "What about the mirrors?"

"What about them?"

"Broken mirror at the Edison and again at the Four Seasons. Not at the bus depot."

"Can't break those," Brayman explained. "They make them from polished stainless steel. Broken mirrors, though. Suggests the killer is ashamed of what they're doing."

"Can't bear to look at themselves."

"Something like that."

"Or they just got angry."

Brayman shook his head. "I don't see anger here."

"You know what else we're missing, if we're assuming all three are homicides?"

Brayman said nothing.

"Escalation. We've got three victims linked together by those marks—that fits the bill of a serial—but serials usually escalate or fine-tune their kills. Make incremental changes as they tweak their fucked-upedness."

"Their—"

Walter cut him off. "If we look at these in order, there's no escalation. If anything, it's the opposite." He tapped the photo of the first victim, the naked man found at the Edison. "With this one, it looks like our killer took time. Not only with the kill, but with the cleanup. Might have lured our vic there. They were together in that room for a while. Then you look at victim number two, in a bath-room stall at the bus depot. That one looks hasty. If the first was calm and planned, the second was a quick kill under far from ideal circumstances." Walter made a gun out of his thumb and forefinger, then added, "Yet this third one…"

"…looks more like an accident."

"Or like the killer tried to cover it up. Didn't want us to tie it to the others. Skipped the fingers. Skipped the theatrics. Damn near perfect murder." He looked up at Brayman. "Think about it. If they had left the body where it dropped instead of dragging it to the shower, we wouldn't have been called there at all. The vic would have just been some guy who clocked out in a hotel room. We were there by dumb luck."

"That single move suggests panic," Brayman agreed. "It's reactionary."

Walter nodded. "The killer won't make that mistake again. He's getting good, which means we might not even find the next one. Not unless all the right people are looking for it. That takes us back to our real problem. There's no gun here. No knife. No known murder weapons. There's no way to induce cancer, right?"

"Not short-term, no. It would take some form of ex-posure."

"And Ackerman already ruled out radiation," Walter pointed out.

Brayman rolled his fingers on the edge of his desk. "So we're back to 'something new,' something she doesn't know, or doesn't know how, to look for."

"What do you make of the salt? Our guy was covered in it," Walter noted.

His partner just shook his head. "No idea."

Both of them went back to looking at the grainy photograph of the girl. Staring at it.

After about a minute, Walter returned to his desk. He had the files for all the known prostitutes near the Edison lying there, the ones matching the description provided by the night manager on top. Nine of them. He flipped through them, and each photo made this more and more frustrating. "You throw a wig on one of these girls, and any one of them could be the woman from the Four Seasons video."

"Or none of them," Brayman replied. "If the girl is our connection, I seriously doubt she's a streetwalker." He pointed at the image. "Those shoes look expensive, and that bag is a Gucci. Looks legit, too."

"A run-of-the-mill pro can't play dress-up?"

Brayman nodded at Walter's desk. "Look at those files, the rap sheets. Track marks. Coke busts. Heroin. All nine have drug problems. It's almost inevitable in that business. It's how most of them cope. Girls with drug problems don't spend a thousand bucks on shoes and a purse; they blow it on smack. If this woman is a pro, she's not some girl turning tricks for twenty bucks. The girls who circle the Edison and the ones who frequent the Four Seasons are from two very different worlds."

He's right. Streetwalkers and—

Captain Hazlett's door opened. He quickly looked around the homicide bullpen, his eyes landing on Brayman. "Come in here for a second."

When both of them rose, Hazlett waved a dismissive hand at Walter. "Just Wes."

Walter didn't think he'd say anything about the drinking,

but he couldn't be sure. For all he knew, Brayman had already said something.

His new partner stepped into the captain's office and closed the door behind him, but not before Walter heard Nadler's familiar voice say *"Still there?"* from the speakerphone on Hazlett's desk.

Why the hell are they talking to Nadler?

He didn't need this.

He didn't need trouble.

Walter started back toward his desk when he spotted Jade standing at the elevator, holding a file. She nodded at him.

Walter gave the captain's closed door a glance and walked over to her. "Did you find something?"

"I pulled what I could from records, figured I'd save you a trip." She handed him the file. "I need to get back before someone notices I'm gone. Call me sometime, we should get dinner, catch up."

She gave him a quick smile, then was gone. Back in the elevator and behind closing doors.

Walter opened the file. A mug shot of Willow stared back at him, wide-eyed and worried.

Her real name was Rebecca Edgecomb, nineteen. Left home at fifteen, a runaway from New Jersey. She had various arrests for theft, shoplifting, vagrancy, and prostitution. The most recent was only three weeks ago. Vice had picked her up in a sting downtown along with twelve other girls. She'd been released on two thousand dollars' bond with a hearing set in three months.

Her last known employer was an escort service operating out of a residential address on Franklin. Not far. There were several known associates listed, but none of those names were Amy Archer or Amelia Dyer.

Walter looked back at the captain's door again. He could see shadows moving around inside.

It was nearly seven o'clock.

"Fuck it."

Walter didn't wait on the elevator. He took the stairs.

A minute later he was on the curb, hailing a cab.

33

"THAT'S IT ON THE right," the cabbie told Walter, his voice slightly muffled by the plastic barrier between them. "Third one in from the corner."

According to her jacket, the last known employer for Rebecca Edgecomb, a.k.a. "Willow," was Elite Escorts, located at 415 Franklin Avenue. Walter had expected an office complex, possibly some type of front business like a nail salon or restaurant, but instead, the cab pulled slowly by a series of large residential brownstones. Each was three stories tall, probably basements below, and either single family residences or apartments. Expensive ones. No doubt the phone number on the missing business card from Michael Driscoll rang a line somewhere inside that building. He could feel it, some unconscious pull telling him he was close.

"Let me out up there on the corner," he told the driver. "Take a right and go a little further down the block so we're off Franklin."

The driver double-parked next to a late-model BMW. "Want me to wait for you?"

Walter shook his head. He handed the driver several bills through the slot in the plastic. "No, I'm good. Thanks. Keep it."

With the sun gone, the air had taken on a chill, not uncomfortable but heading in that direction. Walter wore his suit jacket, should have brought something heavier. He shoved his hands into his pockets and walked toward the brownstone. Rather than stop, he circled the block on foot. Heading in the direction opposite the one the taxi had taken. He wanted to get a better feel for the area before he made any kind of move. He still wasn't sure what that move would be. As a patrol officer, he'd seen his share of illicit businesses, but he had no idea how this one operated. It might just be a call center, remotely managing the escorts. Or the girls might live inside, use it as a base. It was equally possible this was a full-on brothel or that there might not be anything inside but a forwarded phone sitting on a cardboard box along with a handful of strategically placed lights on timers.

The neighborhood was fairly quiet. Several joggers ran by. A woman with a golden retriever gave him a distracted nod before crouching next to her dog and pulling a plastic bag from her pocket. A man and woman held hands as they walked.

As he neared 415, nothing about the building stuck out other than a yellow potted plant on the front stoop. To the left of the door was a brass plate with the house number. Several lights were on inside, illuminating the edges of heavy curtains drawn over the windows. He slowed only slightly as he walked by, his ears straining to hear anything from the other side of the brick facade, hoping to spot movement. He was on his second trip around the block when a Mercedes pulled to a stop on Franklin and a young blond woman wearing jeans and a dark sweater got out, dodged around the parked cars, and disappeared inside.

Several minutes later, another girl came out—a redhead in a black evening dress. She scrambled into the back seat of the same Mercedes and they were gone a moment later. Over the next thirty minutes, Walter watched seven other girls come and go in similar cars. Three men as well. None of them were Willow. None of them were Amy Archer.

That didn't mean they weren't in there.

Walter was rounding the block again when the pay phone at the corner of Franklin and Nineteenth, about twenty feet from where he stood, started to ring. He glanced up at the brownstone, thought he saw someone near a window on the second floor, but couldn't be sure.

The phone rang eight times, stopped for about ten seconds, then started up again.

Walter walked over to the phone booth and stepped inside, leaving the door open. He picked up the receiver and brought it to his ear but didn't say anything. At first, there was only soft breathing, then her voice.

"What are you doing, Walter?"

"Amy?"

She was silent for a moment. *"You're going to get me in trouble. Me and Willow. You need to go."*

"I want to see you."

"You can't."

"Where did you go last night?"

"You don't remember?"

Cradling the phone on his shoulder, he turned slightly so

he could see the brownstone again. "No. Most of the night is a blur."

"Last night was a mistake."

"Don't say that."

"It was."

"Come outside."

She sighed. *"I can't."*

"Then let me in."

She said nothing.

"I've got…" *Money.* He almost said it, then pulled the word back before it slipped out. Even if she was working for an escort service now, whatever happened between them last night had nothing to do with that. He couldn't stumble over that line. "I've got…to talk to you," he said instead.

Again, she said nothing, but he could hear her breathing; she was still on the line.

"I just want to know what happened to you after you ran from my patrol car that night, after Alvin Schalk. I've spent six years worried about you. Hell, I thought you were dead."

"Who?" She dropped off for a second. *"Walter, I think you've got me mixed up with someone else. I don't know an Alvin…what did you say his name was?"*

"Alvin Schalk."

"I don't know who that is. I've never been in a car with you. You said we've met before, and I'm sorry, but if we did, I don't remember you." She went quiet for a second, and when she came back, her voice had dropped lower. *"I just moved here three months ago from New Jersey. I've never been to Detroit before that. I'm only here because Angie…I mean Willow…said I could stay with her until I got on my feet. Working here, doing…this…isn't how I*

*planned things, but it's only for a little while, just until I can afford
an apartment, someplace of my own. Maybe another move. I don't
know. I haven't really decided yet. But the point is, this is temporary;
it's not who I am. And I'm not who you think I am. I'm sorry. I hope
you find her, whoever she is. It sounds like you care about her, but
it's not me. I've got to go…"*

"Amy, wait, I—"

A heavy fist banged against the glass of the phone booth
to the right of Walter's head. When he jerked around, the
largest man he'd ever seen was standing there, an angry
scowl on his face. The angry man was at least six foot five
and pushing three hundred pounds. If he had a neck, the
rolling wall of muscle that made up his chest had swallowed
it long ago. He wore a dark navy silk suit, a deep burgundy
tie, and black loafers polished to a reflective sheen. A prison
tattoo was slightly visible at the base of his jaw under his
white collar. The expensive suit was nothing more than a
uniform, a disguise. This was the kind of guy who'd sooner
stick a screwdriver in your gut than give up his pudding cup
in the chow line.

"I believe the lady asked you to leave," he said in a
gravelly voice.

Walter still had the phone receiver pressed to his ear, but
the line had gone dead. He slowly placed it back on the
cradle and reached for his wallet. "I'm a cop. I'm just getting
my badge."

The man huffed. "I don't care if you're a cop." His large
head nodded toward a white van halfway down the block.
"You're a cop; they're cops. We got cops everywhere. I want
you to fuck off, the whole lot of you. The young lady asked
you to leave, and you're going to leave. If you don't, I call
my boss, they call their boss, and a bunch of people will

start calling *your* boss. They'll light up his fucking phone, and that won't end well for you."

Walter had the badge out and held it up.

The man ignored it. His eyes remained fixed on Walter. "It feels a lot like you're harassing me without cause. Me, a resident of this fine neighborhood. In fact, I feel very threatened by your presence."

" *You* feel threatened?"

The man had a hundred pounds on Walter. His large head bobbed slowly on broad shoulders. "Not just me, but the girls inside. You followed them home, now you're hanging around outside. Lurking, like some freak." His eyes narrowed. "Do you have a warrant or cause to be here? Stalking is a crime, Officer."

"Detective."

"Whatever, shithead."

This guy either had a cursory understanding of the law or had been coached. Either way, Walter knew he was right. Worse yet, this guy might go back inside and take out his frustrations on Amy or Willow or God knew who else was in there.

Walter stepped out of the phone booth. "I'll be back with a warrant."

The guy smirked. "No, you won't."

He didn't move out of the way, and Walter was forced to step around him to leave the booth and get back on the sidewalk. He pictured Amy, standing to the side of one of the curtains, her back pressed up against the wall. Maybe she was still holding the phone.

The man faced the white van. "Go ahead, say hello to your friends before you go."

Walter turned and started toward the van.

"I'll call you a cab," the man said behind him, heading back toward the door.

Walter held his middle finger up behind his back.

The van was a mix of chipped white paint, dust, and rust. While there were no markings, the city plates and a sticker for the Detroit Metro garage on the windshield said enough. Three bulky antennae on the roof didn't help them blend in much, either. Walter went to the back door and gave it two hits with a closed fist. There was a click and the door swung open. A man holding a burrito in one hand was standing there, hunched over, his large belly testing the limits of his shirt. He had shaggy brown hair with a reddish tint and a matching mustache in need of a trim. He was shaking his head. He gave the street a quick survey. "They've got cameras all over this block—surrounding buildings, above their door. They probably spotted you before we did, and we had a bead on you when you started doing laps around the neighborhood. Next time bring a stroller or something, try to blend."

"Get in here," someone called out from deeper in the van. A Black guy sitting in a swivel chair staring up at several bulky monitors, a pair of large headphones on—the left can over his ear, the right side resting behind.

Walter climbed up into the van, and the brown-haired detective with the burrito pulled the door shut and dropped into a chair. "I'm Buncy. That's Wilson. We're with Vice. Who the hell are you, and what are you doing sniffing around our caller?" Buncy offered a hand, then realized hot sauce was dripping down his wrist and pulled it back.

"I'm Detective O'Brien, Homicide," Walter told them.

"Homicide?" Buncy said. "We miss something? Nobody told us about a homicide."

"I'm just chasing a lead."

Wilson gave a short laugh. "Sounded more like you were chasing some tail."

"You heard that?"

"Pay phone's tapped. Same with the other three within a quarter mile of here. We record everything, but if the call isn't connected to the girly operation we're not allowed to listen, have to hit the Mute button. Your call certainly sounded connected," Wilson said. "I listened to every word, even made a note here on my nifty clipboard. Says, 'Cop? Poontang brings out the stupid in all of us.'" Wilson smiled. "Welcome to the official record, Detective. Which one was she?" He gestured up at a series of photographs tacked to a board above their makeshift desk.

Two of the pictures were mug shots; the rest looked like they'd been captured with telephoto lenses. Willow was the third one from the left (mug shot) with *Rebecca Edgecomb* scribbled on a piece of masking tape below the photograph.

Amy was…

Walter took a step closer. He cocked his head and focused on the first one. "This might be her, but I'm not sure. It's a shitty picture."

"Lolita Number One," Buncy replied, nodding approvingly. "She's proving to be a little camera shy, but we'll get her. It's like she's got a spidey sense for avoiding our cameras. She might be the hottest of the bunch. Do you have a name?"

Amy Archer.

Walter hedged. "I questioned a man yesterday who said her name was Amelia Dyer, but I think that's bogus."

"You called her Amy—that some kind of nickname?"

Walter nodded.

They wouldn't understand.

Buncy grunted, scribbled *Amelia "Amy" Dyer* on a piece of tape, and stuck it below her photo. "She's connected to a homicide? That's a shame. Girl like that will get pulled six ways to Sunday in prison."

Walter had no idea what Buncy meant by that but didn't say anything.

He went on. "We've been watching this place for a few months now. They were operating out of another brownstone on Wilmington before that. Three joined apartments downtown before that one…we got them at nine different locations over the past three years."

"Why haven't you arrested them?"

Buncy gave Wilson a sidelong glance, took another bite of his burrito, and spoke with his mouth half full. "We know what they're doing. We know who they're doing it with. We even have most of the *how*s figured out, but they're damn careful. You got their phone number from a business card, right?"

Walter nodded.

"They print them in small lots, probably fifty or so. The numbers are only good for a couple weeks, then they rotate them out. The girls give their customers a new card after each visit, but they need to use it quick or the number goes bad. That helps keep the johns on the hook. Every time they get a new number, we need to get a new warrant. Makes that damn near impossible. By the time a judge comes through for us, the number is dead and they've moved on. We've only gotten lucky a handful of times and got one of those calls down on tape, and they're real careful with what they say or respond to. Anything incriminating comes up, they hang up and burn the number. The calls themselves roll through a series of forwards worldwide. They bounce them through switches, which makes tracing a nightmare. At the moment, they're answered here. But like I said, they move their base location, too. Girls are dispatched but the hanky-panky never happens here, so all we've got are them coming and going. That's not a crime. Living here isn't a crime. The crime part takes place behind closed doors at any number of hotels downtown."

"Why don't you just send in an undercover and arrest them at the hotel? All I did was call the number from the bar at the Huntley, and they sent someone right over. I could have easily busted her when we got upstairs."

At the back of the van, Wilson chuckled.

Buncy smiled at him. "That easy, huh?"

"Yeah."

"We follow them to the hotels, but we don't have eyes and ears in the rooms. What little we've learned, we've had to shake out of johns we picked up on their way out," Buncy explained. "If you'd managed to get your girl upstairs, she would have asked you for your driver's license and phoned it in so they could run a background on you. She would have also asked you flat out if you were a cop. You answer no, and you venture into entrapment territory. You answer yes, and she's gone. Background comes back with anything hokey, and she's gone. You would have found she wouldn't ask you for money. A voice on the phone would have told you how much and where in the room to leave it. Those words would *never* come out of her mouth. She may pick up the cash, but that's not necessarily a crime. Neither is doing the deed with a stranger. The crime comes from all these moving parts, and only if a couple of them align just right.

These people have been running this racket for a long time and are extremely cautious. They don't let those parts align. We think it's probably Russian mob pulling the strings. Maybe Italian, but it smells more Russian. No real proof either way, though. The girls are just players. Busting them doesn't move the needle. They get ten more girls for every one we take off the board. We want to get the people running the operation, and that takes time. Gather evidence, build a case, wait for a break. That's how this works."

Russian mob?

Walter thought of the files still sitting on his kitchen counter.

"Do you have any record of these girls going to the Four Seasons or the Edison this week?"

"The Edison?" Buncy repeated with a hint of amusement in his voice. "These girls don't cross over to that side of the tracks. They leave that neighborhood to the dime-store ho-hos. The Four Seasons, though..." His voice trailed off, and he looked at Wilson, who was thumbing through a notebook.

Wilson's index finger ran down a page. "Three trips to the Four Seasons yesterday." He nodded up at the photographs. "Number one, three, and nine."

Number one was Amy, three was Willow. Number nine was a blond girl with high cheekbones, full lips, and bright green eyes. She looked Eastern European.

Walter said, "I'm going to need copies of whatever you have on those three."

34

THE FOLLOWING MORNING, WALTER managed to get himself to work early, but not early enough. When the elevator doors opened on the homicide bullpen at just a little after seven, Brayman was already at his desk, coffee in one hand and the remains of a breakfast sandwich in the other. He looked up at Walter, studied the files in his arms with a wary eye, then looked back down at his desk.

Walter crossed the room and set the folders down. Jackets on the three girls from the escort service were on top, the mob files were beneath, and all were marked with colorful Post-it tabs. "I think I've got something."

"Uh-huh," Brayman muttered.

He was reading the *Detroit Herald,* open to the crime beat section. The headline was a story about the body at the Four Seasons. "First a story on the Corktown body, now this. Do we need to have a conversation about talking to the press? You know, little things like, we don't talk to the fucking press."

"I didn't talk to anyone."

"Well, they've got all the details here. Our names, a description of the vic. They even mention the aneurysm and how the body was moved and repositioned. The reporter might as well have been holding your hand."

"Me? How do I know *you* didn't talk?"

"Because I don't talk to the press. Ever. I know better."

Walter felt his face burn. "Man, you are a complete ass, you know that?"

"Yeah, I'm the ass." Brayman shook his head. He remained still for a moment, then slowly got up from his chair with the newspaper in hand. "Captain wants to see us."

"He's here already? About what?"

Nadler.

The near DUI.

My drinking.

The list was growing.

Why couldn't they just drop the bullshit and let him do his job?

"Now, O'Brien."

Walter scooped up the files. He'd show them what he found. Then nothing else would matter. They'd forget all this other high school bullshit.

Captain Hazlett was sitting in his chair behind his desk, his hands folded over his own copy of the *Herald*. He looked up at Walter as he came in, his face blank. "Close the door."

Walter shouldered the door shut, then set his folders on top of the captain's desk.

Brayman was standing off to the right, leaning partially

against the wall. He eyed the files and exchanged a quick look with Hazlett but said nothing.

Walter cleared his throat. "I think I've got a bead on our unknown woman from the hotel. I'm not a hundred percent sure, but I've got a link."

The captain's eyes narrowed. "O'Brien, I—"

Walter cut him off. "Have either of you ever heard the name Sergei Turgenev?"

Neither man said anything.

Walter shuffled through the files, found Turgenev, and spread the contents across the captain's desk. "Turgenev is Russian mob. Hard-core, old-school. He operates out of the back of a drugstore on the east end. There's a small pocket of immigrants there. I spoke to some guys in Vice last night, and—"

"You talked to Vice?" Hazlett interrupted. "Who in Vice?"

"Buncy and Wilson. They told me Turgenev has his hands in a number of local operations, but two of them jumped out—Elite Escorts, on the upper end of town, and a series of pimps he runs around Arlington and Edgewater near where our first vic was found. He offers 'protection' for the pimps and their girls in exchange for a piece of their take." From the folders, Walter pulled out the witness statement from the manager at the Edison as well as the photograph taken from the surveillance camera at the Four Seasons. He set them both side by side on the desk. "We've got a girl at the Edison, most likely the last person to see our vic alive. And we've got another at the Four Seasons, same thing. Two girls, most likely pros, but from very different worlds. Both with a single connection."

"Turgenev," Hazlett muttered.

"Exactly. I found a number of links between those two

operations, with Turgenev in the middle. Turns out if one of the pimps gets a girl who can cut it uptown, Turgenev throws the pimp a bonus and places the girl with Elite Escorts. If one of the girls at Elite isn't earning enough or is at the tail end of her career, they bust her down to the Arlington area. The point is, these girls go back and forth depending on their earning potential. Both businesses feed each other."

"How does that connect to our vics?" Brayman asked. "What's the motive?"

"I think they were hits."

"Hits? Seriously?"

"I think the Russian mob wanted these people dead, and they used one of Turgenev's girls to do it."

Brayman looked like he was on the verge of laughing. "What, like some femme fatale? A female assassin?"

Walter ignored him. "All three were murdered; we just don't know how yet. I'd be willing to bet if we dig, we'll find that the victims all have a connection to Turgenev. Maybe they worked for him. Maybe whatever they did for him led to some type of exposure to something toxic, and that exposure is what caused the cancer, the aneurysm. These illnesses that look natural. Maybe he had them killed to keep them from talking to anyone about it."

Captain Hazlett leaned back in his chair. "And what, the woman at the bus depot was one of Turgenev's girls?"

Walter nodded. "Probably running, and they caught up with her." He looked at Brayman. "We talked about that, remember? Her death looked hasty. Something quick to shut her down. At a bus depot, no less. Oh, she was running for sure. Somebody took her out."

Hazlett looked over at Brayman. "You two talked about all this?"

Brayman just raised his palms, shook his head, and said nothing.

Walter let everything sink in before pulling another file from the stack and setting it in front of Hazlett. "I think this is our girl."

Hazlett leaned forward and read the name on the tab of the folder. "Amy Archer." He said the name slowly before settling back in his chair.

Walter didn't want it to be Amy, but his gut told him he was right. He couldn't hold back now. She was the missing piece. It explained why she was pretending to be someone else, too.

He went on. "I don't know if you're familiar with this case. It's an older one, goes back six years. Nadler and I found Amy Archer in an apartment with a dead man named Alvin Schalk. At the time, it looked like Schalk had abducted her and she killed him trying to get away. But the evidence doesn't add up. We found blood on the mattress there, some rope. We figured Schalk tied her up and tortured her, but the blood came back as a match for him, not her. She was in the wind long before any of this was discovered. The detective on the case, Freddie Weeden…I don't know if he just dropped the ball or was sloppy, but he never followed up on her." Walter patted the folder. "Half the information in his report is wrong. Her description is all off. Maybe he got it mixed up with another case or something. I don't know, I shouldn't make excuses for him. If anyone was looking for Archer based on Weeden's report, though, they'd never find her. Then I got lucky and spotted her on the street a few days ago."

Hazlett and Brayman exchanged another glance. Rather than look through the information Walter had laid out, Brayman looked down at his shoes.

Hazlett said, "You found her? Amy Archer?"

Walter nodded. "She's working for Elite Escorts now. For Sergei Turgenev. Using the name Amelia Dyer."

Hazlett considered all of this. He was quiet for a long time. Finally, he groaned, reached into his desk drawer, and took out a pile of reports of his own. "This isn't the first time you've found Amy Archer, is it."

A statement. Not a question.

WALTER RECOGNIZED THE TOPMOST report. He probably still had a copy of it somewhere buried in a box back at his apartment. "That's not what you think," he said defensively.

"No?" Hazlett replied. "Because I think it's a restraining order. You know why I think that? Because it says *Restraining Order* across the top in big blocky letters, and a judge signed it down here at the bottom, all official-like. See?"

Hazlett turned the document around and tapped at the signature.

"That was five years ago. Almost six."

"It was right after she ran," Hazlett said. "I read all that crap before I signed your papers and agreed to take you into Homicide. I know all about that case. The whole damn department knows. Weeden used to bring it up whenever we bullshitted about his unsolveds. How he cut a break to a rookie, some young punk named O'Brien who let a girl get the better of him. Gave him the slip. That's not the part that irked him, though. Mistakes happen. We all get that. What bugged him is you couldn't keep your hands out of the investigation. Wasn't even your job, but you kept nosing around. You bugged some kid so damn much his mother felt the need to take out a restraining order against you." Hazlett tapped the document again, harder this time. "A Black mother, in a shitty part of town, felt the need to go to the police, file a report, and go to court, all to keep you away from her kid. Do you have any idea how bad you need to fuck up to get a Black mother in the projects to ask the cops for help? To trust the system?"

"That kid knew Archer was in there with Schalk," Walter said. "He told us Schalk had a girl in there. He knew who was in that apartment, knew what was going on in there, and he could have helped us find her."

"It wasn't your job," Hazlett repeated flatly.

"That kid saw who came and went. He could tell us whether Schalk had Archer tied up in there or the other way around."

"*That kid* is dead," Hazlett said. "Died of pulmonary atresia five years ago. Heart valve problem."

Walter felt a lump grow in his stomach. He hadn't known that.

Brayman took a step closer to the desk. "Nadler says you have a thing for her. You've never been able to let that one go."

"It's not like that," Walter said dismissively.

Hazlett moved the restraining order aside and showed Walter a stack of fax cover sheets. "How do you explain all these?"

Walter said nothing.

Hazlett spread them out across the desk. "You faxed your

own BOLO out to half the precincts in the state. There must be fifty of them here, and these are just the ones Weeden found. He bitched about this for a month, said you didn't even get the girl's physical description right."

"That's not true—Weeden's the one who had it wrong!"

Hazlett continued. "He said you completely muffed it and *that* was why she got away. Anyone looking for her had the details all wrong. Another cop does this, and they'd get bounced. Lucky for you, Nadler had your back and smoothed things over, kept Weeden from filing a formal complaint against you."

Walter told himself to stay calm. "Go down to records and pull the report. Weeden listed her as a blonde with green eyes. She was a brunette with gray eyes."

"Oh, I've seen his report," Hazlett fired back. "You don't think he showed it to me? He worked for me. You know what else I've seen? Statements from other officers on the scene. Every damn one of them contradicting you. Got to be a joke around here, one nobody told you because you were the butt of that joke. You need to hear it, though, if you've got any kind of future here, at least in my department. It's been years. We all think you've finally dropped it, given up the chase. And why wouldn't you? Got a promotion. New partner. New focus…Perfect time to start fresh, right? That's watercooler talk. That was all rookie crap, a long time ago. Old news. Then Nadler calls me yesterday, says you called him the night before from some club, drunk off your ass, with eyes on some girl you swore was Archer. That's obviously bad. Can't get worse, right? But it does, because he unloads a confession on me, tells me how you used to see Archer everywhere— on the street, at the store, bars at night, running in the park—some ghost you spotted more often than your own reflection.

"He tells me how he kept all this under wraps because underneath it all you're a good cop. Said he cut you slack because you grew up a foster kid and managed to make something of yourself. Told himself that for all those years the two of you were partnered up. Didn't want to make things harder on you by ticking the wrong box in your jacket. So I gotta wonder—how bad of a fuck-up did I make by giving you a desk in my department?"

"I haven't—"

Hazlett shook his head and glared at the folders on his desk. "And now this bullshit? You're going to try and tie her to *this* investigation? I should pull your shield right now."

The phone on Hazlett's desk began to ring. He made no move to answer it, just let the shrill clatter echo over the three silent men for six rings before he finally scooped up the receiver.

"Hazlett."

A female voice spoke. Walter couldn't make out the words. Hazlett glanced over at Brayman several times but avoided eye contact with Walter. After about a minute, he shoved some of the pages on his desk aside and scribbled something down on a notepad.

When he hung up, he tore the page from the pad and handed it to Brayman. "That was Jane Ackerman. She got an ID on your vic from the Four Seasons. Earl Golston. That's a home address."

Brayman pursed his lips and said, "What about…"

Hazlett glared at Walter. "He fucks up one more time, tell me, and he's done."

36

BEHIND THE WHEEL, BRAYMAN appeared both defeated and exhausted. He made no attempt to speak as they drove, and Walter simply couldn't find the words to break the silence.

He'd followed the evidence, exactly as he was taught.

As Brayman insisted, he hadn't made any assumptions.

By the book. Every second of it.

Did he want this to be Amy Archer?

Of course not.

Every time a piece of evidence pointed at her, he'd closed his eyes, saw that frightened girl in the bathroom looking back at him, and tried to convince himself it wasn't her.

His gut insisted, though.

His instincts were spot-on.

The facts backed his theory.

Turgenev.

The prostitution rings.

The similarities between the bodies.

He was right; they were wrong.

What would it take for them to see that?

Goddamn Nadler. Why couldn't he keep his mouth shut? Walter sighed.

"What?"

"Nothing," he replied before turning to the window to watch the neighborhood go from bad to worse.

The address Hazlett had given them was an old four-story brick apartment building in a section of Detroit most referred to as low town, not too far from the Edison. The windows on two of the first-floor apartments were sealed with plywood and covered with so many spray-painted symbols, names, and gang markers it was near impossible to read any of them.

Brayman pulled the Crown Vic to a stop behind the burnt-out husk of an old hatchback and shut off the engine.

Walter nodded at the car and cleared his throat. "Not like patrol to leave something like that in the street, even here."

Brayman didn't reply. Not at first. He wouldn't even look at him. He just sat there, drumming his fingers over the steering wheel. He unfastened his seat belt, started to get out, then settled back down. "I didn't know you were a foster kid."

"It shouldn't matter."

"Hazlett showed me your DCS record."

Walter felt the blood heat his face. "He what? That's supposed to be sealed."

"Not when you work in law enforcement and carry a gun. Not to your superior officer. Everything is reviewed and considered." He drummed his fingers again. "Forget that. Doesn't matter. I'm only bringing it up because I didn't know. If we're going to work together, it's important we understand each other. Not knowing how a partner will react in a certain situation gets people killed. A lot of that *knowing* comes from understanding where we've been. The experiences that shaped us."

Walter fought the urge to get out of the car. Every ounce of his being would rather hit the sidewalk and just keep walking than have this conversation. He didn't want people to judge him by his past. He wasn't that little boy. Not anymore. It had colored his relationship with Nadler; he didn't want that with Brayman. He wanted to be judged by the man he was today, not that kid. Never that kid.

"Just drop it, okay?"

He didn't, though. Instead, Brayman said something that surprised Walter. "My father was shot behind our house when I was five. Stray bullet from a drug deal gone bad. I lost my mother a year later in a car accident. My grandmother raised me until I was twelve, then I lost her, too. Heart attack. I bounced around with cousins after that. I know it's not the same, but my point is you're not alone. There's not a day goes by I don't miss my parents. That emptiness never quite fills in. Not completely."

"Yeah? I bet your parents loved each other."

Brayman looked at his hands and smiled. "Always. They made it a point to say the words every day. More importantly, though, you could see it in their faces. The way they looked at each other when they didn't think the other one was watching."

Walter had no idea what that was like. "My father was a drunk and a cheat. He treated my mother like shit. The night of the fire I saw him outside kissing some other woman. Right there in our backyard. He saw me, too, but didn't care. No way my mother was in the dark. She must've known. He didn't care about that, either. Selfish prick. Dying was the best thing that could have happened to him." He looked over at Brayman. "You read my entire file?"

Brayman hesitated, then nodded.

Walter sighed, shaking his head.

His partner's next words were careful, measured. "I know he beat you. Your mother, too. I saw the hospital reports. Six trips to the ER. I've been around long enough to understand if you went six times, there were probably countless other times it didn't get quite as far. Growing up like that, I can't imagine the hate and fear and anxiety, how that would build and—"

"You want to ask, just ask. Quit beating around the bush."

Brayman turned and met his eyes. "Did you start the fire?"

Walter held his gaze. "No."

"Do you know who did?"

Walter shook his head. He sat there for a long moment, then dug his hand into his pocket, wrapped his fingers around the old dog collar, and took it out. "I don't remember much. I don't know if it's because I was so young or if my mind blocked it. A lot of qualified people have tried to pull what happened that night from my head, but I don't remember that much. My dog alerted me. I woke up coughing and he was on the floor next to my bed making this awful sound— some mix of barking, crying, and howling. My room was full of smoke; I couldn't see much beyond him. He led me to the door, down the stairs, out front. I was standing in the grass before I realized I wasn't dreaming. Then I kept waiting for my parents to come out of the house."

"But they never did."

"No. They never did."

"And you don't know——"

Walter cut him off. "It could have been my father. Or the woman he was seeing. Or maybe my mother finally trying to put an end to things…I have no idea. Or maybe it was just some freak accident. Something left a little too close to the stove. If you read my file, I'm sure you saw the fire marshal's report. They have no clue. Just a bunch of guesswork."

Walter twisted the dog collar around his fingers as he spoke. "I've kept my dog's old collar as kind of a good-luck charm, I guess. Lost him along with everything else when I went into foster care. I like to think he lived out his days on a farm somewhere or with some old lady who spoiled the shit out of him, but the truth is, I don't know where he ended up."

"What was your dog's name?"

"Scritch."

A silence fell between them, and when Walter couldn't take it anymore, he shoved the collar back into his pocket and got out of the car.

Brayman waited a beat and followed.

The two of them stepped up to the abandoned car. There wasn't much left. The scent of charred metal and plastic found him, and Walter told himself that was from the car, not the memories Brayman set stirring in his head.

Brayman bent to get a better look inside. "This is recent."

"Got lit up three nights back," a woman said. She was sitting on the stoop of the apartment building, holding a mug of coffee, wearing a threadbare beige dress, her hair up in rollers. "Waiting for someone to tow it away. Last time we had one of these, it got left out there down at the end of the block for two months. Hoping this one moves faster. Dangerous for the kids, you know."

Walter walked around the back and bent down at the bumper. "The tag's gone."

"Probably sold that," the woman groaned and took another sip of her coffee. "Usually do."

Brayman offered her a thin smile and started up the steps into the building. "Appreciate the information, ma'am."

"Officer," she replied before going back to her coffee.

The vestibule inside the front door, the stairwells, and the hallways all bore the same graffiti as the outside of the building. The walls and ceiling were thick with cracked and flaking paint.

Earl Golston's apartment was on the third floor at the end of the hall.

Brayman froze when he reached the door.

"What's wrong?"

"Do you smell that?"

Walter cocked his head. "Is that gas?"

"Some kind of accelerant, maybe lighter fluid. Do we know if he lived alone?"

"Hazlett didn't say anything about that. Just gave us the address."

Brayman gave the door a hard knock. "Detroit PD!"

Nobody answered.

When Brayman tried the knob, he found the door locked. Walter motioned for him to move out of the way.

"Detroit PD, we're coming in!" Brayman shuffled to the side, took out his gun, and gave Walter a nod.

Walter hit the door with his shoulder and the halfhearted lock gave up.

The smell was stronger inside. Wet lines snaked over the floor, up the walls. Brayman was right—lighter fluid.

The window in the bedroom was open, the fire escape on

the other side. Walter scrambled over and looked out, saw no one. Whoever had done this was gone.

That didn't matter, not now.

The two of them quickly returned to the living room to get a better look at what they had glimpsed coming through the door.

Brayman stood perfectly still as Walter began turning in a slow circle to take it all in.

"Shit," Walter muttered.

"Yeah," Brayman replied. "Shit."

The floor was covered in a thin layer of salt. And nearly every inch of wall space was filled with rough sketches, paintings, and photographs of women.

37

WALTER STEPPED UP TO the nearest photograph, the salt crunching underfoot. The paper, saturated with lighter fluid, curled and pulled away from the wall. A glossy eight-by-ten, black-and-white, taken with a telephoto lens. The subject was walking down a sidewalk. She wore black boots that nearly reached her knees, a short skirt, and a thin tank top. The breeze had caught her hair and sent it wild around her face. Her head was angled to the side, looking in the window of a nearby shop. A candid shot, her face hidden.

The other photographs were no different. In each photo, either the subject was turned away from the camera or her face was obscured by lens flare, similar to what they'd seen with the video footage at the Four Seasons.

"Do you think these are all the same woman?"

"That's a leap," Brayman replied dismissively. "Can't make out a face in a single one of these shots. And look at

the clothes, the hair, the cars…there might be decades between some of these. No way they're the same woman."

Walter hadn't been looking at the photographs when he
asked the question, though. He was studying the sketches.

Although several were inked, most had been drawn with
pencil by a practiced hand—presumably Golston's—that
Walter could only envy. In these, the woman faced the
virtual camera. In some she smiled; others caught her from
a slight distance. Walking, reading a book, sleeping, taking
a bath. Several in various states of undress. One in particular caught Walter's eye—the figure was sitting naked at
a vanity, running a brush through her long hair, her face
visible in the reflection. This was one of the few sketches
done in colored pencil, and Golston had clearly spent a lot
of time on it.

Christ, they all look like Amy.

Well, not *exactly* like Amy, but close. Like he couldn't
quite capture her, as skilled as he was. Walter saw it, though,
a hint of her in each image.

"These are all connected somehow. Similar look, build,
and age, but there are differences in the photos and drawings. Subtle, but there. This guy was a good artist, that's no
mistake. To me, this looks like he was stalking a type, not
someone specific. Screams serial," Brayman said.

"Maybe he was just a looker and not much of a taker."

Brayman turned his back to him, studying the room.
"Looks like he was living out of bags. This guy's got no real
furniture, just that table and a sleeping bag in the bedroom.
One step from homeless. Not the kind of guy you find at
the Four Seasons, not on the regular. If this is his world, he
didn't belong there."

Walter glanced around, and an odd sense of déjà vu

rolled over him. His mind flashed back to Alvin Schalk's apartment—not a home but a temporary way station. He glanced back at the open bathroom door, at the space on the floor next to the sink.

Nobody in there, his mind muttered.

Nobody chained to the sink. That's what you meant.

"What is it?"

"Reminds me of Schalk's place, that's all."

Brayman put his gun away and got a closer look at the pictures on the walls. "Was Amy Archer Alvin Schalk's only victim?"

"There were two unidentified bodies found in the building's basement attributed to him, but too badly decomposed to ID. Archer's the only one they ever pinned on him that I know of, yeah."

"I'm thinking he spotted our girl from the Four Seasons video, saw something he wanted, and lured her there. Aneurysms are like ticking bombs. If he meant to hurt her, the stress and adrenaline might have caused it to burst. The woman, a pro—who doesn't want to get caught in a hotel room with a dead john—drags him to the shower with a towel to try and muddle up what happened."

Walter nudged a duffel bag with the tip of his shoe and dumped it over. Nothing inside but some men's clothing— a couple of shirts, jeans, underwear—everything soaked with lighter fluid.

"There's a good chance that car out front is Golston's."

"Then how did he get to the hotel?" Brayman shot back.

"Cab, maybe? We should check with dispatch."

Brayman went quiet again, slowly walking the room.

Crossing over to a folding table set up in the center of the room, Walter flipped through the items on top. A tattered road atlas, a stack of take-out receipts, some old Philip K. Dick paperbacks. A small notebook buried under those. Everything drenched in lighter fluid. He opened the notebook and flipped through the pages. "What do you make of this?"

"Make of what?" Brayman had paused at several boxes stacked under a window.

"A log, I think. Names, dates, locations…a slew of them going back years. Decades, actually. More sketches of girls."

Without looking back at him, Brayman produced an evidence bag from his pocket and threw it in Walter's general direction. "Bag it."

Walter picked the bag up off the floor, dropped the notebook inside, and slipped it into his pocket.

Golston had run a long cord to get the phone from the kitchen to the table.

Walter picked up the receiver and dialed *69. After three rings, a male voice answered, "Four Seasons. How may I help you?"

He hung up. "Last call was to the Four Seasons. We'll want to pull the LUDs and see who else he talked to. I bet we'll find Elite Escorts on there."

"Oh, Jesus—"

Brayman, still crouching at the boxes, fell back on his hands and stared inside one he'd opened.

"What is it?"

Walter went over and looked down. The box held about a dozen glass mason jars.

Brayman had pulled out one of the jars and dropped it on top of the others when he startled.

The jar was nearly full of human teeth.

Some were old and yellow; others looked fresh, with dried blood on the edges, bits of skin or gums.

Walter felt his stomach lurch. He glanced down at the neat rows of metal lids in the box. "What's in the other jars?"

Brayman said nothing.

"Are you gonna look?"

"Go ahead, nobody stopping you."

Walter gave him a frustrated glance, then reached into the box. He took out the jar of teeth and carefully placed it off to the side, then picked another jar at random. This one was full of blond hair. The next had brown. Auburn in another. The fourth jar had—

"Oh, fuck me," Walter muttered, nearly dropping this one as Brayman had the teeth.

Fingernails.

Some painted, some not. Most likely from women but no way to be sure. Not clippings, but the full nail. No fingers, thank Christ.

"What the hell is this?" Brayman said beside him.

Lighter fluid had soaked through the cardboard and pooled in the bottom of the box.

"It's evidence," Walter muttered. "Somebody was about to make it all go away and got interrupted."

"If these are Golston's souvenirs, he wouldn't just destroy them, not unless he thought he was about to get caught."

"Why would somebody else do it? Somebody trying to protect him?" Walter had a thought. "Ever hear of a serial with a partner?"

"It's rare, but he wouldn't be the first."

Brayman went quiet again, considering all of this. He opened one of the other boxes and found more photographs and drawings inside. Hundreds of them. Several of the pictures had locations and dates written on the backs. "Phoenix. Santa Barbara. Seattle, Miami…These are from all over the country. If he is a serial, we might need to bring in the feds."

"I mentioned blackmail back at the Four Seasons. Maybe the girl got onto him and hit him up for cash or threatened to turn him in."

Brayman went to the phone and punched in a number. "We need to get a team in here. Our boy Golston just became a whole lot more interesting. See if you can find anything else."

"Boxes of human remains and several hundred potential targets aren't enough for you?"

"Check the kitchen. Guys like this sometimes keep trophies in the fridge."

"Lovely," Walter muttered, heading into the other room. "Hey, if this guy is some kind of serial, he's not *our* serial unless one of those jars is full of fingers, too."

In the kitchen, Walter opened first the freezer, then the refrigerator compartment. "Nothing in here but some peanut butter, half a loaf of bread, and a box of baking soda."

Brayman didn't reply. He was speaking into the receiver, his eyes fixed on the boxes and jars.

Walter had another thought as he started pulling open kitchen cabinets and drawers. "If Golston doused everything in fluid and meant to light it up, destroy evidence of…whatever this all is…and assuming that car was his, too, why would he burn the car? Wouldn't he keep that to get away? Torch the apartment and run?"

"Maybe there was something incriminating in the car."

"Burning it out front like that just draws attention to

him. Brings people here asking questions. You don't do that when you're trying to hide something. Maybe somebody was onto him and lit up the car to purposely draw attention? If the blackmail thing is right, maybe the girl torched his car to show him she was serious, take him off-balance." Walter opened another cabinet door and found nothing, kept talking as he went on to the next one. "That all fits. Think about it. This guy is some kind of serial whack job, she figures him out, tells him she knows. Then she demands…whatever…and torches his car to spook him. Imagine him standing up here, surrounded by all this, watching his car burn, waiting for the police to come knocking on the door. He might have grabbed the bottle of lighter fluid himself at that point, soaked everything, and stood there with a match ready to light it all up when that knock came. The knock didn't come, so he backed down, then met her at the Four Seasons to wrap things up—pay her, kill her—doesn't matter, either fits. The stress is too much. His brain pops. But when Golston dies, she panics and drags him to the shower like we said, then runs."

"So this isn't connected to Turgenev anymore?"

Walter shrugged. "Captain told me to drop it, so I'm dropping it and giving you an alternative theory. Can you think of another reason for someone to—"

Walter froze. Every drawer and cabinet had been empty. This one, though—this large lower cabinet to the right of the sink—it wasn't empty. Far from it. There was a body, folded up.

He bent to get a closer look, and the body moved.

A leg kicked out at him like a piston, catching him in the shin.

Walter stumbled back, fell against the counter behind him. Another leg came out. Then an arm, another arm— and a hand holding a can of lighter fluid. The stream sloshed over Walter's wrist as he rolled out of the way, but not before a match flicked to life and sailed toward him.

38

THE MATCH STRUCK WALTER'S wrist and ignited the fluid, and flames leaped up his skin. The match bounced off his arm, hit the kitchen wall, and that caught, too. A whoosh of light and heat.

The figure shot out of the lower cabinet, crashed into him, and sent Walter tumbling back. He tried to keep his footing, but his ankle caught on the kitchen doorframe, and he went down hard. The body, this person who had just set him on fire, ran over him in a blur of jeans, red hoodie, and white tennis shoes. *Stepping on him,* and possibly saving his life because one of those steps smothered the flames on his wrist, and the pain that came a moment later reminded him to roll, and somehow he managed to roll out of the kitchen as that entire room went ablaze.

Walter felt hands on his shoulders pulling him back.

Brayman.

The second he was out of the kitchen, Brayman shouted, "Go after him! I'll get everyone out of the building! Go!"

Walter scrambled to his feet and was out the door.

He caught a glimpse of red on the stairwell, rounding the corner below. He took the steps in leaps—four, five at a time—hit the landing, nearly slipped, crashed into the wall, and kept going. When he reached the small vestibule on the first floor, the building's door was swinging shut. Walter burst through out into the daylight.

The woman who had been sitting on the stoop when they arrived was standing, her coffee puddled at her feet. When she saw Walter, she pointed down the sidewalk to her left. "He went that way!"

"Call the fire department!" Walter shouted back at her as he ran. "Get everyone out!"

The man cut hard to the right and vanished down an alley. Walter reached the opening in time to see his assailant take a right out of the opposite end onto another sidewalk. Dodging bags of trash and boxes, Walter came out the other side and found himself facing the Lawson train station and the crowds that came with it.

At his feet, he nearly tripped over the discarded red hoodie.

Cursing, he sucked down air, filled his strained lungs, and swiveled his head from side to side, scanning the packed sidewalks. Then he saw her—*Amy Archer* herself, ducking through a door into the main terminal. White tank top, same jeans, same tennis shoes, her hair pulled back in a ponytail.

Not a *him* at all.

The sight of her sent another burst of energy through Walter's body, and he was at the door pulling it open before he even realized he had moved. Inside the main terminal he spotted her again, at the mouth of a tunnel leading toward the eastern tracks. She turned, just long enough for their eyes to meet, and that glance might as well have been a bullet, because it tore through Walter with enough force and ferocity to nearly knock him off his feet. He reached for a nearby wall to steady himself, and when he looked back up, she was pushing through the crowd halfway to the platform.

"Amy!"

He started after her again. He wasn't about to let her go.

There was a train waiting at the platform. The doors on the opposite side had opened, allowing passengers to disembark. On this side, they were still closed as a hundred people stood ready to board, inching closer to the train. Her back was to him, but she must have known he was close—the moment he found her she froze and visibly tensed, but she didn't turn, only worked deeper into the crowd.

Walter pushed through the throngs of people, closed the gap, ignoring the stares and those pointing at his injured arm.

He was ten feet away from her when the train doors opened and the large group started to move inside. Only five feet away when she reached up and tapped the neck of the man in front of her, a man of about sixty with wisps of gray hair on his balding head.

The touch was brief, no more than half a second. Anyone watching might have assumed she was only helping him along, or steadying herself as those behind her pushed forward toward the open door.

The man instantly froze, his body rigid. His right hand

reached up and gripped the side of the door; his briefcase dropped from his left.

Three feet away.

Walter reached for the back of Amy's shirt; his fingers grazed over the white cotton but couldn't get a grip as she ducked under the man's outstretched arm and disappeared into the train car.

People pushed behind him, from the left and from the right, as the man collapsed on the platform. His face had gone pale, and he was clutching at his chest.

"He's having a heart attack!" a woman shouted.

The man was lying at Walter's feet, his legs twitching. He'd torn his shirt open, and his fingers were scrabbling at it as his body convulsed.

"Does anyone know CPR?!"

This came from another man standing beside Walter. He'd retrieved the man's briefcase and was looking frantically around.

Amy was gone. Somewhere deep in the train now.

You know where to find her.

Walter dropped to his knees, straightened out the man's body, and began to administer CPR, hoping someone had the good sense to dial 911.

NOW

CHAPTER

39

COMMANDER RIGBY ORGANIZED HER strike teams two blocks down on Woodward in a small private parking lot sandwiched between a Starbucks and a used bookstore. The television networks had taken up a foothold behind the barricades surrounding the club—cameras zoomed and directional microphones swirled around everywhere in the hope of capturing something one of the other networks didn't have. At this point, she didn't know who was watching or where this Walter O'Brien had his people positioned, and she couldn't risk tipping anyone off.

Three teams of six.

All in full tactical gear.

At the sidewalk, a Public Works man pried the manhole cover off and rolled it to the side.

Rigby huddled with the three team leaders, their backs to the street. "Nobody breaches until you get my go, understand? Just get in position, prep, and be ready to move. This is all about stealth."

All three nodded. Each held a map of the utility tunnels with routes highlighted—one to the basement of Moreland Bank, another to 1812 Park, and the third team to Club Stomp. If O'Brien had additional shooters out there, her people hadn't found them and she couldn't risk waiting longer. She needed to get in front of this.

"Any idea what kind of bomb they have?"

This came from Hersh. He'd had three deployments in Iraq and Afghanistan working IEDs. That's why she'd put him on the club.

"None," she replied. "Use the sniffers when you get in position, see if you can pick anything up. Run a camera, if you can, without being noticed. If they brought it through the front door, it would have to be something small to get by the bouncers, but they could have just as easily set up in advance if they got in during off-hours. No way to know. The few people who got out didn't see anything."

She turned to the other two team leaders. "We'll try and pinpoint their shooters with thermal before you go in, but if that doesn't work, you'll need to secure floor by floor. We're blocking transmissions, but their communication still seems to be up. If you line up on a shooter, move fast—if the bomb is on a trigger, you can't give him a chance to tip off whoever is holding it."

"Understood," they said in unison.

"Rigby?" Hurwitz's voice came over her comm.

"Yeah?"

"I've got the deputy chief on the line."

"On my way."

Rigby gave them each a final glance, authorized them to move, and ran back toward the SWAT van. The salt truck rounded the building again as she climbed inside.

Hurwitz put the call on speaker. "I've got Rigby, sir."

The deputy chief didn't waste any time. *You sure it's him? Walter O'Brien?*

"No ID, but we've got no reason to doubt him."

"And he's telling you he's after a woman? A specific woman?"

"No name. No physical description. I don't think he knows what she looks like. But yes."

"Where are you on containment?"

"Their shooters are occupying two buildings. Not sure how many yet, but they're on multiple floors. I've got teams moving into position as we speak. We've got at least two hundred souls inside the club, zero contact, but we can see them on thermal. We're working on access there, too."

"What about the bomb?"

"No color beyond what he's told us, sir. Most likely on a timer, possible remote trigger as backup. We're blocking all radio signals to keep that from happening."

"And he hasn't asked for anything?"

"Only her, sir."

The deputy chief's voice went muffled. Sounded like he was speaking to someone else in the room. Probably several *someones.* He came back after about twenty seconds. *"Keep your eyes on the clock, Commander. Whether or not the bomb is real, that countdown is relevant to him. This needs to end before you reach zero. That gives you thirty-seven minutes. No time for negotiations. The moment your shooters have his gunmen in their scopes, you need to take everyone out simultaneously. Evacuate the club. Locate and disarm the bomb. No hesitation."*

Rigby gave Hurwitz a glance. "He's one of us, sir."

"He hasn't been a cop for a long time, Commander. He's a terrorist. Your focus needs to be on freeing the hostages."

"Understood, sir."

He hung up.

Hurwitz pointed toward his large monitor. "I've got his service record."

"Why did IA have it locked?"

"I left three messages, and nobody—"

She understood. He hadn't gotten it from IA.

The easy way.

Rigby would worry about that later. "What does it say?"

"Beat cop from 1986 to 1992, then promoted to Homicide. Impressive arrest record. Multiple citations. Several accelerated promotions, but..."

"But what?"

Hurwitz let out a soft whistle. "Terminated for cause in 1997. Evidence tampering. Falsifying statements. There are several disciplinary actions in his last year for intoxication while on duty. This guy fell apart at the end."

He scrolled and pointed at another section of the report. The one listing O'Brien's partners. Several were listed as deceased. One guy named Herbert Nadler. Wesley Brayman. The second one was tagged as *extenuating circumstances.* Hurwitz tapped the name. "This might be why the file was with IA. His partner died on the job."

"How?"

"It doesn't say." His glasses had slid down his nose slightly. He pushed them back up. "Most of these older records aren't digitized. The highlights are in the system, but everything else is still on paper. It's a budgetary thing. Too expensive."

Hurwitz brought up another window and entered the name *Brayman*.

At least two dozen files appeared. Nearly as many came up when he keyed in *Nadler*.

"This is the drive he gave you."

A voice boomed from the van's overhead speakers. *"Commander, this is Yellow Team, copy?"*

"Go, Yellow Team."

"We've got zero access to the club from the utility tunnels. The wall terminates at solid concrete. Several pipes pass through, but nothing big enough for a person. Widest is ten inches. Can't risk explosives, we'd have to cut. That would be noisy. No other ingress."

No time, either.

"Understood. Come back out and prep your team to enter the club from the street. You'll have to go through the front door when we move."

"Yes, ma'am."

Images from numerous body cameras filled the upper monitors, slowly looking around two basement spaces in green-tinged night vision. "Blue Team, Green Team, report."

"Blue in position."

"Green in position."

Rigby said, "Prepare to move on my mark."

A cell phone rang

The one Walter O'Brien had given her.

1992

ALIASES?

Amy Archer

Amelia Dyer

Alvin Schalk

Two bodies/basement freezer

John Doe/Edison

Jane Doe/Corktown Bus Depot

Earl Golston/John Doe/
Four Seasons

Man on train platform

Hair

Nails

Teeth

Notebook

Drawings/girls related?

... Walter O'Brien, 28 Years Old

40

WALTER SAW THE BLACK smoke long before he turned the corner back onto Earl Golston's street. He heard the approaching fire trucks and the wail of sirens the moment he pushed back out the glass doors of the train station and started that long walk back.

The building's residents were standing in the street. Some were dressed; others were still in sleep clothes; most were clutching whatever they were able to carry with them as they rushed out the door. He found Brayman sitting on the back of an ambulance, looking up at the fire.

Walter tossed the red hoodie next to Brayman and sat. "Did you get everyone out?"

"I think so. Smoke's everywhere, but I think they contained the flames to his place and maybe the apartment above. Water damage is another story." He nodded back at the building.

Water flowed like a river out the front door and down the steps. The street was partially flooded, and they were all standing in it.

A paramedic returned to the ambulance and went to work on Walter's wrist. With a pair of small scissors, he cut the sleeve of Walter's shirt to his elbow and peeled the material back, fully exposing the burn. Walter sucked in a wisp of air from between clenched teeth.

Brayman pinched the red hoodie between two fingers and picked it up, gently spun it in a slow circle, then set it back down between them. "What happened? You lost him?"

Her. I lost her.

Walter knew he couldn't tell him the truth, not after what had happened back at the precinct. If he did, Brayman would surely have him pulled from the case. Hazlett would put him on leave, or worse.

He'd wait for the medical examiner's report to come back on the heart attack victim. If the ME found a mark on the man's neck under black light, *then* he'd tell him. He'd tell both of them.

"I was close when some guy had a heart attack on the platform and I had to decide—stay and help or keep up the chase."

"Did he..."

Walter shook his head.

The paramedic finished wrapping Walter's wrist.

Walter thanked him, watched him walk back out into the crowd, then flexed his wrist. "You saw what was in those jars. Messed up, for sure, but do you think Golston killed our vics? It doesn't track."

Brayman looked down at his hands and shook his head. "I don't know what to think anymore. We finally catch some semblance of a break, and it's all gone before we really had a chance to look at it."

All gone, except…

He reached into his pocket and took out the notebook wrapped in the evidence bag. "Not everything."

CHAPTER

41

BACK AT THE PRECINCT, Brayman was at his desk. Golston's notebook was open in front of him, several pages marked with paper clips. Walter had scribbled notes of his own on some paper and had several maps splayed out as well; one for the city, the other a large national highway map. The notebook contained partial names, dates, and locations. Brayman marked each location on the map with a red pen as he read. He was only about halfway through, and the map was covered in dots and zigzagging lines crossing back and forth over the country.

Walter was staring up at the board, trying hard to forget about the burn on his wrist and failing miserably. It hurt like a son of a bitch, even after taking three ibuprofen. He knew he should go to the doctor, get something stronger, but he didn't want to leave right now. Not when it felt like they were finally making progress.

The pictures of their three victims (or two victims, if

Golston was, in fact, responsible) all looked back at him from the board with dead eyes. Much to Walter's surprise, Brayman had added an old mug shot of Sergei Turgenev. A still shot of the girl from the Four Seasons' surveillance tape hung there, too.

"I'm not saying your theory is worth a shit, but I don't want to discount anything at this point."

Walter had said nothing to this, only wondered how Hazlett would react when he saw it.

Brayman hurriedly scribbled something else, took a moment to process whatever he had written, then crumpled the sheet and dropped it to the floor. There were a few others down there now. When his phone rang, he scooped up the receiver without taking his eyes from the notebook. "Brayman."

The voice on the other side of the call spoke fast.

Brayman grabbed a pen and blank sheet of paper and began scribbling notes. "You're sure? That's a long time ago. What's he been doing since?"

Walter listened.

"Ah-huh."

When he hung up, Brayman stared down at his notes, processing what he'd just heard.

"Well?"

"Got some background on Golston. You'll love this." Brayman thumbed his notes. "He was a private eye."

"A private eye?"

"He used to work for a firm based out of Chicago called Macallum Associates. They let him go for job abandonment. He took a case that involved some travel and stopped reporting in. Never came back. Vanished."

"What was his last case? Did they say?"

"Cheating spouse named George Grendal."

Walter went back to the notebook and flipped to the beginning. His finger landed on the first entry. "This is dated April 12, 1948. It says, 'GG 19480412, Detroit.'"

A smile filled Brayman's lips. "George Grendal. GG." He paused for a second, then added, "That was forty-four years ago. There's no record of Golston working anywhere else since, at least not with the IRS. He was twenty-six years old when he quit. He's seventy now. Well, was."

Walter thumbed the pages of the notebook. "Who knows how he survived, but he clearly didn't stop investigating. There are probably a hundred entries here between 1948 and the present. The last one is..." He flipped to the back, found the final line, and said nothing.

"What?"

"It's dated two weeks ago, Detroit." Walter swallowed, moistened his throat. "The initials are WO."

Brayman's expression went flat. "Let me see that."

Walter flipped the book around and pointed to the first entry and the last one:

GG 19480412, Detroit

WO 19920814, Detroit

"GG—George Grendal, and WO, Walter O—" Brayman began.

Walter cut him off. "Not funny."

"Little funny." Brayman smirked.

"It doesn't necessarily mean me. Forty-plus years of entries. It's a coincidence."

Brayman thumbed through the pages but didn't say anything.

Walter read over Brayman's notes from the phone call. "What's *Glendale* mean?"

"Cervantes gave me contact information for the last person who hired Golston. She's at Glendale Adult Care outside the city."

"The last person to hire him in 1948 is still alive?"

Brayman grabbed the notebook, the maps, and the marker he'd been using and nodded at the car keys. "I need to keep working on this. You're driving."

"I have a suspended license, remember?"

"So don't hit anything."

CHAPTER

42

THE GLENDALE ADULT CARE facility was located about ten miles outside Detroit off 96 along with a shopping mall, several gas stations, chain restaurants, and lower-priced hotels targeting cost-conscious travelers unwilling or unable to pay city rates.

Walter parked in the visitors' lot.

The plump, graying woman at the front desk eyed them both nervously as she spoke into her phone. "Yes, two police detectives here to see Norma Grendal."

She listened for a second.

"No, they didn't say. Said they could only tell her."

After another moment, she hung up and sighed deeply. "Mrs. Grendal is seventy-nine years old, you understand. We obviously don't want to do anything to agitate her. She had a stroke several years back and recovered well, but her blood pressure has been an issue since she joined us, so we try to keep her stress to a minimum."

Brayman smiled at her. "I promise, we'll be respectful. This will only take a few minutes."

She nodded and pointed down the tiled hallway on her side. "Follow that to the end and make a right. You'll find her in the sunroom."

A nurse in scrubs stood at the end of the hall, propping the sunroom door open. She indicated a woman sitting alone on a couch near a bay window in the back. She appeared to be knitting.

"Let me do the talking," Brayman said to Walter as they approached her.

"What, old person to old person? I guess that makes sense."

"Fuck you, kid. We don't want to spook her. Don't show her your b—"

Walter took out his badge and held it out between her and Brayman, cutting him off. "Mrs. Grendal? I'm Detective O'Brien, and this is Detective Brayman. We're with Detroit Homicide. Would you mind speaking to us for a few minutes?"

Her hands stopped moving.

She only had one needle. Walter was pretty sure you needed two needles to knit.

"Homicide detectives?"

"We'd like to talk to you about Earl Golston. Do you recall that name? It's been a while."

There had been a smile on her face, albeit a halfhearted polite one, but it quickly faded to a scowl. "Earl Golston? Do you know where he is? He owes me twenty-three dollars."

Brayman took a seat next to her. "He's dead, ma'am. He passed away yesterday."

"Well, hell. Now I'll never get my money." She dropped

her project down into her lap and turned to Brayman. "He was a charlatan. Took my money and gave me nothing but a smile and a heap of talk in return. Then he up and disappeared."

Walter eased down into an oversized armchair across from her. "Why did you hire him, ma'am?"

"I hired him to track down that little hussy who took my Georgie and left our kids without a father. He was supposed to find her and help me put an end to that nonsense. Instead, Georgie died, Golston vanished, and I was left to raise two boys and a girl all by my lonesome. The least he could have done was returned what I paid him. I gave him everything I had. My entire rainy-day fund from my crocheting and the bake sales…"

"Can you tell us what happened?"

"That was almost fifty years ago. Why does it matter now? How did he die?"

"That's not important, ma'am." Walter struggled to find the right words. "So you hired Golston because your husband was…stepping out on you?"

She snorted. "My Georgie wasn't just stepping out. He was off doing the horizontal mambo with his little girlfriend when he should have been home. Or at the office. Or out bowling with his league."

Her face had gone red, and her hands were trembling.

We try to keep her stress to a minimum.

Brayman patted the back of her hand. "Take a deep breath, Mrs. Grendal. No need to get worked up. This was all a long time ago. If you don't want to talk about it, you don't have to. We can leave."

She shook her head and pinched her eyes shut for a moment. "It's okay. I'm fine." She looked over at the nurse standing at the door. "Did they tell you I was standing at death's door? That it?"

"They told us you've had some recent health episodes."

She waved a dismissive hand in the air. "No matter. If it's important or helpful, I don't mind telling you." Her gaze dropped down to the yarn at her side. "Georgie started having trouble sleeping. At first, just tossing and turning. Then he went on to mumbling. I couldn't make out what he was saying, not at first. Then I realized it was a name— Jane. I didn't know any *Jane*, and he claimed not to, either, but I knew better. A man doesn't just make up something like that. This went on for more than a month, and I knew Georgie was keeping something from me. I had a pretty good idea of what it was, and at first I wasn't sure I wanted the answer. Then I realized if I didn't put an end to it, he might end up in the hospital or worse, so I hired Mr. Golston. He followed Georgie for me from the moment he left the house until he got home at night. Three straight weeks. Mr. Golston finally sat me down and told me what I expected to hear: there was another woman. But nothing else he told me was expected, not in the slightest."

She paused for a second and took a sip of water from a blue plastic cup on the table beside her, then went on. "He told me Georgie went to the park every day on his lunch break, sat on this rock, and watched some girl reading under a tree. Never spoke to her, mind you, not in Mr. Golston's presence, anyway, only watched her as he ate. At first, I thought this was some midlife crisis, some harmless crush, but Georgie was obsessed. He'd lost so much weight he looked like a walking twig. I began to wonder if the illustrious Mr. Golston was lying to me. I went to the park myself, and sure enough, there was Georgie sitting on a rock, staring at some young thing with long red hair, who was reading a book under a tree. Georgie was always partial to redheads. He just watched her, though, nothing more. If she noticed him, she made no show of it. Twenty minutes later, she closed her book and walked off and he packed up his lunch and went back to the office. I suppose I should have confronted him about it, but what would I say?

"Golston had followed the girl home on several occasions. He said her full name was Jane Toppan and she was renting a small place with two other girls a block from the park. He hadn't seen her go to work or anything, figured she probably had some family money. He started following her, trying to learn more. He didn't charge me for that, which was a little odd, but I wasn't about to say anything. He'd charged me enough for Georgie."

Norma Grendal sighed. "Georgie stopped eating. Stopped going to work. He looked ten years older, twenty even. He barely talked. He started wandering off at night. I'd find him in that park, either on that rock or sitting under the tree. I didn't see the girl again, Jane Toppan. I only saw her that one time, but I couldn't stop Georgie from going back. In the end, he didn't even try to hide it from me, just got up and went. He died under that tree. About three months after this all started. He sat down one day and didn't get back up."

Walter leaned forward. "As far as you know, he never talked to Jane?"

She blew out a breath. "Oh, I don't believe that nonsense for a second. I think Mr. Golston was just trying to spare my feelings when he said that. He wasn't honest about a number of things."

"Like what?"

"For starters, he only followed Georgie a couple of times, nowhere near as often as he said. I learned later he spent far more time following Miss Toppan around, even after I stopped paying him. After Georgie died, I started getting phone calls from his employer. They didn't even know I'd hired him to check up on my husband, not the girl. The handful of reports Mr. Golston submitted were all about her, and his boss said they read like 'raving nonsense.' I went back to that park only one time after Georgie died. Couldn't bear to see it more than that, and I thought I saw Mr. Golston near the tree, but I can't be sure. By the time I walked up, he was gone."

Walter and Brayman exchanged a quick glance. Then Walter asked, "Are you sure the girl had red hair?"

Norma Grendal looked over at him, confused by the question, and Walter understood why. She'd just told them about one of the darkest times in her life and Walter's first question was about the girl's hair? He had to know, though. "Could it have been dyed?"

"I…I don't know. I suppose so."

"What color eyes did she have?"

"I didn't get close enough to see, I'm sorry."

CHAPTER

43

BACK IN THE CAR, Walter's mind was somewhere much farther away. "I need a phone."

"For what?"

"I want to know what was in the last report Earl Golston filed with Macallum Associates before he disappeared."

"What for?"

Walter didn't answer.

Finally, Brayman scooped the radio microphone from the dashboard and pressed the Transmit button. "Dispatch, this is 4197. I need you to place a phone call and connect, over."

"Four-one-nine-seven, this is dispatch. What's the number?"

"You'll have to look it up—Macallum Associates in Chicago."

"Stand by."

There was a dial tone, then several rings followed by a female voice. *"Macallum Associates. How may I direct your call?"*

Brayman said, "Artie Lowman, please."

Several clicks as the line transferred and connected.

A gruff voice came on the line. *"Lowman."*

Brayman introduced Walter and let him explain why they were calling.

"Lucky for you, Golston's file is still on my desk. There's been a lot of watercooler talk about him today with the man turning up dead. He's been a bit of an office mystery for decades."

There was a shuffling of paper from the other line, then Lowman came back. *"Okay, got it. What do you need?"*

"Whatever you have on his last case."

"Yeah, well, there's not much. PI gets obsessed with subject of surveillance and vanishes. They canned him."

"Just read it to me," Walter said. "Whatever you have."

"Okay. We've got a surveillance report on a female subject— Jane Toppan, approximately nineteen years of age, blond hair, green eyes, at Beacon Park, Detroit—"

"Blond, not red or brunette?"

"Yeah, blond."

Walter looked over at Brayman. He was facing away, staring out the window.

"Ah…Beacon Park, Detroit. He's got a series of dates and times written down. Basically her coming and going from the park. There's an address for her but it's for an old tenement building no longer there. Bulldozed twenty years ago to make way for a larger apartment building…Let's see…this is where it gets weird. He goes on like a hard-up teenager peeping through a window — 'she ran her hand down the length of her body and smoothed her dress before settling beneath her tree. I'd taken to calling it her tree because nobody else seemed right beneath it. If I were looking at a painting, it would only be complete when the artist's brush fully rendered her there under the branches, stretched out in the shade, her

legs this golden tan and buttery like…' Are you sure you want me to read this?"

"Read it."

Lowman blew out a breath and continued. *"All right, but I'm gonna skip ahead. My boss is waiting on me for a meeting. Let's see, this is the second-to-last report he filed, and I use the term* report *loosely. Here goes. 'I spoke to her today. At least, I thought I did. I left the safety of my vehicle and crossed the park before the will to do so left me, and I went right up to her and introduced myself. I was shaking, I don't know why, like a nervous boy asking a girl to his first high school dance. Ah, Earl, get it together, man! She smiled up at me and set her book down in her lap, an Agatha Christie novel I'd read several years earlier, and she said hello. Her voice was as angelic as I imagined it to be, the sound of soft chimes ringing in a summer breeze. There was this sweet scent in the air, and at first, I thought it came from the park itself, but it became clear it came from her, this sweetness not unlike a mix of sugar and fresh flowers. I understood George Grendal's obsession then, why he found himself so drawn to her and unable to pull away. For one brief second, I wondered if he watched me now, jealousy boiling, because I found the courage to speak to her when he would not. And then I didn't care. What he thought, what anyone thought, none of that mattered, because I had finally found her. My soul mate. My completing half. My Iele. My angelic, beauteous, bewitching Iele. I thought I spoke to her, but then my eyes opened and I was still in my car, still in the parking lot, and she was no longer under her tree.' That's it, that's all he wrote. I don't get it. I went back and read some of his other casework after seeing this garbage, and it's clear, concise. He was a solid investigator, then he just lost it. He submitted several expense reports after this for some travel, five different cities, just receipts. They finally cut him off. Told him they wouldn't wire any more funds until he*

246

reported in—either in person or over the phone. That's when he vanished."

"You said that was his second-to-last report," Walter replied. "What was in the final?"

"Half a page. He just wrote that word over and over again, about a hundred times. Iele. I'm not sure I'm pronouncing it right."

"It's pronounced *eye-lee*," Brayman said in a quiet voice. *"Eye-lee."*

"WHO'S IELE?" WALTER ASKED after the call ended.

"It's just a figure of speech," Brayman told Walter dismissively. "Like calling someone an obsession or their sole object of desire. That sort of thing. I've known guys like Golston. They spend so much time alone on stakeouts, something in them snaps. Long-haul truckers are like that, too. I once knew a guy who'd carry on complete conversations with the air freshener hanging from his mirror. He spoke to it like they were best friends. Argue, too. That's why PD rotates officers on stakeouts. PIs out in the field don't get that luxury. It's usually a solo gig."

I had finally found her. My soul mate. My completing half. My Iele. My angelic, beauteous, bewitching Iele.

"Can I see that map you were working on?"

Brayman fished the map out from beside his seat and handed it to Walter.

Walter smoothed out the creases. The sun was starting to set, and deep shadows reached across the dashboard toward the paper. "How far into that notebook did you get?"

"A little over halfway. He starts off with a few notes on George Grendal. Then there's nothing but locations, dates, and initials with the occasional drawing."

Brayman had plotted each point with a red marker and written the date next to each dot in small, neat script. Some were connected by lines. "These go all over—Detroit to New York, to Boston, Cleveland, Chicago, New Mexico, Vegas, Los Angeles, Philly—East Coast to West, then back again, hitting the northern cities, west after that, then through the south, like big loops."

Brayman took out the notebook and started flipping through the pages. "The amount of time in each location varies. Some seem to be as short as a few days, and it looks like he holed up in other places for months. But not a single repeat, except for Detroit." He paused for a moment. "Here's the thing—even if he was still following that girl, she'd be what? Sixty-three? Sixty-four now? That's not *our* girl. This could just as easily be Golston logging his own travels. Maybe he got tired and walked away from the job. Just hit the road."

"Collecting hair, nails, and teeth?" Walter pointed out. "Don't forget what we found in his apartment. Have you heard from the fire marshal? Some of that may have survived."

Before Brayman could respond, the radio chirped.

"Four-one-nine-seven, come in."

Brayman picked up the microphone and pressed the Transmit button. "Four-one-nine-seven, copy."

"The ME called. They have an ID on the vic from the bus depot. Want me to patch you in?"

"No. We're not far. Tell Ackerman we'll be there in ten minutes."

"HER NAME'S ANETA KOSTENKO." Jane Ackerman moved fast as she led them through the double doors into cold storage.

"Kostenko?" Walter gave Brayman a narrow-eyed glance. "Hmm. That sounds Russian."

Ackerman tugged open a drawer on the right and gently folded down the teal sheet from the body, revealing the top half of the woman from the bus depot.

"It's a Ukrainian name," Ackerman told them. "Part of the Soviet Union but not quite the same thing. Her ID was tricky. Luckily for us, she had those breast implants. I matched the serial number to a doctor in New Jersey who recently got himself busted by the feds for working on illegals, prepping them for sex trafficking. Bad dude, but he kept good records. The serial number gave me her name. That all tied back to her file with Interpol, where I learned a little more. She's from a small town called Pripyat. She went missing at twenty-four. Four years ago."

"If you decide you'd like to be a detective, call me," Brayman told her. "The ones coming up nowadays can't find their own ass."

Walter ignored the jab and whistled down at the woman's body. "Man, that's a hard twenty-eight. She could be a hundred."

Although it had only been two days, Aneta's skin had taken on a severely dry appearance on her face, neck, and arms and was a deep gray yet nearly translucent, like a thin plastic bag holding her internal organs together.

"The degeneration appears to be accelerating," Ackerman agreed. "The man you brought in from the Edison is worse. We froze him to preserve what's left. We'll have to freeze her, too, pending the outcome of all this. If we don't, there might not be much left in a few more days. From what I can determine, the moisture from the body seems to be seeping from the head and extremities and pooling at center mass."

Brayman reached out and gently touched the woman's face, running his index finger along the wrinkles surrounding her eyes and the corner of her mouth. "Could this be progeria?"

"I considered progeria when they brought in the man from the Edison." She nodded down at the woman. "I gave it serious thought when she came in, so I sent some samples to the lab at Hopkins. I haven't received the results yet. The CDC wants to fly in a specialist out of Atlanta."

"What's progeria?" Walter asked.

Ackerman said, "Hutchinson-Gilford progeria syndrome, HGPS. It's a rare genetic condition that causes children to age rapidly. Most don't live past twelve or thirteen. Their cells degenerate and they die of complications usually not seen outside the elderly."

"Like multiple forms of cancer all presenting at once," Brayman added.

Ackerman nodded. "Progeria usually presents at a very early age, but in some rare instances we see it later—early adolescence or young adults—fifteen to maybe twenty at most. Even then, there are precursors—shorter than average height, thinning and gray hair, age spots on the skin, voice changes. Sometimes even facial tics or weak arms and legs, nonresponsive muscles...similar to stroke victims. This woman is twenty-eight. The man from the Edison was maybe mid-thirties. Both are too old for progeria, at least the way we understand it. We haven't ruled it out, but it's unlikely. The working theory is that this is a mutation."

Walter scratched the side of his head. "You said genetic, right? So whatever killed them, it's not contagious?"

"Not contagious in any way. The odds of two people presenting with it in such close proximity, particularly when you take in the diversity of their backgrounds, are slim to none. That's the biggest concern right now." She folded the sheet back up over the woman, slid the drawer back into the wall, and closed the door. "That brings me to something else I wanted to show you. We might have one more."

Walter's heart thumped.

The heart attack from the train station. The one she *had touched. Had to be.*

Ackerman crossed the room to another bank of freezers and opened the third drawer from the left, pulled out the sliding gurney. This body was also covered in a teal sheet. She folded it back with the same care she had the sheet covering the woman. "No missing fingers this time, but signs of the same degeneration."

Not the heart attack victim.

This body was male and hadn't been autopsied yet. His skin was deeply wrinkled, and he was bald except for a small tuft of thin gray hair surrounded by dark age spots stretched over his scalp and temples. His mouth was open slightly, and several teeth were missing. His fingernails were cracked and yellow.

"He came in about an hour ago," Ackerman said. "His wife said he hasn't been feeling well for the past few days, wouldn't get out of bed. He actually locked her out of the bedroom and wouldn't let her in. When he finally did, she panicked and called 911. She was hysterical, a complete mess. Understandably so. He's only thirty-four. He died en route to the hospital—massive coronary." She took a business card from her pocket and handed it to Brayman. "He had this on him. His wife told the paramedics he'd been mugged recently, said she thought it was connected."

Walter only heard part of this exchange. His eyes were fixed on the man's bruised knuckles. "Holy shit."

46

BRAYMAN'S FACE TWISTED INTO a scowl as he held up the business card.

Walter's business card.

Although the room hovered just above freezing, sweat broke out on the back of Walter's neck, between his shoulders.

"I'm done cutting you breaks." Brayman took a step closer. "You know something, spill it. All of it. Right now."

"You won't believe me."

"I think we're well beyond all that, don't you?"

Ackerman looked away, fidgeted with a temperature gauge, like she was embarrassed for him.

"That's Michael Driscoll," Walter said softly. He reached up and touched the faded bruise near his eye, the healing cut under his chin. "He lied to his wife. He wasn't mugged. He's…he's the guy who hit me."

Brayman shoved the card into his pocket. "And why exactly did he hit you?"

"I saw him…with Amy Archer." Walter wanted to sound convincing as he said this, but he knew he hadn't. The name trailed off as it left his lips.

The look on Brayman's face was enough to tell him he didn't believe him, didn't want to hear this.

"Let's be clear. You saw him with someone *who looks like* Amy Archer."

"No." Walter shook his head. "I saw him *with* Amy Archer. I'm sure it was her. When I confronted him, *them*, he hit me. Knocked me out. But it was her. No doubt."

"Were you drunk?"

Walter didn't answer at first. Then he said, "It was the night of my party at Mig's Tavern." He raised both hands defensively. "But I know what I saw, and it was her."

"You need help," Brayman said flatly, shaking his head.

"It was her!"

"It's a wonder you passed the psych eval."

"She told him her name was Amelia Dyer. The name's bogus. No record in DMV, birth, I couldn't find it anywhere. But I tracked her down. She's working for Elite Escorts."

"So that's how you got onto Sergei Turgenev? You've been chasing all this? Chasing some girl who gave you the slip six years ago?"

Walter nodded reluctantly.

Both of them went quiet for a long while, Ackerman standing there worrying the pocket of her lab coat.

When Brayman finally spoke, he tried to keep his anger in check. "The two of us are going directly to the precinct, and you're going to tell Hazlett all of this."

"He won't see the facts. He'll say I'm chasing a ghost and fire me."

"He should."

Walter glanced at a clock on the wall. It was almost eight o'clock. "He won't be there this late, you know that. Give me until morning to get some proof."

Brayman snorted and shook his head. "I'm not letting you out of my sight. We'll call him at home, go to his house, whatever we need to do. I'm not going to be responsible for you. You're his problem, not mine."

Hazlett will take my badge for sure.

He might lock him up. Hell, Brayman might back him up on that. And if Nadler weighed in, weighed in officially...

Walter's skin crawled, anxiety burning beneath the surface. He turned back to Ackerman. "What did you find with the black light?"

Rather than answer, she looked nervously at Brayman. Finally, he gave her a nod.

"I haven't had a chance to look yet. Give me a second." She pushed back through the aluminum doors and disappeared down the hallway.

When they were alone, neither Walter nor Brayman spoke. Walter stared at Driscoll's withered body. Brayman faced the floor, his left hand tapping on his thigh.

Ackerman returned with the portable black light in hand. "Turn off the lights?" she said to Brayman, who moved to the switch on the wall and flicked it off.

The room went dark, but not completely. The backlit thermostats on each freezer drawer cast the room in a faint yellow.

Ackerman switched on the black light and brought it close to Michael Driscoll's head. "Whoa."

They all saw it.

His lips glowed bright. Not just his lips. There were also marks on his cheeks and several on his neck.

"She kissed him," Walter said in a muted voice. "I saw her kiss him several times."

"That doesn't mean…" Brayman started to speak, but he went quiet before completing the thought. His mind was clearly reeling.

There were no marks on Driscoll's chest, only his face and neck.

Walter pointed toward Driscoll's groin. "She also…you know."

Giving Brayman another glance, Ackerman slowly pulled back the sheet and drew the black light down Driscoll's torso, over both arms, past his abdomen. "Oh, my."

Michael Driscoll's penis and the area surrounding it glowed with dozens of marks.

Minutes ticked by, and the three of them stood there in silence.

When Brayman spoke, it was to Ackerman. "Does he have cancer, like the others?"

"I haven't had a chance to biopsy. Like I said, he just came in. But these spots on his head, his arms, and here on his shoulders, they look like melanoma. That would be consistent with your John Doe from the Edison and Aneta Kostenko. Hold on…"

From a table on her right, she selected a scalpel and made a small incision in the upper part of Driscoll's abdomen, about a quarter inch in length. She then took a needle and inserted it into the opening, maneuvered the plunger with her thumb, and removed it.

"Liver?" Brayman asked.

She nodded and carried the needle over to another table with a microscope and placed the sample on a slide, placed the slide on the microscope, then made several adjustments to the various knobs and controllers.

Ackerman sighed, then stepped aside and motioned for Brayman to take a look.

He studied the sample for nearly twenty seconds, then, without looking up, said, "Did you find any cancer in the man from the Four Seasons? Earl Golston?"

Ackerman shook her head. "Only the aneurysm. Directly below the mark I showed you back at the hotel."

"Could those marks be some type of injection sight reaction?"

"I looked for needle marks. There aren't any."

"She's not using needles," Walter said quietly.

They both continued to ignore him. He didn't blame them. What he was suggesting wasn't possible. He was suggesting that somehow Amy Archer killed these people with only her touch.

Not just killed them, drained them, his mind muttered. *Some slow, some fast, but took the life all the same.*

When Brayman finally looked up, he nodded toward the drawer holding Aneta Kostenko. "You said she was involved in sex trafficking. Did you get that from her jacket?"

Ackerman nodded and went to a desk in the corner of the room. She thumbed through the contents of a folder already open on top. Handed Brayman and Walter several mug shots of a beautiful woman in her early twenties. Couldn't possibly be the same woman, but Walter knew it was.

She went back to the folder and skimmed one of the reports with the tip of her finger. "This doesn't say anything about Turgenev, but that doesn't mean he's not connected.

She was arrested twice. The second time she had a stack of business cards in her purse. No business name printed on them, only a phone number. Somebody set her up with a high-priced attorney; he wouldn't let her talk. Got her off with a slap on the wrist."

Walter quickly said, "Were the cards black with red lettering?"

"Ah." She skimmed one of the reports. "Yeah. Black card stock, red print."

"That's Elite Escorts."

Brayman crossed the room and stared at the drawer holding Aneta Kostenko's body. Finally, he looked over at Walter, the expression on his face unreadable. "Take me there."

He started for the door but Ackerman stopped him. "Wes?"

"Yeah."

"There's something else you should know." She was holding a sheet of paper. She eyed Walter nervously. "I got a call from Lynn Crowley in Evidence the other day. She was trying to track down some information on an old case. Autopsy results…for your partner."

He glared at Walter. "Whose autopsy?"

"Two bodies found in a freezer in Alvin Schalk's basement. The…Amy Archer case."

Walter reached for the paper but Brayman snatched it first. His eyes were flying over the text when Ackerman said, "Both bodies were male, heavily decomposed, cancerous. All their fingers were missing."

47

EVEN THOUGH WALTER TOLD Brayman the people running Elite were well aware they were under surveillance and that the arrival of a Detroit Metro car, even unmarked, would be a surprise to no one, Brayman parked the Crown Vic a block off Franklin and the two of them walked back in the direction of the brownstone.

"They've got eyes all over this block, far more extensive than ours." Walter's hands were in his pockets, and he looked down at the sidewalk. "I'm not sure if they're using cameras or people positioned in the windows, but I can guarantee they're already watching us. Probably made us before you killed the motor."

"That doesn't mean it's okay to pull up in an unmarked and park under their nose. I don't want to kick the hornet's nest; I just want to get a look around."

"You're not gonna spook these guys." Without looking up,

Walter told him, "That's it up on the left. The brownstone with the yellow potted plant out front, number 415."

The white van was parked in the same space. Walter wondered if anyone bothered to move it or if the surveillance van was just a permanent fixture on the street with a rotating string of detectives climbing in and out. With parking at a premium, they probably didn't want to risk losing the space.

The back door swung open before either of them had a chance to knock.

Detective Buncy hadn't shaved in a few days, and he had dark circles under his eyes. "Homicide's back," he told Wilson, who was in the same seat as last time, facing the bank of monitors. "Brought a date this time." He nodded over his shoulder. "Get in here, hurry up. We got weirdness going on up in there."

Brayman climbed up into the van first, Walter behind him, tugging the door shut.

Wilson, headphones on, gave them both a quick nod, then went back to the monitors. There were at least a dozen empty cans of Jolt scattered about, some on the table, others on the floor, one in Wilson's free hand.

Buncy studied Brayman. "You're Wes Brayman, right? We worked together maybe ten years back. I don't know if you remember."

"Lou Buncy, I remember. The girl we pulled out of Lake St. Clair. You were with the Twenty-Third."

"Still am. This case has crossed so many jurisdictions over the years, the higher-ups gave up trying to take ownership; they just keep me and Wilson on along with two other teams. Got someone on them round the clock now."

Brayman moved slowly through the van, studying the

photographs taped to the wall above their desk, his eyes lingering on the one labeled Amelia Dyer on the left. "Weird how?"

"Huh?"

"You said something weird is going on up in there."

Buncy glanced at Walter. "Remember how I told you they only use this place for dispatch? Calls come in, the girls go out, but they never host the johns here?"

Walter nodded.

"Yeah, well, as of a few hours ago, that business model has gone to shit. We've had eight men go in there since sunset, and none have come out yet."

"Nine," Wilson said. "Not eight, nine."

Buncy rolled his eyes. "Whatever. At least six are in our records, part of their frequent-flier program. We're running photos of the other guys, trying to get an ID. None of the girls have gone out on calls for hours. The ones who were out have come back and stayed. Everyone's inside like they got called home for some customer appreciation party or some shit."

Walter pointed at the grainy photo of Amy Archer. "Is she in there?"

"They're *all* in there. Even Turgenev, and he never comes by here. Something big is going on."

Brayman was looking over the various monitors, studying the camera shots, when Wilson said, "We've got another."

He pointed at the monitor on the top right. A man wearing khaki pants and a dark blue shirt was standing at the door next to the potted plant.

Wilson pressed several buttons below the monitor, unplugged his headphones, and audio came out of two speakers mounted in the van's ceiling. They all heard the man knock twice on the door, then watched as he looked up and to the right, speaking into what must have been a camera. "The breakup of AT&T will end badly."

"What's that supposed to mean?" Walter asked.

"Code phrase," Wilson replied, turning up the volume. "They're all saying it, then——"

Then the door opened, the man went inside, and it closed behind him. From their current angle, they couldn't see who opened it.

"Then we lose them," Wilson finished.

"No surveillance inside?" Brayman asked.

Buncy shook his head. "Our warrant covers internal audio and video, but they sweep for wires at least once each night. We've gotten bugs in there before, but they don't stick. The little bit of audio we've recorded on them has been nothing but gibberish, like they know we're listening and they're just trying to screw with us. Phone taps are useless. We explained that one to your partner here the last time he dropped by unannounced."

Brayman took a photograph out of his pocket. It was the woman from Corktown, the teal sheet at the morgue pulled up to her neck revealing only her face. He showed it to Buncy. "Her name was Aneta Kostenko. You ever seen her before?"

Buncy's face twisted into a grimace. "God, no. Get that out of my face."

Brayman gave Walter a sidelong glance, then took out one of the mug shots from Aneta Kostenko's jacket. "What about her?"

This time, Buncy nodded. "Her I've seen. Bolted out of here with a bag a few days ago. Hasn't been back. We figured she ran."

Brayman was looking at Walter again, but he didn't say anything. He shoved both pictures in his pocket.

"Why don't you send somebody in there?" Walter asked. "You've got their secret password, handshake, whatever. Why not send someone in to try and get something concrete and take them down?"

"We've got a requisition in. We're waiting for them to send someone down here. They know both of us. We need a fresh face."

"How long is that gonna take?"

Buncy didn't have an answer for that.

"I'll do it," Walter told them.

Buncy laughed. "You're not exactly a fresh face, either. The fine gentleman who ran you out of there last time told all his buddies about you. Told the girls to stay away from you. No way you're walking in there."

"I could do it," Brayman said. "They don't know me."

Buncy eyed him up and down but didn't reply.

"I don't know," Wilson said. "I think we should wait on whoever our captain sends out."

Brayman sighed. "O'Brien might be right about the timing. If they've got a full house, doing things outside the norm, that means their usual security is lax. This might be your only shot."

Buncy licked his lips as he thought it over. "They'll frisk you at the door. That means no gun, no wire. You'd be going in there blind. Are you sure you're up for that?"

"Wouldn't be my first undercover op, and we've all got a vested interest here. This organization might be tied to at least three or four homicides in the past week. If we've got a chance at busting it, we need to take it. No telling when there will be another window."

As he said all this, another man walked up to the brownstone door, gave the pass phrase, and disappeared inside.

"Now or never, gentlemen," Brayman said.

He must have known what their answer would be, because his backup weapon was sitting on the chair beside him, and he had already started unsnapping his shoulder holster.

A moment later, Walter, Buncy, and Wilson were all huddled around the monitor, watching Brayman provide the pass phrase and disappear inside the brownstone.

CHAPTER

48

FIVE MINUTES TICKED BY.

Ten.

"Want one?" Wilson held a Jolt Cola, his eyes glued to the monitor.

Walter shook his head. "I'm good."

Wilson shrugged, popped the top, and took a long chug. When he set the can down on the table, he wiped his mouth on the back of his wrist and burped. "Love these things."

"This might have been a bad idea," Buncy muttered. "How old is Brayman now? He's probably knocking on the retirement door. Nobody's gonna mistake him for a john."

"He's a smart guy. He'll find some way to play it."

Buncy chuffed. "Like what? 'I dropped my son off here half an hour ago, and he forgot his wallet. Any idea what room he's in?'"

Wilson laughed. "Better to play off the age thing. 'Who are you people? Wait—this isn't my house…'"

Walter was busy studying the other monitors. He noticed a black Mercedes parked across the street. "Is that their car? I noticed one like it dropping off and picking up girls the other night."

Buncy nodded. "Driver's inside with everyone else. He went in about two hours ago."

Fifteen minutes.

"Maybe we should have put a time limit on this or had some signal so we'd know he was okay."

"What, like hang a sock on the doorknob when the charge on your credit card goes through?" Wilson laughed at his own joke, and Jolt shot from his nose. "Oh, Christ, that hurts."

"I'm not worried about Brayman getting hurt," Buncy said. "I'm worried he'll get made and they'll boot him out and ruin our chances of getting someone else in there tonight. They know we're watching. They wouldn't touch a cop."

Wilson pointed up at one of the screens. "Door's opening."

"Is it Brayman?" Walter asked, turning back to the monitors.

Wilson pointed up at the photographs on the wall. "It's your girl, Lolita Number One. She's moving fast."

By the time Walter got eyes on the monitor, he only caught a blur as she walked off camera.

Wilson pointed at two different screens. "Give it a second. We should catch her here or here, depending on which direction she goes."

The three of them stared, but she didn't reappear.

"Shit. I don't get it. There's no blind spot."

Buncy's forehead creased. "Where the hell did she go?"

"Goddamnit, out of the way—" Walter pushed by the large man and scrambled for the door, yanked the handle, and jumped down onto the sidewalk. He spotted her about halfway down the block hailing a taxi. She was wearing a slinky black dress with matching pumps, her dark hair swept back.

Walter ran, closing the gap as a taxi pulled to a stop next to her on the curb.

As she got into the car, Walter jumped in beside her and pulled the door shut.

She startled. "Walter? What are you doing here?"

Walter tried to find the right words. He couldn't risk her running. "I'm gonna give you a choice."

"What kind of choice?"

"Come with me, right now. Testify against these guys. I can get you out of this life, keep you safe. Away from Turgenev, or whoever has a hold on you."

The driver eyed them both in the mirror with a look of complete indifference. "Where to, miss?"

She gave him an address.

He steered the car away from the curb and out onto Franklin, merging with the traffic as he accelerated.

Her makeup had been applied with the skilled hand of a professional, and the sweet scent of lavender drifted from her. She moved aside the small purse she clutched in her hands. A soft smile crossed her lips. "You're going to be my knight in shining armor? Is that your plan, Walter? You barely know me."

"I know enough. I know where this life leads."

"What if I like this life? I've got money. I'm free to do what I want, when I want."

"You know the police are watching that building, right?"

"So?"

"When they arrest everyone, you don't want to get caught up in the sweep. At best, you walk away with a record that follows you forever. At worst, you go to prison for a long time. If they've been coercing you, *forcing you* to do things against your will, you're not at fault. You're a victim."

She looked down at her hands. "People like Turgenev don't let you walk away. He would kill me. Or have me killed. Who knows what he would do to my friends. I can't leave Willow in there."

"I'll find a way to get her out. I can get you into protective custody, both of you. If you cooperate, I can keep you out of trouble. This is your chance to walk away, but it has to be now."

The car pulled to a stop.

She turned toward the window and let out a soft breath. "That's a lot to promise, Walter."

"I can keep you safe," he said again.

Her hand had slipped into his. Or had he taken hers? He wasn't sure, but he felt her fingers tighten around his, felt the warmth of her body beside him, the inches between them feeling like an impossible distance. She must have felt this, too, because she eased closer and rested her head against his shoulder. The two of them sat there like that for a moment. Then a mischievous glint entered her eyes. She smiled up at him. "How about you buy me dinner first?"

Before he could answer, she was out the door and rounding the car.

They had stopped in front of Giovanni's. The same restaurant where he had spotted her on Sunday with Michael Driscoll. Without looking back, Amy Archer stepped inside.

Walter swore under his breath, and when he reached for the door, the driver scowled. "Hey, somebody needs to pay for the ride!"

Quickly fishing some bills from his wallet, Walter tossed them onto the front seat and went after her.

CHAPTER

49

INSIDE, WALTER WAS BOMBARDED by the scent of garlic, Italian music, and voices all talking over one another. Different hostess. About two-thirds of the tables were full. He spotted an older waiter pulling a chair out for Amy at a small table in the back corner partially hidden behind a potted plant. If the kid from the other day was working, he didn't see him.

Walter worked his way through the maze of tables and sat across from her.

Amy smiled, unfolded her white cloth napkin, and smoothed it on her lap. "This is one of my favorite restaurants. I've always had a thing for Italian food, *real Italian food*. There are so many imitators out there, but the head chef here, Luca Giulia, he's from Palermo. Doesn't speak a lick of English, but he is such a talented man in the kitchen. I've told him he should start a chain, but he won't hear any of that. He wants to keep it in the family. I guess that makes sense, but food like this should be celebrated far and wide, not hidden away in Detroit, of all places."

"You speak Italian?"

"Of course. *Parlo molte lingue, tesoro* Walter."

The waiter had filled up two glasses of water. Walter picked up the one nearest him, wiped away some of the condensation from the glass with his thumb, and set it back down without taking a drink. "Why are we even here? We need to go back."

She pouted. "I don't want to leave, not yet. There are bad things waiting for both of us. I don't think you're ready for them any more than I am. So how about this? Let's pretend we're on a date. Our first. I'm from a small farm in Dubuque, Iowa, and we met today in the checkout line at the grocery store. You asked me out, and against my better judgment, I agreed."

"What, like role-playing?"

She settled back in her seat, closed her eyes, and drew in a deep breath. The air washed over her with a shiver, and something within her shifted. Her posture changed. The muscles in her face twitched and seemed to settle in slightly altered positions from only moments earlier, and when her eyes opened, there was something different about them. The color hadn't changed, nothing like that, but *different*. Walter couldn't put his finger on it. She reached up and removed several bobby pins from her hair, letting it drop down over her shoulders, and shook it out. When she spoke again, there was an accent to her voice that hadn't been there before, just a hint of the Midwest but far removed from her normal speaking voice.

"If you hadn't asked me out, I might have made the first move. I don't think I would have let you walk away."

Walter stared at her.

It was like she'd become another person.

He told himself it was only a trick of the lighting, but even her dark hair looked lighter, filled with subtle highlights.

When the waiter came to take their drink order, she didn't drop the pretense. Instead, she played it up. Even her movements seemed to belong to someone else, her body language that of a stranger. "I think I'd like to order, if that's all right. I'm famished. Are you ready, Henry?"

She tilted her head slightly to the side and smiled at him from across the table.

Henry?

"Sure."

She looked back at the waiter. "I'll take Ossobuco alla Milanese with a side of focaccia."

Although she'd spoken with a perfect Italian accent only moments earlier, now she completely butchered it, as if saying the words for the first time.

Exactly like someone who had never set foot out of Iowa might say them.

Walter ordered a small pizza and tried to remember how much cash he had in his wallet as the waiter collected their menus and disappeared into the kitchen.

Under the table, he felt Amy's foot rub against his ankle. "Tell me about yourself, Henry. Where did you grow up?"

He leaned closer to her. "We don't have time for this, Amy."

She leaned closer, too, and her voice dropped to a conspiratorial whisper. "My name is Velma, Henry. Velma Barfield. And if you have any hopes of getting lucky on this first date of ours, the least you can do is call me by my name." She grinned mischievously. "I don't know about you, but I think I'd like to get lucky tonight. That's why my underwear is in my purse."

The waiter returned with a plate of bread, a bottle of white wine, and two glasses. "Compliments of Chef Luca." As he poured first Amy's glass, then Walter's, he told her, "He said to tell you you look ravishing this evening. Our dining room is brighter when you're in it."

She blushed and pressed a hand to her cheek. "He is just the sweetest thing. Please thank him for me."

When the waiter left, she raised her glass. "To those who have seen us at our best and seen us at our worst and can't tell the difference. We, the misfits of the world."

She said all this without dropping the Iowa accent. If anything, it became more complete. Walter had trouble remembering her actual voice. She took a sip of her wine, smiled, and set the glass down. "My daddy makes the best strawberry wine, but this is nice, too."

Walter left his glass sitting on the table between them. "Why did you burn down Earl Golston's apartment? Who was he to you?"

She cocked her head. "Earl Golston? I'm not sure I know who that is."

Walter unbuttoned his shirtsleeve, rolled it up, and peeled back a corner of the bandage. "Does this help you remember?"

She didn't look at the burn. Instead, she smiled, tore off a small piece of bread. "Okay, Henry. If you're not going to tell me about your past, I'm going to guess." She reached across the table, turned his hand over, and studied his palm. "My gran was really good at this, and she said I have the gift, but it's never worked quite right for me. Instead of a fine-tuned engine like she had, I've got more of an old motor that sputters along and doesn't necessarily start on the first pull." Her eyes narrowed as she traced one of the lines from his index finger to his wrist. "I see tragedy in your life. Something horrible as a young child. A loss. A great loss." She looked up at him. "Oh, it was your parents, wasn't it? They died in a car accident? Or, no, wait. Something else." She stroked the outer edge of the bandage. "Was it a fire?"

Night—his father, standing outside the kitchen window, his back against a tree. A woman in his arms. A woman who wasn't Walter's mother. His father's hand twisted in her hair, holding her close as their lips met. Her palm in his shirt, on his chest. His father glancing at the window, seeing Walter, watching him yet unable to stop.

Walter jerked his hand away. "That's not funny."

"I wasn't trying to be." She offered him a consoling smile. "How horrible that must have been. To have to go on after, all alone at such a young age."

"We don't have much time," he told her. "We need to focus on you, or I won't be able to do anything for you. Tell me what happened at the Four Seasons. Were you at the Edison?"

The accent perfected now, she went on. "We've both had some tribulations in life, sadness. I suppose those things are what shape us. Clay can't be molded into something beautiful without pressure from all sides. I think that's what first attracted me to you, the pain you carry right below the surface. You're not unique in that fact. Many people suffer, but there is something different about your suffering, a vulnerability. Like an impenetrable door left slightly ajar. We have that in common, the two of us. When you look at me, I know you see it. That's why you feel this need to help me. I want to be there for you, too. We could disappear.

Start something new. A new life far from here. We could heal each other and learn to move on as one instead of two broken halves covered in jagged edges." She nodded toward the front of the restaurant. "There are two futures outside that door. The first where you take me back to your friends in the white van on Franklin and I'm dragged away from you, put in a box. And a second, where we walk out together, hand in hand, down the sidewalk, get in a car, and go anywhere in the world that is not here. I have money. We could disappear."

Under the table, her hand found his. He knew he shouldn't let her take it, but he did anyway. He knew he shouldn't look into her eyes, but he did that, too, because he also understood what waited on the other side of that door wasn't good and he didn't want to think about it, not then, not in that particular moment.

Her voice fell to a whisper again. "I want you to be the first person I see in the morning and the last one I see each night. I want to know how you feel inside me. I don't want secrets between us, never again."

Walter hadn't heard the waiter walk up, but he was now standing beside them doling out the various plates.

Amy—Velma—cleared her throat, stood, and set her napkin down on the chair. "I'm going to visit the ladies' and wash my hands. I'll be right back."

She was gone before Walter could object, walking off toward the back of the restaurant and down a short hallway, disappearing through the restroom door.

When a minute ticked by, Walter asked the waiter, "Is there a way to get out of the restaurant from back there?"

The waiter looked at him, puzzled. "From the restrooms? No. The only other door is in the kitchen."

He gave Walter another look, one that said, *Is your date really going that badly?*

Walter got up and went to the small hallway in the back. He knocked on the door marked DONNE / WOMEN. When no answer came, he stepped inside.

The waiter had been correct. There was no door, no window, no visible way out—only a single stall with a toilet and a pedestal sink—but the bathroom was empty.

On the mirror, written in red lipstick, big, loopy letters formed the words

Good-bye, Henry.

CHAPTER

50

WALTER RAN.

From the bathroom.

Through the crowded restaurant.

Out the front door and to the sidewalk.

He frantically scanned up and down the block, finding no sign of her. There was a narrow gated-off alley on the right of the restaurant. Walter's waiter was there, leaning against the wall, smoking a cigarette.

Walter pressed against the fence. "Hey, I'm a cop! Did you see my date come out that way?"

The waiter did a slight double take. "No. I told you, she couldn't. Even if she tried, Chef Luca has the key to that gate."

Walter reached through the chain link and shook the padlock.

Locked.

Fuck! Fuck! Fuck!

The waiter shouted something about the check as Walter jumped into a taxi. "Four fifteen Franklin!"

Four minutes.

That's all the time it took to get back.

He threw some bills at the driver, not sure how much, not caring, and ran from the car to the back of the white van, yanked open the door, and scrambled inside.

Buncy glared at him. "What the hell? Where did you go?"

Wilson was still in his seat, fumbling with knobs, headphones on, his eyes fixed on the monitors.

"Where's the girl?" Buncy asked.

"Where's Brayman?"

Buncy leaned his sizable bulk on the edge of the table. "We saw you get in a cab with her. Did you lose her?"

Twice. Three times, if you count the train station.

Or did you let her go?

Buncy didn't say that last part, not out loud, but it was right there.

"Brayman hasn't come out yet?" Walter pressed. He looked at his watch. He'd been in there more than half an hour.

Buncy shook his head. "Not yet. Wilson's been trying to get something on the directional mic, but it's quiet in there. Nobody else in, nobody out. I'm trying to get a warrant to go in. Judge Belton said—"

Walter didn't hear the rest. He jumped out of the van and ran to the door of the brownstone—beat on it with the back of his fist. "Detroit PD! Open the door, now!"

He tried the knob and found it locked.

Above the door, the lens of the small camera glared down at him, unblinking and quiet.

He pounded the door again. "Open the goddamn door!"

On the street, both Buncy and Wilson were leaning out the back of the van. "What the hell, O'Brien?" Buncy said in a loud whisper.

Walter took out his gun, pulled back the hammer, and shot the lock three times.

The first bullet missed its mark and vanished in the wood frame, but the other two tore into the doorjamb between the knob and strike plate, leaving nothing behind but a splintered mess.

Walter grabbed the knob, yanked the door open, and, leading with the barrel of his revolver, stepped into the brownstone.

He nearly tripped over the body of the large man who had run him off the other night. The guard was on the floor, leaning lazily against the wall, one arm at his side, the other bent at an odd angle behind his back. His mouth was open, and a glistening trail of drool hung from his purple lips, down over the tattoo on his neck, and into his shirt, where it pooled on the collar. One dead eye looked up at Walter. The other was turned off to the right, staring at things unknown. Walter was reminded of Earl Golston's body back at the Four Seasons. He had no doubt when they ran a black light over this man they would find a small mark on his temple, a mark no larger than a fingerprint.

"Brayman!" Walter shouted, moving fast down a hallway that opened into a sitting room.

The furniture in here was all antique, obviously expensive. Walter found more bodies positioned on each couch, in each chair. Seven dead men and four women faced each other in silent conversation, heads lolled to the side, hands folded in their laps. The room reeked of something both sweet and acidic, and Walter didn't need anyone to tell him these people had all died recently, probably within the past few hours.

Music drifted down from upstairs. Walter knew the song—"Crying in the Rain" by the Everly Brothers. His mother had played the forty-five so often, the highs and lows had vanished in the worn grooves.

Walter yelled Brayman's name again as he bounded up the steps, taking them two at a time.

Each open door he passed—bedrooms and several bathrooms—revealed more bodies. Walter tried not to look. He only followed the music, the twang of the chorus and the soft strum of a guitar.

He found Brayman in the last bedroom on the left.

His body had been dragged up and positioned in the center of the bed. Fully clothed, and with the same dead look upon his face as all the others. Willow was draped over him, one arm across his chest, her legs twisted in his, her flesh unnaturally white.

The music came from a small turntable on the dresser, and when the song ended, Walter watched the arm rise, move back to the beginning of the record, and lower the needle, starting again. A bit of static followed by the strum of a D chord and a lazy drum.

NOW

51

RIGBY HAD GIVEN THE phone to Hurwitz earlier, and he'd wired it up to a recorder and a system that would help him triangulate the signal and pinpoint the caller. She gave him a soft nod. He keyed in some instructions on his computer, then answered the call on speaker.

It was the same male voice as earlier:

"You need to stand down."

"You know I can't do that."

Hurwitz had a camera fixed on Walter O'Brien, and he hadn't moved. He was still sitting in the battered patrol car, door open, staring at the entrance to the club. If he was listening in on this conversation, he gave no indication of it.

"I know you have people in the utility tunnels and you're preparing to breach. I'm going to ask you to abort so I don't have to shoot them on live television."

Rigby looked over at Hurwitz, who had turned worriedly to the breach-team feeds.

Maybe Walter's people had cameras of their own.

"What makes you think I have people in the utility tunnels?"

"Because that's what I would do. If you didn't, I'd be very disappointed in you."

On a sheet of paper, Hurwitz scribbled *He's guessing. Can't see.*

Rigby looked up at the clock. "According to your friend, I only have thirty-three minutes left. You're not communicating. You haven't asked for anything. I can't let that clock tick down to zero and do nothing."

"I'm not faulting you for doing your job. I'd expect nothing less. But I feel obligated to tell you if your people attempt to come up through those tunnels, they will die. If they somehow manage to reach one of my shooters, I'll have no choice but to detonate the bomb. That's a lot of death on your hands, and as commander of this operation, I feel it's important you consider all the facts before you decide on a course of action. Walter gave you a hard drive. Have you looked at it?"

"No," she lied.

"I'm not sure I believe you."

"I don't really care."

"They're going to tell you Walter's a dirty cop. Delusional. Can't be reasoned with. They'll order you to put him down. All of us. Their only move is to discredit us. What you have there is proof."

"Proof of what?"

"Proof of who we really are. Proof of the things we've seen. Proof of something that shouldn't exist. When this is over, people are going to demand answers, and you have all of them, right there."

On the monitor, Hurwitz was busy scrolling through all the data. He stopped on a folder tagged *Walter O'Brien — Detroit PD.*

Opening the file brought up a series of documents nearly identical to the ones they were just looking at in the IA database, *nearly—*

His jacket didn't say he was terminated for cause. Instead, it simply read *Resigned* with a date of August 12, 1997. No mention of the disciplinary information. The two dead partners were still listed.

Rigby told herself this was meaningless. Most likely fake. It changed nothing. She was still staring at a ticking clock, a hostage situation, and the people responsible were just trying to jerk her chain. She said, "I think you're stalling. I need an act of good faith. You've got a lot of people in that club. The longer this goes on, the tougher that will make things. They'll get hungry. They'll need to use the bathrooms. Some might have medical conditions. Release half. Release two-thirds. Give me something, and make this easier on yourself."

"If she doesn't come out on her own, the bomb goes off in thirty-two minutes. Bathroom breaks and snacks aren't really a concern here."

Hurwitz pointed at something on the screen.

Rigby studied the document as he loaded up others. All of them nearly identical, with the exception of the issue date. She said, "Brown hair. Gray eyes. Early twenties. Does that sound about right?"

"So you are reading."

"Walter O'Brien issued the same BOLO more than a dozen times over eleven years. Wanted in connection to the homicide of some guy named Alvin Schalk in '86.

Multiples in '92. Amy Archer. Is that the woman you're after?"

There was a photo, but it was horrible. Grainy. Couldn't make out much of anything.

"That would make her what, in her fifties now? If she's in there, she wouldn't be hard to find."

"Call off your teams."

"You know I can't do that."

"A week from now, when you're sitting in front of a review board that's holding a magnifying glass over every one of your decisions, I'd hate to see you have to explain some knee-jerk reaction and the resulting consequences, particularly those that could have been avoided. Are you watching the news?"

They had a satellite on the roof, but none of the displays were tuned to television. That was a distraction she didn't need. She'd spotted at least three news trucks beyond the barricades the last time she'd looked. There were probably more now. Reporters paid interns to listen to police scanners. They were never far behind. She told herself they were doing a job, and as long as they didn't get in the way of hers, she'd let them.

"All those eyes are on you. On this. You don't want to do something you'll regret."

"What I want to do—what I *am* doing—is my job."

One of the computers dinged, and Hurwitz loaded up the phone trace.

Rigby mouthed, *Do you know where he is?*

He shook his head. On the paper, he wrote: *I think it's a SAT phone. Only the last leg is running through the cell system. Best guess = he's right here.*

Thirty-one minutes left.

"I want you to let at least ten people out of that club."

"No."

"At the very least, I need to send in a medic to make sure everyone is okay."

"No."

"Let me send in someone with a camera. Try and find her for you. O'Brien can watch the feed, and—"

"That won't work."

"Why not?"

"Review the drive."

He was stalling. Wasting her time.

"We're done." Rigby hung up on him.

Fuck him.

She blew out a breath and pressed the Transmit button on her comm. "Green and Blue teams—breach on my mark. We go in three…two…"

"Whoa, wait!" Hurwitz nearly shouted.

"Hold," Rigby quickly transmitted.

The live body-cam feeds filling several of the monitors bounced—jittery, jerky motions—then settled.

She glared at Hurwitz. "This better be good."

"Walter O'Brien wasn't the only one to issue a BOLO for a twentysomething female with brown hair, gray eyes, and a shitty photograph."

He pointed at another document on the screen.

Specifically, the logo in the corner.

"FBI?"

1997

Amy Archer

Amelia Dyer

Velma Barfield

Iele

Alvin Schalk

Two bodies/basement freezer

John Doe/Edison

Aneta Kostenko/~~Jane Doe~~/
Corktown Bus Depot

Earl Golston PI/~~John Doe~~/
Four Seasons

Man on train platform

Michael Driscoll

BROWNSTONE

Wes Brayman

Rebecca Edgecomb (Willow)

17 others

Covering tracks?

Hair

Nails

Teeth

Notebook – names, dated,
locations

Drawings/~~girls related?~~
~~Same?~~ ???

… Walter O'Brien, 33 Years Old

52

"**KEEP YOUR SHOULDER DOWN**, O'Brien! Lean into the hit! You pull back and you give your opponent an opening, the chance to fully deploy their punch. Lean in, and you cut that punch short, reduce its overall force, *and* take them off-balance!"

Walter feinted left, went right, and thrust out his left leg, catching his opponent in the ankle. The kid stumbled back and tripped, landed on his ass.

Third time now. Take that, you squirmy little shit.

"Better!"

After a second, Instructor Sanchez ripped off his FBI Academy ball cap and threw it down onto the man's chest. "Get up, Desmond! You stay down for more than a beat and you're dead! Sleep on your own time!"

Tim Desmond, a twenty-seven-year-old and self-proclaimed MMA enthusiast from Cleveland, scrambled back up looking at the dozen other recruits surrounding the mat, his face flushed with a mix of exertion and embarrass-ment. He planted both his feet and turned an angry gaze back on Walter. "Come on, old man! Knock off the cheap shots and throw a real punch!"

"Old man" again. At thirty-three, Walter only had six years on this guy.

You're five years older than the average FBI recruit, nearly eleven over those coming in fresh from college, old by all counts, Walter. If the stats don't sway you, how about that growing ache in your gut from a pulled something or other yesterday? Or how about the brace on your knee? I'm sure they've all spotted it under your sweatpants. How long before one of them takes a swipe?

The punch caught Walter square in the gut. Air expelled from his lungs, rushed up his windpipe, and shot from his mouth in a wet gasp. He tried to suck more in but couldn't before another hit caught him in his left kidney. Because Walter did nothing to protect his body, his body did it for him, a spastic bend to the side as a second kidney punch landed, then a third. On his way to the ground, Walter spun and managed to get his leg caught up in Desmond's again. He hooked the man's calf, and the two of them dropped to the mat together in a tangled mess.

Ignoring the pain, Walter jerked his shoulders to the right, brought up his arm, and managed to get his elbow around Desmond's neck. He was about to give the man a good squeeze when Sanchez blew his whistle.

"Time!"

Desmond was first to his feet, and when he got up, he held a hand out for Walter. When Walter reached for it, Desmond pulled away and started back to his place on the mat. "Life can be cruel, Grandpa."

Instructor Sanchez started over to assist, but Walter

managed to get back on his feet all by himself and brushed off. Aches and pains began to sound off all over his body— particularly the tough, tight skin around the burn scar on his wrist.

Sanchez studied the faces around the mat and pointed at Walter. "You see that? Like a damn junkyard dog cornered by three others. That's how you do it. Doesn't matter how bad you hurt, how hard you're hit, you can't stop swinging. The second you do, you're dead. You think some crackhead is gonna fight fair? Some jerk-off staring at life in prison? I don't care if you end up in financial crimes taking down rogue accountants, they'll sooner stab you with a pencil or slit your throat with their pocket protector than go down. When you've got the bad guy against a wall, doesn't matter the reason, they all see you with the same thought in their head—this is the guy about to take my life away, and I'm not gonna let 'im. They get the upper hand, and there's nobody there to blow a whistle, you're dead. Don't *ever* let your guard down."

"I didn't want to hurt him, is all," Desmond said under his breath. "Last thing I need is a lawyer from AARP hounding me."

This didn't bring the laughs Desmond had hoped for. Instead, Instructor Sanchez got in his face. "You know what age gives you, dipshit? Age gives you patience and wisdom. Tolerance and stealth." He took a step closer, and even though Desmond was nearly a foot taller and probably had a hundred pounds on him, Sanchez's gaze didn't falter. He cocked his head slightly to the side and narrowed his eyes. "I'm fifty-two and I haven't lost a fight since second grade. I've been stabbed, shot, and beaten with a pool cue to within an inch of my life. Ain't nobody takes me down without getting bit. You want to give me a go?"

When Desmond made no move to respond, Sanchez stepped closer. "I didn't think so." He jerked a thumb at Walter. "This man worked six years on patrol in Detroit—*Detroit*—plus five more as a homicide detective. That's almost twelve years in the field before coming here. Imagine the shit he's trudged through. If you were to ask me to put a team together, do you think I'm going to pick someone like you—a college boy who read *Fight Club* one too many times—or someone with practical experience behind him?"

Sanchez eyed Desmond for nearly thirty seconds more. Thirty seconds of pure silence, and when the younger man finally relented and blinked, he stepped away and slowly walked around the circle. "If you want to succeed here in the Bureau, there is one single word I want you to remember: experience. Experience trumps will. Experience trumps training. Experience trumps youth. Experience gets you up the ladder, and lack of experience can get you killed. Whenever you enter a situation, whether that's a gunfight, a burning building, or questioning someone's grandmother, you want to position yourself behind someone with more experience than you. Observe them. Learn from them. And eventually, you will be them—you'll become the person others want to follow."

Walter wanted this to be over, because those who weren't watching Desmond or Sanchez were staring at him. The last thing he wanted was attention. When a woman in FBI Academy sweats came through the door of the gym, spotted Sanchez, and went straight for him, everyone seemed grateful for the opportunity to breathe.

The woman whispered something in Sanchez's ear, and Walter's reprieve ended when Sanchez looked up at him. "O'Brien, you're wanted in the principal's office. Go see Assistant Director Harwood. Hustle now."

53

THE FBI ACADEMY IN Quantico, Virginia, was far more than a campus. It was a miniature version of a military base, a small town. Self-contained and isolated, a patch of civilization surrounded by Virginian wilderness.

The gymnasium was located off Bureau Parkway, and while Walter could have reached the administration building by following hallways, crossing through the training center and various classrooms, he chose to dart out a side door and cut across the lawn to save time. It was just a little after seven in the morning, and the air was crisp and cool. He'd been up since four thirty, first on a run through the obstacle course, then training with his classmates in the gym. He was scheduled for a class on hostage rescue at eight, and he smelled ripe. If he wanted any chance at a shower and change of clothes, this stop would need to be fast, and he didn't want to waste precious minutes walking through lengthy halls (where no running was permitted) when he could cut the distance in half outdoors.

He pushed through the glass doors of the administration building and reached Harwood's office in record time. The director's receptionist was on the phone, and after quickly taking in his sweat-stained clothes, she covered the receiver with one hand and pointed at the door behind her. "They're waiting for you."

They?

Walter stepped past her, swallowed, and knocked on Harwood's door.

"Come in."

Although he'd never met Assistant Director Harwood, Walter had seen him around campus several times. Late forties, trim, with dark hair and glasses that seemed a little too large for his long face. He was standing behind his desk, sleeves rolled up and suit jacket over the back of his chair. "Close the door, O'Brien, take a seat."

There was another man in the room. Short, stocky. All muscle, like a package wrapped up a little too tight in his dark-gray suit. Ex-military, maybe. He didn't look much older than Walter but there was no mistaking the air of authority hovering about him. He was in charge, whether it had been spoken aloud or not.

As Walter eased down into one of the wooden chairs, he glanced at the folders on Harwood's desk. There were several, but the only name he could make out was his own, and that file was on top.

"I apologize for my appearance; I came straight from the gym. Pleasure to finally meet you, sir."

Harwood waved him off. "Let's skip the formalities, shall we? I've got another meeting in twelve minutes, so we don't have a lot of time here." He settled back into his chair, pushed his glasses up the bridge of his nose, and looked down at Walter's file. The other man stood there, making no effort to introduce himself, and Harwood went on. "Eleven years with Detroit PD, five of those in Homicide as a detective. Couple minor scrapes on your record, but looks like you were doing well there, so I gotta ask. Why the FBI? Why are you here? Why now?"

"I needed something different."

Harwood took off his glasses and faced him. "We've all lost partners, coworkers, friends…If you're running from that, you're wasting your time. It will follow you here, too."

"I'm not running from anything."

"How exactly did your old partner, Wesley Brayman, die?"

"That was six years ago and we were only partners for about a week. I was very detailed in my report." Walter nodded at the file. "I believe that's a copy right there. Second page down; I recognize the header."

Without looking down at the pages, Harwood took out the second sheet, turned it around, and slid it across the desk toward Walter. "I'm glad you can read it, because I can't make out much of anything."

At least two-thirds of the text had been redacted. The page was barred with black ribbons over names, places, and pertinent details. Walter knew Brayman's official cause of death had been listed as a pulmonary embolism, a blood clot in his lungs. His pension, death benefits, and life insurance all paid out to a daughter nobody had known he had, living in California.

Two days after the events at the brownstone, Walter had been called into Captain Hazlett's office, and a guy who looked a lot like the stocky man standing to Harwood's right had told him the investigation had been taken over by another authority and he was to cease all related activities. Should he continue, his career would be in jeopardy, he could potentially face charges, and the various companies and agencies who paid out the death benefits to Brayman's daughter might reconsider. Sometimes things slipped through the cracks, but if Brayman's cause of death were to be altered to anything but natural, those things that slipped might be pulled back up through those cracks.

Hazlett had said nothing while this was explained to Walter, and three days later, when Walter visited the medical examiner, Jane Ackerman made it clear she'd been given a similar speech and left things at that. Buncy and Wilson had grown equally quiet, and Walter dropped it at that point. Publicly, anyway.

He did take a trip down to the evidence locker in the basement but was only there long enough to confirm all the related information was now gone, including the evidence box from Alvin Schalk's apartment.

Whoever had been following him (and Walter was certain someone was) on those days vanished soon after. By the time he returned to active duty, events had become more memory than fact, not only for him but for the entire squad. Even the framed photograph of Brayman, much younger and in uniform, disappeared from the break room no more than a week after it went up.

Clean and quiet, history rewrote itself, and Walter let it.

The unknown man who had explained these new facts to Walter in Hazlett's office on that particular day (and who had no doubt visited Ackerman, Buncy, and Wilson, among others) wasn't the same man standing in Harwood's office right now, but they were cut from the same cloth.

The report Walter had originally filed had been nearly nine pages long and included everything he could remember, even the bits about Amy Archer. He'd put it all on paper. At the time, he didn't care who read it, what they thought about it, or what it would mean for his career. He just wanted to get the facts out there. Now someone had reduced his report to the single redacted page in Harwood's possession.

Harwood tapped the paper. "Your report doesn't say how Brayman died. At least, I can't tell from the dozen or so words still readable on it, so why don't you tell me?"

"I'm sorry, sir. I'm not at liberty to say."

Walter had always assumed the gag order came down from the federal level, but if the assistant director of the FBI couldn't get an unredacted copy of the report, how high up did it all go?

Harwood stared at Walter a moment longer, then took another page from the file. "The few black marks on your record are alcohol related. Are you still drinking?"

Walter shook his head. "Not since…Not for five years now."

The stocky man placed a hand on Harwood's shoulder and cleared his throat.

Harwood's gaze lingered on Walter a moment longer, then he straightened up the various pages and placed them back in the folder, stood, and put on his jacket. "I'm going to head to my next meeting. I'll leave the two of you to it."

The stocky man waited for Harwood's door to close and the sound of his voice talking to his secretary to fade and vanish. Then he sat in Harwood's chair and leaned back. "You're an odd one, Walter O'Brien."

The man sounded like a long-term smoker or someone who'd spent his life shouting.

"How so?" Walter replied.

The man reached down into a black satchel at his feet and began taking out file folders of his own, spreading them out on the desk. Folders with names Walter recognized— *Alvin Schalk, Aneta Kostenko,* one marked *J. Doe—Edison,* and *Earl Golston.* "You see things where other people don't, and you're not afraid to chase a ghost, even one that bites."

54

WALTER OPENED HIS MOUTH to speak, then abruptly shut it again as the man began taking drawings out of another folder. Most were burned. All smelled like smoke even from a distance, even after all this time.

"How did you get those? The fire gutted Golston's apartment; I walked it myself. There was nothing left." Walter's gaze shot back to the other man. "The jars of hair, teeth, and fingernails—did you get those, too?"

The man didn't answer, just continued spreading out the drawings. When he finished, he reached back into the satchel and took out Golston's original notebook and the maps Brayman had started marking up and never had time to finish. He placed those on the desk, too. He even had several photographs of the large board that Walter and Brayman had set up in the Homicide bullpen, which had vanished while Walter was still on leave.

Walter looked at all these things and forced his expression to remain blank. Ignored the thumping in his chest.

"I want you to tell me what you know about all this."

Walter thought back to the day in Hazlett's office and the threats made, particularly those involving Brayman's daughter. This could be a trap or a test. Even if it wasn't, if this guy wasn't going to give anything up, why should Walter tell him anything? "Those aren't my cases. Haven't been for a very long time."

"No need for the pretense, O'Brien; you're among friends here. We know you worked these on your own time. Summarize what you found."

They were alone in the room, but the use of *friends* and *we*, plural, wasn't lost on Walter.

"Who are you? How about you show me some identification?"

The man rocked softly in Harwood's chair and turned his gaze to the window as a group of about thirty recruits ran by in tight formation. "I think you know exactly who I am, Walter. I'm the kind of guy who isn't really here. Security has no record of me coming on campus. If anyone were to ask Harwood, he'd promptly tell them he met with you alone. I got a kid back at my office whose sole job is to make me *not here*, and he's damn good at it. I so much as buy a Big Mac in New York, and no more than a minute later, he's got three records to prove it couldn't have been me, 'cause I was in Honolulu at the time, working on my tan. I'm that guy. I'm not here any more than I was in Golston's apartment while it was burning to the ground. I'm not here any more than I was in that whorehouse on Franklin long enough to hear that damn Everly Brothers song play three times while I was trying to get a handle on what was what.

I'm the guy who spent two hours tossing your apartment years ago in Detroit when you first started sniffing around all this, and I'm the same guy who just went through your underwear drawer back in your room at the trainee dorm while you were out running through the woods this morning. I probably know more about you than you do. We can play this in one of two ways. We can spend the next hour going through your fucked-up childhood, talking all about you and how I can either help your career or end it—or we can get down to brass tacks, compare a couple of notes, maybe scratch each other's backs." He leaned forward and tapped Golston's notebook on the corner of Harwood's desk. "I think we both know how important this is. Cracked things wide open. I know that's what really roped me in, got the hairs on my neck standing."

Walter tried not to look at the PI's notebook.

Not wanting to risk damage, Brayman had managed to make a copy before returning the original to Evidence. Walter had plucked that copy from the Crown Vic before Internal Affairs towed the car off. He'd considered taking the maps, too, but figured it best to leave those. He'd been able to re-create them in a few hours. Got much further than that.

When Walter still didn't speak, the man continued. "Okay, you want to play it that way? How about I go first?" He found the oldest file on the desk. "Alvin Schalk, killed by blunt force trauma to the skull. In autopsy it was discovered that his left arm, and only his left arm, had multiple tumors. Not COD, but it would have taken him out eventually. I bet you're curious what his arm looked like under a black light, right? Your ME never ran that particular test. It took a few years before anyone outside my group picked up on that. This was taken shortly after we took possession of the body in '86."

Reaching inside the folder, he removed an eight-by-ten glossy photograph of Schalk's arm. In color, the image was filled with purples, blues, and pinks—enhanced to best show the ultraviolet spectrum. Below the carpus bone was a glowing handprint. It wrapped around his wrist, four small fingers clearly visible. He had another photograph of Schalk's inner wrist, where a thumb could also be seen.

The man placed both these photographs side by side, then moved on to the next folder. "This here is Glenn Beede, thirty-one years old, found naked and very dead in a bed at the Edison Hotel. I believe you still know him as John Doe. You also know they found a similar mark on him. Your ME was kind enough to show that one to you. Mr. Beede wasn't anyone special, but he had an affinity for high-end escorts though not hotels that required a credit card, so when he called for a lady friend, he went downtown and found someplace that took cash. He tried to change things up. That was his only visit to the Edison. Fun fact about Mr. Beede—his last phone call was from a pay phone two blocks from the Edison, to Elite Escorts. I'm sure Brayman would have gotten around to pulling the logs on nearby pay phones, but I don't think he would have found this one; the phone was a little too far away. I'm fairly certain you know who Elite sent over to polish his knob, though."

Although the man didn't look at the sketches on the desk, Walter did. He didn't want to, but he did.

The man reached for another folder. "Of course, you're acquainted with Aneta Kostenko. Former employee of the month at Elite Escorts. We think she saw something she wasn't supposed to, it scared the living piss out of her, and she ran. Whoever she was running from caught up with her at the Corktown Bus Depot—that's where she received her glowing handprint and more fatal diseases than the hospice ward at a nursing home in Boca Raton, Florida. I'll let you in on a little secret—she wasn't running from Sergei Turgenev. On that particular day, he was far from being the scariest person in the room, and that's saying something."

The next folder he pulled was Earl Golston, but rather than open it, he put it aside. "We'll talk about our private investigator friend in a minute. He's got more skin in the game than most, and that one will take a while." He turned back to his bag and shuffled through the contents. "Ah, here we go." He took out a manila folder, unfastened the clasp, and removed another stack of photographs and spread them across the desk on top of all the other information. "Nineteen dead in that brownstone. Nice and neat. Every last one of them dead from some natural cause—embolism, stroke, brain lesion, two heart attacks…Christ, so many I had to make a list just to keep it straight." He waved a hand. "Oh, sure, the ME data lists other CODs, but I think you and I both understand I've got the real scoop. I've got the reports that came before the reports, understand?"

Walter felt himself nod and stopped. He didn't want to give this man anything. The other man's hand had drifted over to a photograph of Brayman lying in that bed, Willow draped over him.

"The point is, whether COD is strictly aneurysms or a mix of the CODs I just mentioned, how do you explain nineteen people dying within minutes of each other, all of natural causes? People who were relatively healthy an hour earlier?"

Walter remained quiet.

"Twenty-three people dead of natural causes just on this table."

He let this hang in the air for a long moment, and when Walter still didn't say anything, he lowered his voice. "I know the thought has occurred to you, probably a few times, but it's one of those things you dismiss, because as a detective, it's not possible so it doesn't make the board, but still, I know you thought it. Hell, it was the first thing I thought of when I saw one of those glowing handprints." His voice dropped even lower. "These people were *infected*. Don't ask me how, I don't have that, but somehow, they were infected with *death*. I've even floated the theory that life was taken from them, *drained*, because that almost makes more sense than the other theories tentatively sticking to the wall." He went back to the victim from the Edison. "Take Glenn Beede here—it's like someone put a straw in him and sucked out all the life. Same with Aneta Kostenko. Your buddy Michael Driscoll, too, can't forget about him. Whatever this is may have moved a little slower in him, but there's no mistaking he caught the same bug. Then you got Earl Golston and all these other people in the brownstone. They all got themselves a little tap." He tapped the side of his forehead with his index finger. "Hurried, but just enough to take them out, might as well have been a bullet to the brain. Like someone quickly cleaning house before they skipped town. Fast and efficient."

The man glanced at his watch and started putting everything back in his satchel. He left Golston's drawings of the girl for last. "I know you've got a thing for her, O'Brien. I know the two of you have history. I'm honestly still not sure whose side of this whole thing you're on, but I can tell you, there *are* sides, and it's in your best interest to be on mine."

"I still don't know who you are."

When Harwood's desk was empty, the man said, "My name is Lincoln Sealey and I'm either your new best friend or your worst enemy." He stood and started for the door. "Do you have a go-bag?"

"If you tossed my room, you know I do. It's part of our training here."

"Get it, and meet me in the field near the east gate in ten minutes. There's something else I want to show you."

BECAUSE FBI AGENTS OFTEN have to leave home for extended periods of time, and are usually given little to no notice when expected to take that leave, all FBI recruits are taught how to properly pack and maintain a go-bag upon arrival at the academy. Walter's was a large black duffel containing five changes of clothing, travel versions of his various toiletries, a microcassette recorder, and a box of ammunition for his 9mm. Although most recruits weren't issued personal weapons until graduation, Walter was permitted to keep his due to his tenure in law enforcement prior to joining the Bureau.

Walter kept his go-bag in the closet next to his roommate's, but when he reentered his room now, he found it sitting on top of his bed. Aside from that, there were no visible signs Sealey had been in the room, but that was enough. Plus, when Walter lifted his mattress, he discovered that his copy of Golston's notebook and the maps and notes he'd compiled over the years were all gone.

He'd worry about that later.

Sealey had only given him ten minutes. He'd lost two of those running back to his dorm in the Madison building across the common from Admin. Walter quickly stripped out of his sweaty clothing, took a four-minute shower, toweled off, dressed, and was out the door with two of his ten minutes remaining. Several shuttles continually circled the Quantico campus, and he managed to board one as it was pulling away from the dorms. Walter watched the seconds tick away as the bus lumbered out onto Bureau Parkway toward the east end of campus, and rather than wait to make the full loop, he got off at Hoover Road and ran the rest of the way across the grass to the east gate.

Walter had expected a car, but as he neared, he remembered Sealey had said the field near the east gate, not the gate itself, and sitting in that field, rotors quickly picking up speed, stood a white-and-blue Bell 206 helicopter, back door open, and Sealey motioning for him to get inside.

"There's an accident on the parkway holding up traffic; this will be faster," Sealey shouted out, handing Walter a pair of headphones before closing the door and tapping the pilot on the shoulder. They were airborne a moment later, swooping over the academy.

Walter's headphones had a microphone, but when he spoke, Sealey didn't appear to hear him. When he saw Sealey's lips move, maybe speaking to the pilot, he realized he was on a different channel. Walter reached for the selector above his head, but when he attempted to adjust the dial, Sealey shook his head and mouthed the words *leave it*.

Less than three minutes later, they touched down at the Marine Corps Air Facility adjacent to the academy.

Before the rotors had a chance to slow, Sealey had the door open and motioned for Walter to follow as he jumped out, hunched down low, and ran toward a small jet parked on the tarmac about fifty feet away, his black satchel thumping against his leg. Duffel in hand, Walter ran after him, up the stairs, and into the plane. It might have been a Gulfstream, Walter wasn't sure, but aside from Sealey and the two pilots up front, it was empty. Sealey dropped into one of the seats and placed his bag at his side. He motioned for Walter to take the seat across from him and told the pilot, "Let's go, we're on a ticking clock here."

The copilot rose from his seat, went to the door, and pressed a button. There was a hydraulic whoosh as the steps retracted into the side of the plane. Then he pulled the door closed and manually engaged the lock, double-checked everything, and returned to the cockpit. A second later they were moving. Less than a minute after that, they were in the air.

"Where are we going?"

He didn't expect Sealey to answer, so he was a bit surprised when the man did.

"Atlanta. Well, just outside Atlanta."

"What about my classes?"

Sealey didn't answer that. Instead, he opened up a small compartment next to the table, revealing a minibar with a wide assortment of beverages and snacks. "Do you want something to drink?"

Walter had had enough of the cloak-and-dagger shit. "I want you to tell me what's going on."

Sealey shrugged, scanned the bottles, and took one out. "I'm gonna have some Scotch."

"I don't drink, remember?"

Sealey rolled his eyes, took out a can of soda, and set it on the table in front of Walter. "Coke and a smile it is."

He unfastened the clasps on his satchel, removed Golston's file and notebook, and placed them on the table. Then he reached back in and removed Walter's copy of Golston's notebook, his personal notes, and the various maps he had marked up over the years. Thumbing through the notebook, Sealey let his finger linger on several of the entries—dates, initials, and cities. "So, how many did you manage to track down?"

Fairly certain Sealey already knew the answer, Walter told him. "Six."

Sealey flipped back through Walter's copied notebook again, slower this time. "Which six? You didn't mark them."

"No, I didn't."

Sealey pursed his lips and placed his palm on top of the pages. "Well, considering what you had to work with, I suppose six in five years isn't bad. I know about Lou Morter in Tampa. I had you followed when you flew down there a couple years back. Jim Malerman, too. In Austin. We already had George Grendal in '48. Who were the others?"

Walter still said nothing.

Sealey sighed, took a drink of his Scotch, and looked out the window at the white clouds below them as they continued to climb. "If you're not willing to help, I might as well let you out right here."

Walter felt his ears pop from the altitude, stuffed a finger in one, and tried to open it back up, but it did little good. He settled back in the seat. "How many did you find?"

Sealey set his glass back down on the table and gave it a quarter turn. "A good number of the local law enforcement offices are computerized now, but the data is a mess. Nobody is using the same software. There are about a half dozen systems available off the shelf and who knows how many proprietary databases in use. The FBI is working to try and tie it all together, bring it all into NCIS or something like it, but we're still a few years away from that. Those aside, you've got all the smaller municipalities who just can't afford to computerize and are still working with paper. Then there are the outfits somewhere in the middle—they have a computer system, but they're still keying everything in. That could go on for years. We've developed flags. Based on the locations in this notebook, the dates and initials, we've got people searching all those databases as they come online, matching things up. Between NCIS and several other federal databases, my team has managed to track down twenty-three, and we're close on at least nine more. All dead by natural causes, which doesn't make things any easier since we have to search hospital and coroner records, too."

"There's a hundred and forty-nine entries."

Sealey nodded. "Yeah. Spanning almost fifty years and hitting nearly every state in the union. You saw it with your maps—back and forth across the country. Hits one coast, heads back, then reverses again. Just back and forth, back and forth." He waved his arm around to illustrate, then took another drink of his Scotch. "Here's the thing, though. The more names we figure out, the less important I think identifying them all might be. Whether I've got a real name or not, I know each entry represents the same thing— a dead man between the ages of twenty and forty—found dead of natural causes under unusual circumstances. We've got her trail either way."

As he said *her*, he tapped one of the sketches in the note-book, traced the girl's dark hair with his fingertip.

"All male?"

Sealey rolled his hand. "In the notebook, yeah, but we've found a handful of female vics throughout the years. Motive seems to be different, though. They seem to be women who got in her way, like your bus depot vic, Aneta Kostenko—we think she saw something she shouldn't have and your girl shut her down quick and dirty."

"My girl?" Walter said softly. "Amy Archer wasn't alive for most of the entries in Golston's notes. He was chasing something, but it wasn't her."

"I'm not so sure. This is bigger than that. This is bigger than just her." Sealey finished off his Scotch and poured another. "Could be a family, like a string of women related by blood. Mothers, daughters, sisters…Amy Archer isn't even your little girlfriend's real name."

This last bit felt like a punch to Walter's gut. "What?"

A glimmer entered the corner of Sealey's eye. "All these years, all the pseudonyms, and still you actually believe she told you her real name? Maybe I put more faith in you than you deserve, O'Brien."

Sealey reached back into his satchel, took out a pad, and placed it on the table between them. Several names were written on the first page. "The first name we have on record, the one with George Grendal, was Jane Toppan, right?"

Walter nodded.

"Well, Jane Toppan is the alias of a woman named Honora Kelley, born in 1854. She was arrested in 1901 and confessed to thirty-one murders. Get this: she told the cops who brought her in that her goal was 'to have killed more people—helpless people—than any other man or woman who ever lived.' She was a prize, that one. The name your girl initially gave you—Amy Archer—that's one pulled from the history books, too. The real Amy Archer, better known as Amy Duggan 'Sister' Archer-Gilligan, killed five people that we know of, probably more, between 1910 and 1917 in Connecticut. Nursing home fraud. Then we got the name your girl gave to Michael Driscoll."

"Amelia Dyer."

"Yeah, Amelia Dyer. Another winner. They've pinned three to four hundred murders on the real Amelia Dyer over in the UK between 1880 and 1896. Kids, mostly. She'd adopt them for money from wealthy families of daughters with 'accidents,' then she'd kill the kids after she got paid and dispose of the bodies. Fucking monster, but she had a good racket going. Made her a rich woman. Bought her a good defense at trial, but not good enough—they still hanged her."

Sealey turned the list around so he could read it. "Let's see, who else we got? What was the name she gave you during your play-date at that Italian place?"

"Velma Barfield."

"From Dubuque, Iowa, right?"

Walter nodded.

"Well, that's not quite right. Iowa, I mean. The real Velma Barfield was born Margie Velma Bullard in South Carolina back in 1932, executed by lethal injection in 1978 with six murders behind her. Married into the Barfield name." He met Walter's gaze. "The point is, she played you. Every name she gave you was bogus. I think she picked the names of female serial killers throughout history as some private joke. Maybe she wanted to see if you'd catch on, who knows. Not just you, though; that's my point here. Golston has records dating back to 1948, and I don't think that was the start of it. He stumbled into the middle somewhere, just like you, like me. Who knows when this really started. I think what we're dealing with here is a long line of female serial killers, black widows, all related somehow, operating together like a cult. Like a mother who passes the bug on to her daughter…multiple generations. Golston followed them most of his adult life, got obsessed. Tracked them to your doorstep. That's why his last entry has your initials, then they killed him. I'm guessing he arranged a meet at the Four Seasons, and they took him out. That's why his death is staged to look more accidental. I think they wanted to cover that one up."

Walter slumped back in his seat and thought about all this. It was a lot to take in. "Black widows are usually motivated by money, right? Did you find—"

Sealey cut him off. "Nope. If they're stealing from their vics, we haven't found proof. That doesn't mean we won't, but we haven't yet. But there's a distinct pattern here, and we're on it."

"How do you explain the other things we found in Golston's apartment?"

"The hair, nails, and teeth? All the salt?"

Walter nodded.

"No clue. But we'll figure it out," he told him. "They're like that bottle of wine you found in Golston's room at the Four Seasons with the needle marks."

"Opus One," Walter remembered. "It came back from the lab negative for poison. We never figured out what he injected."

"Our lab found low levels of something called oxenberry."

A puzzled look filled Walter's face. "What the hell is oxenberry?"

"It's a berry that grows in Asia. Might give you the shits but not lethal. We never could figure out why he went through the trouble. Someday we'll tick that box, but not today." Sealey looked at his watch, took his black satchel from the seat beside him, and placed it on the table. "Pick through what you want. I don't have any secrets from you. The sooner you understand that, the better for both of us. We've got a few more hours, and I need to get some shut-eye. I suggest you do, too. We're gonna hit the ground running."

With that, Sealey pulled down the window's plastic shade, leaned back, and closed his eyes.

No way Walter was going to sleep. He started pulling everything out of the bag before Sealey changed his mind.

BY THE TIME LINCOLN SEALEY'S eyes opened again, Walter had picked through every scrap of paper in the man's bag, memorized what he could, took notes (which he carefully hid away in his pockets) on the rest, and put everything back where he'd found it. He didn't want to give Sealey the satisfaction of knowing which items drew Walter's focus (particularly which ones were new to him) and which didn't. The only item still on the table was the notepad with the various aliases. Aside from Amy Archer, Jane Toppan, Amelia Dyer, and Velma Barfield, the list also contained the names Gesche Gottfried, Nannie Doss, Myra Hindley, Leonarda Cianciulli, Dagmar Overbye, and nearly two dozen others. But Walter couldn't help but think of her as Amy Archer.

The plane had started its descent, Walter felt it in his gut.

Sealey licked his dry lips and pulled himself back up into a sitting position. "I'm guessing you didn't get any sleep?"

"Not a chance. My brain is running on overdrive right now." Walter had found a coffee maker near the back of the plane and was on his second pot. That probably hadn't helped. "How many do you think are involved here?"

"Victims?"

"No, killers."

Sealey shrugged. "Best guess? One for every five years we have on record, so at least ten but most likely more. Golston had the most complete record, but like I said, this machine was in motion well before he stumbled into it. I wouldn't be surprised to learn they were operating ten, even twenty years before he found them in '48. Their motive is the key to this whole thing. We figure out why they're doing it, then we can get in front of them."

The plane lurched as the wheels made contact with the pavement.

Before they stopped moving, Sealey was on his feet and working the controls at the door. "Grab my bag, let's go."

Walter slid the notepad back into Sealey's satchel, threw his own bag over his shoulder, and followed him through the door and down the steps to a black Suburban parked on the tarmac. They scrambled into the rear seat and pulled the doors shut.

"Is this Hartsfield?"

Sealey shook his head. "Dobbins in Marietta about sixteen miles northwest of Atlanta. I try to avoid civilian airports whenever possible." He tapped the driver on the shoulder. "Go."

They sped off through a series of access roads, through two gates, onto Cobb Parkway. A few minutes later they were on 75 heading north running at least thirty miles per hour over the posted limit. Walter hadn't noticed any markings on the Suburban, nor were there lights on top, but nobody pulled them over as the driver expertly weaved through the traffic for nearly an hour before leaving the interstate for a quiet exit near some town Walter had never heard of called Cuman. They passed an abandoned gas station, several overgrown farms, and a rusted-out pickup truck with a maple tree growing through the center, surrounded by tall grass. The driver took several more turns before they left the pavement for a gravel road that became a dirt road about two miles in.

A sickening feeling began to swell in Walter's gut. They hadn't seen another vehicle in nearly twenty minutes. Sealey could very well be driving him to his final resting place—a bullet to the back of the head out here and he'd never be found. Aside from Harwood, there was no record of him leaving Quantico. Certainly no record of travel to Georgia. He instinctively tightened the muscles around his shoulder and felt his 9mm in the holster under his arm. If Sealey was armed, Walter hadn't spotted a weapon.

The Suburban bounced as the wheels dipped down into a rut. The driver slowed, rounded several holes, then began to pick up speed again. Branches from the encroaching trees scraped against their ceiling and thumped along the sides.

"Where exactly…"

Before Walter could get the sentence out, they topped a hill and came down the other side, where a large field carved out an open space in the heavy woods. At least a dozen vehicles came into view with forty or fifty people bustling about. Most were wearing FBI windbreakers, while some were in sweat-drenched T-shirts wielding shovels. A mobile trailer, several large tents, and white canopies had been set up, and the first thought that entered Walter's head was that this was some type of archaeological dig.

The black body bags strewn about told a different story.

"Oh, my God."

Sealey cleared his throat. "We've been calling it the Garden."

57

THEY PARKED NEXT TO the trailer and got out of the Suburban in silence, rounding the front to get a better look.

Walter opened his mouth to speak, but nothing came out except a soft gasp.

Some of the black bags clearly contained bodies; others looked empty but were near recently dug holes or next to one of the dozens and dozens of small yellow flags that sprouted from the earth. More than Walter could count. Multiple generators buzzed nearby.

Sealey said, "The first body was discovered completely by accident. It had rained for three straight days, and this place had turned into a giant mud pit. Some kids had come out here to screw around on their four-wheelers. One of them spotted a shoe—a black, red, and white leather limited-edition Air Jordan from Nike. I don't know shit about shoes, but apparently kids pay upward of a couple hundred for these, and this particular kid knew exactly what they cost, so he got off his ride to get a better look, then probably wished he hadn't. Somebody's foot was still in the shoe, but the rest of that person's leg had failed to join the party. The local sheriff found the body about twenty feet away, partially dug up by some animal. He got a crew out here to excavate, and a member of his team walked off about a hundred yards to take a piss back by the tree line over there and saw what looked like a mound of displaced dirt, possibly another fresh grave. The sheriff broke his team in half and got digging over there, too. That's where they found body number two."

Sealey wiped his nose and gestured back in the direction they'd come from. "Those farms we passed on the way in, years back a couple of the farmers got together and bought a GPR. Do you know what that is?"

Walter shook his head.

"Ground-penetrating radar. They hoped to use it to map out some of the terrain, get a better handle on where the water was coming from and maybe get it under control. That plan went to shit when the money ran out, but the sheriff remembered they had it and sent a deputy out to borrow the machine. So they got the GPR out here, and anytime they found a disturbance, anything that looked like a possible grave, they planted one of those yellow flags. When the sheriff was on his third box of flags, he called in the staties, and when they opened up the fifth box of flags, the state police called the feds. By the time we got out here, this entire field was covered in those little yellow flags like the devil's daisies. I don't know who called it the Garden first, but the name stuck. Follow me…"

Sealey led Walter around the side of the trailer to the large white tent and held the flap open.

A rush of cool air floated over him as Walter stepped inside. One or more of the generators must have been running air-conditioning units, but the circulation they provided wasn't enough to mask the familiar scent of death. The space was thick with it.

Five bodies on stainless steel gurneys surrounded by bright halogen lighting rigs stood on the left. Four doctors in masks and scrubs appeared to be in various stages of autopsy. Several people looked up as they entered. The others went on with their work. They all looked exhausted. On the right, stacked in neat rows, were dozens of body bags like the ones outside.

"How many?"

"We've been moving them to a local hospital post autopsy, but between those, the ones in here, and the ones still out in that field, we've got sixty-three at last count. Like you saw, though, we're still digging. There's more. Best guess is close to eighty by the time we get the last one out of the ground."

"Eighty?"

Sealey nodded. "Most are nothing but skeletons, but some, like the one wearing the Nikes, are fresh. The few we've found with tissue to work with were diseased. Various cancers, mostly, but we got a couple fatal blood clots, even three heart attacks, and I use that term loosely because the last heart one of the docs showed me looked like it exploded in the chest cavity."

Walter was staring at the body bags. "Have you IDed any of them?"

"That's the million-dollar question that led me to you," Sealey said. "We're taking dental casts to compare to missing persons, but that's all gonna take some time. They're all missing their first metacarpals, between the first and second knuckle. Sound familiar?"

"Like the guy from the Edison, Glenn Beede, and Aneta Kostenko from Corktown."

"Don't forget the two in Alvin Schalk's freezer," Sealey reminded him. "We haven't found any females out here yet, all males. That tells us something."

Sealey gave a moment for all this to sink in, then turned and started back toward the door. "I can't take the smell of this place, reminds me of failure. There's something else I want to show you."

Walter followed him back out and over to the trailer, up a ramp and inside.

58

THE TRAILER WAS A mobile command center. On the way in, Walter caught a glimpse of the trailer's license plate and noted that it hadn't been issued by a state, but simply said *Federal* across the top.

Inside, Sealey tossed his black satchel onto the folding chair behind a cluttered desk. He scooped up several McDonald's bags and sandwich wrappers from a table in the middle of the room, balled them up, and threw them into an overflowing trash can near the door. "I'm gone for a day, and the kids leave the house in complete disarray. Do you want some coffee?"

"I'm good."

He shrugged and went over to a coffee machine in the corner, filled the tank with several bottles of water, dumped some grounds in the top from an open can, and hit the Brew button.

Walter caught this from the corner of his eye as he

stepped up to a topography map on the wall surrounded by dozens of sketches and photographs—images he'd memorized over the years. The map looked like a blowup from something much smaller. The lines and details were blurry, not meant to be this size, barely readable.

"Not a lot of maps available for Jerkwater, Georgia. That's the best we could get on short notice. It's from some local farmer's almanac," Sealey explained, stepping up beside him. He traced the outer edges with the tip of his finger. "We came in right here; this is the path we followed. We've done a preliminary search of the surrounding woods but didn't find anything out there. All the bodies seem to be in this open field. The yellow thumbtacks match all the remaining flags. Red means we already dug and found a body." He shook a box of blue tacks on a table next to the map. "These are for the false positives. Haven't opened it yet, because so far we *have* found a body in every hole identified by GPR."

Walter flicked a small piece of paper under one of the red tacks. It read: *M-1906 7'.* "What does this mean?"

"Male, found seven feet down. Approximate year of origin based on depth."

"Nineteen oh six? Is that possible?" Walter was still going through the notes under the thumbtacks. "This one says 1841."

Sealey nodded. "I wanted you to see this before I told you, didn't make sense to go into all of it on the plane. The oldest one we've got here appears to be from the 1720s. This group, whoever they are, has been actively dumping bodies out here for more than two hundred years."

He'd gotten tired of waiting for the coffeepot to fill up, and was now holding a mug under the thin stream. "This is the perfect dumping ground. This entire field floods every year, turns into a swamp for about three months. It's low land, so the water eats away at the surrounding dirt, encroaches on the tree line. Throw a body out there when it's wet, weigh it down, and Mother Nature does the heavy lifting, buries it for you. Every year when things dry out, there's a little more dirt on top. Between that and the local wildlife treating the place like a buffet, it's a wonder any of these bodies turned up. Without that hard rain, without those kids, we wouldn't be standing here right now."

As he said this last part, he gestured at the images on the wall surrounding the map. Blowups of the drawings and sketches from Golston's notebook. There were also images captured from the surveillance system at the Four Seasons of the girl who looked a lot like Amy Archer, but wasn't quite her, coming and going. Although they were still blurry, these had been enhanced since Walter had last seen them. Sealey clearly had better tech than Detroit PD. There were also surveillance shots taken outside the brownstone on Franklin, most likely from Buncy and Wilson. Each photograph or sketch was tagged with a date. There were several police sketches, too. Walter had never seen those before.

"The dates on the surveillance images are exact. With Golston's drawings, I had to use the surrounding notes and make an educated guess. There's a clear family resemblance between all of them. You see that, right?"

Walter did, and he nodded, but none of them looked like Amy Archer, either. Not exactly. Even the ones at the brownstone only seemed to have a passing resemblance.

"Here's what I don't get," Sealey said. "Golston was a good artist, damn good. I couldn't draw a person like this to save my life. So, if he were drawing the same person,

I've got no doubt they'd look the same. These subtle differences aren't the result of an unskilled hand unable to capture his subject; it's the opposite—he's skilled to the point where he *can* isolate those subtle differences. Understand?"

"Backs up your theory that he followed multiple women over the years, all with a look similar enough to be family."

Sealey nodded. "What I don't get is the age thing."

"The age thing?"

"Every girl here looks like she's maybe early to mid-twenties. Golston followed them for well over forty years. Why no drawings of the mothers or daughters? What about boys? One of them must have had a son at some point. Yet Golston's focus was always on the girls, and only for this narrow age range. It's like they hold one of them at a time as the public face of the group, then when she reaches a certain age she goes reclusive and someone else takes over? Mothers passing on the bug to their daughters, like I told you on the plane."

Walter was standing in front of the last photograph. A grainy black-and-white of Amy Archer leaving the brownstone. He recognized the dress and knew the picture had been taken moments before she hailed a taxi, moments before he went chasing after her, he was certain of that, but it didn't look like her. The shadows didn't help—the whole image was marred in them. "I never saw her again after this night. Not after she disappeared from that restaurant."

"You'd recognize her, though, right?"

"Yeah. Of course."

"That's important. More so than you might realize, because as far as I know, you're the only person still alive who has had contact with her and can make that claim." As he said this, Sealey's eyes drifted back to the map, all those colorful tacks.

She wouldn't hurt me.

The thought popped into his head, and Walter didn't want it to be there. He didn't want to think of Amy that way. He felt Sealey's hand on his shoulder.

"Come with me. There's one other reason I brought you here."

59

SEALEY LED WALTER DOWN a worn path through the dirt, around a tent filled with crates and supplies, and past a group of people huddled together studying what looked like an old alarm clock covered in rust and dirt.

As they rounded the corner, another tent came into view and two men in army fatigues holding AR-15s straightened up. One was a Black kid, no more than nineteen. The other man was about ten years older, with short reddish blond hair that had begun an aggressive retreat on his freckled, pale scalp.

"Sir," they both said in unison, pulling their guns in tight against their chests and moving to either side of the tent's closed flap.

"Gentlemen." Sealey tugged the flap open and motioned for Walter to step inside first.

Two more soldiers were stationed at the interior, and Walter noticed the barrels of their rifles tick in his direction until they spotted Sealey coming in behind him. Then they stepped aside like the others.

The tent seemed larger on the inside than Walter had expected, at least thirty feet square. Near the center, three more soldiers were busy assembling what looked like a large cage, complete with barred floor and ceiling, a metal box about seven or eight feet on each side. In the center of that nearly complete cage, a small person sat on a metal folding chair, hands and ankles cuffed to the metal frame and a black bag over their head, drooping loosely over their shoulders.

An oily substance dripped from the cuffs.

"What is that?" Walter asked.

"Oxenberry. I mentioned it on the plane. We've been … testing it."

"Testing how?"

"Never mind that." Sealey stepped inside and reached for the black bag. "You're the only one to ever get a good look at her. That's why you're here." He pulled the bag off the handcuffed prisoner's head and held it at his side.

The girl's head jerked from side to side. Gray eyes—dark and frightened—darted up and quickly scanned the room, taking in everything, taking all of them in, before glimpsing Sealey and settling on Walter, dropping into place as if that's where they belonged—her eyes on him, his eyes on her.

There was a piece of tape over her mouth and, judging by the puffiness of her cheeks, something beneath. Most likely a piece of cloth. She was wearing white canvas tennis shoes, no socks, a pair of jean shorts, and a white tank top—all filthy, as if she'd been dragged through the dirt. Her hair was pulled back in a ponytail. Several loose strands fell across her forehead and the sides of her face.

Sealey tapped his foot, a single impatient thump. "Well, is this her?"

Walter felt a hard thump in his chest. "No."

The word dropped from Walter's mouth before he gave it a second thought. As if placed there, trapped, and wanting to get out.

And it isn't her, is it?

This girl was too young.

But, damn, she does look like Amy. Could easily be her little sister.

Amy Archer had been in her early twenties the first time they met, and that was eleven years ago. That put her in her late twenties when he last saw her sitting across from him at Giovanni's. This girl was maybe nineteen, and that was being generous. There was a strong resemblance—the eyes in particular—no denying that, but it wasn't her.

Sealey's face filled with frustration. "Are you sure?"

Walter forced his mind to go back, pictured her sitting there across the table, smiling at him, her ankle rubbing against his.

My name is Velma, Henry. Velma Barfield. And we're on our first date.

That wasn't true, though. Velma Barfield was a killer—tried, convicted, and sentenced to death. And he wasn't *Henry*. And the Velma Barfield who sat across from him at Giovanni's, that girl from Iowa, didn't quite resemble Amy Archer, and neither of them was the girl tied to this chair.

She tried to lean away from Sealey, those gray eyes pleading with Walter to set her free. To help her. This girl, whoever she was, was terrified.

"Can't be her."

"That's not the same thing. *Is this her?*"

"No."

"Are you sure?" Sealey repeated.

Walter felt his head nod, and let it.

"There's a resemblance, though, right? Like we discussed? Family?"

Behind the tape, her mouth twitched and she grunted, jerking her hands, ankles, and torso in a violent shudder. The chair wobbled, threatening to topple, but remained upright. The metal cuffs clattered but didn't give. She tried again anyway, then a third time. Her eyes never left Walter's, as if to say, *I'm here because of you, and only you can get me out.*

One of the soldiers raised the barrel of his rifle slightly, enough to get her attention, and she stopped.

Please, help me.

"You need to let her go. This isn't right."

"She's not going anywhere."

There was a filthy metal bucket on the floor beside her. Walter didn't want to think about what that bucket was for. Several empty water bottles littered the ground.

Two of the soldiers maneuvered the cage roof into place and began tightening the bolts—one every six inches.

Walter's head filled with so many thoughts, they became a jumbled mess.

All the graves.

The bodies.

The dead in Detroit.

Alvin Schalk.

Wes Brayman.

The sketches—her but not her.

If you get me out, I'll tell you everything.

This thought screamed louder than all the others in a voice that was not his own, and he turned back to her.

She was no longer looking at him but at the ground, tears streaming down her face.

He forced himself to turn away and back to Sealey. "What makes you think this girl is part of all this?"

"I'll show you."

60

SEALEY LED WALTER AROUND to the other side of the clearing, to a smaller tent set up near the dirt road they'd followed driving in here. Inside, the air was stifling, fueled by four pairs of large halogen floodlights mounted on portable rigs surrounding a muddy, rusty Toyota Camry. The trunk and hood were both open. So were all four doors. The car was resting on risers that held it about eighteen inches above the ground. Plywood was spread out beneath, covered in small tracks from something Walter had once been told was called a creeper.

As he stepped closer, he realized some of the mess on the car came from fingerprint powder, but it was still in bad shape, a couple of oil changes away from the junkyard.

Sealey gave the dented hood a tap. "She was pulled over last night for speeding in this beater, about four miles from here, heading back toward Atlanta, we think. Tire treads match samples taken here. We sent some of the mud from the wheel wells back to the lab—I'm confident we'll prove it originated here, too. The car is registered to a man named Barney Simpers. He's an orderly at a retirement home in Mableton, just west of Atlanta. He's been missing for three days. Called in sick the first day, then nothing after that."

Stepping around the Camry, Sealey led Walter to the trunk and pointed to rust-colored stains in the carpet to the left of the bald spare. "Luminol confirmed that's dried blood. I'm pretty sure it's gonna match Barney."

"No body?"

"We haven't found him yet, no. But I'm confident he's out there." He gestured at the wall of the tent, in the general direction of the Garden. "We're focusing our search on a marshy part toward the back right now—beyond the tree line, far from where we've been working. That's her most likely dump spot. I'm guessing she spotted us and didn't want to risk getting closer. This piece of shit wouldn't have made it any further without getting stuck. Found a drag trail there, about the width of a grown man, that disappears off into the mud. We think she parked and hauled him the rest of the way. About two hundred meters."

"That girl weighs a buck nothing. No way she dragged a grown male six hundred feet."

Sealey gave Walter a tired look that said he knew well how hard it was to move a dead body; he'd probably moved his share over the years. "It's also possible she walked him out there and killed him when they reached the other side, but that wouldn't explain the drag marks."

"Without a body, you've got nothing."

"We got a lot of circumstantial, I'll give you that." He sighed. "But it's solid circumstantial. For starters, she told us her name was Mary Clement. The name's bogus. The real Mary Clement died in 1944 after being convicted of attempting to poison her sister's family in Rose Hill, Illinois. Did a year in Joliet for that one. Cut her teeth by killing her parents and two other sisters when she was just a kid back in Dubuque, Iowa."

When Amy Archer pretended her name was Velma Barfield on their "date," she said she was from Dubuque, Iowa.

"On top of that, the retirement home where Barney Simpers worked reported sixteen deaths in the past five months. All men. All natural causes. The girl in the other tent, 'Mary Clement,' worked there, too."

"It's a retirement home. People die," Walter reasoned.

"It's been triple their norm since she started there."

"You can't charge her for someone dying of natural causes in her presence. None of this means anything."

Sealey frowned. "Whose side are you on exactly?"

"I'm just playing devil's advocate. You know none of this will stick if you run it by a judge. You won't even get an indictment."

"It sticks if the blood in the car comes back as Barney Simpers's, or if we find his body out there somewhere." Sealey ticked off several more points on his fingers. "Her prints aren't in the system. She's got a fake driver's license. The retirement home has a fake résumé on file. Her nursing license is bullshit. It's all quality paper, can't fault them for buying it, but none of it is real. We have no idea who or what she is, but this is all clearly tied together. She knows how all those bodies got out there, and she can tell us what happened in Detroit."

"So you're gonna keep her chained to a chair in a cage until you can figure it out?"

Sealey didn't reply to that, but the look on his face told Walter that was exactly what he planned to do.

There was a lot more to this. The man was clearly holding back.

"Let me talk to her."

CHAPTER

61

"I'D LIKE ALL OF you to step outside," Walter told the guards as he reentered her tent.

The hood was back on. Beneath it, the girl's head bobbed up at the sound of his voice. She shuffled slightly in the chair and sat upright.

The soldiers had rotated—the Black kid and the one with red hair were now inside the tent. The other two had taken their positions outside. Work on the cage was nearly complete—one soldier was working a screwdriver on the final wall; another was testing the locking mechanism on the heavy door.

"We're under orders to keep eyes on her at all times, sir," the soldier with the red hair told Walter. When he spoke, his grip tightened on his AR-15. His finger played over the trigger guard.

"Sealey okayed this. Ask him if you want."

Redhead nodded. "Give me a moment."

As the soldier pressed the Transmit button on a radio fixed to his shoulder and spoke softly into the microphone, Walter pulled the girl's hood off and dropped it to the ground beside her chair.

She blinked several times, adjusted to the light, then studied Walter and the others in the room.

One of the straps from her tank top had fallen from her shoulder, and Walter slipped it back into place. He expected her to shy away from him, but instead she pressed against his palm and nuzzled closer for a brief second before Walter pulled away, conscious of the Black soldier watching.

The redheaded soldier released his radio and made a circle gesture in the air with his finger. "Everyone outside, we're taking five."

"I gotta hit the head anyway," the soldier with the screwdriver said, pocketing the tool and starting for the door, the other soldier on his heels.

The Black soldier didn't move, still looking down at the girl, lost in a reverie.

"Thompson, quit daydreaming. Out."

When he still didn't move, the redhead punched him lightly in the shoulder. "Now, Romeo."

The kid's eyes blinked back to life. He frowned for a moment, as if unsure of where he was, then turned slowly on his heels and shuffled out.

The redhead stepped up to Walter. "She stays in that chair. Cuffs on. Understand?"

Walter nodded. When they were alone, he knelt down beside her, peeled the tape from her mouth, and removed the gag.

She looked directly at him, pleading. "They're gonna kill me!"

"Nobody is going to hurt you. I won't let them." Walter tried to assure her, but he knew it was an empty promise. "Tell me about Barney Simpers."

"I don't know who that is." She tugged at her chains. The handcuffs, dripping in that oily substance, clanked against the chair. "Do you have a key for these?"

"They found you driving his car."

This seemed to confuse her. "What car? I was hitchhiking on 75, working my way to Chattanooga to see my cousin. This white van stopped—I thought they were gonna give me a ride—and when I tried to get inside, the back door opened and three guys jumped out and grabbed me. They threw me in the back, tied me up, and brought me here. You need to help me, call the police, find help, *real help*," she begged. "These guys are gonna kill me. That man you were talking to…Seaton…Sarley…"

"Sealey."

"Sealey. He said when they were done with me I'd end up out there in the mud with all the others. He said nobody's looking for me—he made a point of telling me that—then he…he grabbed me…my…he told me how much fun we were all gonna have. You gotta get me out of here!"

"These are federal agents. FBI. Nobody is going to hurt you."

She smirked. "These people aren't FBI. They kidnapped me, and they're *lying* to you. Why would the FBI be working with people dressed up like soldiers? Why are they building a fucking cage? You need to get me out of here. Have you even seen a badge? Do you seriously think they're FBI just because they've got a couple windbreakers and T-shirts that say so? If you don't believe me, call someone, check them out." Her voice dropped lower, and her gray eyes filled with tears. "Who are you, exactly? How did they get you here? Do you have a car? What did they tell you? I don't know what's going on, but it's not what it looks like. For all we know, *they're* responsible for all those bodies out there."

"Do you work at a retirement home with Barry Simpers?"

She frowned. "A what? No. I'm a student at the University of Florida down in Gainesville. My last job was in a coffee shop near campus. Like I said, I was just hitching my way north to see my cousin when these psychopaths grabbed me."

"How old are you?"

"Nineteen."

"Who is Amy Archer to you?"

"Who?"

"Amy Archer. Jane Toppan. Amelia Dyer. Velma Barfield. What do those names mean to you? I know you know what I'm talking about, so cut the bullshit."

"I'm telling you the truth!" She tugged her arms up, pulled the handcuff chains tight. "Get these off of me."

Walter studied her eyes, facial expressions, body language, looking for any sign of deception, and found none. He wanted to believe her even as a twinge in his gut told him not to.

"What's your name?"

She opened her mouth to speak but couldn't hold it together anymore. She began to sob. "I don't want to die here! Not like this! Please, not like this!"

She seemed to fold up in the chair, shrink into a small ball.

Behind him, a throat cleared.

Walter looked back and found Sealey at the mouth of

the tent. Sealey bobbed his head toward the outside. The soldiers filed back into the tent in silence, none of them willing to look at the hysterical girl chained to a chair.

No one but the young Black kid. She was all he could look at.

62

FOLLOWING SEALEY THROUGH the tent flap, Walter realized he had completely lost track of time. Although the air was still hot and muggy, the sun was gone. Halogen lamps on large towers buzzed around the outer edge of the clearing, casting a yellow glow over everything. Insects swarmed each of them like dark clouds.

The guards eyed Walter but said nothing.

Sealey slowly paced off to the side, a portable phone held loosely in his hand. When he glanced up, a large mosquito buzzed by his face. He swatted at it, frowned, and faced Walter. "She's good, I'll give her that, but don't let her bullshit you."

Walter gestured at the phone. "Can I use that?"

"Sure." Sealey handed it to him. "Have you seen one before? It's a satellite phone. Can make a call from anywhere as long as you've got a clear shot to the sky. Damnedest thing. Just dial and press that button marked Send. It'll take a minute to connect."

The phone was heavier than Walter expected, bulky. He keyed in the number for the FBI Academy's main switchboard from memory, pressed Send, and lifted the phone to his ear, his eyes never leaving Sealey. When about thirty seconds went by with nothing, he looked at the display— the red numbers had vanished. "It's not working."

Sealey took the phone and studied the blank digital screen for a moment. "Shit, battery's dead again. I only get a few hours of talk time between charges. Feels like I'm always plugging the thing in. I've got another in the Suburban—you can use that one."

He expected Sealey to ask him whom he wanted to call, but the man didn't pry. Part of Walter hoped he would. That would have made this next part a little easier. "You haven't shown me a badge. Nothing since we left Quantico."

"A badge? Seriously? I picked you up from a secure facility—from your supervisor's office—brought you here on federal transport. You're surrounded by federal agents, and you want to see my badge?"

Walter nodded. "I want to know who exactly you are and who you're working for. If you can't provide that, I'm taking that girl out of here until I can get a better handle on all this."

Sealey whistled. "Damn, *she is good*. A couple of minutes, and she's got you wound around her cute little finger like a lap dog. Don't feel bad, she seems to have that effect on everyone. That's why we keep rotating the guards."

"This doesn't feel right."

"Well, I think we can agree on that much," he agreed. "Don't let her cloud your head. We need to focus on why you're here. *Is that her?* Is that the girl you've been chasing on your downtime?"

"Why do you keep asking me that? I told you it wasn't. She's too young. Sister, maybe. She said she was going to visit her cousin, so maybe that's it—some cousin of Amy Archer— a relative of some kind, like you said. *Or she just looks a hell of a lot like her, and you've got the wrong girl.*"

Even as Walter said this, he wasn't sure if he was trying to convince Sealey or himself.

"Well, that's a narrative I know you've been accused of once or twice. Were *you* wrong all those times?"

Walter opened his mouth to speak but said nothing.

Sealey kicked at the dirt. "Look, I brought you here to ID her. But I think we both know that IDing her is only about half of why you're really here. This is a very…unique and delicate…situation. If we're dealing with some family cult working together, she can tell us who they all are, where they're operating out of—why we've got a field of bodies out here planted in the mud. She's a door, a way in."

"Or you've got the wrong person chained to a chair."

"Given the circumstances under which we picked her up, I've got *zero* doubt about what landed her here."

"You've got her pissing in a bucket. When she gets an attorney, they'll have a field day with all this."

"This is all temporary. We're transporting her back to Atlanta in the morning."

That's bullshit. If it's true, why the cage?

"Why not tonight? Why hold her here instead of the state police barracks or the local sheriff's office? There's got to be something better nearby."

"They're not equipped. I've got an armored transport coming in the morning."

"For her?"

"For her," Sealey said flatly.

"What aren't you telling me?"

Sealey fell silent for a long moment. When he finally spoke, he kept his voice low so no one else could hear. "Her operating as part of a group. One of many makes sense. It explains everything. I know it clears things up for you, too. Years of questions bouncing around in that head of yours. Ties things up with a neat little bow. But it doesn't feel right." He went quiet for another beat, then added, "I brought you here for a very specific reason. One that scares the shit out of me."

"What exactly is that?"

"To determine if you've been right. Confirm what you thought all along," Sealey said flatly. "What if all of this is…her. Only her. All these years, somehow, the same woman."

A sharp gunshot cracked from inside the tent.

Two more after that.

Weapons raised, the two guards rushed back through the flap, followed by Sealey and Walter. Sealey produced a small .380 from an ankle holster. Walter's 9mm was out and in his hand in a single fluid motion that came to him as instinctively as breathing. He ducked through the opening, low, ready to roll, and quickly took in what was happening.

The redheaded soldier was on the ground—a bullet hole above his vacant right eye, two more in his chest. The young Black soldier was standing over him, smoke still trailing from the barrel of his AR-15.

The two soldiers who had entered first had their rifles trained on the shooter.

Sealey tightened his stance and shouted, "Drop it!"

In the chair, the girl watched all of this, frozen.

The Black kid's mouth fell open, his gaze bouncing from the body at his feet to his fellow soldiers to the girl to Sealey. "It just went off," he stammered. "I didn't mean to—"

One of the other guards fired at nearly point-blank range. The bullet entered the kid's neck above his Adam's apple and burst out the base of his head in a fan of red.

He went down.

The soldier who had fired the shot looked down at the rifle in his hands, released the gun, let it dangle from the shoulder strap, and stared at his hands in confusion. "That wasn't…I wouldn't—"

Beyond the tent walls, the steady hum of the generators went silent.

The lights went out.

Gunfire began to crackle from all around.

CHAPTER

63

SOMETHING BUZZED PAST WALTER'S head, and before his brain registered exactly what that something was, the soldier standing less than two feet from him was struck twice in the chest. His body jerked and crumpled to the ground. Several more bullets tore through the fabric of the tent. The other guard fell.

"Down!"

The shout sounded like it came from Sealey, but Walter couldn't be sure. He had lost track of the two men working on the cage.

"Down, damn it!"

All of this felt like minutes, but in reality no more than a millisecond had ticked by. Walter dropped to the ground as several more bullets whirred over his head. He came down beside the girl in the chair, thought he heard her screaming, then realized those particular cries were coming from outside the tent—screams, shouts, more gunfire—

all of it escalating, growing louder, chaos from all over the camp.

Is Sealey right? Is she part of a cult? Is this her people coming to free her?

Having somehow tipped the chair, the girl was lying beside Walter on the ground, her face blank and still. For a quick moment, he thought she must be dead. Then her lips moved, and although he couldn't possibly hear her over all the noise, the words found him anyway—

Get me out of here before they kill me!

Walter shimmied across the floor and fished around in one of the dead soldier's pockets, came out with a set of handcuff keys, and quickly made his way back to her.

Pressed tight to the ground, a half dozen paces away, Sealey was glaring at Walter, his gun hand coming around, targeting the two of them. "Don't touch her! Get away from her!"

The wall of the tent split open as automatic weapons fire cut through the fabric, the bullets struck the dirt between them, and Sealey scrambled back several feet, positioning himself behind the body of one of the fallen soldiers as Walter made his way back to the girl and fumbled the key into the lock on her ankles.

"Hurry!" she shouted.

Several more bullets struck the ground nearby. One hit the metal of the cage with a resounding *clang!*

How many people are shooting out there?

Walter twisted the key. The lock snapped open, and the cuffs dropped from her feet.

Another pair, the kind with a long chain typically found in prisons, wrapped around her waist and secured her to the chair. He keyed that lock, too, and yanked the clasp open.

Wrists still handcuffed but free of the chair, she shuffled toward the tent flap.

Walter grabbed her leg, pulled her back toward him, and pointed toward the far end of the tent where there was no door.

With a frantic nod, she scrambled off in that direction, Walter behind her, the two of them rounding the frame of the cage.

"You're blocking my shot, O'Brien!"

This came from Sealey, and when Walter risked a look back, he saw the man crab-walking after them, trying to stay low to the ground as he closed the distance, bullets flying everywhere.

Walter didn't expect him to fire, but he did—the bullet went high, sailed over Walter's head.

"She can't leave! Stop her! If she—"

Another round of automatic fire cut through the tent, missed Walter's foot by inches, and sent dust, dirt, and rocks through the air as the bullets cut a line through the ground between Walter and Sealey.

The girl had reached the back wall of the tent and was clawing at the steel pegs holding the fabric to the earth. She'd gotten two out.

Through all this, Walter had managed to hold on to his 9mm—he pointed it back in Sealey's direction and considered firing a warning shot, but he could no longer see him through the dust in the air. If anyone else was still alive in the tent, he'd lost track of them, too.

A third peg came free, and she slipped under the heavy canvas fabric, Walter on her heels.

They huddled together as Walter tried to get his bearings.

At first, he thought the shots were originating from the

tree line, but it was impossible to know for sure. He knew there were at least fifty agents here, and although he'd seen only a handful of soldiers, where there were some there were always more. He imagined whoever had attacked the camp must've come from the trees, and that those in the camp were firing back. Because the clearing was low ground, surrounded by trees on all sides, every shot echoed. There was no moon, and with the lights out, the only illumination seemed to come from muzzle flashes, dozens, but even those were difficult to pinpoint; they seemed to be everywhere. Bright pops of light. Between the cracks of gunfire were the voices—shouts to stop, screams of pain, cries for help.

Bodies littered the ground. Some moved; others didn't. He couldn't tell who'd been hit or was taking cover.

Walter and the girl crawled around the side of the tent, and he spotted the outline of the command trailer. "That way!"

He led with the 9mm, the fingers of his other hand twisted around the chain of her handcuffs, pulling her with him. They reached an SUV, but two of the tires were flat and a line of bullet holes cut through the side, ending near the engine block. Useless.

Sealey's Suburban stood beyond that, and Walter pulled her toward it as several shots struck the ground no more than five feet away. A soldier came out of nowhere, crouched, and returned fire. Walter didn't know if the man was firing blindly, and he didn't care. The cover fire gave them the precious seconds they needed.

When they reached the Suburban, Walter yanked the passenger door open and caught sight of the keys dangling in the ignition. He practically launched her inside. "You drive!" he told her, pushing her over the center console and climbing in beside her.

As he pulled his door shut, the glass shattered. He leveled his gun and fired in the direction the shot had come from. Fighting against her handcuffs, the girl twisted the key, threw the Suburban into reverse, and stomped down on the accelerator. They collided with the SUV behind them in a hard crunch of metal, and she shifted into drive, jammed the pedal down again, and yanked the wheel in the direction of the dirt road leading out.

Another bullet took out their rear window. Walter returned fire and saw a woman in an FBI windbreaker drop.

He'd just shot a federal agent.

CHAPTER

64

AS THE SUBURBAN BOUNCED down the road, Walter stared out the missing back window, unsure of what he'd just witnessed. The gun felt so heavy in his hand.

"She got up," the girl told him, glancing in the rearview mirror. "She was wearing a vest. You didn't kill her."

He turned to her. "Are you hit?"

She shook her head.

"What the hell was that? Someone coming for you!?"

She gave the Suburban more gas as the dirt road made way for gravel.

"I can't help you if you don't talk to me!"

She rattled the handcuffs. "Take these off."

"No," he fired back. "Tell me that wasn't someone coming for you!"

"Do you see anyone behind us? Are they following?"

Walter didn't see anyone, but he wasn't about to let her

take control of the situation. She was in custody. He had the gun. "Pull over up here somewhere, off in the trees. We need to wait for backup."

She jerked the wheel hard to the right, avoiding a fallen tree branch in their path, then back left. The Suburban fishtailed, but she managed to maintain control.

How fast are we going?

"Slow down."

She didn't. Instead, she picked up speed and leaned forward to get a better view over the steering wheel.

Walter heard a phone ring and realized it was coming from a briefcase on the back seat. The spare satellite phone Sealey mentioned he'd left in his car.

Reaching between the seats, Walter thumbed the briefcase latch, grabbed the phone, and pressed the flashing Talk button. Before he could speak, Sealey's panicked voice came from the small speaker.

"Walter, listen to me carefully. I don't know how she did it, but that shooting…that was her. It wasn't a raid—somehow she got my own people to turn on each other. All people she touched…or touched her…I think—"

"Don't listen to him, Walter," she said. "He's lying."

"You need to bring her back."

The phone pressed against his ear, Walter slowly turned back toward her, and for one brief instant, he saw it—it was her eyes, those dark gray eyes, eyes he knew as well as his own. This *was* Amy Archer. This was *her.*

He raised the gun, pointed it at her.

When she saw this, she sighed. "Damn you, Walter."

She jammed her foot down on the accelerator, the Suburban lurched forward, and Walter slammed back into his seat. He glanced out the windshield an instant before they roared into the old pickup truck with the maple tree growing through the middle.

There was a loud boom followed by an intense silence, then nothing at all.

CHAPTER

65

RUNNING WATER.

That was the next thing Walter heard, and for some reason it reminded him of a fort he'd built as a kid with two of his friends in the woods behind his childhood home back in Dearborn. Nothing fancy. They'd stolen some sheets of plywood from a nearby construction site and pounded them into the sides of a couple of trees to form walls. The one they'd used for the roof had a hole in the center, and the water would stream down whenever it rained. None of the other plywood sheets had holes, so how that particular piece ended up on the roof was anyone's guess (or fault), but rather than swap it with one of the walls, they'd positioned pots and pans beneath to catch the water like primitive indoor plumbing. Rain filtered down through the trees, hit the roof like handfuls of gravel, and flowed down through that hole into the metal pot below with a tinny sound. They'd use that water for drinking and, more important, to douse the firepit whenever they left because none of them were supposed to have matches and they sure as shit didn't want to set the woods on fire.

That tinny sound.

Running water.

When Walter's eyes opened, he half expected to find himself lying on the floor of that fort. When his mind quickly reminded him of the crash, he then expected to find himself in the passenger seat of the Suburban. But he was in neither of those places.

Walter woke to find himself in a bed, naked, a stained ceiling above him. His arms were splayed out above his head, held there with ropes tied around his wrists and secured to the headboard. When he tried to move his legs, more rope bit into his ankles—they were tied, too.

"Nothing's broken, but you got banged up pretty good!" the girl who didn't seem to have a name of her own called out.

Walter turned his head in the direction of her voice and found the source of the running water.

A bathroom on the opposite side of the room, the door partially closed. Steam drifting out.

She was in the shower.

The faucet squeaked as she twisted it off.

Through the opening, Walter watched her reach out from behind a green plastic curtain for a towel hanging over the side of the sink. A moment later, she pulled the curtain aside and stepped out, the towel wrapped loosely around her torso, one hand clutching it at her breasts. Water dripped from her dark hair and down her back. She ran her free hand through her hair and brushed it back over her shoulders.

Above the sink, where the mirror should have been, was an empty frame. Only a single shard of glass in the upper left corner remained. If the rest of the mirror was in pieces on the floor, she made no attempt to avoid it as she stepped out of the bathroom and went to the dresser opposite the bed.

Walter's go-bag was sitting there.

She tugged the zipper open, riffled around inside, and came out with one of his shirts. With her back to him, she draped it over her shoulders and let the towel drop to the floor. As she worked the buttons, she said, "The shirt smells like you; it's nice. I hope you don't mind. I don't have anything of my own."

"Where are we?"

Walter barely recognized the sound of his own voice. His throat was so dry the words hurt coming out.

Think of this as our place, Walter. I'll always be here for you.

"A small motel outside Garson. Room 402. You needed to rest, and I desperately needed that shower. With your friends out there looking for us, I figured it best to find someplace quiet, where we could regroup and come up with a plan."

"What happened?"

Her back was still to him, and he looked at her legs, still glistening and wet from the shower, her smooth thighs vanishing under his shirt.

"You saved me, Walter. I think we should focus on that, not the part that came after. You risked your life to help me. I'll never forget that."

She turned toward him then, and any doubt he may have had about her identity vanished. She was Amy Archer. He didn't understand how that was possible, but there was no denying it. She didn't look a day older than she had the last time he'd seen her—their dinner at Giovanni's—nor did she look as young as he'd first thought back at the Garden. She was simply *her*. The girl he knew, the one he remembered.

Amy stepped across the room and knelt on the edge of the bed between his legs. She'd only fastened three of the buttons, and as she moved, he caught glimpses of her naked body beneath, the shirt clinging to her wet skin, her nipples erect and her gray eyes burning with mischief.

"It's you," Walter heard himself say.

"It's always been me, Walter. It's always been you and me. Always will be. Isn't that what you wanted?"

"It's not possible. Can't be…" He pulled at the ropes as she drew closer.

She put her hand on his knee and gently squeezed. A sharp pain raced up his leg to his groin.

"The ropes are for your own safety, Walter. Like I said, you got banged up pretty good. It's best you don't move. Let me do all the work. I'll be careful. I promise. I want to thank you. Let me do that."

Over her shoulder, on the wall behind the dresser, was an ugly floral wallpaper Walter swore he'd seen before. The ropes seemed familiar, too, the bed.

The mattress was covered in stains and stunk, and Walter was reminded of apartment 2D, Alvin Schalk's apartment back in Forest Park. Or was it the room in the Edison, where they found the man named Glenn Beede, every ounce of life drained from his body, leaving nothing behind but a disease-ridden husk?

"I had to cut your clothes off," she told him as she gently kissed his thigh. "With the ropes, there was no other way.

I'm sorry for that, but it had to be done." She edged closer, and he could feel the warmth of her body, her weight pressing down on him. "I asked you once to run away with me, and it's not too late. You and I can disappear, find someplace to call our own. But we need to move fast; they'll be coming for us soon. I don't want to say good-bye again. I really don't."

She teased him with her hand, her fingers brushing against his manhood, alive with heat, then going to the burn scar on his wrist. "I'm so sorry for this. I never meant to hurt you."

She bent down and traced the edges of the scar with her tongue.

Walter jerked against the ropes and shrieked—her tongue felt like the tip of a blade digging into his flesh, trying to get under the scar to scoop it out.

She looked up at him and pouted. "I'm sorry, baby, did that sting?"

The breath caught in Walter's throat, every muscle in his body tensed and pulled tight.

Blood dripped from the tip of her tongue, from the corner of her mouth, from the grin on the corner of her lip. "You'll learn to like it. They all do."

When she lowered her head again, Walter screamed.

CHAPTER

66

"**HE'S AWAKE! NURSE! DON'T** move, Walter! Don't move!"

Walter's body jerked, that kind of spastic movement that sometimes finds you in the moments before sleep, the sense of falling some great distance, then smacking into unseen ground. A series of involuntary jumps.

"He's having a seizure!"

Voices now.

Other voices and hands.

Unfamiliar.

"Get back! Get back!" A woman's voice. "Five cc's midazolam and diazepam, now!"

Hands.

Hands holding him down.

"Sir, I said get back!"

"Sorry. Sorry."

Sealey?

"Somebody tighten those! Get a bite guard in his mouth. Moreno, can you reach?"

"Got it. Hold on—"

Ten seconds passed, or it may have been ten minutes. Time seemed very fluid in those first few moments, and Walter could no more easily grasp the passing of it than he could grab a stream of water from a garden hose and hold it still in his fist. There was a sensation of floating in the instant before his vision went from black to pink; then his eyes opened on bright lights burning down from above—hot halogen lights like the ones surrounding the Camry, only those lights had been square, and these were round and—

"Walter, can you hear me?"

The female voice again.

Walter saw her now, a form hovering over him. She pulled his eyelids back with the tip of her finger and shone a penlight directly into his pupils.

"Can you follow the flashlight? Try not to move your head, only your eyes."

Walter wanted to blink but couldn't, not with her holding his eyelids, so he did what she asked, then blinked about a dozen times when she finally let go.

At least three others were standing there.

"Where am I?"

"Atlanta General. I'm Dr. Logan. You gave us quite a scare."

He caught movement from the corner of his eye and tried to turn, but his head wouldn't move.

"You've been restrained. Try to remain still. It's for your own good. You're heavily medicated."

A wash of pain rolled over him, but it felt muted, like a scream under water.

"What hap—How bad?"

The doctor looked from Walter toward the corner of the room, then back again. "Seat belts save lives, Mr. O'Brien. Unfortunately, you chose not to wear one. We've had you in an induced coma for three days to give us a chance to put you back together again. You sustained numerous lacerations when you went through the windshield. Those will heal with time. There will be scarring, so you may wish to consult with a plastic surgeon—early on is best. We have one here on staff, Dr. Collins. He's fantastic. The bones, though, those will take some time. You shattered your pelvis, your left humerus, your right ulna, radius, and wrist. Both femurs in your legs, but your right is worse than the left. In your right leg, in addition to the femur, you have a single break in the tibia and multiple in the fibula. Your right patella is a mess, too, your knee. You'll walk again, but it's going to take time and physical therapy. Somehow, your spine managed to remain intact, and that's a miracle. Your rib cage did what it's meant to do and took the bulk of the impact for your torso; that spared your vital organs. You did rupture your spleen, though, and we had to remove it. You probably feel pressure in your face; that's from—"

"Doctor?"

She looked up and back to the corner of the room.

"I can fill him in on the rest," Sealey said, walking over to the side of Walter's bed. "Can you give us a few minutes?"

A worried look washed over her face, then she nodded. "A few minutes, then I need to run some tests." She gently rested a hand on Walter's arm. He saw her do it but didn't feel her hand. "I want you to understand, you're a lucky man. It may not seem like it right now, maybe not in the months to come, but you are. You need to hold on to that."

With that, she left the room. The other three followed after her, murmuring softly to one another.

When they were gone, Walter said, "Why can't I feel my arm?"

Sealey's brow furrowed. Then he understood what Walter was really asking. "Probably because you're in a cast that looks like it's about an inch thick, and they've got you on enough painkillers to take down a rhino."

He pulled a chair up beside the bed and whistled. "She did a number on you."

"Where is she?"

"Gone. I have no idea how. She hit that truck and tree head-on, running at least sixty. Both of you went through the windshield. You missed the tree, went over the truck, and hit the mud; that probably saved your life. If you'd've bounced off the tree at that speed, we'd still be scraping you out of the bark. Best we can tell, she hit the ground, too, but just kept on going. Somehow got up and out of there. We didn't find so much as a speck of blood on the driver's side, nothing in the glass. Just a set of footprints through the woods. We brought in some dogs, but they came up with nothing. Followed her trail for about a hundred feet, then lost it in the general direction of the highway. She must have caught a ride from someone."

"Who would..."

Walter started to speak the question; then his mind put the answer right out in front—a pretty girl flags down a car on a dark highway, she's handcuffed and looks like she's been held somewhere, she wouldn't have to spin much of a tale. Food, clothing, money...people could be generous. Most would lend a hand without a second thought.

Three days. She could be anywhere.

Sealey held up three bullet fragments. "I think these hit her; found them in the driver's seat. Little good they did. Might as well have been bug bites."

That wasn't possible.

"You're not FBI," Walter managed to say. "Who are you?"

Sealey let the question hang. "Want to know what we found in the apartment two doors down from Barney Simpers's? An apartment that should have been vacant?"

Walter tried to nod, but when his head wouldn't move, he said, "Tell me."

"Barney Simpers's body. He'd been tied to the bed for days, with no food or water. She didn't even let him up to use the bathroom, made him go right there. In the end, that probably didn't matter much to him." Sealey cleared his throat, forced out, "She bit off his fingers while he was still alive. I'm sure he screamed, but his tongue was nothing but a swollen lump of cancer cells. Damn near filled his mouth; any sound he made would have been muffled. He was like the others. We found extensive signs of aggressive cancer everywhere—arms, legs, vital organs, brain. My experts are still trying to figure out how he lived as long as he did, still arguing about what exactly killed him, since any one of these things should have done the job. The one thing they can all agree on is that it was inflicted by someone else. Black-light tests back that up—he's got handprints at the center of each cancer cluster. The worst of it was on his face, his mouth, like a death kiss."

Sealey went quiet for a second. "She touches these people and somehow takes the life from that part of their body. The cells go cancerous, then degrade, rapidly age. The cancer isn't so much an infliction as it is a symptom, a byproduct.

It's what's left when she's done…taking. She *milked* these people. She did this, with a touch."

"That's not…"

"Possible?" Sealey set the bullet fragments on Walter's chest. "I'm done trying to figure what's possible and what's not. I'm focusing on *what is*. She did this."

"She," Walter managed to get out. "You're sure of that. Not *they?*"

Sealey's eyes fell to the floor. "When I started on this, I figured it had to be a group, so that's been the company line. But the truth is that every time we told ourselves it was a group, the evidence gave us ten reasons to believe it was a single individual. It's only her, and she's been at it for a long, long time. Logically that's horseshit, but I got a stack of reports as tall as me saying otherwise. Let me ask you a question. Describe for me the girl in the tent. What did she look like?"

Speaking was difficult, and Walter didn't want to play this game again. He wanted to sleep. He forced his mind to work through the sludge. "Nineteen. Maybe twenty. Shoulder-length brown hair. Gray eyes. Fair complexion. No visible marks, bruises, or tattoos."

Sealey nodded, then took a small folded piece of paper from his breast pocket. "I want to read you something. We pulled this from that kid who fired the first shot and killed his fellow soldier." He cleared his throat.

"They got me guarding my future wife, Mama. I don't know what she did and don't much care. From what I gather, this is all some misunderstanding, and as soon as they figure it all out, I'm gonna whisk this girl off to the nearest chapel and get her home before she gets a chance to up and disappear on me.

Mama, you gotta see her—beautiful skin and silky black hair down half her back. Perfect almond eyes. Like someone took the best parts of Diana Ross, combined them with Whitney Houston, and produced a ten, maybe an eleven. I know, I know, that shouldn't matter, but it's her personality that got me, Mama! She—"

"She wasn't Black," Walter interrupted. "He's describing someone else."

Sealey lowered the note. "It's a letter to his mother. Why would he lie?"

"He's describing someone else," Walter repeated.

Sealey sighed. "I saw a blonde, about twenty-five. Blue eyes. Long, tan legs. From the moment she was brought in until she ran off with you, that's who *I* saw."

Walter didn't reply to this.

"Twenty-three people injured, four dead. That's what we got back there. Not one of them can explain to me why they started shooting *or* why they felt it necessary to shoot at people they knew. The levelheaded, sensible part of my brain says this was all a big accident—panicked friendly fire in the dark. The other part, the part that seems to be making better sense of all this, says she somehow compelled these people to shoot. Not a single one of these people can agree on what she looked like. The cop who picked her up said she was Spanish—went so far as to say Guatemalan, same place where he grew up. I've got three people who swear she was Asian. You, me, *all my people,* not one of us saw the same person. I got a gay kid who won't even swear we had a woman in that chair—he says it was someone who looked like an androgynous cross between Demi Moore and Rob Lowe. Nobody can agree on a damn thing other than that she was the most beautiful person they'd ever laid eyes on. Whoever, *whatever,* she is, she's not something normal. She's not something *natural.* She's something...else. But whatever she is, she's somehow responsible for every body we pulled out of that place and who knows how many more.

"We'd like you to work with us. Track her down, stop her before she hurts someone else. Or you can walk away. Heal up, forget the two of us ever met, and go back to your life. I don't know about Quantico—work as a field agent might be out with a bum leg—but I imagine they'd find a place for you somewhere in the Bureau if that's what you want. But I think you want to find her as much as I do, and I need that. I need that drive. I need you on my team."

"Who exactly do you work for?"

"That's complicated. We fall under the umbrella of national security but not a particular agency. Our budget is pieced together. A little from here, a little from there...We have oversight, but it's a closed-door committee. For all intents and purposes, we don't exist and we track others who *shouldn't* exist. For the past decade, we've been tracking her and I want you to help us."

Sealey crossed the room and came back with a hand-held mirror.

"There's something else, Walter. No easy way to tell you, so I'm just going to show you." He lifted the mirror to Walter's face and held it there, his hand trembling slightly.

Walter took the mirror and a gasp left his lips. He couldn't speak. His brain couldn't form the words. All he could do was look at the image staring back at him from the round, smudged glass. Wrinkles branched out from around his eyes and mouth, wrinkles that hadn't been there just days ago. And his hair—it had thinned and gone stark white. The man looking back at Walter in that mirror was a much older version of himself, one he barely recognized.

A memory came back to him, just a quick, fleeting moment, but he had no doubt it was real. Seconds after the crash, after his battered body stopped rolling, Amy Archer bent down over him and brought her soft lips to his.

A good-bye kiss followed by a brush of his cheek; then she was gone.

NOW

67

"**THE FBI IS LOOKING** for this woman?" Commander Rigby said, reading over Hurwitz's shoulder.

"I'm not exactly sure what this is. It's all marked classified. Some kind of investigation outside Cuman, Georgia, back in '97..." His voice trailed off as he cycled through documents on the screen, flipping through and reading far faster than Rigby could keep up. "This can't be real."

"What's in Cuman, Georgia?"

He didn't answer her. Instead, he stopped on one particular document, a field report, and highlighted the case number with his cursor, then opened another window on his computer: NCIC—FBI, National Crime Information Center. He keyed in his user name, badge number, and password and opened the encrypted law enforcement landing page. He pasted in the case number from the document and hit Enter.

No results found.

He ran another search, this one for all activity in Cuman, Georgia, for the past forty years.

No results found.

Hurwitz paused a beat, then opened another window. "You may not want to watch this."

"Why not?"

"Sometimes it's good to have plausible deniability."

He flashed through a series of windows and screens, his fingers moving fast. At first, the text was nothing but gibberish, then the FBI logo appeared at the top along with the text *Office of Budgetary Responsibility—House Appropriations Committee, Subcommittee on Commerce, Justice, Science, and Related Agencies. Washington, DC.*

Before Rigby could speak, Hurwitz repeated, "Plausible deniability," under his breath.

She didn't need him to tell her what it was. The little bits she caught as he maneuvered the menus gave her enough—he'd accessed the FBI's financial records. Spending and receipt data. He quickly clicked through to 1997, expanded the text, and ran a series of keyword searches, a frown deepening on his face. "There's nothing here to support an operation of this size."

Rigby asked, "What specifically are you looking for?"

He continued reading as he spoke. "The documents on this drive detail a substantial operation in Georgia in 1997. Over one hundred federal agents and troops deployed and on-site for more than a month." He looked up at her. "Nearly one hundred corpses found in some kind of mass grave. Excavation. Removal. Identification efforts...That's what's on the drive, but there's no record of anyone paying for all that."

"But the documents on the drive are marked classified."

"You can't hide the dollars, not in real life. That only happens in the movies. There would be a line item on this ledger tied to a classified case number without any descriptive details, but the bucks coming out of the bank, that would be here." He loaded up an internet browser window and keyed in *Cuman, Georgia*. A map came up, a couple of links to local headlines, but nothing else. "No way something like that happened and the press didn't pick up on it. That kind of federal presence popping up in the middle of nowhere, people would notice. There would be something. It would have made national news. Hell, there'd be a movie of the week."

"So the documents are fake."

"Gotta be."

She looked back over at the field report. The signature at the bottom. "What about him? Lincoln Sealey."

Hurwitz went back to NCIC and opened a search for federal employees, keyed in the name and ID number on the report. "Permitted to resign in 2009. Evidence tampering. Falsifying statements. A couple disciplinary actions in his final year for intoxication…" He looked up at her from his chair. "These are all the same reasons we found on O'Brien's record. Nearly word for word."

The phone line in the SWAT van rang.

It was the deputy chief.

Rigby drew in a breath and answered. "Sir?"

"Why haven't you breached yet?"

"He knows we're there, sir. He threatened to detonate the bomb if we move on his shooters."

"Then take them out with your snipers. Have you isolated their positions?"

Hurwitz brought up the thermal images of the two

buildings. There was a clear heat signature on the fourth floor of the bank and another in the office building, this one on the top floor. Four others.

"You've located their shooters, right? Hit them and O'Brien at the same time. End this."

Rigby's eyes bounced from the thermal images to the windows with the data from the USB drive and back again. Something felt off.

"Commander?"

She swallowed. "Sir, they knew we'd use thermals, so they turned up the heat in both target buildings when they first arrived. We shut down power, but it's still too hot for us to get a clear position on the shooters. We have eyes on at least six and reason to believe there are more. I'm not comfortable with that course of action without more intel."

Hurwitz knew she was lying, but he didn't say anything. He was digging through the drive data.

"I'm eleven minutes out. I want an alternative by the time I arrive."

The deputy chief hung up.

To Hurwitz, she said, "Something's off. I just bought you ten minutes to make heads or tails of all this. I need to understand what's real here."

He'd gone back to the root directory and was quickly scrolling through the folders.

"What's that one?" Rigby pointed. "Bakersfield?"

2009

ALIASES

Amy Archer*

Amelia Dyer*

Velma Barfield*

--iele--

Jane Toppan*

Gesche Gottfried*

Nannie Doss

Myra Hindley*

Leonarda Cianciulli*

Dagmar Overbye*

Mary Clement*

*BLACK WIDOWS/BOGUS

Hair

Nails

Teeth

Notebook – names, dated, locations

Drawings/~~girls related?~~

~~Same?~~ ???

VICTIMS

Alvin Schalk

Two bodies/basement freezer

Glenn Beede/ ~~John Doe~~/Edison

Aneta Kostenko/~~Jane Doe~~/ Corktown Bus Depot

Earl Golston Pl/~~John Doe~~/ Four Seasons

Man on train platform

Michael Driscoll

BROWNSTONE

Wes Brayman

Rebecca Edgecomb (Willow)

17 others

~~Covering tracks?~~

THE GARDEN

80+ bodies

Some over 200 yo

Dumping ground

... Walter O'Brien, 45 Years Old

68

FOR NEARLY TEN MINUTES, Walter watched the man through the one-way glass but said nothing to the doctor standing beside him. It was clear the doctor wanted answers. Had their roles been reversed, he'd be curious, too. When Walter did speak, he simply said, "Would you consider Mr. Larson to be a religious or superstitious man?"

The doctor—Dr. Patrick Frazer, he had introduced himself—took off his round wire-frame glasses and made a quick show of cleaning them with his tie before placing them back on the bridge of his nose. "Red? No, never."

"Why encourage this? Why give him chalk?"

"For his own safety. When he first started, he wrote on the walls in his room with his fingernails. Chipping the paint, scratching at the drywall. When his nails were gone, he used the blood from his fingertips. We gave him the chalk, and he permitted us to bandage him. He hasn't slowed down, but at least his injuries are improving."

The man's hand was bandaged in a thick swaddle.

"Why not restrain him until this passes?"

"In my experience, it's best to let these things work themselves out. You try to stop them, it's like putting a cork on a bottle of expanding gas. He's not harming anyone. Eventually this, too, will end, but it was peculiar enough I felt it was important to reach out to you."

Walter peered through the glass. In various colors of chalk, the phrase

Fuck you, Lilin — I am not Walter O'Brien

covered the floor and two of the walls, and this man, Red Larson, was busy working on the third.

"Any idea where he learned my name?"

The doctor shook his head. "Not a clue. I questioned the staff; nobody seems to know. He's had a long, storied life, so he may have picked it up anywhere. While in our care, he's never appeared delusional, so we assumed the name was real and set about tracking you down."

A sharp pain shot up Walter's right leg, like a needle to the ball of his foot, and he tried not to think about the bottle of Percocet in his pocket. Barely an hour had gone by since the last pill. He needed to get off his feet.

"How long has this been going on?"

"Consistently, for a week now. Prior to that, I only heard him mention your name twice in our regular sessions."

Walter shifted his weight from his cane back to his left leg. The pain that had become as constant to him as breathing dulled for a moment, then began to build again on the opposite side of his body. When his pelvis screamed, he shifted back again.

The man they were watching appeared to be in his late fifties. His gray hair was cropped short and his face showed the lines of someone who had lived a hard life. He wore loose-fitting beige scrubs and scruffy white canvas shoes.

"Why is he here?"

"Mr. Larson joined us for the fourth time about three months ago," Dr. Frazer explained. "He's been in and out of facilities like ours since returning from Vietnam."

"Is he dangerous?"

"Only if you put a rifle in his hands. He was a sniper in that past life. Red Larson simply wants to forget, and his mind will not permit him to do so. Over the years, we've found delicate mixes of medications able to put up a wall strong enough for him to leave us, function out in the world, but over time that wall crumbles and he returns to our doorstep. Like I said, this being his fourth visit with us, one of his longest—going on three years now. We will always welcome him back here with open arms with the hope of finding the means to set him free again."

Here being Bakersfield. A private psychiatric facility located in Bumass Nowhere, Michigan, just outside a small town called Broken Creek.

"You weren't an easy man to find," Dr. Frazer continued. "There are a lot of Walter O'Briens in the world."

In the one-way glass, Walter's reflection stared back at him, the thin scars diffused by time. The white hair bothered him most. He'd tried dying it over the years, but the color—black, brown, blond—never took. In a day or two it always went white again, changing as quickly as it had all those years back.

"How exactly did you find me?" Walter asked.

"Sister Mary Susan spotted your name in a story about a fire back in Detroit some time ago. Realized you were with law enforcement."

"I haven't been with Detroit PD for some time."

"Yet of the dozen or so Walter O'Briens we contacted, you're the only one who dropped everything to come here after our call. That tells me all I need to understand that you are the correct Walter O'Brien. The others either politely dismissed us or outright hung up."

In the cell, and there really wasn't a better way to describe it, Red Larson continued to write on the third wall, his handwriting surprisingly neat, steady, and quick.

Fuck you, Lilin—I am not Walter O'Brien

Fuck you, Lilin—I am not Walter O'Brien

Fuck you, Lilin—I am not Walter O'Brien

"I'd like to speak to him."

The doctor nodded. "I assumed as much."

69

DR. FRAZER LED WALTER down a wide hallway with a steepled brick ceiling. Beneath the scent of bleach and floor wax was the smell of urine and decay.

"This was once a single-family home," the doctor told Walter as they walked, "the summer home of a well-known textile manufacturer who helped fund the automobile industry. His daughter suffered from mental illness, so upon the patriarch's death in 1911, the family donated the home to the care and well-being of those suffering from similar ailments. There was a trust once, but it's long gone now, so we survive on a budget strung together from donors and government handouts. The hope is to one day restore the house to its previous glory, but taking care of our patients comes first, of course. Here we are…"

Dr. Frazer gestured into a room not unlike the interview rooms back at Detroit PD.

"Take a seat. I'll have Red brought in."

Walter carefully lowered himself into one of the chairs, doing his best to ignore the pain screaming from every mended bone and muscle and failing miserably. The metal pins in his right femur were worst of all. He wouldn't take another pill, though, not yet.

Larson arrived in restraints, which Walter found odd considering the doctor had just finished telling him the man was harmless.

"Are those necessary?"

The orderlies helped Larson into the chair opposite Walter and fastened his restraints to an eyebolt in the center of the table. "Procedure, sir."

Larson didn't seem to mind. Judging by the blank stare in his bloodshot eyes and the glisten of drool on the corner of his mouth, it was clear the man was heavily medicated. He swayed slowly back and forth in the seat.

The orderlies left, followed by the click of a heavy lock.

Walter wondered if anyone was on the other side of the one-way glass.

He pointed toward the cup of water near Larson's hand. With the restraints, the man wouldn't be able to lift it to his mouth on his own. "Are you thirsty? I can help you."

Larson only stared at him. The drool worked down the side of his chin and dripped to his shirt.

Walter took a handkerchief from his pocket and dabbed it away.

Larson remained still, those eyes of his looking more through Walter than at him.

Walter settled back in his chair. "Do you know who I am?"

When Larson finally spoke, the words came slowly, a gruff drawl. A mix of medication and a deep Southern accent.

"You're the one Lilin wants. The one she talks about." His eyes dropped to the restraints on his hands. "I'm not good enough for her."

"Who?"

"Lilin."

"Who is Lilin?"

"Her. She is Lilin."

"I'm afraid I don't know that name."

Behind the dull eyes, Walter could see the man's mind attempting to work, trying to fight through the haze. "Lilin...*Preta*."

"Is that her last name? Preta? Lilin Preta?"

It wasn't a name Walter had ever heard before.

Larson's head slowly shook. "*Preta*...a Vietnamese word. Hungry ghost. Eater of life. *Preta*."

"Is that where you first heard the name? In Vietnam?"

Larson nodded. "In Vietnam."

"How do you know my name?"

"She speaks of you. Her Walter. Her Walter O'Brien. We've spent many hours talking about you. You're all she ever wants to talk about. All she ever...wants. Doesn't matter how hard I try, always, Walter, Walter, Walter."

"Is she here? In this place?"

"Always. Here. Everywhere. Always."

"I'm not sure what that means. Can you describe her for me? What does she look like?"

What does she look like...to you?

Larson's gaze dropped to the burn scar on Walter's wrist, and his eyes filled with a brief moment of clarity. "She misses you, Walter. Told me to tell you she wished it was just the two of you. The two of you forever in your place."

Our place, Walter. Don't you remember it?

A heavy hand knocked on the door.

When it opened, Lincoln Sealey was standing there. He motioned for Walter to step back out into the hallway.

CHAPTER

70

WALTER ROSE AND STEPPED back out into the hallway. There was no sign of Dr. Frazer.

Sealey closed the door behind him and twisted the dead bolt. When he spoke, he kept his voice low. "I'm not sure what to make of this place. You think she's here?"

"Good spot to hide." Walter gave a sidelong glance to a nun standing silently in the hallway, still enough to be part of the shadows.

"Better than Albuquerque, that's for damn sure."

They'd nearly gotten her in Albuquerque. She'd been living in student housing near a large community college with twenty-plus other girls. A constant rotation of new students in, older students out. They weren't exactly sure how long she'd been there, but the first body they found on record was a male student, nineteen, dead of a massive brain tumor behind a small convenience store in 2003. Under the black light, his lips lit up the room. Their team had found seven others, and they were still looking for more. The last had been an English professor, though, three years ago. They lost her after that. She'd stopped using the female serial killer aliases back in the late '90s, probably knew they were watching for that now. Despite 24/7 surveillance, she'd never been seen returning to her dumping ground in Georgia, either. Walter was certain she had others; they just hadn't found them yet. There were too many bodies.

"She's gotten downright obsessed with you, cowboy," Sealey said.

"It's just another one of her games."

Outside Nashville in 1999 they had found the body of a missing accountant covered in dead roses in an old fishing cabin, a Valentine's card in his fingerless palms. Inside she had written, *For my lovely Walter. I miss your touch. Do you miss mine?* In Oakland, California, there had been an entire biker gang. Nine altogether, five men, four women. They'd been handcuffed to chairs in a warehouse, no doubt a nod to Sealey and his tent back at the Garden. She'd taken her time with them. A few weeks at least, draining them of life in slow increments—a touch here, a longer hold here, a kiss there. There'd been a security system and she'd covered the cameras, but the audio had captured every scream. Between the cries of these men were her desperate whispers—*Why didn't we just go to Iowa, Walter? If you wake with a nightmare, is there anyone there to dry your tears?* The victims had been unrecognizable by the time the bodies were discovered. Sealey had said she was getting sloppy, disorganized. Walter had thought, how long can anything survive in isolation before the loneliness begins to eat at whatever is left? That had been in 2005.

"If she's here, why hasn't she just killed this guy like

the others? Sounds more like she's been confiding in him," Walter said. "Keeping him alive so she has someone to talk to."

Lonely.

Sealey just shrugged. "I've given up trying to understand her. I didn't see any marks on him, did you?"

Walter shook his head. "We know she can dial it back when she wants to. There's *something* here. Did you hear him? He called her a *preta*."

"'Hungry ghost. Eater of life,'" Sealey quoted. "Not an inaccurate description, although most *preta*s are believed to be invisible to the human eye, unless..."

"Unless drugged, fevered, or in a hallucinatory state," Walter finished for him. "I've seen that report, too. Tell me he doesn't fit *that* bill. Legend has *preta*s eating their victims to replenish their strength and reverse aging, particularly body parts associated with the senses—eyes, ears, and—"

Sealey cut him off with a wave of his hand. "I'm not saying it's wrong; I just don't get why he's not dead."

Same reason I'm not dead, Walter thought. *She found something she liked. Only difference is she kept* this *pet in a cage.*

Walter didn't want to go there so he changed the subject. "What's *Lilin*? Ever hear that name?"

"Sure." Sealey scratched at the scruff under his chin. "It's a play on Lilith, a name that appears in all sorts of religious texts. In ancient Mesopotamia, the lilin were hostile night spirits that attacked men. Wraiths, sirens, banshees, that kind of thing. Means a similar thing in Hebrew. In Targum Sheni Esther 1:3, King Solomon commanded Lilin to dance before him."

"Dance?"

Sealey waved a hand. "You can't take that stuff literally.

In context, I think it meant bow down, obey him, do his will, a subservient thing. His way of proving he was stronger than her."

"Her, though. Not it, or them? A person, not a thing?"

"It's been a while since I read all that, I'd have to look it up, but if I'm remembering correctly, I read it in the Tanakh, the Hebrew Bible. Something about Lilin and her children, they were called the lilim, I think." Sealey paused as a little more came back to him. "There's a couple stories, but the gist is King Solomon captured Lilin and tried to bend her will, use her for his own gains. I don't think it worked out well for him."

Walter looked back at Larson through the small window in the door. He was hunched over the table. Still awake, but barely.

Sealey continued. "Lilith is apocryphally considered to have been Adam's first wife in the Bible, too."

"Adam's first wife?"

"Before Eve, yeah. Lots of nasty lore tied to that name and different takes on it, like Lilin. Numerous cultures link both to variations on succubi." He followed Walter's gaze through the small window and studied the man inside for a moment. "Larson is a Scandinavian name, and Sweden has a larger Jewish population than you might expect. If his parents or grandparents were from there, that may be how he picked it up. We'll know when his background comes back. The name Lilin might just be some word floating around in the back of his head, something he heard long ago and plucked out to fill some fantasy. We don't know this man's mental state. Sounds like he was a complete wreck when he came in, and now he's hopped up on who knows what. Just because he believes it doesn't make it real. This might be a delusion based on some story he heard."

Because he's alive. She wouldn't let him live.

"He's not delusional. Red's not like that."

This came from the nun. They'd barely spoken above a whisper, but she had heard them anyway.

She took several steps closer. "Red is a deeply disturbed individual, but he's not prone to delusions, fantasies, or hyperbole."

Sealey narrowed his eyes. "And you are?"

"Sister Mary Susan." She nodded at Walter. "I'm the one who found you."

"Do you have anyone on staff here who goes by a name that sounds like Lilin?"

"No."

"What about another patient? Any patients named Lilin, Lilith, or some variation?"

She shook her head. "We currently have twenty-seven female patients, none who go by that."

"Who specifically has access to Mr. Larson?" Walter asked her.

"He stays in his room by choice. I've never seen him in the community room or the outdoor spaces. He takes his meals alone. If he's had contact with other patients, I'm not aware of it. His interactions are limited to staff."

"What is he on?" Sealey asked the nun.

"Clonidine, Prozac, and propranolol."

"We need him clearheaded," Walter told her. "Can you discontinue his meds?"

"Not without Dr. Frazer's approval, and I seriously doubt he'd authorize that."

"Okay, can you *delay* his next dose? Buy us an hour?"

To this she didn't reply. That was better than saying no.

At the opposite end of the hallway, Walter caught the shadow of one of the orderlies who had brought Red Larson to the interview room—a large Black man, at least six four and probably pushing three hundred pounds. Their eyes met for a moment, then the man rounded the corner and disappeared again.

The nun said, "That's Canton Brown. He played pro ball for the Bills until his knee blew out about eight years ago."

"Shit," Sealey muttered. "Thought he looked familiar."

Walter said to her, "You've been here awhile, then?"

She nodded. "I was on staff the last time Red Larson came in. Something has changed within him, and not for the good. I can also tell you that change occurred *after* he arrived. This business with Lilin presented recently and has only escalated since."

"We'll need access to patient and staff records, visitor logs," Walter told Sealey. "Everyone in and out of this place over the past year, maybe more. I can write off the biblical references as coincidence, but not knowing my name. He got that from somewhere."

Sealey agreed and looked up and down the hallway. "Where did that administrator go?"

"Dr. Frazer returned to his office," the nun said. "I was told to bring you there when you finished with Red."

"We need to lock this place down. Nobody in or out." Taking a cell phone from his pocket, Sealey gave Walter a resigned glance. "I'll move our people into position and get a warrant."

71

"THIS IS A MEDICAL facility, first and foremost," Dr. Frazer spouted from behind his large oak desk. "I can't allow you and your people to traipse around in here upsetting our staff and patients any more than I can grant access to confidential records. Not without a warrant. We could lose our license. The state could lock our doors. I can only imagine how our donors would view such an intrusion."

Sealey was out in the hallway, still on his phone, working on the warrant, but he hadn't gotten one yet. Sister Mary Susan stood silently, her back against the administrator's door.

"We're working on it, but it takes time," Walter told him. "If the person we're looking for is here, and she realizes we're searching for her, we may lose her. Speed and surprise are key."

Dr. Frazer's face grew red. "Let's talk about that. I just got a call from our front gate. There are two men out there claiming to be federal agents turning away deliveries and visitors—not allowing anyone in or out. Two more at our main entrance, and several more around our perimeter. Care to explain who authorized all that? I know it wasn't me."

"There's an urgency to—"

"My chief of security phoned not two minutes ago," Frazer interrupted. "He said someone waved a badge at him and demanded access to our camera footage, our logs."

"I don't think you fully understand the—"

"What I understand is that, badge or no badge, you're taking actions here without the authority to do so." Frazer picked up his phone and quickly dialed a number. He looked down at the receiver, thumbed the disconnect several times, and glared at Walter. "It's dead. Did you cut our phone lines?" He tugged open a drawer and took out a cell phone, tried to place a call, then frowned at the display. "I'm not getting a signal. What's going on? Are you doing this?" He gestured toward Sealey, visible through the window overlooking the hallway. "How did he dial out?"

Walter ignored the questions. Instead, he asked, "How many people have died here in the past year?"

Dr. Frazer replaced the handset, dropped the cell phone back in the drawer, and slumped angrily down into his chair. "What does that have to do with anything?"

"How many?"

"Fourteen."

This came from Sister Mary Susan, not from Frazer. The doctor shot her an angry look.

"How many the year before that?"

"Three," she replied before the doctor could stop her.

Frazer's face grew stiff. "That's meaningless. There was no foul play. The county coroner autopsies anyone who dies in our care. If he'd found anything remotely suspicious or problematic, I would have heard about it from a half dozen different people."

"Tomorrow's headline could easily read 'Federal Authorities Investigate a 400 Percent Increase in Death Rate at the Bakersfield Psychiatric Facility.'"

Dr. Frazer didn't miss a beat. "And you'd be sued for libel."

Walter shrugged. "Maybe. But it will take a couple years for all that to play out in court. What happens to this place in the meantime? Think the government, the one you want to sue, will continue to send you checks? How about your donors? How many of them will want their name attached with a cloud like that hanging over the place?"

"You're insinuating the woman you're looking for is killing patients like some angel of death," Frazer said. "I can assure you every death on record has been natural."

"So are all the others we've attributed to her."

This wasn't exactly true, but it was true enough.

"Only Larson has seen her," Frazer reasoned. "I use the term 'seen' loosely because patients like him tend to see a lot of things. Presuming she's real and not some figment, how do you explain her movements around the hospital? Completely unnoticed by staff and all others. This is a secure facility. Everything and everyone accounted for at all times."

Because she can alter her appearance at will, Walter thought. *Appear different to different people.*

If he told the truth he might just earn a room in this place.

Walter tried a different angle. "I'm going to ask you something very specific, and I need you to be honest with me. If you lie, I'll know. Understand?"

The administrator didn't reply, only stared at him.

"Have you ever found patients secured to their beds and tortured? Maybe over an extended period of time?"

A disgusted look washed over the man's face. "Half the patients here have been secured to their bed at one time or another. But tortured? No. Of course not. And if you leak something like that to—"

Walter cut him off. "Would you know?"

"I know everything that happens here."

"What about missing fingers?"

"Missing?"

"Bitten off."

He was clearly taken aback by this, too stunned to answer.

The nun's mouth was hanging open slightly, but when Walter glanced at her, she quickly shook her head. "He's telling you the truth. The deaths we've had were heart attacks, several late-stage diseases. I recall a stroke. Nothing as horrible as you're suggesting. Certainly no foul play."

"What about cancer?"

"Certainly."

Walter recognized that these people wouldn't know what to look for. Not if she was being careful. She hadn't survived this long without knowing how to hide when she needed to.

Walter rested one hand on Frazer's desk. The top of his cane dug into his other palm as he leaned closer to the man. "The warrant is coming. Give us a head start on the search. Let us get in front of her. We can't allow this woman to escape. If you help us, tomorrow's headline could just as easily read 'Local Administrator Instrumental in the Capture of Serial Murderer.' The ball's in your court, Doctor."

Walter could see the gears working behind Dr. Frazer's eyes when someone knocked on his door.

72

"WHAT?" FRAZER BLURTED OUT.

When nobody responded, Walter hobbled over and opened the door.

Dressed in black with a gun on his hip and a badge hanging around his neck, a member of their team was speaking softly to Sealey in the hallway. Both of them turned, and Sealey said, "We've got something. Staff quarters upstairs."

Frazer rose from his desk, his face somehow growing redder. "Who gave you permission to look upstairs in staff quarters? I want all of you out of my facility immediately!"

Sealey raised his hand and waved his cell phone at the administrator. "The warrant's been approved. They're faxing you a copy. Who does room 27 belong to?"

Dr. Frazer ignored him and crossed his office to the fax machine on a table in the far corner. When he didn't find anything in the tray, he picked up the receiver, frowned, and held it toward Sealey. "This line is dead, too. I can't honor a warrant I haven't seen. Why is your cell phone working and mine isn't?"

Sealey dropped the phone back in his pocket. "Mine is satellite based. It doesn't rely on local towers for a signal."

"We haven't touched your phone lines," Walter told him. Actually, most likely, Sealey had had the lines cut and activated a cellular blocker, just as Frazer suspected, but Walter certainly wasn't going to tell him that. "If she knows we're here, there's a good chance she did something."

"Room 27, Doctor," Sealey repeated. "Who does it belong to?"

The nun let out a frustrated sigh. "For heaven's sake, testosterone will be the end of us all." She went to a tall file cabinet against the wall and tugged open one of the drawers. "Room 27, you said?"

Sealey nodded.

She thumbed through several files, pulled one out, and opened it across the others. "Room 27 belongs to Sister Mary Daria. She came to us four years ago as a novice. She's twenty-five years old, real name is Madelyn Johnson."

The name meant nothing to Walter, and by the look on Sealey's face, he didn't recognize it, either. "Do you have a photograph?"

The nun frowned. "It should be clipped to the inside flap of her file, but it's gone."

"Let me see that." Dr. Frazer stomped over, took the folder from her, and flipped through the contents. "Almost everything is missing. Photograph is gone, so is her résumé, background check, and references. There's nothing in here but her last few evaluations." His eyes narrowed. He pulled out several more folders, growing increasingly frustrated. "Somebody's gone through all of these. All the photos are gone, personal details, it's all been removed." He looked up at Walter. "My office is always locked when I'm not in here. Only a handful of people have access."

Why would she take the photographs? She's never been captured on film. Did someone finally manage to get a shot of her?

Then the answer came to him—if they used photographs to eliminate everyone else, leaving only her, she'd be the only one *without* a photograph. This confused the issue.

Walter glanced at Frazer. "You'd recognize her, right? You could point her out to us?"

"Of course."

Walter knew that was probably meaningless, too, but at least the man wasn't arguing with them anymore.

Sealey turned back to the man dressed in black. "Show us what you found in her room."

Several nuns watched them as they quickly made their way through the facility. A few brazenly followed. Sister Mary Daria's room was on the second floor, about halfway down a long hallway. The door stood open, a second man dressed in black standing guard. He moved aside as they stepped into the small space.

There was a single bed, the sheets and quilt free of wrinkles, made with military precision. A small wooden cross hung above the headboard. A table and single chair occupied one wall, and a large armoire stood against the other. The armoire had been pulled away from the wall and several clear plastic bags sat on the floor in a neat line.

"Those were hidden behind," the man in black told them.

The nun gasped and covered her mouth. "Is that…?"

Sealey bent to get a better look.

Walter hovered above him, not willing to test his knees right now. His grip tightened on the cane.

There were four bags in total—teeth, hair, fingernails, and brown clumps that might have been skin. Unlike the jars found in Earl Golston's apartment all those years ago, the items weren't separated here—each bag contained a mix, the clear plastic marred with brown stains, inside and out, most likely blood.

Walter hadn't known it at the time, but Sealey's team had recovered the jars from Golston's. In recent years they'd analyzed them and compared the DNA, determined everything came from the same source, not multiple victims. She was keeping pieces of herself.

The color that had been so prominent on Dr. Frazer's face was gone. He was stark white.

"If you're going to throw up, please step outside," Sealey said before taking a pen from his breast pocket and using it to turn one of the bags on its side. Without looking up at the man who'd led them to the room, he asked, "Anything else?"

"No, sir. Nothing else in this room. None of the other staff rooms, either. Just those."

"Where is Sister Mary Daria now?" Walter asked.

"She's on cafeteria duty," the nun replied.

They headed to the cafeteria where another nun told them that Sister Daria hadn't reported yet. None of the people in the kitchen had heard from her.

"We've got this place locked down," Sealey told Walter and the others. "She couldn't have gotten out. She's here somewhere."

Looking around the large cafeteria, Walter only half

heard him. He had an idea. "Do you have an intercom or PA system?"

Frazer nodded.

"We need you to gather all the nuns and your staff together in this room. Everyone who's not a patient. Now."

73

IT TOOK ABOUT FIFTEEN minutes and three announcements over the PA system to gather everyone. Seventy-two employees at this time of day. Dr. Frazer called it a staff meeting in an attempt to avoid raising suspicion. Sister Mary Susan's idea. There were hushed conversations as the group eyed Walter and Sealey warily.

Dr. Frazer stepped over to them, tugging nervously at his tie. "Warrant or not, I'm not comfortable leaving my facility unstaffed like this. We have patients to tend to. Do what you need to do quickly, so I can return these people to their posts."

Sister Mary Susan leaned close to Walter and spoke softly, her breath warm on the side of his face. "Sister Mary Daria isn't here. At least six others are not accounted for."

"Are you sure?"

She nodded.

The orderly, Canton Brown, stepped into the cafeteria

then. He held the door open with one arm and guided Red Larson with the other. Although he was still in restraints, Larson moved with more purpose and agility than he had earlier. The shuffle was gone, and he stood upright. The nun had told them he'd last been given his medication three and a half hours earlier. He was due again in thirty minutes.

Canton Brown led Larson to where Walter and Sealey stood and held him there with one hand resting on Larson's shoulder.

"How are you feeling, Red?" Walter asked him.

Larson's head swiveled toward him, his eyes following on a slight delay. "I've got the worst hangover. Are you my new doctor?"

Walter shook his head and offered a smile. "I'm just a friend."

A spark lit then as he remembered more. "Oh, Walter O'Brien. Her…her…"

Walter gestured toward the line of nuns against the wall on their left. "I need you to point out Lilin to us. Can you do that for me?"

Canton Brown glanced at Dr. Frazer, who was standing beside Sealey.

Frazer gave a dismissive wave. "It's fine, Mr. Brown. Just keep an eye on him."

Larson worked his way across the room, with the orderly at his side and Walter one pace behind them.

Standing side by side, the nuns went quiet as they approached. Some clasped their hands; most averted their eyes and looked down at the ground.

Walter and Sealey had walked the line twice while they waited for Larson. Neither of them recognized Amy Archer among the faces; neither of them expected to. All the women wore full habits, their hair and bodies completely covered. That didn't make things any easier, but Walter knew it was of little consequence. He only needed to remind himself of the several times he'd been unable to identify her himself to realize she could be standing right there, and he wouldn't know. Under most circumstances, she appeared differently to everyone, as their *ideal* woman, something that could (and often did) change over time. That was her natural state. When she needed to, she could willfully alter her appearance. They'd learned that much, too.

Walter wasn't sure what this meant for Red Larson—the man might point her right out, or he might walk the line as they had and not see her. They had to try, though. They had nothing else.

Larson reached the start of the line, gave the first woman a quick glance, then continued on. She was older, probably in her late sixties. The second woman was Asian, and he moved by her quickly, too. Walter remembered the note from the soldier back at the Garden, the one he'd written to his mother. He'd seen her as a Black woman. The cop who had pulled her over back then, just a day earlier, thought she was from Guatemala.

To those who have seen us at our best and seen us at our worst and can't tell the difference. We, the misfits of the world.

The toast Amy/Velma gave at dinner in 1997 came back to him for some reason. The little smirk on her lips as she said it.

Walter shook the thought away.

"Take your time, Red. She may look a little different than you remember."

When Larson reached the fourth nun, Walter realized he wasn't just looking at them; he was *smelling* them. Larson leaned close to each woman and inhaled deeply. Several of the nuns seemed taken aback by this; others eyed him curiously. Others still grew tense, whispered uncomfortably to one another. One opened her mouth to object, but a look from Frazer silenced her.

When Walter had chased her back at the brownstone, when he'd cornered her in the taxi, she'd smelled like lavender. Fresh flowers. That wasn't the first time he'd noticed the scent, either. At the time, he wasn't sure if his mind was just playing tricks on him, but he'd be damned if he didn't smell lavender way back in Alvin Schalk's apartment, when he'd first found her huddled under that sink. In the taxi with her. In his apartment. Even in the dream after the accident—tied to that bed as she hovered over him, damp and freshly showered.

Our place, Walter. Don't you remember it?

Scent might be her only tell.

Walter reached into his pocket and gave the dog collar a gentle squeeze. "There you go, Red," he said softly, barely aware he'd spoken.

The orderly wasn't sure what to make of all this. He grew visibly tense every time Larson leaned toward one of the women.

When Larson reached the end, he started back the way he'd come, checked again. He would have doubled back a third time, if Walter didn't put an end to it.

"She's not here, is she, Red?"

He shook his head. "I want her to be, but that's not enough."

Walter patted him on the shoulder. "It's okay, you did good. Wait here."

He went back over to Sealey, Sister Mary Susan, and Dr.

Frazer. The three of them huddled together near the door. To Frazer, he said, "Are you sure this is everyone?"

"We're missing four orderlies."

"Four?"

He nodded. "Hernandez, Galloway, Morton, and Bloomington. All four clocked in this morning, but they didn't report in with everyone else. I could see maybe one staying behind, but not all three, and not without at least checking in."

Sealey still had one hand in his pocket; the other was clutching his phone. "Nobody's left the building. I sent Gorman up to try and track them down, and he's not answering now. It could be the building, reception is bad, even with the sats, but—"

"Where were they last?"

"Third floor," Dr. Frazer said.

74

WHEN THE ANCIENT ELEVATOR groaned to a stop on the third floor and opened, they found the security desk deserted with no sign of the three men.

Larson tensed. A small vein throbbed on the side of his neck, and his head moved ever so slightly with a fast mechanical tick—right, left, then back again. His breath caught.

"Take off his restraints," Walter said softly.

"I wouldn't advise you—" Frazer began.

"Take them off. We need him. Take them off now."

There was something in the air. Something not right. The orderly must have noticed it, too, because he didn't wait for Frazer to give him the okay. Instead, he fumbled the keys from a clip on his belt and quickly released the various clasps on Larson's bindings.

As they fell away, Larson rubbed at his wrists and shucked

the thick leather from his ankles. "Thanks for that," he said softly to Walter, his eyes still fixed on the empty hallways.

The six of them stepped out of the elevator, Walter and Larson first, Sealey last. He took the gun from his holster and held the weapon at his side. Both Dr. Frazer and the nun saw it, but neither said anything.

A mechanical whir hummed somewhere off in the distance. There were soft pings and beeps; machines keeping time, nothing else.

Walter drew closer to Dr. Frazer, spoke as low as he could. "What's on this floor?"

"Immobile patients. Bedbound."

"Who has access?"

"Same as the other floors. Patient doors are all kept locked. Only the orderlies and I have keys. Routine checks are scheduled. If someone needs access to a particular patient, they have to go through proper channels, and it's logged. The orderlies accompany the sisters and doctors on rounds of any kind, no exceptions."

The nun was looking down at the desk near the elevator. A wisp of steam rose from a half-full cup of coffee. A partially eaten chocolate doughnut sat on top of the comic section from today's newspaper. A fly perched on top, its legs twitching.

Sealey cupped a hand over his mouth and shouted, "Gorman!"

Frazer gave him an irritated look, no doubt worried about disturbing the patients.

No response came, though.

Sealey's voice echoed once in the small vestibule.

Nobody moved.

The phone rang.

The clattering bells of the old mechanical phone must have been turned up to full volume in order to be heard from a distance. They were deafening and everyone jumped.

Walter reached for the phone, but Larson beat him to it, snatching the receiver off the base with reflexes far faster than the sluggish movements he'd demonstrated up until that point. He brought the handset to his ear, and all of them watched as his eyes grew wide.

"Who is it?" Frazer asked. He tried to sound authoritative, but the wobble in his voice betrayed him.

Larson listened for a long moment, looked to Walter, and held the phone out to him.

Walter took the handset and brought it to his ear. Before he could speak, her voice came from the small speaker.

"I'm glad you're not dead, Walter. I've often wondered."

Amy Archer's voice. Not the Midwest accent she'd used at Giovanni's. Not the voice she'd used at the Garden outside Atlanta. This was the girl Walter had found huddling under a sink so many years ago, a voice as familiar as his own.

"Where are you?"

"Close."

Walter turned slowly, looked up and down one hallway, then the other. There was no movement. "Why don't you come out? Talk to me in person."

His eyes met Sealey's, and the two exchanged silent words. Walter extended two fingers and quickly pointed at the other man, then down each of the hallways. Sealey nodded and started down the hall on the right, both hands on the gun, systematically checking each locked door.

From the small speaker, she said, "You took my plaything. Can I have him back?"

Walter glanced over at Larson. The man's gaze was fixed

on him. If there was a string tied between him and Archer, someone had just pulled it tight. "He seems to have a nose for you, like a bloodhound."

"You need to let me go, or I might have to hurt someone."

"I can't do that."

She sighed again. "That's okay. I don't mind hurting someone. I think I want to. It's so good to see you again."

The line went dead.

Walter held the phone against his ear for several more seconds before replacing it on the cradle. "Is there any way to tell where she called from?"

Frazer shook his head. "The button that lit up was an internal extension. She could be anywhere in the building." He hit the Speaker button on the phone and pressed several others. "We still don't have a dial tone on the external lines."

"Walter!"

The shout came from Sealey, somewhere down the hall.

THEY FOUND SEALEY JUST beyond a bend in the hallway, standing in front of an open storage closet. On the floor, partially wrapped around a yellow plastic mop bucket and surrounded by various bottled cleaning products, was a young nun, vacant eyes looking off in directions that were all wrong. Thin wisps of blond hair trailed out from under the white band of her black coif.

Walter knelt and pressed two fingers against the side of her neck, knowing what he'd find but checking anyway. He gently lifted her hand, then set it back down. "She's still warm, and rigor is just now starting to set in. She's probably been dead about three or four hours."

"That's Sister Mary Lucinda."

Walter glanced back at the nun standing behind him. "You're sure?"

She nodded, her mouth covered with one hand.

Sealey got down on his knee next to Walter and tapped the side of his forehead.

Walter nodded. "Probably. We'd need a black light to know for sure. Didn't touch her fingers."

If Sealey had any thoughts on that, he didn't share them. He grunted and got back to his feet.

Violence was nothing new to the large orderly who had been escorting Larson. Canton Brown's face betrayed no emotion as he stepped up to get a better look. "It takes a lot of force to break someone's neck like that. Are you sure we're dealing with a woman?"

Dr. Frazer looked like he might be sick.

"All of you should go back downstairs," Sealey told the group. "Make sure the staff stays put."

Frazer glared at him. "We need to call the authorities! You have a working phone, use it!"

"We are the—"

"Hey, Walter!"

A large man dressed in white burst out of the room two doors down, hand above his head, tightly gripping a large screwdriver. He lunged across the hallway, his legs somehow pushing his considerable bulk into the air, launching him.

Walter tried to sidestep, but his bad leg twisted instead and his weight fell against his cane.

Canton Brown moved with tremendous speed. He got himself between the man and Walter as the man brought his arm down, slashing toward the place Walter had stood a moment before. The screwdriver cut the air and buried itself in Canton Brown's upper back, just below the base of his neck. Both men fell to the ground in a pile of rolling limbs.

Sealey pointed his gun, prepared to fire.

"No!" Walter shouted. "He might know where she is!"

Sealey fired anyway. The bullet went high, landing about four inches above the two men as they rolled into the wall and came to a stop.

The man yanked the screwdriver from Brown's neck and tried to kick out from under him. When he couldn't, he howled.

Brown wasn't moving. Blood sprayed out from the open wound in his neck.

"Drop it!" Sealey screamed at the man wielding the screwdriver.

A twisted grin slipped over the man's face. His head swiveled up toward Walter—when he spoke, the voice wasn't his. It was hers, sickly sweet. "I'm planting a new garden, Walter!"

He slammed the screwdriver into his own eye, buried it halfway to the hilt, and went still.

Sister Mary Susan screamed.

Canton Brown was dying.

Ignoring the pain in his leg, Walter dropped down next to the orderly and tried to pinch the wound shut, but it did little good. Blood poured out from between his fingers. "Doctor! Help him!"

Frazer took a step closer, then stopped.

"What are you doing? Help him!"

"He's already gone…"

"No, he's not, he…" Walter saw Brown's eyes then and realized the blood that had been forcibly flowing only a moment earlier had stopped. Canton Brown's neck had gone dark purple beneath his skin.

The man had most likely saved his life and lost his own in the process. This was his fault.

"That's Rand Galloway," Frazer told them, staring down at the other man. "One of our missing orderlies. He's worked here for nearly eight years. We've never had any disciplinary problems with him. I don't understand why he'd do this."

Walter understood, though. He'd seen it before. "She's in their heads. Just like back in Georgia," he told Sealey.

After Georgia, they'd tried to piece things together. Between interviews with survivors and surveillance footage, the best they could tell was that she'd been able to influence or outright control others after nothing more than a touch.

Possession.

Sealey had used that word.

Walter had thought *infection* was more accurate.

"She's in their heads?" Dr. Frazer repeated. "What's that supposed to mean? Give me your phone—I'm calling the police."

"What you need to do is get back down to the cafeteria like I asked and keep everyone there before someone else gets hurt," Sealey replied. "This man shouldn't have been up here in the first place."

"If you won't let me use your phone, I'll find another that works, and I'll be sure to tell everyone how you tried to prevent me from doing so."

Sealey's hand twitched, the one holding the gun.

"Is that supposed to frighten me?"

"We're still missing two other orderlies," Sister Mary Susan pointed out in a quiet voice, her damp eyes fixed on the dead men. "Three were stationed on this floor. Maybe we should focus on that." She looked over at the body of Sister Mary Lucinda still in the closet. "And we should move Sister to someplace with a little more dignity. She deserves better than to be seen like this."

"We can't move her," Walter muttered. He tried to stand and slipped in the blood, his bad leg folding under him.

Red Larson took several slow steps around Dr. Frazer and reached a hand out to Walter, helping him to his feet. He picked up Walter's cane, wiped the handle clean on his pants, and leaned in close as he returned it to him. "She'll be in other heads. I can feel her trying to get back into mine."

Before Walter could respond, a loud chime rang out from the PA system, followed by an urgent woman's voice, "Code Blue in 234! Repeat, Code Blue in 234! Dr. Frazer to 234!"

"What's a code blue?" Sealey frowned.

Frazer looked up at the speaker on the wall. "Patient death. Patient death on the second floor."

NOW

76

READING FAST NOW.

Craziness. Fiction. Fabrication. Mental illness. Conspiracy theories. Delusions. Fantasy. Hallucinations. No other way to describe it.

Possessions?

Some demonlike thing that "fed" on people?

"Click on that one," Rigby said softly, pointing to a video file dated August 12, 1968.

A window opened up. A grainy image of a soldier in dirty fatigues. Shot on film. The fabric of a green canvas tent at his back.

"Can you state your name for the record?"

"Alfred Theodore Larson."

"Date and location of birth?"

"March 14, 1952. Fayetteville, Arkansas."

There was a slight pause. "That would make you sixteen."

"I lied on my admissions paperwork, sir. I wanted to fight. Joined up about a year ago."

A pause again.

"You arrived in Vietnam. Got assigned to D Company, Second Battalion?"

"Yes, sir. Sniper duty." He had a fresh scar on his cheek. Red. Inflamed. Covered in grime. A fly landed on it and he swatted it away. "Grew up with a rifle in my hand, was always a good shot. Seemed like a good fit."

"When did your squad arrive at My Lai?"

"March 14, 1968."

"Your birthday?"

"Yes, sir."

"Did you know Lieutenant William Calley, Jr.?"

"No, sir."

Another pause. "Were you *aware* of him?"

"I didn't hear the name until...after."

"After what?"

"After I got back."

A shuffling of papers, then: "You weren't part of the fighting on the sixteenth?"

"No, sir. Me and two other snipers set up camp the night before on a ridge overlooking the village. She attacked that night."

"She?"

At first, Larson didn't answer. His gaze seemed to focus on something off camera. Or maybe he was just remembering. "Yes, sir. She."

"Can you describe her for me?"

"Blond hair. Green eyes. Maybe sixteen or seventeen."

"American, though? You're certain of that?"

He nodded. "Midwest accent."

"You understand how unlikely that is? An American teenage female, in the jungle?"

"Yes, sir."

"Tell me what happened."

"I'm not sure that I can, sir."

"Try."

"It's just…I didn't see much."

"Tell me what you did see."

Larson swallowed, considered his words. "I woke up around three in the morning. She was on top of Garner. Naked. They were…you know. At least, I thought they were, until I saw what she did to his hands. Two of his fingers were gone…she had another in her mouth…and he was just…laying there. I tried to get up and couldn't move. I don't know why. It was like a nightmare, where you can only watch, but—"

"You're certain this wasn't a dream?"

The soldier frowned and held up his left hand. His index finger was missing.

Hurwitz paused the video. "Holy shit."

The phone rang again.

The deputy chief again.

Rigby answered. "Sir?"

"Did you access files for a federal employee named Lincoln Sealey?"

She exchanged a look with Hurwitz. There was no point in lying. He obviously knew. "We think he's involved, sir.

Working with O'Brien. He may be the one who's been calling me, possibly one of the shooters."

Another voice came on the line. *"Commander, my name is Omar Lussion with the Department of Defense. You need to listen to me very carefully. Lincoln Sealey was fired for cause when an operation went bad in '09. A number of people lost their lives because of his actions. He cut a deal, skirted jail time, then we lost him. He dropped off our radar. If he's there, this is most likely retaliation. He cannot be trusted. Do not operate under his terms. I've got agents en route to assist."*

Rigby frowned. "All due respect, sir, but this isn't a federal matter."

"One of your shooters is in 1812 Park, correct?"

"Yes, sir."

"That's a federal building. Which makes it our jurisdiction."

Shit.

"I'm not asking you to hold. We have no intention of taking command. We only want Sealey. Dead or alive."

"Sir, I—"

"How many shooters have you located?"

Rigby looked at the digital maps of the various buildings. "Eight heat signatures, sir. Scattered around two buildings. We don't have visual beyond thermal, blinds are closed, but we're confident on center mass."

Her snipers would aim at center mass. She'd been told they were firing .408 CheyTacs—rounds that would remain supersonic out past two thousand yards. At this distance, they'd pass through walls, furniture, and anything else in between.

"No more delays, Commander," the deputy chief said. *"You move now. Instruct your snipers to shoot in coordination with your breach teams. I want this over when I get there."*

"What about the bomb, sir?"

The other man responded to that: *"If Sealey has a bomb, he's going to detonate it either way. This man is not rational. Your only chance here is to surprise him. I concur with your chief—strike on both fronts, clear out the club, and get a bomb squad in there."*

If he doesn't blow it first.

"Is that understood, Commander?" the deputy chief said.

She looked at Hurwitz again, then nodded. "Understood."

When they hung up, she let out a deep breath and found herself staring at the frozen image of the soldier on the screen.

If she waited, she'd be in violation of a direct order.

She couldn't wait.

Rigby pressed the Transmit button on her comm and flicked the small switch that would leave the channel open. "All teams, we go in two. Snipers, go for kill shots. Green and Blue teams, clear both buildings, confirm all shooters down. Yellow team, enter the club from the front, clear any hostiles. I'm on O'Brien. I'll distract him. Everyone moves on my mark. Code word, *litany*."

On her way out the door, she told Hurwitz, "Alert the bomb squad. Tell them to prep—I want them inside the moment Hersh with Yellow gives the all clear."

"What about all this?" Hurwitz said, pointing at his monitor.

"They're right. We don't have time."

2009

ALIASES

Amy Archer*

Amelia Dyer*

Velma Barfield*

--Iele--

Jane Toppan*

Gesche Gottfried*

Nannie Doss

Myra Hindley*

Leonarda Cianciulli*

Dagmar Overbye*

Mary Clement*

*BLACK WIDOWS/BOGUS

Hair

Nails

Teeth

Notebook – names, dated, locations

Drawings/~~girls related?~~

~~Same?~~ ???

VICTIMS

Alvin Schalk

Two bodies/basement freezer

Glenn Beede/ ~~John Doe~~/Edison

Aneta Kostenko/~~Jane Doe~~/ Corktown Bus Depot

Earl Golston Pl/~~John Doe~~/ Four Seasons

Man on train platform

Michael Driscoll

BROWNSTONE

Wes Brayman

Rebecca Edgecomb (Willow)

17 others

Covering tracks?

THE GARDEN

80+ bodies

Some over 200 yo

Dumping ground

... Walter O'Brien, 45 Years Old

WHEN THE ELEVATOR DOORS opened on the second floor, an older nun was standing there. She quickly scanned the five of them, her eyes lingering on Walter's bloody shirt and pants before focusing on Frazer. "I don't understand. The room was empty. There shouldn't be anyone in there."

"Why are *you* up here?" Sealey asked.

"How long do you expect us to leave patients without care?"

Without further clarification, she turned and shuffled down the hallway, her scuffed black shoes squeaking on the waxed floor.

They followed after her.

Unlike the other doors on this floor, all of which were closed, the door to 234 stood open. The nun stopped in the hallway.

As Walter stepped by her, she simply said, "I can't."

Frazer froze behind her. He gripped the wall to steady himself.

Gorman was in the bed, naked from the waist down. Dead.

Both his arms were secured to the bed frame above his head with rope, his gun belt, pants, and underwear on the floor. His right eye looked straight ahead while his left was cocked so far off to the side, the pupil was barely visible.

His fingers were gone, nothing but nubs.

Larson had followed Walter into the room, but Sealey managed to stop the others at the door when he realized who was in the bed.

Gorman's shirt was torn open, half the buttons missing, and resting on his chest was a small sheet of paper. Walter stepped closer. He didn't touch it, he didn't want to disturb evidence, but he could still read the words written in play-ful, loopy letters—

Darn. He's not Walter, either!

Beneath the words, there was a smiley face and a little heart.

"Do you smell that?" Larson said from behind him.

Walter did. "Lavender."

Larson drew close to Gorman's right hand and sniffed. "It's her. But you already know that. She's gearing up for something. This is fresh, probably within the last fifteen or twenty minutes."

Larson's meds were clearly wearing off. He was far more lucid than he'd been even minutes earlier.

"You can tell that by the smell?"

"No. I can tell that because the blood on his knuckles hasn't congealed completely. Dead or alive, that takes about fifteen or twenty minutes." He nodded up at the corner of the room, above the door. "You'll want to check that."

Walter turned.

A security camera looked down on him.

Sealey instructed Sister Mary Susan to keep everyone downstairs and coordinate attendance so they could figure out if anyone else was missing. Frazer stayed behind in order to help Walter and Sealey with the security footage. Larson stayed, too—Walter wasn't about to let him out of their sight.

"There!" Walter pointed at the screen.

Frazer hit Stop. "I'm going to rewind just a little bit."

This time when the video started, the room was empty. Several seconds in, the door opened and Gorman leaned in, looked around, then stepped into the room, crossing over toward the bed. A moment later, a nun stepped into the room and closed the door behind her.

Sealey pointed at the screen. "Stop there. Can you zoom in on her face?"

"I can try, but this equipment is far from state of the art." Frazer turned the wheel on the mouse until her face filled about a quarter of the screen. "I'm sorry, that's the best we can do."

Walter and Sealey exchanged a glance.

The lines of her black habit, the coif on her head, those were perfectly clear, but her face was impossible to make out.

"How did they get in there? I thought all the doors were kept locked."

Frazer shot Sealey an irritated glance. "Occupied rooms are locked. Two thirty-four is supposed to be vacant. I think the better question is why one of your men was leading one of our nuns into a vacant room. Was he operating under your instructions?"

Sealey rolled his eyes. "Just hit Play."

Frazer zoomed back out, clicked the Play button, and the video began to advance again.

The nun placed a palm on Gorman's chest and pushed him back several steps, until his legs reached the side of the bed. Then her hands went up to the base of her neck, unbuttoned her black habit, and let it drop to the ground. She wore nothing beneath and stood naked before him for a moment, then pulled her coif off and dropped that, too. She shook out her shoulder-length dark hair and stepped toward Gorman.

Gorman kicked off his boots.

In the wooden chair, the doctor shuffled uncomfortably but said nothing.

With both hands, she gripped the sides of Gorman's shirt and tore it open, then brushed her fingertips down his chest until she reached his belt. A moment later, that was open, too, his pants and underwear were at his ankles, and Gorman was busy shucking them off into the corner of the room. When he reached for her breasts, she took a step back and shook her head, saying something.

"Do we have audio?"

"Privacy laws don't permit audio."

Whatever she said, it drew a smile on Gorman's face, and he dropped both arms to his sides.

She stepped close again, ran a hand through his hair, then stroked his cheek. She stood on the tips of her toes and pressed her lips to his. Her right hand drifted back up the side of his face, and her index finger circled his temple, then pressed.

Gorman's body went stiff, as if he'd suffered a jolt of electricity. Then he fell back onto the bed. Dead.

They watched her grip both of Gorman's legs and heft him completely onto the bed with so little effort, the large man might as well have been weightless.

When Gorman's body was in place, she retrieved two lengths of rope from the pocket of her habit on the floor, secured his arms, then scribbled out the note on a pad beside the bed and dropped it on his chest. She leaned over his left hand and systematically began biting off his fingers. She didn't spit them out or discard them.

She swallowed them.

Walter felt his stomach lurch. They suspected she gained strength from this—ingesting the senses of her victims— but some bit of understanding didn't make it easier to watch.

When finished with his left hand, she rounded the bed to his right. This was over in a matter of seconds. She took a moment to study what she'd done, then she turned toward the camera, brought her hand to her mouth, and blew out a kiss, her face somehow obscured behind a blurry haze of light.

"She wanted us to see this."

Walter nearly vomited. "It's all a game to her."

Gathering her clothing, she opened the door and stepped out into the hallway, disappearing from view.

"Nobody saw that?" Sealey asked. "A naked woman walking down the hall?"

Walter tapped the screen near the time stamp. "We were all in the cafeteria."

Frazer glared at Walter. "The note she left on this man, Larson's scribblings on his wall. What is all this about? What is she after?"

Walter knew he had to tell the man something. He was busy trying to choose the right words when Sealey swore and quickly glanced around the desk, up and down the hallways. "Where'd Larson go?"

78

THEY WERE HALFWAY DOWN the hall when Larson stepped out of the room where they'd found Gorman. His shoulders were slumped and he was holding the agent's gun.

Frazer froze.

Without the slightest hesitation, Sealey drew his .380 and leveled it on Larson's chest.

Larson gave Sealey a dismissive glance and looked back down at the gun in his own hand. "You can't hurt her with one of those."

His thumb clipped the release, and the magazine dropped to the floor. His index finger tripped the takedown lever and slide stop simultaneously, and with a quick jerk of his palm, the slide and body came apart. He dropped both pieces to the ground at his feet.

Walter had never seen someone dismantle a gun one-handed before.

Reaching into his pocket, Larson took out a bloody

screwdriver, wiped both sides of the blade on his pants, and held the tool in a tight underhanded grip.

"Why don't you put that down," Sealey told him, his weapon still trained on the man.

"A gun's not gonna do you a lick of good."

"A bullet through *your* chest will do just fine."

Larson loosened his grip on the screwdriver but didn't put it down. He cocked his head to the side, appeared to be listening to something. Then he stepped over to a closed patient door and placed his hand just below the small window at its center and frowned. He didn't look inside, only bowed his head. After several seconds, he scraped an *X* into the white paint of the door, then moved on to the next one. He didn't mark that door but he scratched *X*s into the two after that. He worked his way down the hallway, picking up speed.

Dumbfounded, the three men stood still and watched all this. He'd marked six of nine doors by the time Frazer finally spoke. "What the hell are you doing, Red?"

Larson was at yet another door. He shook his head and scratched another *X*. "She's building her strength."

"She's building…" Frazer's voice trailed off as the meaning of this settled over him. Then he scrambled over to the nearest door and peered through the glass. "Oh, no…oh, no." He tried the handle, found it locked, and fumbled for the keys in his pocket. It took several attempts before he managed to get the correct key into the lock and open the door.

The room's occupant was sprawled out on the floor, dead, fingers missing. Most of his hair was gone, lying around his head in gray clumps. His skin was dry and ashy, stretched over his bones.

Dr. Frazer moved quickly back out into the hall and opened another door. He looked inside only long enough to find another dead patient, then went to a third door, then a fourth. "This can't be happening," he muttered more to himself than to anyone else. "This can't be real."

Larson reached the end of the hall and was coming back, the tip of his screwdriver covered in chipped white paint. "It's not just on this floor. We need to get everyone out of here."

Walter managed, "How are you able to…"

"She's showing me," Larson told him. "I think she wants you to know."

Walter and Sealey exchanged a look. If she was in Larson's head, maybe she was doing more than just *showing*.

Sealey tightened his grip on his gun and began pacing back and forth, his mind churning. "Nobody leaves. We keep this place buttoned up and force her out. That's the only way we catch her."

Larson chuckled at this.

Sealey turned on him, anger broiling. *"You think that's funny?"*

"You don't *catch* her."

Walter held up both his palms. He knew how hot Sealey could get. They needed to stay calm and maintain control of this. Over his shoulder, he called out, "Doctor…can you move all your patients and staff so our people can search the facility from top to bottom?"

Frazer stepped out of a room near the end of the hallway and shook his head. "Many of our patients are dangerous, to themselves or others. I can only imagine what would happen if—"

Sealey cut him off. "What do you do in the case of an emergency? What's your evacuation plan?"

Frazer blinked. "Evacuation plan? We've never had to…"

Sealey shook his head. "All right, I want everyone brought down to the cafeteria where my people can secure the group. We'll vet everyone, one at a time, and move them to another space, maybe outside, but only after we're sure of who they are. If she doesn't try to get out with the group, we conduct a room-by-room and find her that way. Either way, we get her."

Frazer was shaking his head again. "I don't see how…"

A crackle came from the PA system, through all the overhead speakers.

"Come play with me, Walter."

Walter looked up at the speaker mounted on the wall. "Where's she transmitting from?"

Frazer didn't answer. He was staring at the speaker, too.

"Doctor!"

The administrator went back to the desk and looked down at the phone. He ran his finger over the clunky buttons. The first one was lit in red. "The PA system can be accessed from any phone in the building, this button here."

"I've missed you so much, Walter."

Walter turned back to the speaker. "Where are you?"

When she replied, it was in his head.

"I'm upstairs, Walter. The attic. It's just like our place. Do you remember our place? Every inch of me aches for you. I've so missed your touch. Come up here, you alone. We have so much to catch up on. I should never have left you. Let me make it up to you. I've been naughty. Sometimes I can't help myself, but if you come alone I promise I won't hurt anyone else. You're all I want."

Walter heard her voice as clear as if she stood right next

to him, and he thought he was alone in that until he realized Larson was staring at him. When their eyes met, Larson gave him a knowing nod and looked up at the ceiling. Walter saw it then. At some point, Larson had discarded the bandages that had been covering his left hand—his index finger was missing, the tissue long ago healed over. There was also a mark on Larson's wrist not unlike the one on Walter's chest where she had touched him all those years earlier. That spot that had never quite healed.

I'm upstairs, Walter. It's just like our place.

"Is there an attic?" Walter asked Dr. Frazer.

Frazer nodded. "It runs the length of the building. Ever since the basement flooded in '74, we've used it for storage."

"How do I get up there?"

CHAPTER

79

"**YOU CAN'T GO UP** there alone," Sealey said, following Walter back toward the elevator. "She'll kill you. That's what she wants."

Walter pressed the elevator Call button. "She hasn't killed me yet."

"Not for lack of trying."

Larson and the administrator followed several paces behind them. Every few feet, Larson stopped and scratched a symbol into the wall. Not an *X;* this was more intricate. An odd combination of circles and triangles.

"What is that?" Frazer asked.

Larson didn't answer. He finished the current symbol and started another on the wall opposite the desk near the elevator.

"What the hell is that?" Frazer asked again.

Walter glanced back and got a look at it. He'd seen the

symbol before. Egypt. Asia. Italy. Numerous Mesopotamian texts. "Where did you learn that?"

"A witch in 'Nam."

"I thought it was pagan," Sealey said.

"Some things are older than language. Older than countries or religions. They don't belong to any one place or people. It should help repel her."

Frazer smirked. "A drawing is going to repel her?"

Larson ignored him and looked around the hallway. "I need salt, too."

"Of course you do."

There was an abandoned food cart in the corner near Sealey. He grabbed a handful of salt packets and tossed them toward Larson. They skittered across the floor.

Larson scooped several up, nodded approvingly, and tore one open. He began pouring the packets out at the threshold of each door, creating lines of salt under the symbols he'd drawn. "She won't be able to pass over these. We can contain her."

The elevator dinged and the doors slid open. Inside were four of their team—one woman, three men—all dead and lying on the floor. They'd been killed the same way as the others: a touch to the temple.

Frazer's mouth fell open. "How many people did you bring with you?"

Not enough, Walter thought.

The doors started to slide closed, but Walter blocked them with his foot and reached back. "Give me the key."

The administrator had told them an elevator service key was needed to reach the fourth floor. He located the correct key on his ring and handed it to Walter.

Walter slipped it into the slot, then pressed the Emergency

Stop button to keep the doors open. "Do you have security cameras on the outside of the building?"

They'd lost Frazer again. His eyes were locked on the bodies, the blood dripping from the woman's severed fingertips.

"Doctor!"

He snapped back. "Ah…yes. Of course. Cameras."

Frazer rounded the desk on shaky legs and nearly fell into the chair, sat there stunned for a moment, then seemed to remember why he'd sat down. Through all this, he attempted to project an air of authority. He no doubt told himself he was still in charge, but he was clearly in shock and might just as easily slide under the desk to the kneehole and hide.

"Doctor…" Walter said again.

Frazer cleared his throat, reached for the mouse, and began clicking through the software. He loaded several shots of the building's perimeter, and when they saw no one, he brought up the front gate.

At first, nobody was visible there, either. Then an orderly stepped out of the small guardhouse.

"That's Lewis Morton. He works on this floor with Galloway. He's got no business at the gate."

There was blood on Morton's shirt, and the cuff of his right pant leg was torn.

"I had two people stationed at that gate," Sealey said. He took out his phone and punched in a number. When nothing happened, he frowned at the screen. "I'm not getting a signal on this floor."

Frazer picked up the handset from the desk and punched in a number. "If the PA is working, internal extensions should still work, too."

On-screen, the orderly's head jerked up. He looked up and around, glanced inside the guardhouse, then stepped through the door.

The speakerphone on the desk rang twice, then stopped as someone picked up, and disconnected a moment later after an audible *click!*

The orderly stepped back outside, a phone receiver in his hand with a cut cord dangling from the end. He tossed it into the bushes next to the guardhouse, then went back to looking out over the long driveway with the stillness of a statue.

A grim look washed over Sealey's face. "I have eight people positioned around the exterior. Check the other cameras again."

The exterior appeared deserted.

Flipping back through the various cameras, they found another missing orderly from the third floor in the grassy garden area behind the facility. He was dragging a body by the legs, hiding it behind a thick hedge.

Larson gave the screen a quick glance before returning to the salt. As he worked, he said, "She can get in the heads of anyone she touches, but only those she's touched."

"Or those who've touched her," Sealey pointed out.

"Or those who touched her," Larson agreed. "She's had four years here."

"You honestly believe Sister Mary Daria is some..." Frazer seemed to slip deeper into the wooden chair. "Do you understand how crazy what you're saying sounds?" He seemed to remember he was talking to a psych patient at that point and laughed nervously. "Why the hell am I listening to you? Any of you?"

Larson opened another salt packet and started creating

a line at the edge of the elevator opening. "When I was in 'Nam, I heard a story about a man who slit his own throat. Cut himself ear to ear in a bar after telling a few of his fellow soldiers about this girl he met in Da Nang. Said she was the most beautiful girl he'd ever laid eyes on, said he wanted to do something special for her; then…" With his free hand, Larson dragged a finger across his own neck, then went back to the salt.

"You heard a story," Frazer muttered. "Do you know how many stories I've heard during my career? Fairy tales and monsters. I've seen the right combination of medication and therapy make them all go away. Maybe she's paying these men, made them promises. Sexual favors or whatnot. Maybe they've been drugged. There's an explanation here, one not originating in lore or superstition. There always is."

Walter had seen this before, the rational mind in denial. He'd been one of those people once. "Doctor, feel free to accept whatever explanation makes you comfortable. Just don't get in our way."

The PA speakers crackled with static, then her voice came again, singsong. *"Walter…Oh, Walter…"*

Walter leaned in close to Sealey so the others couldn't hear. "He's useless to you, you know that, right?"

Sealey nodded.

"All the outer doors are chained?"

Again, Sealey nodded.

Other than the front entrance, they'd placed industrial chains and padlocks on every door and emergency exit, purposely locking everyone in the building, creating a funnel. One way in, one way out.

"I moved our snipers in place nearly an hour before you and I even stepped foot inside," Sealey told him. "Nobody saw them position. They avoided all the cameras—they're ghosts."

"Let's not lose focus, then, we got her."

"Christ, after all these years…"

Walter stepped into the elevator, released the Lock button, and turned the key to the service position. "Get Frazer downstairs with the others. Contain everyone. Then take Larson and figure out who we've got left—finish buttoning up everything below us just in case. Make sure none of those chains got cut. You'll want to be ready for her if she gets by me. This ends today." He pressed the button for the attic floor and the door started to slide shut.

Sealey gripped the edge, stopped it, and handed Walter his .380.

Walter felt the weight of it in his hand. It was a light gun. "What if Larson is right and bullets don't work? Remember the truck?"

"What if he's wrong?"

Sealey released the door, allowing it to close, and the elevator began to ascend.

Walter heard her say his name again, and this time, he wasn't sure if it came from a speaker in the hall, a speaker in the elevator, or somewhere in his mind. She sounded giddy, excited.

Walter wasn't sure what the feeling was coursing through his body, but it certainly wasn't excitement.

WHEN WALTER STEPPED OUT of the elevator on the attic floor, recently disturbed dust swirled, filling the space up to the peaked and trussed ceiling. On the dirty pine floor, a line of lit candles formed a path, winding away from the elevator and disappearing between old hospital beds, boxes, and large pieces of medical equipment.

"A gun won't do you much good here," Amy Archer said.

Her voice came from everywhere and nowhere all at once, and this time Walter was certain the voice was in his head.

"I guess you won't mind if I carry it, then."

"I would have preferred you brought me flowers."

"This isn't a date."

"But I lit candles and got all dressed up for you... What's a girl got to do?"

A burly rat raced by Walter's feet, up the leg of an

old mannequin, and vanished in its stomach, its pink tail
flicking against—

Walter swayed.

Not a mannequin, but a woman's nude body, dry and
decomposed. She was leaning against an old dresser, legs
splayed out and both arms at her sides. Her eyes were gone.
Most of her hair, too. As Walter drew closer, he spotted
some strands of hair littering the ground around her, long
strands of black, some of them still bunched together, others
twisted and balled into a makeshift nest.

The rat appeared again in the open stomach cavity, one
paw resting on the tip of a rib.

*"I like it up here, Walter. Although these things are not mine, all
possessions hold memories. They're age defying. They take me back
to another time, another place. Sometimes happier, sometimes not, but
always different, and it's important to escape, don't you think? For
one's own sanity, just get away?"*

Walter found two more dead women in the kneehole
of an old upright piano. A third was sitting on the bench,
hunched over, fingerless hands resting on the dusty keys.
All three looked like they'd been there a long time, but
Walter knew when dealing with Amy Archer, appearances
meant little.

He rounded the piano and followed the candles, their
flickering light filling the space with dancing shadows,
apparitions hovering with him in lockstep, an audience.

*"I was happy here, Walter. I was. This hospital of the forgotten,
the damned, the unwanted. I found a home among the sisters. I was
so fond of some, my closest friends. I brought them up here."*

"This is how you treat your friends?"

His voice sounded much louder than he expected. The
echo boomed off the harsh angles of the ceiling.

"It wasn't hard to disappear in a large group of nuns, but a couple of them realized I didn't belong, and of course, they had to go, too. Their stories joined the others up here. The thing about a place like this—the nuns come and go as often as the patients. Most don't take the time to get to know each other; some don't speak. Others are here to hide; they left their real lives off in some soon-to-be-forgotten place. There were a few, though, who were a little more observant, caught me with some of the patients, so I asked them to join me up here, too. Sister Mary Hazel was a gossipy sort. Who knew she would be such a virtuoso on the piano!"

A harsh chord rang out behind him, and when Walter turned, he saw the rat perched on the edge of the piano keys, its nose twitching.

"If you ask her nicely, maybe she'll play something. Will you dance with me if she does? Remember when we danced?"

Walter followed the candles around several stacks of old mattresses and crates and found himself at the entrance to a room in the shape of an octagon. The ceiling was vaulted and round and came to a peak at the center.

He froze at the threshold, his eyes fixed in horror on what lay inside.

"I can't seem to shake you, Walter. Why is that?"

81

Walter

THE VOICE HADN'T COME from Amy Archer. Not this time. And it wasn't in his mind, either. This was something else entirely.

Walter stepped into the room, carefully avoiding the dozens of candles placed haphazardly on the ground, wax melding them to the floorboards. His legs shuffled along as if they had a mind of their own. He didn't stop until he reached the center, and even then, it wasn't because he wanted to. He *wanted* to turn and run; he wanted to shout; he wanted none of this to be real. He stopped in the center because that was precisely where she wanted him to be.

On the ground, their backs up against the walls, sat six nuns. Arms limply at their sides, legs splayed out, and their heads all cocked slightly to the left side. Their twelve gray eyes were fixed on him, and Walter knew if he were to approach any one of them and tear the veil or bandeau from their head, he would find shoulder-length brown hair beneath, tied back and hidden.

The youngest was perhaps twenty-one or twenty-two and was a dead ringer for Archer the day he first found her under that sink in Alvin Schalk's apartment. There was no fear in her eyes, not like then, no silent plea for help. This Amy Archer simply stared at him, blank and indifferent.

On the opposite wall was another Amy Archer, this one every bit the forty-some years old she would be today—slight lines around her eyes and mouth, a thin wisp of gray in the hair peeking out near her left ear.

There were other Amy Archers, too. The one on Walter's left was easily in her seventies. She had the same blank stare as the others, but her mouth hung open slightly, revealing teeth that had spaced out and gone crooked over time. Her gray eyes sunk deep in her skull.

The other nuns, the other Amy Archers, they were all her at various ages, and Walter wondered if Sealey had been right all those years back when he said she was part of some cult, a family, mothers, daughters, and sisters all sharing some dark— But no, he knew it wasn't that. She was showing him she could be whoever she wanted to be, whenever she wanted to be. Just another game to her. She wasn't just in Larson's head; she was in his.

Walter's hand found its way into his pocket again and he brushed the edge of the dog collar with his thumb.

"I've missed you, Walter."

Their lips moved in unison, and the words came from all of them at once. A chorus of six different voices, yet similar enough in tone to sound like one, and Walter turned in a slow circle from one to the next.

"It's me, Walter. I'm me."

"I don't understand."

"No, I suppose you wouldn't."

"Who are these women?"

"Who do you want them to be?"

"Don't hide behind whatever this is," Walter told her. "Are you so afraid of me you need to use parlor tricks?"

The six nuns laughed at that. This singular voice in unison. "I'm not afraid of you, Walter. I haven't felt fear in more years than you could possibly understand. I'm honestly not sure I've ever felt fear, not the way you do. And you *are* afraid. I can hear your heart right now, pounding like a fist. You have this little vein on the side of your temple throbbing in time with it. You're sweating, too, I can smell it. The sweat is making the burn scar on your arm itch, but you refuse to give in and scratch. Your heightened blood pressure makes your worthless leg ache. I see you trying to hide all this from me, trying to hold that poker face of yours. You don't have to do that with me, Walter. We shouldn't have secrets. I've made you the man you are. I've broken you over and over again, yet somehow, you rebuild. You pull yourself back up and find your way back to me. Should I fear that? No. If anything, I'm flattered. It's nice that you care."

"I'm here to stop you," Walter told the nearest Amy Archer, his grip tightening on the gun.

All six smiled. "I know, it's sweet."

He took several steps closer to the youngest-looking of the six, raised the .380, and pressed the barrel against her temple. "One or six, it makes no difference to me. I have enough bullets for everyone."

"Including yourself? If you shot them all and then learned you killed six innocent women who happen to look alike, putting a bullet in your own skull might be your next decision. Regret can be a bitter fuel, but a powerful one." The smiles on their six faces twisted slightly into mischievous smirks. "Wouldn't you rather have a little fun?"

The Amy Archer nearest him reached down with her left hand and slowly pulled the hem of her skirt up, over her knees to her thighs. The others did the same, their legs spreading apart as they all raised their knees to their chests.

"Pick one. It's all the same to me. I want to feel you inside me. I know you want to."

"Is this what you did to Glenn Beede back at the Edison? Or that private investigator, Earl Golston? Is this how you got them in your bed?"

They all laughed. "Glenn Beede. He was a nobody. But Earl Golston? Oh, I miss dear Earl. He was a bloodhound. He followed me everywhere, with his nose to the ground and one hand trying to get up my skirt. New York to Los Angeles. San Francisco to Chicago. He even managed to find me in Greece, then Germany, and the Netherlands. Earl knew how to keep a secret, though; he never told anyone. He kept everything to himself. All the men in my life. Sure, he wrote down places and dates, tried his hand at questionable artwork, and picked through my trash, but he never shared any of what he discovered with anyone. I always found that endearing. Earl was a gentleman. He knew how to treat a lady. You, though, you're a different kind of animal. Not only have you talked about our little trysts; now you're bringing friends to the party. I'm not that kind of girl, Walter."

Walter was turning again, a slow circle, as these words came from the Amy Archers on the ground at his feet.

Although they all spoke, none seemed to see him. He looked for subtle differences between them. Anything to indicate which were puppets and which was the master, but as they spoke, as they moved, there wasn't the slightest delay. They were perfectly coordinated.

"Are you even in this room?"

"Of course, Walter. I'm close enough to taste you."

All six reached out, but only the hand of the oldest Archer found him. She brushed his ankle with fingertips as cold as the dead.

Walter jerked his foot away, and three of her fingernails tore off. Two fell to the floor, and one caught in his sock. He shook it away in disgust, and all six laughed again, a deep cackle. The teeth were loose in that one's mouth, he was sure of it. Walter thought of the jars they'd found in Earl Golston's apartment, the bags hidden away in the nun's room downstairs—hair, teeth, nails.

She's shedding.

"I'm evolving, changing, altering. Always," she said, somehow in his head again. "Oh, the jars and bags and boxes I've filled over the years as the unused and unneeded flakes away. If you only knew. Golston loved to pick up after me. Became quite the collector, that one. These things hold power, you know. Ask anyone familiar with the old ways. Not as fulfilling as a gifted finger but they'll do in a pinch. I've never understood why you humans discard such treasures. They're delectable."

All six Amys licked their lips with a quick, lizardlike slurp of their tongues. "You should put the gun away. We both know you won't use it. I'd hate for you to hurt yourself by accident."

Walter didn't, though. Instead, he rolled his index finger

over the trigger. "If you walk out of here with me, I can keep you safe."

"You made me that promise before, do you remember? In a taxi back in Detroit. It's chivalrous of you, but we both know it's empty. This place has been good for me. I've been contained here, all these years. Not a peep from me in your world. Are you sure you want me to leave?"

"You can't stay here, not after today."

"No, I suppose I can't. I've been a bad girl. I deserve to be punished."

"Do you even know how many you've killed here? What you did today, that was blatant. But how many before that? How many have you hidden over the years?"

All six shrugged. "The fact that you have to ask should tell you how little it matters. Nobody cares what happens to these people. They're burdens, the unwanted. Society's discarded waste. You should be thrilled I've found such a place to call home. Are you sure you want me out there again?"

"You wouldn't be free."

"No?"

"I'd find someplace where you'd be safe."

"I have needs, Walter."

"I'd take care of you."

"You'd lock me in a cage and toss in murderers or prisoners or maybe the homeless, like raw meat to a lion in the zoo, while your scientists poked and prodded me...Don't for a second believe I haven't taken a peek in your friend Lincoln Sealey's mind. You may have learned to put up walls, but he's an open book."

"This needs to end."

"*It* doesn't end any more than time ends. I think you're looking at this all wrong. Your view is so shortsighted. *I could make you like me, Walter.* I could take away all your pain, and I could show you what it truly means to live. You and I together for all time, can you imagine such a thing! I'm lonely, Walter. There's nothing I want more than to share my life with you. I've made this offer before, but the clock is ticking. You're so frail now; how much time do you belicve you have left? How long before death gets his hooks in you?"

Another hand brushed Walter's foot, and this time he kicked it away. This was the fortysomething Amy Archer, but they all smiled up at him, and for one brief second, he didn't think of these six as her at various stages of life but instead he thought of them as her at various stages of *death*. Each one slowly dying, rotting away.

As he turned in that slow circle, he stepped on something and realized it was a tooth. Yellow, with a crimson root still attached.

She must have felt the disgust roiling in his gut. She said, "I don't want you to think of me that way."

"How else—"

Walter's vision snapped white.

"Is this better?"

WHEN HIS VISION CLEARED, Walter was twelve years in the past—back in the run-down motel near the Garden outside Atlanta. He was tied to the bed and Amy Archer was kneeling between his legs wearing nothing but one of his loosely buttoned shirts, her hair damp from the shower, steam still coming from the open bathroom door.

"This isn't real," Walter said flatly.

She tilted her head. "Maybe it is. What if this is real, and everything you believe came next was all just in your mind? You bumped your head pretty hard in the accident. Wouldn't that be so much better? All the pain you suffered. The years of rehab trying to piece your frail, broken body back together. Chasing after me from this place to that with your little band of friends…Wouldn't life be so much better if all that had been a blip in your mind and this…the two of us right here…was real? *This* could be our truth." Her fingers rolled through his hair, and she massaged his temple. Her voice dropped to a whisper. "It's not too late for you to be Henry and me to be Velma Barfield from Dubuque, Iowa."

Light from the neon sign near the street filtered in through the window blinds, painting the ugly floral wallpaper in stripes.

Where have I seen that wallpaper before?

She lowered her head and kissed his chest. Walter expected a shooting pain, some injury they'd find on him later when someone ran a black light over his dead body, but no pain came. Instead, there was only the moist warmth of her lips. "I pulled you from the Suburban and managed to get you through the woods. You regained partial consciousness, enough to walk with my help, obviously not enough to remember everything. A man in a red truck picked us up at the road and brought us here. He wanted to take us to the nearest hospital, but I managed to talk him out of that. I got you in the bed and cleaned you up; you've been sleeping ever since."

Walter tugged at the ropes on his arms. "Then why am I tied up?"

She nuzzled against his chest and traced up his arm to the rope with the tip of her finger. "You were delirious. Tossing and turning. I couldn't risk you hurting yourself."

"I'm fine now. Untie me."

"What fun would that be?" She pressed her knee down between his legs and spread them apart, then slipped her palm down to his thigh.

Although he tried to fight it, Walter felt his erection grow against the warmth of her touch.

"There you are," she said softly.

"What exactly are you?"

Her fingers worked the last two buttons on her shirt and the soft cotton fell open, revealing her full breasts. She bent forward just enough to allow one of her pink nipples to brush over his lips, then pulled away again. "I'm whatever you want me to be, Walter. I'm the girl who wants to kiss you at sunset atop the Eiffel Tower. I'm also the girl who will drop to her knees and give you head in the middle of a crowded subway car. You can take me home to visit Mom, but it's Dad who will perk up when I enter the room. I know how to make you happy in every conceivable way. There's nothing I wouldn't do for you." A glint filled her eye. "That day you followed me from Giovanni's into the alley with that cheating scumbag, Michael Driscoll, when he had me pinned up against the wall, when he was fucking me, I was watching you. I was thinking about you. Just knowing you were right there, hiding in the shadows, wanting me but not able to have me at that moment, that was such an incredible turn-on. You have no idea how I hoped you would tear him away and take his place. I'm patient, though. I knew our time would come."

"This isn't real," Walter said again, shaking his head.

"No?" She crawled backward, down the length of his body, and playfully kissed his thighs in a slow circle.

"No..." he replied. The insistence he wanted in his voice wasn't there, though. Not only could he feel her; he could feel his right leg. Not the dull, aching throb he'd grown accustomed to over the past twelve years, the pins-and-needles feeling left behind by broken bones and severe nerve damage, but he could *feel* his right leg as much as the left. He felt them like he felt them *before* the accident. He knew if he were able to sit up and look at them, the surgical scars would be gone. The uneven lines of the patched and pinned bones beneath his skin would be gone, too. The broken ribs. His shattered knees. All of it.

Twelve years of physical therapy, pain, and medications. *What if it really is gone?*

Running the tip of her finger up his abdomen, around his belly button, to his chest, she said, "In your dream, they removed your spleen. The scar would have been right here, but there's nothing now. See?"

Walter cocked his head, tried to look, but couldn't get the angle with his arms tied up behind his head.

"You could waste your life, alone, hunting me, or we could be Velma and Henry…We could live on that farm in Iowa, make strawberry wine and sell it to the tourists. We could have children. Grow old together in matching rocking chairs out on the wraparound porch. It's not really a choice when you compare the two, is it? Nobody wants to be alone. Life is so precious, why waste a second on anything that doesn't bring happiness? You couldn't possibly be happy, in that nightmare dream-life of yours…"

Walter stared over her bare shoulder at the wallpaper, the thin stripes of light that seemed to slice it into pieces.

No, that isn't right, either. Not sliced, but—

She smiled up at him, drew closer again. "I've loved you from the first moment I saw you, Walter. I knew you were the one. Running away from you that first time, that may have been the hardest thing I've ever done, but I knew I had to; you were too young. I had to wait. Your mortal years, they would move fast. I told myself I could wait, and wait I did. Every second I spent away from you, all those years between as I jumped from this place to that, you never left my thoughts. I waited for you. I've never known patience, but I waited for *you*. Then it became this game, you and

I." Her voice dropped conspiratorially low. "I'll let you in on a little secret," she whispered. "I only continued to run because I knew you'd follow."

She kissed him then, her full lips pressed into his; he felt her tongue against his and he welcomed it. He pressed into her, testing the ropes, getting as close as he could and wanting to get closer.

When she drew her lips across his neck, near his ear, he pressed his nose into her hair and breathed in the sweet scent of lavender. He hadn't smelled it a moment earlier, but he did now. As if it weren't perfume but her scent, drifting up from her pores.

You know that smell, too, his mind muttered. *It's like the damn wallpaper. That ugly-ass floral-print wallpaper.*

He remembered a similar print in Alvin Schalk's apartment. Similar, but not the same. There had been peeling wallpaper in the room at the Edison, where they'd found Glenn Beede, and where he'd first met his old partner Wes Brayman. Even the room at the Four Seasons—didn't it have floral wallpaper? He couldn't remember for sure. But the other two, yes. Both of those places had floral wallpaper, but neither quite matched this one. The wallpaper here. The wallpaper he remembered from—

The neon sign outside flickered on and off several times, and the light on the walls did, too, and then it came to him. How had he forgotten? He must have blocked it from his mind as a child; nothing else made sense.

His childhood home.

This wallpaper, this *exact* wallpaper, had been in the house where he'd spent the first seven years of his life. His mother had put it up in the kitchen, on the wall behind the stove. His father had complained. Had said nobody uses wallpaper for a backsplash—the grease and heat will destroy it in a week—but she hung it anyway. It was the flickering light that reminded him. The flickering light on that wallpaper, because it looked like—

Fire.

Walter saw the stove then. Flames leaping up from all five burners, catching the oil on the counter, the cabinets, hungrily climbing up the walls, chewing away at that wallpaper. His mind flashed to another memory, the moments before he had gone down to the kitchen.

Walter remembered hearing something downstairs, not sure what it was. He remembered climbing from his bed, tiptoeing down the hall to his parents' room. He wanted to wake them. He wanted to tell them he'd heard something or someone downstairs, but when he crossed their room to their bed, he found them already awake, but...

No. That isn't quite right, either.

They weren't awake, but their eyes were open. Both his parents were lying in bed, staring up at the ceiling. And he remembered the look on his mother's face—her left eye focused up, her right pointing off to the side. They weren't breathing.

And their room smelled like lavender, didn't it? You didn't know what that flowery smell was back then, but now...

That was when Scritch had barked and jumped into Walter's arms.

Downstairs, flames licking at the wallpaper.

The kitchen window was open, and through that window, beneath the tree where he had seen his father kissing a woman who was not his mother, stood that same woman. She was facing him now, her long dark hair fluttering behind her in the night breeze. Her lips moved, and although she was too far away to possibly be heard, Walter heard her voice anyway, angelic, the sweetest voice he'd ever heard, as she said —

"Like father, like son."

Scritch saw her, too, and his little frame grew tense; a growl rose in his throat. He wriggled from Walter's grasp, jumped to the floor, and ran for the door, turning once, beckoning for Walter to follow.

Back in the motel room, Amy Archer drew herself up Walter's body, kissing the length of him as she worked her way back to his ear and softly said, "There's nothing cuter than a boy and his dog."

Walter drew away as these words sunk in, as the long-buried memories flooded back. He tried to speak, but nothing came out.

She kissed him again. "I suppose it was selfish of me, to want you all to myself. And the fire was reckless; I nearly lost you…"

He tried to push her off at that point but couldn't. The ropes held him down.

She sat back on his knees before he could buck her off. "Your father was in our way, Walter. Your mother, too."

"You set the fire."

"How it came to be doesn't really matter. It brought us together. Surely you see that. The fire. The car crash. Alvin Schalk. Earl Golston. This was fate bringing us together. I can't run from you any more than you can escape me. I realized it then, the first time I ran from you, when I left you and your dog standing in the street. We're two halves bound by forces much stronger than either of us. I've accepted that, Walter. I *want* it. I know you do, too."

"That was you…" Walter mumbled. "It's always been you… I was just a kid…"

"Souls are so much older than the bodies, the husks, they inhabit. *That's* what I saw. Your soul. Not the frightened child. I saw the soul meant to be with mine and at first that frightened me and maybe that's why I ran, too, but it all became clear with the years. You and I were always meant to be together."

She leaned down and licked his chin. "Kiss me, Walter. Please. That's all you need to do, and this can be our reality. Our future will start from this moment, and all the pain and heartache will become nothing but a bad dream. You don't have to dwell on the past. I can make you forget, if that's what you want. All you have to do is kiss me. *Give* yourself to me."

The stillness of the air folded over him, thick and unforgiving.

She leaned in toward his lips and froze. A panicked look entered her dark gray eyes. "Walter, do you smell salt?"

A cut appeared on her naked shoulder, another across her cheek, and she screamed.

83

WALTER'S VISION FILLED WITH white again, a bright flash, like lightning behind his temples, and when it cleared, he was back in the turret room of Bakersfield, standing in the center of the six nuns positioned against the walls. Disoriented, he nearly fell over. If not for the cane in his hand, he surely would have. He stood motionless for a moment and waited for the world to right itself.

Sealey shouted something from behind him at the door. When Walter turned, he spotted him hastily dumping salt packets in a jagged line at the opening. "—out of there, damn it!" he screamed over his shoulder.

Larson was hovering over one of the nuns, the screwdriver in his hand. With a quick motion, he scratched the side of her neck. Her face registered no pain, but she began to bleed, and that seemed to be enough to satisfy him because he moved on to the nun next to her—the fortysomething Amy Archer.

Only, it wasn't Amy Archer anymore.

None of them were.

He had seen what she wanted him to; now he saw the truth—she'd somehow projected her image onto the women.

Two of the nuns were Black. One was Asian; another was Hispanic. Larson was blocking his view of the other two, working the screwdriver, but he knew they wouldn't be Amy, either. At least, not the Amy he knew. She had put the images in his head as easily as she'd slipped in her own voice.

Walter realized four of the other nuns had already been cut. Shoulder wounds, like the other. Blood dripping over their clothing. Hastily carved in the wall above each of the nuns' heads was the symbol Larson had carved downstairs in the hallways and doors. There was salt on the floor, too, just scattered around, as if someone had haphazardly thrown a handful into the center of the room.

Larson scuffed the salt with his shoe, tried to get it closer to the nearest nun. His face was red and dripping with sweat. He shouted over his shoulder back at Sealey, "Hurry up with the door! Get the salt around their bodies—you can't just dump it on the floor—you need a complete, unbroken line or it won't work!"

He swiveled quickly toward Walter. "Whatever you're seeing is bullshit! It's not real. It's her. It's all just her!"

Walter watched as Larson swung down with the blade and cut the woman in front of him with no more emotion than someone slicing the tape on a delivered package. She didn't so much as flinch as he opened a wound at least six inches long from her shoulder to her breast.

Sealey finished at the door, maneuvered around the

candles to the nearest nun, and began emptying salt packets around her body, tracing her limbs and torso. As he worked, he tossed a handful of packets in Walter's general direction. "Help me! Hurry!"

"Don't let them hurt me, Walter. Hit that man with your cane. Beat him. Crack his skull open like a rotten melon. The other one, too. They just want to keep us apart. They're jealous because I want you, not them. Neither of them are Walter O'Brien, neither of them are you. They're beneath you, beneath us. Crush them like a roach under your shoe."

Walter tightened the grip on his cane and glared at the back of Larson's head.

He could do it.

One quick swipe at Larson with the cane's heavy silver handle, then maybe a two-handed backswing at Sealey. He'd clip him in the chin like a Major League hitter going for the fence. One, two…it would all be over in under a second. He didn't have to kill them, just hurt them a little.

"Do it for me, Walter. Do it for us."

Walter raised the cane.

Out of breath, Larson was still bent over the fifth nun, both his hands resting on his knees. Blood dripping to the floor from the screwdriver.

"I love you, Walter. I always have. Please…"

Sealey hit him first, a solid right hook across Walter's jaw. He staggered, nearly fell.

"Get the hell out of here if you're not gonna help!" Sealey shouted.

Larson ignored them both and brushed the sweat from his brow. He went to the sixth nun and raised the screwdriver again, prepared to cut her.

The mouths of all six nuns fell open, and a guttural

scream unlike anything Walter had ever heard shook the beams. Impossibly loud, high-pitched, shrill. With it came a wind—how that was possible, Walter had no idea—but a wind swirled out of each of them, spun around the room, and gained intensity with each passing second.

"The candles!"

This came from Sealey, and by the time Walter understood what he meant, it was too late. The wind tore through the space with enough ferocity to send the candles tumbling over. The flames met the waxed floor and leaped across the dry wood, racing for the walls, where they quickly climbed. The room filled with a hungry heat. The women's screams grew louder.

Larson tried to ignore all of it, tried to cut that last nun with the screwdriver—this time, aiming for her neck rather than her shoulder—but the wind blew him back. He stumbled, nearly fell. He regained his balance, but not fast enough.

All six nuns shot to their feet, moving in perfect unison. Their heads swiveled toward the door, but only long enough to take in the salt at the threshold before turning in the opposite direction.

"The window!" Larson shouted. "Get the window!"

The nuns were faster. The first crashed through the glass and vanished, followed by the next four in quick succession. The final nun, having to round the salt spread around half her body, was last.

The same realization must have occurred to all of them at once. They were four stories up. It was at least forty or fifty feet to the ground.

All three ran to the window's edge and peered down at the expansive lawn.

Five bodies littered the ground, bent at horrible angles. No doubt dead.

Five.

The sixth nun was gone.

Larson shouted something, but Walter couldn't make out what he said.

The window was at least four feet across and five feet tall—twenty square feet. With the glass gone, the fire behind them sucked in the fresh oxygen, fueling flames that had engulfed not only the turret room but nearly all of the attic. The entire building would go.

"Come on!" Sealey grabbed Walter by the shirt and dragged him back through the black smoke and flames, toward the elevator on the far side of the floor, with Larson following close behind.

NOW

lele

ALIASES

~~Amy Archer*~~ *lele*

~~Amelia Dyer*~~

~~Velma Barfield*~~

--lele--

~~Jane Toppan*~~

~~Gesche Gottfried*~~

~~Nannie Doss*~~

~~Myra Hindley*~~

~~Leonarda Cianciulli*~~

~~Dagmar Overbye*~~

~~Mary Clement*~~

Lilin

~~Sister Mary Daria~~

*BLACK WIDOWS/BOGUS

lele

Hair?

Nails??

Teeth???

Salt

Notebook – names, dates, locations

Drawings/~~girls related?~~

~~Same?~~ ???

lele

VICTIMS

Alvin Schalk

Two bodies/basement freezer

Glenn Beede/ ~~John Doe~~/Edison

Aneta Kostenko/~~Jane Doe~~/ Corktown Bus Depot

Earl Golston PI/~~John Doe~~/ Four Seasons

Man on train platform

Michael Driscoll

BROWNSTONE

Wes Brayman

Rebecca Edgecomb (Willow)

17 others

All lele <u>Covering tracks?</u>

lele

THE GARDEN

80+ bodies

Some over 200 yo

Dumping ground

… Walter O'Brien, 57 Years Old

84

COULD A BUILDING SWEAT?

The answer was yes, it could. When it was sick.

When there was a cancer inside.

Walter understood that what he was seeing wasn't sweat, not really, only a trick of the streetlights off the smooth surfaces. Awnings, metal flashings, glass. Maybe some kind of sealant on the brick. His mind was projecting—it was turning this place into a living, breathing thing when it was nothing but a container, a vessel, a wrapper around his prize. It was her final disguise. The last place she would ever hide from him.

He looked down at his watch.

Nineteen minutes.

It would all be over in nineteen minutes.

"What's she doing in there?" Red asked over the earbud.

Walter shifted his weight and did his best to ignore the television cameras cropping up around the outer perimeter of the police barricades, the shouts directed at him from reporters. "Our girl or the SWAT commander?"

"Either."

"I have no idea."

"Do you think we have enough? They're getting ready to move. I can feel it."

Walter shifted slightly and tried to get a better look at the crowd behind the barricades without being too obvious about it. "I see at least six networks set up out there, and the same three choppers keep darting around up top. I can't tell if they are press or unmarked PD. We told them no air support, so I'm sure someone found a work-around. Maybe they put a spotter in a press chopper. That's what I would do. But yeah, to answer your question. We have enough."

Sealey said, *"Rigby's coming out."*

Walter turned again. Pain screamed up his back. He'd been sitting still too long. Didn't think to bring water, either. His throat felt like he'd been swallowing sand, and the mucus coming up from his lungs gummed up the entire works. He coughed into the crook of his elbow, cleared it as best he could.

Her stance was different.

Tense.

Red was right. They'd move anytime now.

He had less than nineteen minutes.

Walter watched the salt truck start on another lap as Rigby crossed the intersection and stepped up to the damaged patrol car.

She said, "Lincoln Sealey, Alfred Larson. Who else do you have out here?"

"I've got a small army. And Larson prefers to be called Red."

"We need to talk about the people inside that club," she replied. "I just hung up with my boss, and the people I answer to are getting nervous. They think you've got that bomb on a timer and that you plan to set it off no matter what happens. They think this business with the girl is bogus. Got a dozen people poring through your service record, and they're all telling me you're nothing short of psychotic. Delusional."

Walter knew what she saw—an old man. Frail. Broken. A cripple with a cane, beaten down, covered in scars. "I take it you're on board with that assessment?"

Rigby said, "Give me an alternate theory. Why don't you tell me what you've been doing for the past twenty-four years? Let's start there."

"Would you believe I'm an agent with an elite government unit operating off the books for the DOD?"

Not even a smile. "No."

"Then stick with delusional."

Her eyes narrowed slightly. "You're serious? You want me to believe you're all part of some off-the-books DOD op?"

Walter shrugged. "I don't expect you to believe anything."

"You're forcing my hand. I can't let you blow up that club."

Walter looked down at his hands. "How many snipers do you have on me right now?"

She didn't hesitate. "Six."

"And you've got shooters watching my shooters. You've got teams in the tunnels, ready to go. Ready to take my people out. Sounds like you've got all the bases covered. So why are you standing here?"

"Truth?"

"Why not."

"Because you don't seem the least bit worried about all that, and that scares the hell out of me."

"Some things are more frightening than bullets." He looked up at her. "Did you watch Red Larson's video?"

The look on her face told him she had.

He went on. "CIA shot that. Sent a man to the middle of hell to talk to him when he was found. Not sure if you caught the dates—the night he talked about, the night he went missing, was March '68. He didn't turn back up until August. Vanished for five months. That thing that attacked him killed the two men he was with and got a good start on him before some locals stumbled onto their camp and ran it off. Took five months in their care to nurse him back from that. Physically, anyway. I'm not sure his psyche ever recovered. They called it *preta*. Means *hungry ghost*. Eater of life." He looked her dead in the eye. "Here in the States, we call it a succubus."

She almost said it.

He caught the twitch in her mouth.

Not real. Bullshit.

But she didn't.

That told him two things—first, she'd seen enough of the drive to at least pique her curiosity. And two, Red was right—they were prepping to move and she was stalling, maybe here to distract him. None of that mattered.

Walter cleared his throat. "Don't ask me to explain the hows of it all; I'm not sure anybody can. There's only theories. Legends. Lore. Campfire tales. I can tell you, nobody sees the same thing when they look at her. Best I can describe it, they see their ideal woman. That's how she draws them in. Then she feeds. Give her enough time, and she'll suck a body dry. Savor it like wine. Can do it with just a touch." Walter wrapped the fingers of his right hand around his left wrist and flashed back to the ME's office all those years earlier. God, he had been naive back then. "Kills surrounding tissue. Causes cells to go haywire. Looks like cancer, but that's only part of it. She drains the life out. Give her enough time, and she'll leave nothing behind but a dried-out husk. If she's in a hurry"—he tapped the side of his head—"instant aneurysm or blood clot. She'd been taking her time with Red when the locals in 'Nam got him out, left him in a bad way. They somehow nursed him back with something called oxenberry. Reverses things to a certain extent. Poisonous to her. Took all of those five months to get him back on his feet again, sans one digit." He held up his left index finger. "Still don't know why she takes them. At first, I thought they were souvenirs, but Red found some old texts out of Italy that said, and I quote, 'Consumption of a victim's senses increases strength and vitality.' Nose, eyes, fingers—smell, sight, touch—she just happens to have a thing for fingers." He paused for a moment, gathered his thoughts. "We almost had her at Bakersfield, then things went bad. Sealey took the heat for that one, but we all got shitcanned. Some pencil pusher in Washington caught the ear of the right senator and convinced him our little operation was bad for business. Consequences be damned, best to let the monsters roam free than risk negative press."

"The date on Bakersfield was what, '09? What have you been doing since?"

"Trying to forget. Trying to walk away. And failing at both," he said flatly. "She's my white whale, and this particular Ahab is dying. I can't let it go. Can't let *her* go."

Whether she believed any of this or not, she couldn't help but ask, "And you think she's inside this club?"

"I know she is."

"How?"

Walter thought of the text. "She contacted me. Wanted to see me."

"If she knows you're trying to kill her, why would she do that?"

"Same reason she didn't kill Red when she found him again in that hospital. Same reason she didn't kill me all those other times. This is all some kind of game to her. Like I said earlier, I think she gets bored. Something like her, something older than dirt...how would you fill the time?"

"This is it, fellas," Red said in Walter's earbud. *"Go time."*

"It's been a pleasure working with you both," Sealey replied.

Red chuffed. *"Stow that shit. Ain't over yet."*

The commander looked Walter dead in the eye. "So Sealey and this Red Larson are in those buildings? Who else? We identified eight. Who are the others?"

He had no reason to lie to her. It wouldn't change what was about to happen. "If I told you it was just the two of them, would you believe me? When I learned she'd be here, I got the band back together for one last show. Just me and the boys playing our old hits."

"We know you have more. Who do you have in the club?"

"Nobody."

"Why aren't they answering the phones?"

Walter didn't have an answer to that, so he said nothing.

There it was again, that twitch at the corner of the commander's mouth. Her hand was resting on the butt of her service weapon, and the movement of her eyes told him a million thoughts were passing through her head, riding a wave of adrenaline.

In a voice that didn't waver, slowly and perfectly

enunciated, the commander said, "You do understand you'll go to jail for this? Possibly for the rest of your life? Won't matter that you're sick. If you don't surrender, if you don't tell your people to step down, you'll face a *litany* of charges."

And that was when they went.

RIGBY'S GUN WAS OUT of the holster and on him in one swift motion, inches from Walter's head. From several rooftops, shots cracked from high-powered rifles. Sharp snaps quickly followed by the sound of shattered glass as Detroit PD targeted all locations simultaneously.

In his mind's eye, Walter pictured the bullets tearing across the intersection, bursting through windows, and burying themselves in center mass as Sealey and Red huddled over their weapons. Hearts exploding. Bodies falling. Both men dead in an instant. Or maybe they were head shots. No way to know for sure.

From the lower floors of the two buildings housing his friends, flash-bang grenades went off. More windows shattered, and it wasn't difficult to see these highly trained SWAT officers quickly moving on the locations identified by thermal imaging cameras, clearing all as they went. Moving fast but with caution, even though someone on their radio channel was most likely reporting all shooters down.

Oblivious to all this, the snowplow truck rounded the club again, belching dark smoke.

Without lowering her gun, Rigby shouted out, "Shut that thing down, now!"

Several officers surrounded the truck, weapons drawn. The taillights glowed red. The engine switched off, and the driver leaned out the window, extending both hands toward the sky.

In a low voice, Walter said, "Go easy on that guy. He's not part of this. I found him in a homeless shelter on Eighteenth and gave him a couple hundred bucks to drive the truck. *We* stole it, not him. I figured he would have stopped a long time ago. He's just a kid."

She heard him, but she was listening to the chatter on her comm, too.

Walter could only imagine what that sounded like, an operation this big.

More flash-bangs went off.

He glanced over at the reporters. One was ducking down, pointing over her shoulder behind her while rattling off something in her microphone. Two others were obviously live on the air, standing, with the chaos as their backdrop, as if they were safe because they were behind those flimsy barricades. Cameras swirled around everywhere—not just the press, but the crowd—a hundred-plus arms holding up cell phones and twisting them around to capture whatever they could. The choppers had moved in closer, too. One cameraman was hanging out an open door with a harness holding him in place.

Chaos.

Exactly what they wanted.

Probably a million or more eyes watching now.

The flash-bangs stopped.

The echo faded and died.

Commander Rigby's face went from frustrated to confused and back again. To someone in her comm, she said, "Bring him down. I want him right here." The grip on her gun tightened, and she glared at Walter. "Where are the rest? Who has the detonator? Fucking Sterno cans? *Are you kidding me!?*"

The Sterno had been Red's idea. They lit up cans of Sterno behind desks, places without direct line of sight, to mimic heat signatures.

Bring him down. They'd caught at least one.

With her free hand, she plucked the earbud from Walter's ear and jammed it in her own. Listened.

"My people are off comms now," Walter told her.

Walter heard Sealey then, shouting.

He turned to see three officers pulling him from the federal building where he'd been holed up. He was in handcuffs, and one of the officers was carrying his rifle. They brought him over and forced him to his knees on the pavement at the commander's feet.

Sealey glanced at Walter but didn't say anything. Nothing to say.

Commander Rigby cupped a hand over her ear, listening to all the communications chatter. Her frown deepened, and she trained her gun on Sealey. "Where's Larson? Does he have the detonator?"

Walter exchanged another look with Sealey, then said, "There is no bomb. We lied."

"You lied."

For a second, Walter thought she might pistol-whip one of them. But she was fully aware of all the cameras on her and smart enough to hold back. "Out of that car, on the ground, now!"

"Come on, I have a bad—"

One of the SWAT officers who had brought Sealey over grabbed Walter by his heavy vest, yanked him out of the battered police cruiser, and forced him to the ground next to Sealey. Walter's leg and back both screamed, and he felt a sharp pain in his chest. A ball of phlegm rolled up his throat and he choked it out, spat it to the pavement. Red, black, and diseased.

The commander ignored this, pressed a finger to the ear-bud she'd taken from Walter. "Alfred Larson—surrender immediately to the closest member of Detroit PD!"

Sure, that would bring him out.

In her own comm, she growled, "He's in one of those buildings. Look again." She looked back toward the SWAT van and the mass of uniformed officers and patrol cars around it. "Unit commanders, coordinate with the team leaders, assist. No way he got out of here. I want a complete canvass."

Around the west corner of the club, Walter spotted six more SWAT officers in full tactical gear huddled against the wall and crouched low. Commander Rigby turned toward them. "Hersh, Yellow team—you're a go on the club. Bomb squad, I want you on their backs. Clear everyone out as quickly as possible and search every inch of that place. Hurwitz, bring in the buses. I want every person searched and placed on a bus. Nobody leaves our custody. We'll interview them back at HQ. Use caution—any one of them could be part of this."

Walter had figured they'd use buses. There were at least two hundred people inside the club. He wouldn't let anyone go, either. It was all a complete waste of time, but necessary.

Procedure.

Procedure.

Procedure.

Six SWAT officers crossed the pavement and rounded the valet stand at the front door soundlessly. More went around to the back—welded shut or not, they covered all egress points. Uniformed officers lined up behind SWAT, weapons out.

At the front door, one of them held a large battering ram. He quickly set it aside when he realized the door wasn't locked. Using a small mirror, he checked all edges of the door for potential traps, switches, or triggers, then nodded back in the commander's direction and mouthed something into his radio Walter couldn't hear.

Commander Rigby nodded. "Go," she said into her comm.

An eerie quiet fell over the crowd of bystanders, the press—all eyes on the club as the officer in the lead pulled the door open and the others quickly filed inside.

86

RIGBY'S BODY TENSED. IF she was breathing, Walter didn't see it. There was only a slight tremble in the corner of her jaw as she stared at the club, stone-faced, one hand over her ear.

Listening.

Thirty seconds ticked by.

One minute.

Two.

In a low voice, she said, "Yellow team, report."

Although she spoke in an even tone, there was a slight waver just beneath the surface.

She tapped on her earpiece, as if the device had stopped working and she was trying to coax it back to life. "Hersh, I said report."

Nothing.

"They're dead, Commander," Walter said softly. "She killed them. Probably the second they stepped inside. They didn't even get a shot off. That's why nobody's answered the phone. They're all dead. We need to stop her before she gets out."

Sealey bobbed his head toward his rifle; it was hanging around the neck of one of the men who had brought him over. "Your guns are useless. The bullets in that weapon are coated with oxenberry. They're deadly to her." He paused a second. "Commander, everything we told you about her is true. We're equipped to deal with this; you are not. I strongly suggest you back down and let us do our job before you lose additional personnel."

If Rigby hadn't connected Sealey to the voice on the phone earlier, she certainly did now. Walter saw the recognition flood her gaze. That realization only served to anger her more. "Why isn't this man in restraints? Get cuffs on him. Now."

Two officers quickly tugged at Walter's wrists, and he felt zip ties tighten in place.

Commander Rigby tapped her comm again. "Breach team, report."

No reply came.

"Anyone have visual on the interior? Hurwitz—what do you see on the body cams?"

Walter couldn't hear what was said in reply, but whatever it was, it caused a frown to deepen on Rigby's face.

Another minute ticked by.

One of the officers standing on Walter's right pointed at the club. "There!"

The first person to stagger out was maybe twenty-five, wearing a tight satin T-shirt and dark jeans. His hair was mussed, and he looked like he hadn't slept in a month. He looked out at the large crowd outside the club and froze in the doorway. A SWAT officer appeared behind him and gently urged him on. The man stumbled out. Another officer pointed him toward one of the buses. It took him a moment to understand, then he started toward it, slowing only when he encountered the thick swath of salt. The crowd was still so quiet, Walter could hear the salt crunching under the man's feet. Then he was on the bus, and three more people appeared at the club's door.

Four more behind them.

Men and women, all appearing exhausted, formed a line from the club to the buses in a rushed evacuation as members of the bomb squad darted in the opposite direction, vanishing inside.

Walter knew they wouldn't find anything.

Near the SWAT van, a gray Ford Taurus screeched to a stop and an older man in a dark suit got out, seemed to assess his surroundings, then flashed an ID wallet and badge at the nearest officer, who pointed him at Commander Rigby, and the man started over.

"Feds are here," Walter said.

The man's eyes locked on Sealey as he approached the commander. "Are you in charge here? I believe someone told you I was coming?"

Rigby offered a quick nod, then spouted off orders into her comm. Bomb squad, no doubt searching room by room.

To Sealey, the man said, "A lot of people want to speak with you."

Sealey shifted his weight but said nothing.

Rigby turned away from the club only long enough to ask, "Where are you taking him?"

The man eyed Sealey for another moment, then fished a business card out of his pocket and handed it to Rigby. "McNamara Building on Michigan. We'll hold him there until we can arrange transport to DC, about forty-eight hours or so. If you need to question him, call that number on the back; that's my cell. I'll get you the proper clearances."

She pocketed the card and hurriedly told one of the officers, "Help get this man into his car."

A uniformed officer gripped the zip tie on Sealey's wrists, placed a hand on his shoulder, and pulled him to his feet.

When the officer tried to push him in the direction of the Taurus, Sealey dug his heels in and instead looked down at Walter. *"Are you sure?"*

Walter could only nod.

Sealey closed his eyes and let out a resigned breath. "Okay, my friend. Okay."

The federal agent was staring.

Walter turned away from all of them. He couldn't look. He'd just get choked up.

"Go," the patrol officer said, shoving Sealey forward.

They wormed their way back to the car. Walter watched as Sealey was loaded into the back, the agent climbed behind the wheel, and a moment later they were gone.

He was still watching when he heard the scream at the club's door.

87

TWO SWAT OFFICERS WERE in the open doorway, their weapons hanging loosely at their sides. A young woman was standing between them, her arms draped over their shoulders for support. Her feet were bare and she wore a short black dress that barely reached her thighs. She'd been crying— her face was red and puffy, streaked with tears and snot. The three of them moved slowly, her legs offering little if any support, the officers taking the brunt of her weight. She stared out across the intersection at the police cars, SWAT van—taking in the plow truck, the news vans, the helicopters above, and all the people watching. When her gaze landed on Walter kneeling on the ground, hands cuffed behind his back, she grew visibly tense and stiffened. She scrambled, tried to get back inside the club. One of the officers holding her said something, tried to calm her, but she shook her head and planted her feet firmly on the ground.

They tried to move her forward, but she refused.

"I can't go out there! Let me go!"

Even though she was near hysterics, clawing at the men holding her, screaming out these words as her head thrashed from side to side, Walter knew that voice as well as he knew his own.

Amy Archer.

Jane Toppan.

Amelia Dyer.

Velma Barfield.

Gesche Gottfried.

Nannie Doss.

Myra Hindley.

Leonarda Cianciulli.

Dagmar Overbye.

Mary Clement.

Sister Mary Daria.

Her.

She.

It.

Iele.

She looked exactly the same. This was the girl he'd known as a child with his father; the one he saw again under that sink in Alvin Schalk's apartment; at the brownstone brothel; at that restaurant, Giovanni's; in her killing field, the Garden outside Atlanta; dressed as a nun in Bakersfield; and so many other times and places between they became a blur in his head. A swirl of memories all dipping in and out of one another. A lifetime of thoughts all stacked together in a single pile as transparent and fluid as a glass of water.

"Tell them to get away from her," Walter said to Commander Rigby. "Right now. Tell them."

Rigby said nothing. Her gaze remained fixed on the club's entrance.

The two SWAT officers pulled Amy Archer—Iele—forward, down several of the granite steps at the front stoop. She grew more agitated with each inch. Her legs shot out, and she tried to dig her heels in. The two men were stronger, though. They simply lifted her off the ground and got her to the winding cobblestone sidewalk at the base of the steps, then started across the lawn.

She looked so weak. This little waif of a thing. Fighting with every ounce of strength she possessed.

Frightened.

Terrified.

An act, all of it.

"You don't understand..." Walter said. But he understood. Walter understood perfectly.

Although her eyes remained fixed on him, Walter knew it wasn't him Amy feared; it was the salt. Salt she could not cross. Salt she *would not* cross.

"Tell them to stop there, before—" Walter started.

With her arms still draped over the shoulders of the two men, Amy brought her fingertips to both their temples simultaneously. A quick, sudden poke that happened so fast that if Walter hadn't been expecting it, he might have missed the motion altogether. Both men crumpled to the ground into lifeless puddles at her feet.

A sudden hush fell over everyone, nobody really sure what they'd just witnessed. Several of the police officers hunched lower behind their vehicles, but most appeared stunned, unmoving.

There were at least two dozen guns pointing at her in an instant, and Walter knew if just one of them took that first shot, the others would follow. They'd unload thousands of rounds in only a handful of seconds. Most would miss; many would not.

Walter waited for that first shot to come, and it probably would have, if not for the uniformed patrol officer who appeared in the doorway behind Amy. They wouldn't put their own in danger.

The officer had his own weapon out, and as he approached her slowly from behind, he leveled the gun at her head. Only a few feet away. He wouldn't miss.

She turned toward him, said something in a hushed whisper, and leaned forward.

Her fingertips gently stroked his arm. She stood on her toes and kissed him.

The scene was so bizarre, Commander Rigby's mouth dropped open and the world managed to grow a little quieter.

When Amy pulled away, the officer turned toward them, a stunned look on his face. Still holding his gun, he stumbled past the valet station, over the salt, and reached the intersection. His pace increased with each step, picked up an urgency. His blank stare locked on them.

"Shoot him, Commander!" Walter shouted.

"I'm not gonna—"

The officer shot first.

The commander wasn't his target. Instead, Amy had sent him after the man holding Sealey's rifle. Somehow she knew it contained their modified rounds. The possessed officer fired three quick shots into the man's face and snatched the rifle from his hands before his dead body hit the pavement. With a flick of his wrist, he spun the rifle around, pressed the barrel against the blacktop, and leaned into the stock with the bulk of his weight as he pulled the trigger.

The barrel exploded, and the shot backfired.

Something wet slapped against Walter's cheek.

He didn't remember closing his eyes, but he did, and when he opened them the officer's dead body was on the ground beside him. Half the man's torso was missing; blood pooled out from where bits of the rifle had torn through his chest and arm. All of it mixed around Walter's knees. His ears rang with a sharp metallic sound over all else. That was quickly replaced by the commander's voice shouting.

"—on the ground! Right there! Don't take another step!"

Walter had seen all this before.

He knew what she could do.

Amy—Iele—stood there for a moment, inches from the thick swath of salt across the lawn; then she turned toward them and wiped the fake tears from her face with the back of her arm and called out, "I've missed you, Walter. So much!"

Bending down, she grabbed one of the dead SWAT officers by the back of the neck as if he were nothing but a weightless rag doll and tossed him out into the salt at her feet. The other body followed, an impossible throw of nearly seven feet, this man landing facedown beyond the first.

Her first step was tentative, onto her makeshift bridge of bodies. When nothing happened, when she realized she could stand above the salt without harm, she took another step, then another. Her gait was downright playful by the time she reached the body of the second man, crossed over, and jumped down onto the blacktop, the salt safely behind her.

Amy dug her toes into the pavement, tilted her head to the side, and looked out at all the people—law enforcement, first responders, bystanders, all the television cameras and reporters—then turned back to Walter as if no one existed but them. "I've missed your face." She smiled.

88

WALTER TRIED TO STAND, but with his cane on the ground and his hands secured behind his back, he only managed to get halfway up before dropping. He slammed into the pavement, the rough asphalt tearing open his chin.

"Get these goddamn cuffs off me, now!"

Commander Rigby didn't hear him. She was frozen, maybe in shock. Like all the others, she only stared at Amy, her mind no doubt unwilling to accept any of what had just happened. She might have been contemplating the fate of the other police officers who hadn't come out of the club, the bomb squad, maybe the civilians still inside. As commanding officer, a million thoughts might be going through her head in that particular moment, none of which would be as loud as the one telling her to run.

None of that would matter if Amy reached them.

Walter craned his head back toward the SWAT van,

toward all the patrol cars and the officers huddled behind them lining the streets. "Fire! Everybody fire!"

Walter had no idea where the first shot originated, a single isolated pop somewhere off to his right; it sounded so small, but that was followed by a barrage as every officer started shooting.

Amy's body jerked and twitched. The ground surrounding her erupted in an explosion of dust and chips of asphalt. The glass door of the club shattered. The neon tubes fastened to the brick walls, too. Shell casings shot through the air like metal hail, bouncing off the cars and pavement.

Somehow, she staggered forward.

One step.

Two.

It was all over in less than ten seconds.

Although Walter could hear nothing at first, he knew the sound of gunfire had been replaced by empty trigger pulls and the various clicks of slides locking back on automatics. Some officers struggled to reload while others only stared forward, dumbfounded.

She was still standing.

The gunfire had shredded portions of her dress. She'd no doubt been struck many times, but her skin appeared flawless. Not so much as a bruise.

The plow truck was behind her now, off to the side.

Something within Rigby sparked, and she came to life. The commander mumbled something Walter couldn't make out, dug a small knife from her pocket, and threw it to the ground near Walter's hands, then started toward Amy in quick strides. As Rigby moved, she scooped up an assault rifle off one of the patrol cars and brought up the barrel. She squeezed off three shots in quick succession, continued toward Amy, and fired two more. All five hit her in the stomach. She bent with the impact and started to straighten back up when Rigby fired three more shots, closing the distance with each step.

Walter knew the weapon. It was an AR-5, and each of those bullets should have torn right through her. Eight shots at such close range should have cut her in half, but other than cause her to totter slightly, they did nothing.

The commander fired again.

Walter fumbled for the knife, managed to get a grip on it, and began to saw at his plastic restraints.

"You're getting too close!" Walter shouted, but it didn't matter.

Amy was far too fast.

She grabbed the barrel of Rigby's rifle and yanked the weapon toward her, throwing the commander off-balance. She stumbled and fell to the ground. Amy crouched beside her and gripped Rigby's head between her palms.

Walter thought she was going to snap her neck, but instead, she kissed her. As she had with the officer back at the club, she planted her lips firmly on Rigby's and kissed her.

A string of expletives poured out of Walter's mouth as his restraints dropped away. He found his cane and managed to get to his feet.

Rigby's body tensed and jerked, but she couldn't break free. There was nothing anyone could do but watch as her skin went chalky white, the veins and tendons of her neck grew dark, lined her flesh. Her hands and feet twitched; then she went still as all life left her.

Iele stood, lifting Rigby's body with her, and tossed it to the side—aged a thousand years in seconds, nothing but a dried-out husk.

89

MORE GUNFIRE.

Walter swiveled on his cane in time to see two of the SWAT officers coming around the plow truck toward her, both firing in semiautomatic mode, their rifles kicking out shots in threes—*Crack! Crack! Crack!* Two of the patrol officers were coming at her, too. They rounded several patrol cars and ran directly toward her, nine millimeters leading from stiff arms as they fired.

Oblivious to the shots, she grabbed the first two men, on them in a blur. She pulled the assault rifles from their hands with enough force to break the clasps on the nylon straps. The arm of one man cracked with it, the shoulder dislocated on the other, both spun, and she caught them just long enough to press her palms against their temples. The life left their bodies, and she was on the second two men before the first had time to hit the ground.

Nine millimeters empty, one managed to wrangle his stun

gun from his belt and press the probes into the exposed skin at her midriff. There was a crackle and sparks, but she only smiled, and when she placed her fingers against the side of his head, she took her time with him, as if savoring the life force as it drained from him to her. The stun gun fell away, and he followed. The other officer had his baton out. He swung it with a two-handed grip and caught her in the chin as she turned to face him. Her head jerked to the side.

If the blow stunned her, it was only for a moment. She looked back at him, her hand shot up and grabbed him by the neck, and she lifted him from the ground.

"Stop!" Walter shouted. "Enough of this bullshit!"

Her fingers twitched, snapping the man's neck, and she dropped him.

"Enough!" Walter shouted again.

She took a step toward him and pouted. "Can't blame a girl for defending herself, can you?"

Walter met her gaze and raised his voice. "We've got people in all these buildings," he lied. "We've been positioning for hours. All their bullets are soaked in oxenberry. A little something Red heard about back in Vietnam. Maybe not one shot, but I guarantee if everyone we've got out here opens up at once, you're not walking away."

Without taking her eyes off him, she eyed the remains of the officer on the ground next to Walter, the destroyed rifle. She sniffed the air and her nose crinkled. "This whole place reeks of it. How is Red?"

Walter coughed.

He tried to hold it back, but it came up his throat and forced its way out. He didn't bother to cover his face.

When it was over, her eyes narrowed and she sniffed the air again. "Walter, are you sick?"

"Lung cancer," he told her, wiping his mouth. "I got maybe a month left. Probably less."

"I'm sorry."

"I'm sure you are."

For the first time, her face softened. "You hate me, don't you? You're dying, yet you have the space in your heart to hate me?"

Walter nearly answered her. The words came to the tip of his tongue, but he didn't let them out. He couldn't, not with all these people watching him, listening. They wouldn't understand. And how could they? Walter wasn't altogether certain he understood. Because he should hate her. He wanted to hate her. But he couldn't. He felt more alive today than he had in a decade.

We can tell ourselves who to despise, but none of us get to choose who we love.

He wasn't sure what fortune cookie he'd pulled that from, but it popped into his head.

The sight of her brought feelings he didn't want. Feelings he hated himself for having. Walter fought them with every ounce of his being because they contradicted what he had to do. He couldn't love her any more than she could really love him.

"You're not human," Walter said in a low voice. "You're a monster. A devil."

She took a step closer and smiled. "I'm an equalizer. I bring balance. I'm a necessity."

"I don't want to kill you, but I will. If you don't give me a choice."

"I can't die, Walter. The fact that you think I can illustrates just how little you know. You can't kill me any more than you can kill the wind."

"This needs to end."

"I don't *end*. I don't die. I simply am."

"You need to answer for your crimes," Walter told her.

"And your court is to be my judge? What gives you the right? Don't you see how narrow-minded that is? To attempt to judge me based on what? Insignificant rules created by an infantile society? You're children. You're specks of dust."

"And yet, we've got you trapped."

"You really believe that, don't you?" She gestured toward the club behind her. "I brought you here, Walter, not the other way around. Asked you to come here…so easy to manipulate, the whole lot of you."

Walter looked around at all the television cameras, wondering how much of this they were actually capturing. Any at all?

She went on. "I don't want to run from you anymore, Walter. I'm tired of running. Do you know how many times I've tried to forget you? I've tried to replace you? I've known so many people over the course of my…life…I guess we can call it that. My life. Most are terribly boring. Most are predictable. But you? I don't know what it is about you, but you interest me. You always have, even when you were a child. You've always intrigued me."

Walter coughed again. He knew there was blood on his lips, probably his cheeks. He didn't care. "Am I supposed to feel flattered by that? Touched somehow? I've lost count of all the bodies behind you. Do you understand that? The hurt you've caused? Do you even feel remorse for what you've done?"

"I have no choice in what I do. You can't blame me for existing. I'm fulfilling a purpose."

"Whose purpose?"

She cocked her hip and shifted her weight. "Do you really want to go there?"

All around them, the remaining officers crept up, drew closer. They spoke in hushed whispers and subtle hand gestures, a practiced language known only to them.

She eyed them warily. "Step inside with me, Walter. Maybe we should speak in private."

Before he could respond, she turned and crossed the human bridge back over the salt and disappeared through the shattered club's door.

Walter drew in a deep breath and watched her go, watched her walk away from him as he had so many other times in his life. He willed his shattered body to work, to move.

Are you sure? Sealey had said.

He was.

Walter squeezed the handle of his cane, heard a soft click, and crossed the intersection to the club, the weight of his thick bulletproof vest making the movement all the more awkward.

90

THERE HAD BEEN A mirror on the wall behind the cash register. It was shattered now. The glass crunched under Walter's feet as he stepped through the entrance. The frame still hung there, several shards still clinging to the cardboard backing, but most on the floor. The remains of the club's phone were on the floor, too—an old wired landline, yanked from the wall and crushed.

She stood deeper in the hallway, held by the shadows, watching him move with pity. "Oh, Walter. What the years have done to you. The real enemy here is time."

Not just time, Walter thought. For one brief moment, he felt her hand on his chest again in that alley all those years ago, the mark she left behind.

Walter looked beyond her, toward the quiet dance floor and seating areas off to the sides. Several people were still back there, at least three police officers, too. Probably whatever was left of the bomb squad. "I want them all out. Let them go."

"I'm not stopping them."

Walter met the eyes of one of the officers. "Get everyone out. Now."

There were bodies, too. Walter couldn't tell how many. Several were missing fingers; others had been drained like Rigby and so many others Walter had found in this woman's wake.

As the police officers rushed the remaining people outside, Amy followed Walter's eyes and almost looked embarrassed. "I had to, Walter. I needed the strength. I only took a few of them. No more than I had to. I'm glad you're here."

"Goddamnit, Amy…"

"Amy," she repeated. "You and all your names."

She looked down at her feet as the last of the clubgoers ran by them for the door. Outside, officers hurried everyone onto the buses, warily watching the door.

In a voice so low no one else could hear but her, Walter asked the question that had nagged him for as long as he could remember. "What's your real name?"

She seemed to consider this, and for a moment, Walter thought she'd feed him some other bogus name rather than answer, but in a voice equally low, she told him, "Isabella."

Isabella.

When they were alone, she said, "I'm so lonely, Walter. Aside from you, I have no constant in my life. I've gone months without speaking. Years, even. When I learned you were here, in Detroit again…I couldn't resist."

Walter remained still.

She sniffed the air again, scenting the death emanating from his pores. "But oh, my poor Walter."

Several of the news crews had repositioned in order to get direct shots into the club. The remaining police officers had gotten bold, too, drawing close. All these eyes watching them.

He'd given them enough.

There was a red velvet curtain on a rod over the destroyed door. He tugged it closed and sealed them all out.

When he turned back to her, much of his weight on the cane, she said, "You might be the only one who's ever understood me."

Walter had denied it. His entire life, *denied it*. He didn't want to understand her. Didn't want to care for her. He didn't want to love her. But he couldn't switch off those things any more than he could will himself to no longer breathe or taste. He'd never married or found in another what he felt for her. She'd given him life even as her touch stole it away. She gave him purpose. She'd occupied his every waking thought since the first moment he laid eyes on her all those years ago. Was that love? Was that understanding? At the very least it was a bond. An unbreakable bond linking them together. She completed him as much as he completed her, and without the other there was nothing. He couldn't exist without her. The thought of that was unbearable. He knew how foolish that all sounded, but knowing didn't make it any less true. Love was never meant to be understood.

From somewhere in the distance, the steady *chop, chop, chop* of multiple helicopters drew near.

Backup arriving.

There would be armored vehicles. Large weapons. Possibly soldiers. The feds knew they were here, and given the chance, they'd take her someplace, cage her, study her. Try to make sense of something that shouldn't exist. That had been Sealey's original mission, and with him out, that meant someone else was in charge. That someone else was coming.

Walter didn't have much time.

From the corner of his eye, he saw her reflection in what was left of the mirror. This hideous thing for which there were no words. In the image, a clump of hair fell from her head, the roots moist with glistening black blood. It landed at her feet and joined a fingernail and two teeth on the carpet. If Golston were still alive, Walter imagined those things would quickly find their way into jars. If she were alone, she might scoop them up and hide them.

But it was only them now.

He turned away and tried to wipe the terrible image from his mind. He didn't dare look down at the carpet, because he knew those things would be there. He didn't want to think of her that way. He understood why she always smashed the mirrors, why there was always a trail of broken mirrors behind her.

Walter looked back at her, standing in the shadows. This beautiful woman, with flowing brown hair and gray eyes deeper than the darkest night, her flawless skin and body sculpted to perfection.

His Amy.

His Iele.

Isabella.

This was how he wanted to remember her.

Not the thing in the mirror.

Never the mirror.

It had been some time since Walter had been willing to look into a mirror, either. She was studying him, too, and he didn't want her to.

She walked up to him slowly and pressed her palms against the thick vest on his chest. "You are so broken. Let me show you something?"

She raised a finger to his temple, and for one instant, Walter thought that was it, the moment he would die, but he didn't.

His vision shifted.

He saw them, him and Amy, standing atop a hill overlooking a small cabin in a green valley below. She was wearing a light cotton dress. It fluttered in the breeze, and the sun twinkled over her. Her hand was in his and she was smiling, this infectious smile brighter than all else. He had no cane. He didn't need it. His body was young again, strong. Life coursed through his veins and filled him with energy, vibrance. A small child, a little girl of maybe five or six, stepped around the side of the cabin, saw them both and waved, then started off toward a creek about a hundred feet away, a bucket and shovel in her hand.

Amy looked up at him, stroked his hair. "This is what I've always wanted for us. Thousands of years I've searched for some kind of meaning. Since the day we met, this is the image that carried me. Sustained me. The simplicity of it. The completeness. This is ours if you want it, too, Walter. Please tell me you do. I can make it real for us. I can make it forever, *for us.*"

With a blink, they were back in the dark club, their bodies so close, her looking up into his eyes with a longing matched only by his desire for her.

His hand slipped into his pocket; his fingers searched for the familiar leather of the dog collar he had carried with him every day since he was a child, they but found nothing. It wasn't there. Not anymore.

He pictured the cancer growing in his lungs, reaching out across every inch of his body. As if in response, it answered him with a twinge of pain in his lower back, another in his leg, more in his chest.

The helicopters were loud now, either hovering directly above or landing. Shouts came from outside. The *clang* of heavy metal weapons moving, targeting.

She heard it all, too, and repeated something she had told him all those years earlier, as they sat in that Italian restaurant together. "There are bad things waiting for both of us outside that door. I don't think you're ready for them any more than I am. So how about this? Let's pretend we're on a date. Our first. I'm from a small farm in Dubuque, Iowa, and we met today in the checkout line at the grocery store. You asked me out, and against my better judgment, I agreed."

Walter looked down at her, met her gaze, got lost in it. "I can't think of anything I want more right now."

She rose on her toes, brought her soft lips to his, and kissed him.

Walter wrapped his arms around her, drew her close, and felt his life force shift from him to her, felt all that he was move from him to her. And as the club vanished one last time, replaced with that sunny vision on the hill, he released his grip on the cane.

He heard the soft click of the dead man's switch embedded in the handle and wondered if she heard it, too. In his mind's eye, he saw the spark of electricity triggered by the wireless transmitter, saw it ride the wires concealed beneath the fabric of his bulletproof vest into the explosives packed tight. The thousands of ball bearings soaked in oxenberry. He saw a blinding white light. Then he saw nothing at all.

91

THE FORD TAURUS PULLED into a parking garage near Comerica Park, pausing only long enough to get a ticket from the automated kiosk at the entrance before speeding forward and up the ramp, the sound of the engine echoing off the concrete walls.

Sealey felt his stomach tighten. "Why are we stopping here?"

The man driving didn't answer. Didn't even acknowledge him. Instead, he pulled into a space on the third floor between two unmarked white vans, running over the orange cones that had kept it vacant, and shut off the engine.

"Why are we stopping?" Sealey repeated. His heart thumped, and he felt a bead of sweat form on his brow. He didn't like this one bit. He pulled at the restraints on his hands, fully understanding what a waste of effort that was, but doing it anyway.

The man got out of the car, looked in the side window of the van on their left, then opened Sealey's door. "Get out."

Sealey did, only because he understood resisting would do nothing but waste time.

Whatever this was, he wanted it over fast.

"Turn around."

Again, Sealey obeyed.

There was a soft tug on his wrists, then a snap as a blade sliced through the plastic restraints, cutting them free.

Sealey spun and smacked the man in the shoulder. "You just couldn't resist, could you?"

"What do you mean?"

"You handed that woman your business card with your left hand. You wanted her to see your missing finger, you dumb shit."

Red Larson grinned. A mischievous, childish grin. He felt more alive than he had in years.

He had gotten out of the office building early, within a minute of firing his last shot at the officers trying to stop the salt truck. About the same time Walter was handing that USB drive off to the SWAT commander. He wanted to wait. It felt good to have a gun in his hand again, but he was no idiot. He saw them rolling out their spotters and knew if he didn't get out of the building before they got organized — got a solid handle on the heat signatures and positions — he was done. It was one thing for them to zero in on the Sterno cans, another entirely if they saw him scuttle across the roof and down the chain ladder to the next building over. At his age he wasn't outrunning anybody. They'd eventually find his clothes up there. He'd left them in the bag where he'd stashed the suit. Unfortunately, he had to leave the rifle, too. He liked that rifle. He couldn't walk out the front door with it and that's precisely what he did. Down the chain ladder to the roof of the next building over. Through the access door. Elevator to the lobby. And right out the front to the growing crowd and down the sidewalk and around the block. He'd waited things out in the Taurus until it was time to play FBI, close enough to remain on comms in case things went wrong.

Sealey was still shaking his head. "That woman was sharp. You're damn lucky she didn't figure you out."

"What are they gonna do, lock me up for life? I'm not opposed to living out my days in a box with three squares."

"Good for you. But you're not alone in this, and I enjoy my freedom. You jeopardized the entire operation."

"Blow me," Red replied, before pulling off his tie and tossing it into the back seat of the Taurus. He pointed out over the concrete railing at the thick plume of dark smoke rising against the night sky in the west. "Op's over. He did it."

Sealey rubbed his wrists and stepped over to the railing.

He'd known Walter for nearly thirty years, almost half his life. The man was like a brother to him. "I just hope he finally found peace."

His hand slipped into his pocket and wrapped around the tattered leather dog collar Walter had given him.

Within an hour of receiving the text from Amy Archer, Walter had told him what he wanted to do. He'd laid it all out step-by-step with care and precision, and Sealey understood this wasn't something he'd come up with on the fly but something he'd been thinking about for a very long time.

"We go in there," Walter had said, "and try anything else, and she'll slip away again. You know she will." He was emphatic. "We phone in the bomb threat, shoot up the entrance as people come out, make her think we're willing to shoot every female who comes out that door in order to identify her. When that falls apart, she'll think she's got the upper hand. That's when I go in wearing the bomb."

"Why not just plant a bomb in advance? Blow the place while she's inside?"

Even as Sealey suggested it, he knew Walter would never agree to kill civilians. He wouldn't leave things to chance or risk someone finding and disarming the bomb. He'd thought it through.

"I go in, *wearing* the bomb," Walter repeated. "I make sure everyone gets out. I get nice and close before detonation. That's how we end this."

Sealey knew Walter was dying, but that didn't make this any easier.

"They'll crucify you in the press. Make you out to be some nutcase or terrorist. All of us. Our old employer's been tearing apart our reputations for years to cover their own involvement. They'll just build on that."

A glint had entered Walter's eye, one Sealey hadn't seen in a very long time. "I got an idea about that, too."

Watching the dark smoke, Sealey said softly, "Op's *almost* done."

Red nodded and pointed at the van on their left. "That one's yours. I've got the other one. Clothing, IDs, and some money are in a bag in back. We split up here, and no contact until Iowa."

Dubuque, Iowa.

A spot on the map.

They'd picked it because Walter had mentioned it once a long time ago. Seemed fitting.

From the trunk of the Taurus, Red removed a plastic gas can and began splashing the car's interior, soaking the seats and floor. "I'll finish this up, you make the phone call."

"They took my sat phone."

"There's a burner on the driver's seat of the van."

Sealey looked out at the smoke for a moment longer, then rounded the van and found the phone. He gave the dog collar another squeeze and dialed.

This one's for you, buddy.

CHAPTER

92

THE EXPLOSION NEARLY KNOCKED Russell Hurwitz from his chair. His knees cracked against the bottom of his desk, his half full can of Red Bull taking an epic flight across the interior of the SWAT van and spilling across the floor. All his equipment flashed bright and went dark as something not meant to be rattled by a blast that size snapped and disconnected. Most likely the main circuit connecting the hardware to the van's generator on the roof. He couldn't hear it running anymore.

He sat there in the dark, the only sound coming from the ringing in his ears.

He'd listened to that ringing for nearly twenty seconds before he realized it wasn't actually coming from his ears but from the phone Walter O'Brien had given to Rigby, still wired up to his tracing equipment.

Through the video feed, Hurwitz had seen what happened to Commander Rigby; he'd seen everything that had happened outside the club right up to the explosion. He still wasn't sure exactly *what* he'd seen, because none of that could have possibly been real, but that didn't change the fact that he had seen it.

She'd come out of the club like some ancient goddess. Maybe the most beautiful woman he'd ever seen. The thought struck him as odd, because he hadn't been able to make out her face, not clearly. Even when he zoomed in— shadows, blur, floodlights—something obscured her, but he somehow knew. He couldn't explain what came next—she threw people around like they were dolls. Took enough rounds to take down an army. And Rigby—*what the hell had she done to Rigby?!* If he hadn't seen it…he captured it, though. Recorded all of it.

He'd watch the footage back when he got his equipment online again. Slow it down, clean it up. He had a feeling a lot of people would be asking him for that footage. Then he remembered all the cameras outside. The newsfeeds. Had they captured it, too?

Of course they had. Shit, half of them were probably broadcasting live.

Ringing.

The SWAT van was empty.

He was alone.

The door had banged shut with the blast.

He reached forward with a tentative finger and pressed the Answer button. "Yes?"

The voice was silent for a moment, then: *"Where is the commander?"*

"I think Commander Rigby is dead." He said the words, but Hurwitz was numb to them. He realized he might be in shock. His voice sounded like it belonged to someone else and he was just listening in.

"I'm sorry."

"Thanks." A stupid thing to say, but he said it anyway.

"Who are you?"

He saw no reason to lie. "Russell Hurwitz. SWAT tech."

"Russell Hurwitz, SWAT tech, are you in possession of the hard drive we gave to your commander?"

He looked at the drive, still plugged into his rig. Christ, that explosion had rung his bell. He'd forgotten about the drive. "Why?"

The voice on the other end of the line cleared his throat. "Do you believe in monsters?"

Hurwitz didn't answer, not because he didn't want to, but because he wasn't so sure anymore.

"We only have a minute, so I need you to listen to me carefully," the voice said. "Somebody asked me that same question about five years into my time with the Defense Department, and I shrugged it off. Then I saw things. Things no one should see. I was asked to investigate those things by people far higher up the food chain than either of us. Those same people took everything away from me when they decided the optics were bad. Walter O'Brien saw something where nobody else did, too. He was a good cop, better than most. I suppose we both were. A lot of people are going to tell you otherwise, but the contents of that drive prove it. Everything we've found over the years is on there. Every document, photograph, video, statement, report—everything on that… woman. About five minutes ago, copies of that drive went out to press all over the world. Some automated IT hocus-pocus you probably understand better than I do. We also sent them the number for that phone, the one Walter gave you. I strongly suggest you prepare a statement. Don't let them do to you what they tried to do to us. Tell the world about her. Tell them the truth about Walter."

"Who are you?"

"...she might not be the only one."

He hung up.

Hurwitz stared at the little screen, his mind reeling.

Two loud knocks echoed through the van, and the back door opened. The deputy chief was standing there with four men wearing FBI windbreakers and matching scowls.

"Where's Commander Rigby? These people are here for that man, Lincoln Sealey," he shouted. His eyes were red and he held a cloth over his mouth, trying to filter out the smoke. Behind him, a dozen reporters were lined up on the sidewalks. All the major networks. The local channels. Arms flailing. Pointing. Shouting over one another. Hundreds of civilians held up cameras.

Hurwitz opened his mouth to answer when the cell phone started to ring.

Coming in June 2022

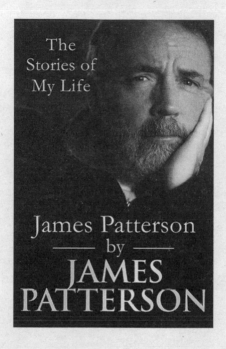

The Stories of My Life

James Patterson
— by —
JAMES PATTERSON

His first novel was turned down by thirty-one
publishers. Now, he is the world's most
successful storyteller.

His best stories are the stories of his life.

Turn the page to read an exclusive extract...

hungry dogs run faster

TIIIS MORNING, I got up at quarter to six. Late for me. I made strong coffee and oatmeal with a sprinkle of brown sugar and a touch of cream. I leafed through the *New York Times, USA Today*, and the *Wall Street Journal*. Then I took a deep breath and started this ego-biography that you're reading.

My grandmother once told me, "You're lucky if you find something in life you like to do. Then it's a miracle if somebody'll pay you to do it." Well, I'm living a miracle. I spend my days, and many nights, writing stories about Alex Cross, the Women's Murder Club, Maximum Ride, the Kennedys, John Lennon, young Muhammad Ali, and now *this*.

My writing style is colloquial, which is the way we talk to one another, right? Some might disagree—some vehemently disagree—but I think colloquial storytelling is a valid form of expression. If you wrote down your favorite story to tell, there might not be any great sentences, but it still could be outstanding. Try it out. Write down a good story you tell friends—maybe starting with the line "Stop me if I've told you this one before"—and see how it looks on paper.

A word about my office. Come in. Look around. A well-worn,

hopelessly cluttered writing table sits at the center, surrounded by shelves filled to the brim with my favorite books, which I dip into all the time.

At the base of the bookshelves are counters. Today, there are thirty-one of my manuscripts on these surfaces. Every time journalists come to my office and see the thirty or so manuscripts in progress, they mutter something like "I had no idea." Right. *I had no idea how crazy you are, James.*

I got infamous writing mysteries, so here's the big mystery plot for this book: How did a shy, introspective kid from a struggling upstate New York river town who didn't have a lot of guidance or role models go on to become, at thirty-eight, CEO of the advertising agency J. Walter Thompson North America? How did this same person become the bestselling writer in the world? That's just not possible.

But it happened. In part because of something else my grandmother preached early and often—*hungry dogs run faster.*

And, boy, was I hungry.

One thing that I've learned and taken to heart about writing books or even delivering a good speech is to tell stories. Story after story after story. That's what got me here, so that's what I'm going to do. Let's see where storytelling takes us. This is just a fleeting thought, but try not to skim too much. If you do, it's the damn writer's fault. But I have a hunch there's something here that's worth a few hours. It has to do with the craft of storytelling.

One other thing. When I write, I pretend there's someone sitting across from me—and I don't want that person to get up until I'm finished with the story.

Right now, that person is you.

passion keeps you going...but it doesn't pay the rent

WHEN I FIRST arrived in New York, I would force myself to get up at five every morning to squeeze in a couple of hours of writing before I went to work at the ad factory. I was full of hope and big dreams but not enough confidence to quit my day job and write for my supper.

I'd play some music, maybe a little Harry Nilsson ("Gotta Get Up"), and do my first stint of scribbling sentences, cutting sentences, adding sentences, driving myself crazy.

The book's getting better, right?

The book's getting worse. Every sentence I write is inferior to the last.

I'm going to be the next Graham Greene.

Don't quit your day job, chump.

You start thinking you're a fraud, "a big fat failure." Okay, okay, so that's a line out of the movie *You've Got Mail.* So is "You are what you read."

As I said, I was driving myself crazy. It goes with the territory. I think that's what first-time novelists are supposed to do. Our rite of passage. Every night after work, I'd come home in a daze of jingle lyrics and cutesy catchphrases, sit in my kitchen, stare around at the tiny antiseptic space, then start writing again. I'd go till eleven or twelve. That's how I wrote *The Thomas Berryman Number*.

I did the first draft in pencil.

But then I typed. The two-finger minuet. I had to reach up to the counter to peck at the keys of my faithful Underwood Champion. Eventually, I hurt my back. That's when I stopped typing and started writing everything in pencil again.

I still write in pencil. I'm writing this with a number 2 pencil. The pencils were gifts from my old friend Tom McGoey. They each say *Alex Cross Lives Here*. My handwriting is impossible to read—even for me. Hell, *I'm* not sure what I just wrote.

After about a thousand revisions, when I thought the manuscript for *The Thomas Berryman Number* might be ready for human consumption, I mailed it out myself. No agent. No early readers. No compelling pitch letter.

I got rejections. Mostly form letters. A couple of handwritten notes from editors that were encouraging. One publisher, Morrow, held on to the manuscript for two months before rejecting it. With a form letter.

Then I read an article in the *New York Times Book Review* about the literary agency Sanford Greenburger Associates. Sanford Greenburger, the founder of the agency, had died in 1971. His son Francis took over the business. Francis was in his twenties, not much older than me. The article in the *Times* said they were accepting manuscripts from unpublished writers. That would be me.

I sent over the manuscript that had already been rejected thirty times. We're talking four hundred typewritten pages secured in a cardboard box. Two days later, I got a phone call from

Greenburger Associates. I'm thinking to myself, *I can't believe they turned my book down so fast!*

The caller turned out to be Francis himself. He said, "No, no, no, I'm not turning your novel down. Just the opposite. Come on over and see me. I want to sell this thing. I *will* sell your book."

So Francis hooked me up with Jay Acton, a hot young editor at Thomas Crowell, a small, family-owned New York publisher. Jay and I got along beautifully. He worked with me for about a month on the manuscript. He helped the book take shape and we cut some fat.

Then Jay rejected it. My thirty-first rejection.

But Francis Greenburger talked me down off a ledge of the thirty-story Graybar Building, where J. Walter Thompson had its offices. "Don't worry your pretty little head. I'm going to sell it this week."

And he sold it to Little, Brown. *That week.*

norman mailer and
james baldwin—fisticuffs

MY FIRST NEW YORK literary party taught me that, like a lot of secret societies, the inner world of literary people was borderline crazy and completely overrated.

That first lit party was at the home of Jay Acton, the editor who had helped me with but then rejected *The Thomas Berryman Number*. Jay and I had stayed friends and I liked him tremendously.

(Years later, the weirdest thing happened to Jay. He'd switched over to being a literary agent, and one of his clients was bestselling romance writer Helen Van Slyke. She was a friend and also a big moneymaker for Jay. Then Jay got the terrible news that Helen had died, suddenly and apparently without much warning. Next, Jay got some very different news. Helen Van Slyke had left Jay pretty much everything. Suddenly he was rich. I think he bought a minor-league baseball team and a radio station.)

I remember sitting in Jay's living room the night of that party. It was before *Berryman* was actually published. I was in the middle of a conversation with Wilfrid Sheed, whose novel *People Will Always Be Kind* I'd read and loved.

Sheed was, well, *kind*.

He gave me the best advice as I waited for *The Thomas Berryman Number* to be published. "Write another book. Start tonight. You can—" We were interrupted midsentence by some kind of hubbub happening elsewhere in the apartment. People were filing back into a rear hallway. I excused myself and followed the noise and the crowd.

I entered a large bedroom.

The room was packed with people. Noisy people. Sweating people. Tense people. *Fight fans!*

In the middle of the room stood these two small men. They were arguing loudly, fists clenched, looking like they were ready to rumble. The bedroom had become a pint-size boxing ring.

The men were Norman Mailer and James Baldwin. Two little guys who looked about as athletic as French poodles. Especially Baldwin. I remembered that Mailer had actually done some prizefighting, but he didn't look like much of a fighter to me. The two men were squared off at center ring.

Mailer and Baldwin were arguing about what should be considered good literature and what shouldn't. It seemed clear they weren't big fans of one another. Weird, because I was a fan of both of them, especially James Baldwin.

You could not have dragged me out of that noisy, stuffy, overcrowded bedroom. No fisticuffs yet, but lots of heated words. The literary crowd gathered in the room was *abuzz*. The pugilists were circling, looking for an opportunity to pounce, maybe throw the first punch, but definitely win the war of words.

I have to admit, I found the whole thing hilarious. But I knew I would never forget that scene, and obviously, I haven't.

It set the tone for the absurdity of literary warfare—which I've tried my best to avoid.

Wilfrid Sheed may have written *People Will Always Be Kind,* but I learned that wasn't always the case.

speaking of bookstore windows

OKAY, I AM walking along Broadway in New York City. I'm walking pretty quickly. I arrive at my local Barnes & Noble on the corner of Sixty-Seventh Street. I see three copies of my novel *Along Came a Spider* in the window. This is good stuff.

I've been pretty much waiting for this to happen since I first came to live in New York in the 1970s. It's now January of 1993.

I go inside the bookstore. I'm hyperventilating a little. I want to make this moment last.

It's a Sunday. I've just seen that *Along Came a Spider* is number 6 on the *New York Times* bestseller list. I don't think that could be a mistake, but I'm a little afraid it might be.

I walk toward the fiction section and I can already see the cover for *Along Came a Spider*. It features big type and an illustration of a spider hanging over a suburban-looking house.

Now here's what some writers do. We count the number of copies of our book in stock at the local bookstore.

I know there were twelve copies of *Along Came a Spider* here a few days ago. Now there are six copies.

So maybe the *New York Times* bestseller list is accurate. I'm feeling a little dizzy. I don't know how to handle this. I'm starting to get hopeful—and hope is not a strategy.

While I'm heading toward *Along Came a Spider,* a woman picks up a copy.

I stop walking.

Now, here's another thing that happens with some writers: If we see you pick up a copy of one of our books at the store, we watch you. If you buy the book, I swear, it makes our whole day. But if you put the book down, reject us, as it were, it breaks our hearts. Seriously. I think it hurts our souls.

So I'm watching this woman, practicing spy craft the way I've read about it in John le Carré mysteries.

She reads the flap copy, then she reads the author blurbs on the back cover. Then she puts *Along Came a Spider* under her arm.

I'm trying to be cool about this, but I want to go over and give her a big hug.

I watch this wonderful, wonderful person walk down a long, narrow aisle—and then she slides *Along Came a Spider* into her hobo bag.

She stole the book.

And all I can think is *Does that count as a sale?*

dolly, hello

I'LL TELL YOU one more love story, the most recent one. I fell head over heels in love with Dolly Parton the first time I met her in Nashville.

I had a half-baked but potentially really good idea for a story about a country singer. I suggested to Dolly's manager that she and I consider writing a novel together. Dolly was interested but she wanted to meet—face-to-face—before deciding. We needed to talk, to get to know one another, if we were going to be writing partners. That made perfect sense to me.

So I took a plane ride to Nashville, a city I've loved since I attended Vanderbilt. Her driver picked me up at the airport. You can tell a lot about rich or famous people by talking to the folks who work for them. The driver had been with Dolly for over twenty years. He told me she was the best, the kindest person on the planet. He loved her and said everybody did. I believed him because of the way he said it. Also because Dolly's reputation precedes her.

That day at her very homey office, I found her to be down-to-earth, genuine, thoughtful, smart as a whip, funny, and self-deprecating. Those are qualities that are right up my small-town alley. There's a line that was used to promote the *Friday*

Night Lights TV series that I like a lot: "clear eyes, full heart." That's Dolly Parton.

I guess she was okay with me too because we shook on a deal on the spot to write our book. No agents, no lawyers, nothing but a promise between the two of us. That's the way things should work, in my opinion. Get rid of the middlemen.

Dolly's one concern had been that there wouldn't be enough for her to contribute, and she refused to just put her name on the book. I told her that wasn't how this would work. I wanted her help with the outline and then the book itself. She would make our story authentic, because she knows *everything* about the music business. She would make the story strong, because that's what Dolly does best, tell stories. In fact, that's what country music is all about, storytelling.

Plus, there were a dozen or so songs in the novel. I needed a whole lot of help with those. Dolly said, "Jim, I've written thousands of songs. I can write a country song standing on my head. Want to see?"

Two days after I got home, I received an unbelievable surprise. Dolly already had some good ideas about the first draft of our outline. And she'd sent me the lyrics for *seven* original songs. She'd already written seven songs. Can you believe that? Well, it's how it happened.

I still remember sending her pages one Friday night and on *Saturday* getting back this note:

Hey Jimmy James,

Loving it, loving it, loving it!!! Love our red-headed twins and the community guitar at the Nashville roadhouse. Nicely done. No notes on this batch—keep it coming!

Love,
Dolly

Sue wants me to frame the damn note. She can't stop talking about "*Dolly's* novel."

Dolly and I became friends during our collaboration on *Run, Rose, Run*. She calls me "Jimmy James" or "JJ." For her birthday, I sent her one of those silver cups people give to a mom after she's had a baby. I had it inscribed HAPPY BIRTHDAY, BABY.

For my birthday, Dolly sang "Happy Birthday" to me over the phone. She also sent me a beautiful guitar. She inscribed it TO JIMMY JAMES, I WILL ALWAYS LOVE YOU.

How cool is that?

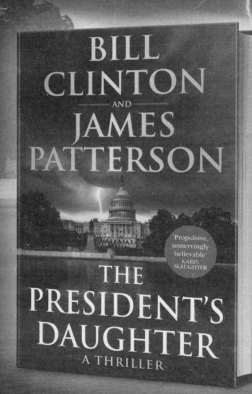

Also by James Patterson

ALEX CROSS SERIES

Along Came a Spider • Kiss the Girls • Jack and Jill • Cat and Mouse • Pop Goes the Weasel • Roses are Red • Violets are Blue • Four Blind Mice • The Big Bad Wolf • London Bridges • Mary, Mary • Cross • Double Cross • Cross Country • Alex Cross's Trial (*with Richard DiLallo*) • I, Alex Cross • Cross Fire • Kill Alex Cross • Merry Christmas, Alex Cross • Alex Cross, Run • Cross My Heart • Hope to Die • Cross Justice • Cross the Line • The People vs. Alex Cross • Target: Alex Cross • Criss Cross • Deadly Cross • Fear No Evil

THE WOMEN'S MURDER CLUB SERIES

1st to Die • 2nd Chance (*with Andrew Gross*) • 3rd Degree (*with Andrew Gross*) • 4th of July (*with Maxine Paetro*) • The 5th Horseman (*with Maxine Paetro*) • The 6th Target (*with Maxine Paetro*) • 7th Heaven (*with Maxine Paetro*) • 8th Confession (*with Maxine Paetro*) • 9th Judgement (*with Maxine Paetro*) • 10th Anniversary (*with Maxine Paetro*) • 11th Hour (*with Maxine Paetro*) • 12th of Never (*with Maxine Paetro*) • Unlucky 13 (*with Maxine Paetro*) • 14th Deadly Sin (*with Maxine Paetro*) • 15th Affair (*with Maxine Paetro*) • 16th Seduction (*with Maxine Paetro*) • 17th Suspect (*with Maxine Paetro*) • 18th Abduction (*with Maxine Paetro*) • 19th Christmas (*with Maxine Paetro*) • 20th Victim (*with Maxine Paetro*) • 21st Birthday (*with Maxine Paetro*) • 22 Seconds (*with Maxine Paetro*)

DETECTIVE MICHAEL BENNETT SERIES

Step on a Crack (*with Michael Ledwidge*) • Run for Your Life (*with Michael Ledwidge*) • Worst Case (*with Michael Ledwidge*) • Tick Tock (*with Michael Ledwidge*) • I, Michael Bennett (*with Michael Ledwidge*) • Gone (*with Michael Ledwidge*) • Burn (*with Michael Ledwidge*) • Alert (*with Michael Ledwidge*) • Bullseye (*with Michael Ledwidge*) • Haunted (*with James O. Born*) • Ambush (*with James O. Born*) • Blindside (*with James O. Born*) • The Russian (*with James O. Born*)

PRIVATE NOVELS

Private (*with Maxine Paetro*) • Private London (*with Mark Pearson*) • Private Games (*with Mark Sullivan*) • Private: No. 1 Suspect (*with Maxine Paetro*) • Private Berlin (*with Mark Sullivan*) • Private Down Under (*with Michael White*) • Private L.A. (*with Mark Sullivan*) • Private India (*with Ashwin Sanghi*) • Private Vegas (*with Maxine Paetro*) • Private Sydney (*with Kathryn Fox*) • Private Paris (*with Mark Sullivan*) • The Games (*with Mark Sullivan*) • Private Delhi (*with Ashwin Sanghi*) • Private Princess (*with Rees Jones*) • Private Moscow (*with Adam Hamdy*) • Private Rogue (*with Adam Hamdy*)

NYPD RED SERIES

NYPD Red (*with Marshall Karp*) • NYPD Red 2 (*with Marshall Karp*) • NYPD Red 3 (*with Marshall Karp*) • NYPD Red 4 (*with Marshall Karp*) • NYPD Red 5 (*with Marshall Karp*) • NYPD Red 6 (*with Marshall Karp*)

DETECTIVE HARRIET BLUE SERIES

Never Never (*with Candice Fox*) • Fifty Fifty (*with Candice Fox*) • Liar Liar (*with Candice Fox*) • Hush Hush (*with Candice Fox*)

THE BLACK BOOK SERIES

The Black Book (*with David Ellis*) • The Red Book (*with David Ellis*)

STAND-ALONE THRILLERS

The Thomas Berryman Number • Hide and Seek • Black Market • The Midnight Club • Sail (*with Howard Roughan*) • Swimsuit (*with Maxine Paetro*) • Don't Blink (*with Howard Roughan*) • Postcard Killers (*with Liza Marklund*) • Toys (*with Neil McMahon*) • Now You See Her (*with Michael Ledwidge*) • Kill Me If you Can (*with Marshall Karp*) • Guilty Wives (*with David Ellis*) • Zoo (*with Michael Ledwidge*) • Second Honeymoon (*with Howard Roughan*) • Mistress (*with David Ellis*) • Invisible (*with David Ellis*) • Truth or Die (*with Howard Roughan*) • Murder House (*with David Ellis*) •

The Store (*with Richard DiLallo*) • Texas Ranger (*with Andrew Bourelle*) • The President is Missing (*with Bill Clinton*) • Revenge (*with Andrew Holmes*) • Juror No. 3 (*with Nancy Allen*) • The First Lady (*with Brendan DuBois*) • The Chef (*with Max DiLallo*) • Out of Sight (*with Brendan DuBois*) • Unsolved (*with David Ellis*) • The Inn (*with Candice Fox*) • Lost (*with James O. Born*) • Texas Outlaw (*with Andrew Bourelle*) • The Summer House (*with Brendan DuBois*) • 1st Case (*with Chris Tebbetts*) • Cajun Justice (*with Tucker Axum*) • The Midwife Murders (*with Richard DiLallo*) • The Coast-to-Coast Murders (*with J.D. Barker*) • Three Women Disappear (*with Shan Serafin*) • The President's Daughter (*with Bill Clinton*) • The Shadow (*with Brian Sitts*) The Noise (*with J.D. Barker*) • 2 Sisters Detective Agency (*with Candice Fox*) • Jailhouse Lawyer (*with Nancy Allen*) • The Horsewoman (*with Mike Lupica*) • Run Rose Run (*with Dolly Parton*)

NON-FICTION

Torn Apart (*with Hal and Cory Friedman*) • The Murder of King Tut (*with Martin Dugard*) • All-American Murder (*with Alex Abramovich and Mike Harvkey*) • The Kennedy Curse (*with Cynthia Fagen*) • The Last Days of John Lennon (*with Casey Sherman and Dave Wedge*) • Walk in My Combat Boots (*with Matt Eversmann and Chris Mooney*) ER Nurses (*with Matt Eversmann*)

MURDER IS FOREVER TRUE CRIME

Murder, Interrupted • Home Sweet Murder • Murder Beyond the Grave • Murder Thy Neighbour • Murder of Innocence • Till Murder Do Us Part

COLLECTIONS

Triple Threat • Kill or Be Killed • The Moores are Missing • The Family Lawyer • Murder in Paradise • The House Next Door • 13-Minute Murder • The River Murders • The Palm Beach Murders • Paris Detective

For more information about James Patterson's novels, visit www.penguin.co.uk